# OPEN SECRET

JAMES LEASOR, who has written many successful novels, three of which were made into films, was born and brought up in Kent where much of the action in this book takes place. He has one wife, two homes – in Wiltshire and Portugal – three sons and four cars. His interest in motoring and property is most fruitfully exploited in *Open Secret*.

JAMES LEASOR

---

# Open Secret

FONTANA/Collins

First published by William Collins Sons & Co. Ltd 1982
First issued in Fontana Paperbacks 1983



Made and printed in Great Britain by
William Collins Sons & Co. Ltd, Glasgow

'You must understand man as he is, and not demand of his nature something it does not possess.'

Sergei Timoveyovich Aksarov
to Gogol

Comrade Vasarov's funeral procession took two hours to pass through Red Square with a dozen bands playing sombre marches. The commentator spoke in a reverent voice.

'Asimir Vasarov was one of Russia's most important and most feared men – yet almost unknown to the outside world . . .'

Max Cornell, watching the scene on television in his penthouse in Grosvenor Square, 'the most luxurious private flat in London', as the *Standard* called it, raised his brandy in an ironical toast. A green light fluttered on his telephone. He picked up the receiver.

A man's voice said: 'Confirming your instructions, Mr Cornell, we will commence selling your holding in Katyn Nominees at ten o'clock tomorrow. Minimum expectation, after commission, is in the order of four million pounds.'

A half-track carried Vasarov's coffin across the square. Old men, faces as hard as Moscow's granite buildings, heads bent beneath black fur hats, followed in slow step.

'As agreed, we are also selling Quendon Construction. Estimated return after commission, another four million. Give or take.'

'Take,' said Cornell drily. 'I have given enough in taxes.'

The man laughed awkwardly. You could never tell when these rich bastards were joking.

'Oh. Very good, sir. Now, Beechwood Garages and International Motor Auctions. An American investment trust has offered three million sterling. Half in cash, half in shares.'

'Accept four, like the others. Nothing less.'

'Very good, sir. Four it is.'

The flag that covered Vasarov's coffin turned Cornell's screen crimson, the colour of blood.

'Vasarov's remarkable career spanned more than forty years of political life in communist Russia. He seemed to have a charmed life, surviving the purges that brought down so many of his contemporaries. He served under Stalin, Malenkov and Khrushchev. Now . . .'

Cornell sipped his brandy.

'I will give instructions about placing the capital tomorrow,' he said.

'Very good, sir. I will await your call.'

Cornell replaced the receiver.

Snow was falling, shrouding Lenin's mausoleum, dusting the shoulders of the patient, orderly crowds and the troops who lined the route. Snow always reminded Max Cornell of events he wished to forget. Why should he be watching Vasarov's state funeral fifteen hundred miles away in Moscow when he was meeting Vasarov again at the Connaught half an hour from now?

# One

How different from the first time he had seen Vasarov!

There had been no iced drinks then; the only ice lay one inch thick on the windows of the prison hut in Katyn, up in the hills, ringed by forests of freezing firs. Max had been inside that hut, his flesh hot and dry from fever, his body raw with pain, as he peered nervously through a hole that another prisoner had scraped in the ice.

Vasarov was outside, inspecting two ranks of Russian soldiers; a magnificent figure, head and shoulders above them all. His thick blue greatcoat with its blood-red NKVD epaulettes emphasised the shabbiness of the soldiers. Vasarov's contempt was as obvious as his arrogance. He was commandant of that camp; his wish meant life or death for guards and guarded alike.

Vasarov passed out of Max's line of sight, but the impression of total ruthlessness remained, unchanging down the years, although so much else had changed – even Max's name.

In 1941, he had not been Max Cornell, but Maximillian Kransky. That hut was not in England, either, but at Katyn, the Hill of the Goats, in Russia. The Bolsheviks had built a camp there after the 1917 Revolution for opponents who had seen too much. They had lined up obediently, along deep trenches, and then, as firing squads shot them unexpectedly from behind, they had toppled obligingly into the newly-made grave.

Max was rich now, beyond all earlier dreams, but recollections of Katyn still lingered, making him flinch at an unexpected knock on his front door or a strange voice on the telephone. Cocooned by wealth and all that money could buy him, basic unease remained, would always remain, like the original indestructible speck of grit surrounded by pearl within the oyster's heart.

Max rarely thought about the past; that was too painful. He kept such things locked away, as spinsters locked away letters from fiancés killed in war. Now, looking across Grosvenor Square, above the rush of the cars heading home, he allowed himself to recall events before Katyn, when he was a boy in Prague. His father was a doctor, who had married late. His mother, Max realised now, thought she should have married the man he called Uncle Sam, who took the name of Harris when he escaped to England before the war.

'Sam Harris will always be a good friend to you,' she would tell Max earnestly. 'He and his son Paul had the sense to get out early. Like we should have done.'

'But *this* is our home,' his father would reply stubbornly. 'These are our people.'

He could not accept that a Jew in Prague in 1939 had no home, no people, no future.

At first, the Kranskys were not interfered with; she was Catholic, and maybe that helped. Then, late one evening, a German civilian came to visit the doctor.

They were listening to Strauss's 'Voices of Spring' on their gramophone. The violins squealed as his father lifted up the arm. He looked pale and shaken.

'The Gestapo are going to take us tomorrow afternoon – and you know what that means. That man came to warn me because in the old days I saved his child's life. It is his way of thanking me.'

'But what can they possibly want us for?' Max asked his father.

'We are Jews, convenient scapegoats. We've had a lot of practice in this role. We're always the lodgers in someone else's country. We never own the freehold.

'I had hoped that you would follow my career as a doctor. Helping other people is a satisfying way to live. But now you had better look after yourself first.'

'If they're coming tomorrow afternoon, we've little enough time to get ready, without all your talk,' admonished his wife.

'We have to go East,' said Dr Kransky. 'To Poland. My brother Mischa is in Lvov. He will help us. The Nazis aren't there yet, thank God. And the British and French have a treaty with the Poles.'

'They had one with us, too, remember?'

'We'll need money,' Max interrupted. He hated to see his parents argue.

'We will sell our furniture. I have a patient who buys good stuff.'

Some of the prices the patient offered for silver ornaments were so poor, however, that the doctor crammed them into a suitcase, to sell, piece by piece, as they needed money. They set off in the family Adler just before ten.

Thirty kilometres from the frontier a policeman flagged them down, and checked the car's registration number against his notebook.

'That dealer must have shopped us. No-one else knew we were leaving.'

'You mean, you told him?' asked his wife in amazement.

'I trusted him.'

'You fool!' she exclaimed bitterly. 'Trust no-one! *No-one!*'

The doctor offered his open silver cigarette case to the policeman.

'Cigarette?' he asked him. The policeman's leather gauntlet reached in through the window. He grabbed the case, put it in his pocket.

'Get out,' he ordered. 'All three of you.'

Behind them a truck had stopped, and another car, a Horch, black, with its canvas hood folded down to reveal leather seats, red as new-spilled blood under the August sun.

For Max, this combination of red and black, the national colours of Nazi Germany, came to symbolise power. Sometimes he wondered whether there was a deeper significance: the black earth in the long grave at Katyn, bright blood on the snow, and the fate he had somehow escaped . . .

Two SS officers in uniform climbed out and began to walk towards them.

'Jews, eh?' said one, examining their papers.

The policeman opened a suitcase and held up a set of silver spoons.

'Removing articles of value from the country without permission, are you?'

'We're only going on holiday.'

'People don't take family silver on holiday. Or can't you Jews afford hotels that supply knives and forks, eh?'

One SS man suddenly hit the doctor in the stomach. The old man staggered back against the car, lost his balance and fell. As he crawled to his knees, the other officer booted him in the groin. He collapsed on the hot tarmac, writhing in pain.

The policeman began to throw the suitcases into the back of the truck.

'Get in,' he ordered.

Suddenly, Max's mother seized a case, ripped it open, and flung the contents across the road.

'Max!' she screamed to her son. '*Run!*'

Max hesitated for a second. Then, he ran. He vaulted a fence and raced across a field. Cows lifted their heads to stare stupidly at him. He heard the crack-crack of pistol shots and zigzagged as he ran. Beyond the field lay a forest. He plunged deep into this and sank down among the nettles and docks and brambles. He heard the motor cycle start up, and, raising himself on his elbows, watched the vehicles follow it down the road. He was alone.

One name hammered in his brain. Sam Harris. Uncle Sam. He will help me if somehow I can get to England. But – how? He waited in the forest all day, eating blackberries, chewing green weeds, pondering the problem. At dusk he decided it was safe to leave.

He walked all night, across fields and rough ground, trying to keep parallel with the road, aiming for the frontier.

There was little traffic on the road, mostly trucks. When he heard them approach, or saw their distant headlights, he hid until they had passed. On one long hill, the driver of a truck missed his gear change and stopped to engage bottom gear. Max ran out and climbed up among huge, rough sacks of apples. He burrowed beneath them, and lay full length, seeing only a dim patch of sky. The motion of the truck lulled him to sleep. He awoke when it stopped and he heard men talking, in Polish as well as German. Then the engine started again and the truck moved forward; he had crossed the frontier.

In the early morning, the driver pulled into a wayside café, and Max jumped down to relieve himself. He walked along the side of the road more confidently. A passing van stopped and the driver offered him a lift until he turned off the main road to a village.

The place seemed atrophied by summer heat; dogs slept in the dust and did not move as Max walked by. A bicycle was propped against the wall, and Max seized it. By evening, he was in Lvov. His uncle's house was grey, sombre, uninviting, its windows shuttered, the gardens overgrown. He banged on the front door with his fist. Bolts squealed, a safety chain rattled, and an old woman peered out at him.

'Mischa Kransky?' Max said eagerly. 'I want to see him.'

'Gone away,' she replied shortly, and shut the door in his face.

Disappointed and bewildered, he slept that night in a shed behind an empty house. Next morning, soldiers were standing at every street corner. Max asked a corporal what was happening.

'Don't you know? It's war. The German army has crossed our border. Total mobilisation has been ordered.'

Sooner or later someone was bound to ask him for his papers. He saw a queue of men waiting in the street outside a recruiting office. This gave him hope; he would join up. In fact, no-one asked him for any papers; there was not even a medical examination. Max took a hurried oath of allegiance, was issued with a uniform and boots, and then marched with others, raggedly and seldom in step, to a barracks. A few days' hasty basic training followed, as the German army swept on invincibly through Poland from the west. Then, as Polish resistance cracked, the Russians invaded from the east. The war was over. Max and other captured recruits were put to work repairing shell-damaged roads and bridges.

They worked in groups of twenty under two guards who counted heads regularly.

Early in the New Year, snow began to fall. Cold killed all feeling in feet and hands. Max's lips cracked and bled. To speak became an effort. The flurrying snow made it almost impossible for the guards to count accurately.

One afternoon, through a haze of falling flakes, he saw two men in another group begin to fight. Max's guard peered anxiously through the snow towards them, wondering whether he should investigate. In that second of indecision, Max ran.

He ran along frozen streets, towards the fields, where his pounding feet made no sound on the thick snow. He heard several shots behind him, but no guard dared to follow in case others also fled. He ran until he was too weary to run any farther, and then, at a walk, he struck out along a track that led to a barn full of cows, standing hock-deep in their own dung. He lay down in a corner on a pile of hay and almost instantly fell asleep.

He awoke next morning to see the landscape through the barn doorway stretch away, white and featureless, to infinity. It was too risky to move against that background. He stayed in the straw, grateful for its warmth. At dusk, he climbed down, found an old pan, and milked the nearest cow into it. He gulped down the warm milk and headed out into the snow.

He walked for several hours along the empty track. It brought him eventually to a railway halt, simply a concrete platform and a wooden hut built from railway sleepers. A line of trucks waited in a siding. One door had a smashed window. He put his hand in through the jagged hole, opened the door and climbed inside. Half a dozen wooden barrels were stacked against the opposite wall. Whitish streaks showed where salt had seeped through the seams. He found a wrench strapped to the wall and smashed a hole in the nearest barrel. Caviare. How ironic for an alien slave on the run to be gorging himself on the food of the rich! Max ate until the salt revolted him. Then, feeling full and slightly sick, he lay down on the floor and, drugged by unaccustomed food, he fell asleep.

Hours later, he awoke, cramped and cold. A pinkish glow lit up the sky; it was time to leave to find a safer hiding place before daybreak. He climbed down stiffly from the truck, crossed the rails – and immediately someone pinioned his arms behind him so tightly that he staggered and fell. A torch blazed in his eyes, dazzling him. Beyond the haze of light, he could just make out two soldiers in Russian uniforms.

'Who are you?' one asked him.

Max was so dazed that he could not find words to reply. They marched him to a shed half a mile away. It stank of animal droppings; a naphtha pressure lamp lit up bare wooden walls. Behind a table sat two men wearing the blue uniforms and red epaulettes of the NKVD, the secret police.

Their questions began immediately. Was he a Polish deserter? A German? Why had he come here? Who did he know? Endlessly, they repeated the same questions.

'You are a deserter from the bourgeois Polish army,' one declared at last. 'You will be taken to a camp for rehabilitation.'

Max spent that day and the following night crammed with others in a cattle truck. They were forced to urinate and defecate as they stood. Finally, they reached a railhead where two army trucks waited in the station square, engines running to prevent their radiators from freezing solid. Each had a machine gun on a tripod mounted in the back, beneath the vehicle's canvas roof. Soldiers lowered the truck tailboards and began to unroll chains, covered in thick black grease to prevent rust. A corporal ordered the prisoners to stand in line on either side of these chains. Soldiers then handcuffed them to the links.

Truck wheels spun in freezing snow, bit, gripped and turned. The chains tightened, and slowly, with the machine guns aimed at them, the lines of men began to move forward, heads down against the driving snow. Once or twice the column halted, for a man had collapsed. His wrists were unlocked, and other prisoners seized his clothes and boots for themselves. Then the column moved on. The fallen were left behind in the freezing snow.

Dawn succeeded night, grey morning merged into blinding noon, then drifted into dusk. The creak and clank of chains, the exhausted sobs of older men, a hum of engines and a whine of gears – these were the only sounds on their journey.

Finally, they reached a camp of wooden huts, surrounded by two parallel wire fences. Armed guards with alsatians patrolled the space between them.

Soldiers unlocked the handcuffs. A colonel came to address the new arrivals.

'You are here as guests of our beloved leader, Comrade Stalin,' he explained. 'Under his wise guidance we will make good communist citizens of you all. First, we demand total discipline. Second, you have no possible chance of escape. Even if you somehow crossed both sections of wire, *and* evaded the dogs, the cold or the wolves would soon kill you.'

Max was detailed to a wooden hut that contained sixty bunks arranged in three tiers. The bottom and middle levels were already taken up by Russian criminals: murderers and thieves serving long sentences. He climbed to his bunk and lay down thankfully on the bare boards. He was exhausted and slept so heavily that it seemed only minutes before he was being shaken awake. Then out to line up at a cookhouse door for a bowl of weak vegetable soup, a slab of bread, a cup of sugarless tea. Afterwards, he and other new arrivals collected saws and axes and were marched under guard to the forest to cut down trees and trim the branches. The work was needed to extend the camp. More prisoners were expected.

So days merged wearily into weeks, weeks into months. Then on an April morning, in 1941, the colonel had unexpected news for all former Polish army men.

'You are to be repatriated to your homeland under the protection of the Soviet Union,' he announced. 'You will leave tomorrow as returning prisoners-of-war.'

This news was so amazing that at first they looked at each other in total disbelief. Then they embraced each other joyfully. Soon, God willing, they would be reunited with their families.

Next morning, they left in trucks, crammed again, body to body, but nobody minded, for now they were going home. At Smolensk, other Polish prisoners joined them from similar camps. The train chugged on for miles until it reached the edge of a fir forest. Here, it stopped. After the cramped, foetid conditions in the trucks, the fresh smell of the firs was almost overpowering.

A corporal marched them under guard up the hill towards a row of wooden huts near the forest. Smoke spiralled up into the cold clear air from crude tin chimneys.

The corporal halted the column outside the nearest hut, and several female orderlies came out. They walked slowly down the ranks, looking at each man appraisingly. One paused in front of Max. She had a plain face, with a slight Mongolian slant to her eyes.

'Fall out,' she told him sharply.

Two men were already being marched into the hut. The rest of the column stood firm.

Max paused in the doorway to kick frozen snow from his boots – and heard two cries of startled agony. He entered the hut to the embrace of welcome warmth from the red hot metal stove. On the floor, the other two men writhed in pain, crouched up, hands gouged into their groins. He turned in surprise to the woman orderly, and at that moment a man stepped from behind the door and, grinning, kicked him viciously in the crotch. Max collapsed in a red, roaring sea of pain.

Hours later, still in agony, and drawn up into a foetal position of instinctive protection, he opened his eyes. He was lying on a hay mattress on the floor covered by a rough blanket. The woman orderly came across to him.

'What happened? Who kicked me?' he gasped.

'One of the guards,' she said simply.

'But why?' She did not reply but handed him a bowl of soup. He sipped the scalding liquid gratefully. For nearly a week, he lay in bed, his testicles swollen and split. To pass water was excruciatingly painful, and the urine was flecked with blood. His groin ached with every movement.

One morning, Max heard Polish voices outside, and thinking that they might be his comrades from the other camp, he pulled himself up to a window.

That was when he had seen Vasarov for the first time, inspecting the Red Army soldiers, facing the vast trench. As he watched, prisoners began to march between the soldiers and this trench. Some sang Polish songs. They halted and turned towards the trench. Then, on Vasarov's command, the soldiers raised their rifles and fired.

With a great cawing and beating of wings, terrified birds flew out of the fir trees. Prisoners staggered, and dropped into the trench. Some had been virtually decapitated with the force of the bullets; bright blood spurted across the trodden snow.

Prisoners not hit by this first volley, but spattered with other men's blood and flesh and tatters of cloth, started to run towards the trees. They were weak and hungry and stumbled in the soft snow. Calmly, the soldiers reloaded and fired a second time. Within two minutes three hundred men had died.

'Seen enough?' the woman orderly asked. He nodded numbly, shaking with disgust and misery. She handed him a bowl of watery gruel. Gobbets of fat and gristle tufted with hair floated on the surface, but it was food.

'Now you will sleep,' she told him, and led him, still trembling, to his bed space. He sank down thankfully on the straw palliasse.

The promise about going home to Poland had been a lie. But, like the others, he had believed what he had been told; they had trusted the word of a colonel, and their trust had been betrayed. As Max sank into uneasy slumber, he remembered his mother's bitter advice when the policeman stopped them near the frontier. He would never trust anyone again.

Vasarov wrinkled his nose with distaste at the sharp smoke from the cigarettes lit by the firing party. He saw a woman orderly's face in a hut window, hastily ducking out of sight as he approached. He was aware that these women, who cooked for the soldiers, took as a right some of the younger, healthier prisoners as lovers. Their crude but effective method of avoiding pregnancy was to have a lover from an earlier draft kick or punch the newcomer in the groin. These blows had the effect of destroying the vitality of the man's semen. The prisoners who had kicked the newcomers were told that their own survival could depend on the force of their attack. They were, of course, killed as soon as it was established that their successor was a more satisfactory lover; no sentiment marked these brutish animal relationships.

Vasarov had been in Katyn for three weeks, supervising the systematic elimination of thousands of Polish officers and men, formerly doctors and lawyers and engineers, on Stalin's orders. Stalin wished to eradicate a whole generation of Poles who had been trained to think for themselves, in order to make the eventual subjugation of their country infinitely easier to accomplish.

He turned over a wallet that he had picked up. The leather felt sodden, and smelled of sweat and rot. Inside he found an icon, a yellowing photograph and a Polish officer's identity card. He threw away the wallet and the icon. The identity card he placed in an inner pocket; it might prove useful should thc NKVD need a true Polish background for a spy. The photograph, he looked at more closely. A woman in her late thirties sat between two girls, probably her daughters, on a low wall in front of a house. Their clothes implied it was summer. He turned over the photograph; a name was written on the back.

He put the photograph in his pocket. Behind him, the fir forest loomed. It reminded him of other woods around Tiflis, the chief city of Georgia, where he had studied briefly at the Orthodox Theological Seminary. This was not because he had wished to become a priest, but because his father had once been a student there with Stalin, until both had been forced to leave because of their continual subversive political activities.

Several older monks still recalled Stalin, under his real name of Josif Dzhugashvili, as an enthusiastic wrestler, although he was deformed. The second and third toes of his left foot were joined together, and his left arm was several inches shorter than his right. Whenever he won a bout, he would jump on the back of a friend, and shout triumphantly: '*Ya stal! Ya stal!* I am steel! I am steel!'

After the Revolution, Lenin suggested he adopt this name

permanently. So, after several earlier aliases to confuse the Tsarist secret police, he became Stalin, the Man of Steel.

When the monks expelled Stalin from the Seminary he became a clerk in the Tiflis Physical Observatory. After office hours, with Vasarov's father as his loyal helper, he worked at his real career of revolutionary

Under the name Koba (The Indomitable), he and Vasarov's father helped to organise strikes and local uprisings in the Caucasus. Steadily, Stalin became more powerful. Rarely did he personally lead an attack or take a risk; he acted at second hand, by remote control. In this way he could take personal credit for all successes, and denounce the failures as the follies of others.

He also ruthlessly eliminated anyone who might conceivably pose a threat to him as leader. Lenin, poisoned; Artem, murdered in a railway train; Zinoviev, executed; Trotsky exiled and murdered in his fortified home in Mexico. By the time Stalin assumed complete power, there was a huge propaganda network praising the 'Wise and Beloved Leader'. The poet Rodina Schostlivykh summed up Stalin's almost divine image in lines all Russians of that generation knew by heart:

'If he tells the coal to turn white,
It will be as Stalin wishes.'

Inevitably, Vasarov's father also fell from favour. He was arrested and condemned to death on charges of uttering criticisms of Comrade Stalin.

Vasarov was allowed to visit him on the eve of his execution.

'My trial was a charade,' the old man said, 'just like the trials of everyone else who knew too much for Stalin's peace of mind.'

'Do not speak in that way,' Vasarov replied nervously. Had his father forgotten that all prison cells contained hidden microphones? The prospect of imminent death loosened tongues as regularly as it loosened bowels.

'I made my confession because I had to,' Vasarov's father continued. 'They simply gave me a document to sign – and I did so, although it contained several ridiculous errors. I even admitted to being in towns I have never seen.'

'I did not come here to listen to such talk,' Vasarov told his father sternly. 'I came to say farewell to a parent.'

Vasarov wanted to add words of comfort, even of love, but he feared the microphones. His father had already said too much, so he simply shook his father's hand and left him in his cell.

At six on the following morning, the hour of his father's execution, a sudden ringing of the bell at the door of the two rooms he shared with his wife and her parents jarred him into wakefulness. Two strangers in dark suits and heavy overcoats gave him time to dress and then pushed him into the back of a car. He had no need to ask who they were.

In Lubyanka Square, in the centre of Moscow, the driver turned through the high entrance of the Ministry of Internal Security, the People's Commissariat of the Interior or NKVD, who acted against treachery and subversion. They handled agents within Russia, in every factory, office and rooming house, and also a vast network of spies in other countries.

Vasarov was relieved to be going up in the lift, not down to the basement dungeons. He was taken to a big room with double windows and thick curtains overlooking the square. It was carpeted and opulently furnished. No traffic rumble penetrated this sealed and silent luxury. A small round man with a bald head, polished like an ivory billiard ball, sat at a vast desk. His hands were folded, the fingers pudgy, nails cut very short and bitten at the edges. Vasarov's two guards bowed, and walked backwards through the double doors as though from an audience with royalty. Vasarov was alone with the head of the secret police, Lavrenti Beria.

'Your father died this morning as a traitor to the state,' Beria began without preamble. 'You visited him last night and he made certain subversive comments to you. You reprimanded the traitor. Your loyalty is to be rewarded.

'You will leave your post in our educational publishing house, and will join my Ministry of Internal Security. You speak and read German and English?'

'Yes, Comrade Beria.'

'You will also report to me personally any criticisms of my Ministry you may hear, and who makes them. You, of course, will be under similar observation. That is all.'

In his new job, Vasarov learned with a mixture of surprise and pride of the enormous ramifications of the Soviet secret service. And yet some discoveries disturbed him. How could such a loyal and faithful friend of Stalin as Dimitry Shmidt, who commanded the cavalry in the Revolution, or the equally distinguished army commander Tukhachevsky, whose legendary exploits he had learned in history lessons at school, suddenly face denunciation as traitors and imperialist lackeys and be executed? Nor were they alone; he handled lists of thousands of apparently loyal Party members who had been deported to Siberia or shot without trial. Now the wind from the forests of Katyn brought back this early unease. The scent of the firs was also the odour of exile, of loneliness and death.

Only one antidote existed for his growing fear of sudden denunciation, without knowing his accuser or why he was being accused – flight to the West. That, of course, could never come about.

Freezing flakes of snow began to fall, shrouding the forest. But although Vasarov could no longer see it, he knew that it was there. Like the miles of electric fence along every frontier, the machine gun and searchlight posts, the trip wires linked to alarms, and the vast distances involved; all combined to make escape to freedom impossible.

Max awoke.

The hut was dark and fusty with charcoal fumes from the stove. Outside, wind moaned across the empty land, blowing snow over the newly-made graves. As he prepared again for sleep, he felt a slight, furtive movement. The woman orderly eased herself in beside him. She pressed her naked body against him, and when her mouth found his, her lips were wet and warm. He knew what he must do. His hands groped for her huge breasts. Slowly, she moved across him and laid her great weight upon him.

'There is a saying,' she whispered, lips against his ear, 'that Poles are made for death and love. Is that true?' She giggled at the thought.

Max's comrades in the long grave had proved true the first part of that saying. If his survival lay in providing the second, then he must survive.

'You will see,' he answered her with assumed enthusiasm, and embraced her gaping, willing body, thrusting into her with the despair of a man whose life depended upon an entirely commercial exchange: sexual satisfaction to secure a stay of execution.

One evening, the orderly brought unexpected news.

'You may be leaving,' she told him. 'This morning Comrade Molotov, our Foreign Secretary, made a special broadcast from Moscow. I heard it myself. The Nazis have invaded our country. We are at war with Germany, and you are an ally.'

'How many allies like me have died here?'

She pouted. 'Thousands, I think. But then, I told you, Poles are made for death – or love. Prove this true again.'

Early the following morning, before sunrise, a Red Army corporal shook Max awake. He was to dress immediately. He was leaving, without even time to say goodbye to the woman orderly.

In the half-light the corporal marched half a dozen prisoners to the station. A train with two engines was waiting, packed with former Polish soldiers released from other camps. They leaned out of the windows, singing cheerfully.

The train took them, with many stops, to the Persian frontier. They crossed and climbed into army trucks that transported them to a camp outside Tehran. Next day, by another train, they began the hot, tedious journey to yet another camp in the desert outside Cairo. Here the details of Max's birth and background were checked.

The Polish officer interrogating him knew Lvov well, and grew suspicious when Max could not answer his questions. He turned to the British captain who sat at his side.

'This man is not Polish,' he said grimly. 'He is an impostor.'

'Are you a Pole?' the captain asked Max.

'No, sir. Czech.'

He explained how he had reached Lvov.

'We don't want you,' the Polish officer told him firmly.

'*We* might,' said the British captain. 'We have what we call an Alien Pioneer Company of Germans, Czechs and Hungarians. You could join that.'

So Max was put on a troopship bound for Southampton. After more interviews, he was posted to Bideford in Devon. From here, with others, he was moved around the country, laying foundations for latrines in Bristol, or clearing bomb damage in Liverpool.

After several months, the commanding officer called him into his office.

'A new unit is being formed of anti-Nazi Austrians and Czechs and Germans,' he explained. 'You speak several languages, you're medically fit and better educated than many of the men here. Care to volunteer?'

'Certainly, sir.'

'I see from your records that you have an uncle, Sam Harris, a British subject apparently, living in north London. Have you contacted him?'

'I have tried to, sir, but I have had no reply. I discovered his telephone number, but it's no longer in use.'

'He must have moved,' said the major. 'Lots of people have, of course, because of the bombing and so on. Still, it might help if he could give you a character reference. I'll make a few enquiries, and in the meantime put you down for X-Troop. Quite harmless name, really. As the men are technically enemy aliens, their behaviour is still an unknown quantity. The algebraic symbol for that is "X". Hence its name.'

A week later, the major called him again into his office.

'You will have an interview in London, and then, if all goes well, you will be posted for training to North Wales,' he told him. 'One bit of advice. I would not mention this Mr Harris of yours.'

'Why not, sir?'

'Our people have managed to locate him, but he disowns you altogether. Says he's never heard of you.'

'But how *can* he, sir? My mother has many times spoken about him. He is her sister's husband.'

'Unfortunately she isn't here to speak for you.'

'Can you give me his address, sir?'

No, I can't, for the good reason that I haven't got it myself.

'He has a son, sir,' said Max. 'Up in the north of England somewhere. He calls himself Harrow, I believe. He wanted an English name. He could be contacted.'

'Very likely,' replied the major. 'But if I were you, I wouldn't waste the time.'

Max took his advice and within days began training with his new unit in the seaside town of Aberdovey, with the ultimate aim of becoming attached to a British Commando unit. His duties would be interrogation and translation. Like the others, he was told to take an English-sounding name. If he were captured by the enemy it would be fatal for his real identity to be discovered. He chose Cornell, from an article about that university in an American magazine.

Three times a week, the newcomers attended lectures on Nazi and communist espionage and other political subjects given by Professor Tobias Tobler, from Cambridge. Tobler was in his early forties, and a heavy smoker. He usually had a cigarette in his mouth and would dust ash from his lapels in an almost automatic movement as he talked. Sometimes, he would be seized with a fit of coughing and his voice would tail away to a dry whisper.

'Cigarettes will kill me,' he would remark in an aside to his audience. 'But then every man is said to kill the thing he loves, so that particular death will not be inappropriate.'

Tobler would often invite several of the men for a drink at the Dovey Inn. They were under strict orders never to speak German or any other foreign language in public. Sometimes, however, the temptation to talk in their own tongue became overwhelming, and then the professor would hold up one hand in warning – and invite them all back to his flat to continue the discussion in any language they wished.

When the conversation went on very late, Tobler offered Max a bed in his spare room. He was generous and warm-hearted. Max found qualities in him he wished his own father possessed; not only the gift of words, but the even rarer ability to listen.

Until these lectures and discussions with Tobler, Max had never thought much about politics. But Tobler appeared to think of little else.

'What we need is *genuine* democracy. Government by the people, for the people, *all* the people,' Tobler would say to him earnestly.

'But that's impossible, sir.'

'As things *are*, yes. As things *will be*, no. Monarchy means a hereditary ruling class. Fascism and Nazism represent rule by the middle classes. The only real alternative is communism. Government *by* all the classes, *for* all the classes.'

'But in Russia, things are terrible. I was a prisoner there.'

'So you have often told me. But if you were arrested in England now as an alien without identity papers or money or anyone to vouch for you, I daresay you'd have a pretty rough time.'

'But not be shot in the back of the head.'

'No. But then I find your account of events in Russia rather far-fetched. In that cold, at that altitude, one's susceptibilities become very vulnerable. I can't believe it was *quite* as bad as you maintain. And, after all, we also have the death penalty.'

'But for murderers. Those men were not criminals. They were doctors, lawyers – perhaps even professors.'

'I know a number of professors who should have qualified! Now, another gin?'

'Thank you, yes. But I can't accept what you say about Russia, Professor. Newspapers here have been critical of much that goes on there.'

'And who decides what you read and what you see, dear boy? The capitalist owners of newspapers and newsreel companies. Millionaires with a vested interest in seeing that truth is distorted. I have also been to Russia several times, and at each visit I was more impressed. There *are* things to criticise, of course, but much, much more to admire.'

Max did not agree at all; a casual visitor could not assess a foreign country like a resident – or a prisoner. But as a guest in the professor's home, as well as in his country, he had no wish to argue.

He was not converted by Tobler's idealistic ideas; in this world, he decided, the prize went to the wealthy. The more Tobler talked, the greater grew his determination to become rich.

One night, they sat alone in Tobler's flat listening to a record of Chopin.

'I have never married,' said Tobler suddenly, 'and I never will, but like all men I have the urge to mould a young person. When I first saw you in the lecture room, tall, broad-shouldered, open-faced, I felt instantly that you were someone I would like to help and influence.'

'You have. A great deal,' Max assured him.

'I think so. At least, you will never be gauche again. You know exactly what you want and what price you are prepared to pay for it. Everything has its price, dear boy.'

'You mean, in money?' asked Max.

'Sometimes. Money is, after all, the lubricant of life, and I gather you place a high value on it. But there are other currencies in which dues can be paid. Loyalty. Courage. Devotion. As an academic, I am paid little in monetary terms. That does not worry me, because I inherited a fortune.

'But if you do not inherit money, or marry it, then I agree you must take the hardest course of all – and make it. One person can paint a great picture. Another can design a great building. Yet another, who can barely write his own name, may become richer than either – and patron of both.'

'I will be that third person,' Max told him, grinning.

'Possibly. Money always made me feel guilty,' Tobler went on. 'I used to see men out of work as I drove past in my Delage on my way to a dinner that would cost more than a month's dole.'

'Then why didn't you sell your car?' asked Max.

'What difference would the price of one car make?' Tobler retorted sharply. 'It's the principle that's wrong. The fact that I had so much and they had so little. I wanted everyone to be able to buy a car like mine. But that will never happen under our present system.'

'You say you have never married,' said Max, to change the subject, aware that his remark had irritated the professor.

'Women revolt me,' Tobler said.

'You must have a reason to feel so strongly?'

'A very good reason,' Tobler agreed. 'One night, when I was about thirteen, I woke up suddenly. I heard a cry. My mother was calling out to me for help. I ran to her bedroom. My mother lay naked on the bed. The sheets were thrown back and my father, also naked, was humped above her. His face was turned to one side and saliva was running out of his mouth. His eyes were staring, wide open. He was dead.

'He had been making love to her and had suffered a fatal heart attack. It was a horrible experience. My mother seemed unclean, diminished in my mind. I shall always remember the sight and the smell of it. . . . My own parents.'

Tobler paused, reliving the moment once more, his face contorted with revulsion.

'I have only ever told that story to one other person,' he said at last, 'so you are honoured. By an absolutely astonishing coincidence, he had discovered his parents in exactly the same situation – his mother screaming, his father dead. He was an undergraduate at Cambridge, who came to me for tutorials.'

Max felt embarrassed at the unexpected and unwanted confidence.

'Where is he now?' he asked, for something to say.

'He worked for the Rothschilds for a time when he came down. Now he's in the Foreign Office. Hush-hush work, you know. No-one you're ever likely to meet. Man called Guy Burgess.'

# *Two*

When Max finished his training he was given seventy-two hours' leave before joining his permanent unit. An Austrian on the course recommended a small hotel in the Pennines where he had spent a week before the war, and looking through the Manchester telephone directory for its number, Max saw, in black type: 'Harrow Radio (1937) Ltd.' Instantly, he forgot all about the hotel. If Sam Harris disowned him, then he'd see what his son had to say. He immediately telephoned the number, spoke to a secretary, and finally a cautious male voice came on the line.

'Mr Cornell? You wish to speak to me personally? What company do you represent?'

'None. Only myself. Kransky used to be my name. Like yours was Harschmann. Your father is my uncle.'

'My father? Your uncle?'

'Yes. In Prague.'

A pause, then Harrow's tone of voice changed.

'Where are you?'

'In North Wales. In the army. I've got three days' leave. I want to see you.'

'It's difficult at the moment,' Harrow said quickly. 'We've a lot of work on, and trouble with our suppliers. They keep saying, "Don't you know there's a war on?"'

'I do know,' said Max with feeling, suddenly remembering the long graves at Katyn. 'I needn't stay with you. I just want to make contact. My mother used to speak highly of you and your father.'

'We could put you up, I suppose. When would you get here?'

'There's a train that arrives in Manchester at seventeen-thirty this afternoon.'

'Get off at Stockport. I'll be at the station.'

Paul was fatter than Max had expected and somehow disappointing. Max had not seen him for years and would never have recognised the man who now shook hands with a limp grip. Why had the young boy he remembered grown middle-aged so quickly? He wondered whether Paul thought the same of him.

Private motoring had been banned because of the petrol shortage, but a black Wolseley 25 with a uniformed chauffeur waited outside the station.

'I'm an essential user, you see,' Paul explained, as though reading Max's thoughts. They drove in awkward silence through shabby streets. A queue of women with head scarves waited for a fish shop to open. At a bus stop, middle-aged men in cloth caps regarded them with hostile eyes.

'What sort of work are you doing?' Max asked his cousin.

'Secret stuff, mostly,' Paul replied shortly. 'Radios for the army, the air force.'

'I'm glad you saw me,' Max told him. 'When I arrived here a few months ago I tried to get in touch with your father, but I couldn't get any answer. My company commander then tried, and Uncle Sam said he'd never heard of me.'

Paul looked straight ahead.

'I can't imagine why,' he said. 'Lines crossed somewhere, I should think. Maybe the man tried the wrong Harris?'

'It's possible. However, we can easily clear up the matter. You must have an address for him. I'll get in touch myself.'

'I'm terribly sorry, but I don't know my father's address. We were never close, you know. And since we came to England, we've had even less contact.'

'You mean you've no idea at all where he is?'

'That is so. But don't think too badly of him – or me. We've both had our problems. What about your parents?'

'The Nazis took them off in a truck. That's all I know.'

'But you escaped, obviously?'

'I ran away,' Max admitted.

'Wise boy,' said Paul approvingly.

The car turned into an entrance between two stone gate posts. A house with too much red brick and white pointing stood at the end of a tarmac drive. The tarmac was tinted pink to match its brickwork.

'My little place,' Paul explained proudly. 'And all on cost plus ten.'

'What's that?'

'The rule of business here these days. There was to be no profiteering out of this war, as there was in the last, so manufacturers can only make ten per cent profit on their costs.'

'Nothing wrong with that, surely?' said Max, vaguely irritated by Paul's self-satisfaction.

'Nothing at all,' agreed Paul quickly. 'It simply means that I make far more than I'd have made otherwise, because now everything goes down to costs. Car, chauffeur, entertaining, house. The more we can show we've spent, the more we make.'

'Very lucky for you.'

'Agreed. But I've worked, too. Started at two pounds a week in north London, assembling rotten little wireless sets in cheap wooden cabinets. Then I found a better job up here, met a bank manager's daughter – and married her. That's Rachel. Her father organised a bank loan so that I could start up my own business. Now, I want you to meet her.'

Rachel was dark-haired and slim, and wore a loose cashmere sweater that showed off her figure to its best advantage.

'I didn't know Paul had any relations over here,' she said as they shook hands.

'Ah, lots of things you don't know about me,' said her husband archly. Rachel smiled, but just for a second Max saw contempt in her eyes.

'Rachel's brother is in the army,' Paul explained.

'A prisoner,' Rachel added. 'Captured in Norway.'

Paul smiled at his wife, as though he needed her approval, and she smiled back at him, but only as a muscular contraction of her face. Paul turned to Max.

'First, the good news. I've three steaks for tonight of a size you won't see these days, even in the Commandos,' he said conspiratorially. 'Got to keep in with the right people. The butcher, the garage owner. I see they're all right – slip them a buckshee radio or a gramophone – and they look after me. Now, the bad news. I can't be with you after today. Got to go to Glasgow tomorrow morning. Trouble with a battery supplier. Must sort it out myself.'

Next afternoon, Rachel and Max – wearing Paul's flannels and sports shirt – played tennis on his grass court. Afterwards, they had tea together, and then played records on the gramophone: Jack Hylton, Geraldo, Ambrose.

They were on their third gin and lime, sitting side by side on a wide pink settee.

'I hear your father lent Paul money to start his business?' Max said.

'Well, the bank he works for did.'

'Amounts to the same thing. A professor in Wales taught me that a bank – or any other company – isn't a building or a letterhead, but the people who make it work – or don't. How do you get on with *your* father-in-law?'

'I have never met him. He and Paul parted soon after they arrived here.'

'Do you know where he is living now?' he asked.

'Not a clue. Why the interest?'

'Well, he is my uncle.'

'What about your parents, then? Where are they?'

Max told her.

'I'm sorry,' she said softly. 'I had no idea. It's difficult when you've never been out of England. You read things in the papers, but they don't register. Not until you meet someone who's actually involved. Like you.'

She put her hand on his. Outside, dusk painted the lawn with shadows. Rachel had not turned on the lights in the lounge. Carrol Gibbons and the Savoy Hotel Orpheans began to play 'South of the Border'.

'Women envy me,' said Rachel musingly. 'They think I've got everything. And in the middle of a war, too, when other husbands are away in the army and wives struggle to bring up children on pennyworths of whale steak and dried egg powder.'

'You don't want children?'

'No. Well, Paul doesn't.'

'And you?'

She shrugged and did not answer. Rachel had filled her glass too full. As she reached out for it gin slopped over her white shorts. She did not appear to notice.

'I like the luxury Paul provides. I admit that. But I don't like all the fiddles when so many others are having a terrible time.'

'Then get yourself a job. Help in a hospital, a canteen, anywhere you feel you'd be doing something worthwhile.'

'Paul won't hear of it. Says I must be here to entertain his friends, to help him get permits he needs for glass, sheets of metal, copper wire. That's my war work.'

Her voice was rising. Max put his other hand on hers and stroked it gently to soothe her. Rachel leaned towards him, grateful for sympathy. Her shoulder brushed his, and as she turned he felt the unexpected weight and warmth of a breast through her thin blouse. Their faces moved towards each other. Lips brushed, lightly at first, and then more fiercely. Tongue sought tongue, and Max felt Rachel's long, soft fingers on his body. He was already unbuttoning her blouse, unclipping the hooks on her white brassiere. He cupped her left breast in his hand, feeling her heart beat, and the nipple harden beneath his palm. His other hand was now on her thigh.

'I'm sorry,' he said hoarsely. This was not Katyn, where to refuse could mean death.

'Whatever for?'

'You're my cousin's wife. This is impossible.'

'You think so? Then let's work at it and make it possible. I'm ready to try.'

Rachel unbuttoned his shirt as she spoke, running fingers down his rib cage. Then, more slowly, she unfastened his belt and loosened his trousers. She gripped his other hand and guided it beneath her shorts.

My God, thought Max, I'm bloody mad. My cousin's wife. In his house, as his guest. He drew away sharply.

'What's the matter?' Rachel asked in a voice thickened by gin. Her eyes were wide and clouded with need. In the dimness, Max could see the two globes of her breasts. The room suddenly felt hot, airless, oppressive. He was acting like a lunatic. Paul could come home at any moment – and what chaos would that bring?

'I'm sorry,' said Max thickly.

'Sorry? Is that all you can say? Sorry? For what? For being a bloody fool? You're only a boy, and I thought you were a *man.*'

She picked up his glass of gin from the side table and threw it angrily in his face. Max gasped as the spirit stung his eyes.

'What are you? A virgin? A homo? My *God!*'

Rachel filled her own glass with neat gin and began to gulp it down.

'Get out! You're no good to me! All your bloody cousin thinks about is making money. I want a man! When you came through the door, I thought I'd found one. Do you know that? Sex is a *need,* like food and drink. And who do I get? You!'

She gulped the gin greedily. Some slopped down her chin and between her breasts. Her damp skin shone like oiled silk. Another record dropped, and a thin high voice began to sing: 'Run, Rabbit, Run, Rabbit, Run, Run, Run.'

'You bloody well run off, too! Get your kit bag packed! Brush your teeth and clean your nails like a boy scout! Get out of this bloody house and stay out!'

Rachel began to blunder blindly about the shadowy room. She fell against a chair. The gin bottle had fallen over and the spirit glugged onto the carpet.

Max went up to his bedroom. A maid had pulled the blackout curtains. He washed his face in cold water, changed into his uniform, and scribbled a note to Paul: '*Have had to dash back to camp. Sorry. But thanks for everything. Max.*'

Thanks – for what? For the chance to seduce his wife? For an opportunity declined, an enemy made of Rachel?'

He walked downstairs, kit bag over his shoulder, and paused briefly at the doorway.

'I'm going, then,' he said.

Rachel called out, her voice thickened with self-pity and gin, 'Well, don't talk about it! Get out! Be like that bloody rabbit – *run!*'

The word cracked in Max's mind like a whip. He saw the SS officer kick his father as he lay on the ground and heard his mother shouting '*Run!*' Suddenly, the past erupted in him: all the insults, the humiliations, the fear and the danger. He tasted the stolen caviar, and the Siberian winds made his joints ache. He heard Vasarov order the soldiers to fire, and began to walk towards Rachel as though she was responsible. He would be the master now; the slave would have his revenge.

'Get out!' Rachel called again, but far less loudly. As he reached her, she raised her glass in a taunting toast. He flicked it out of her hand, then gripped both her wrists, pushed out her arms and, releasing her suddenly, ripped off her blouse. She faced him, eyes wide, breasts bare and firm, jutting towards him. He unbuttoned his battledress slowly. Rachel stood nearly a foot shorter than him. He bent and kissed her, gently at first, and then more fiercely. She wriggled out of her tennis shorts and stood naked. Her face was blotched with lust and drink and fear. He took her, not as he had coupled with the women orderlies, not dutifully, but fiercely, hungrily.

Then he forced Rachel back against the sofa, half over one of the tasselled arms. Castors squealed with the harshness of his approach, and the sofa slipped on the highly polished floor. He picked her up, flung her down on a thick white rug. A glass-topped table toppled and china figurines cascaded around them. He did not even notice as they writhed, mouth on mouth, limbs entwined, body in body.

Afterwards, hours later it seemed, they lay sated in the darkness of the room amid the debris. Max was the first to move. He picked up the gin bottle, still nearly half full, and drained it. Rachel lay on the floor, one hand across her eyes.

Max dressed quickly.

'Sorry about this,' he said, indicating the broken ornaments all around them. He was not sorry for what he had done. About that, he had no feeling whatever.

'Sometimes I drink too much. Things get broken,' said Rachel vaguely. 'Clara understands.'

'Clara?'

'The maid. I make it worth her while. She likes a tipple herself sometimes. She also gets lonely.'

'Then, goodbye. I've left a note for Paul saying I had to return to camp. Tell him anything you like.'

'I'll tell him nothing. He won't even ask. He trusts me.'

When Max reached Aberdovey the company clerk was in the troop office, in a requisitioned house, drinking a mug of tea.

'What about a posting?' Max asked him.

'But you already have one.'

'That's in two days. I want something quicker. *Now!*'

'Sorry, no luck, mate. You'll have to sweat it out. What's the hurry, anyway? Husband come back and find you?'

Max smiled grimly.

'Might have been better if he had.'

Paul turned his car off the Preston road across the edge of the common. He drove a Wolseley of the type the police used, because he believed that a police patrol would be less likely to flag it down late at night. And when the boot was crammed with black-market meat and eggs and bottles of whisky, immunity from being stopped and searched was invaluable.

Now the heavy car bumped over rough, sandy tracks. Gorse bushes in blossom flared yellow in its masked headlamps. When Paul was thirty yards off the road, he stopped and switched off the engine and lights. He opened his cigarette case and offered a cigarette to the man in the front seat beside him. Dougie Carton shook his head.

'I've a bad throat,' he explained in a north-country accent. 'And I have to address a meeting in half an hour.'

There was a rustle of a paper bag as he put a cough lozenge in his mouth. Carton was a heavily built man with a sallow complexion and pale eyes and hair. Rachel had once told her husband that he was the most unattractive man he had ever brought home.

'I'll see you're there on time,' said Paul reassuringly. 'A drink, then? I keep a flask in the back.'

'No thanks. It smells on the breath. And half these Labour Party people are teetotal.'

'Well, I won't keep you. It's a matter really of a yes or a no.'

'I'll help you if I can. You know that. What is it this time?'

'I have just landed a new contract to build receivers for the army. They have to be strong enough to be dropped by parachute and able to survive all kinds of shock. Think of the commercial off-shoots after the war.'

'Let's *finish* the bloody war,' replied Carton irritably. 'Survival is more to the point.'

'Now America's in, we can't lose. And I don't want to be left behind when the fighting stops. I can easily adapt the circuits to make portables that would stand up to rough treatment – and still be *really* small. A very big market there.'

He paused deliberately and added, as an afterthought, 'We could even sell a few now. Test public reactions.'

'So what's stopping you?'

'Aluminium for the chassis. I can't buy any. No dockets.'

'That's no problem. There's an over-supply of ali at the moment in the aircraft industry. I read a memo in the ministry this week. Some could be switched. So long as it's put down for essential work. How much do you want?'

'Say twenty tons. In thin sheet, if possible.'

'A hell of a lot of ali. It's pretty light metal, you know.'

'I know. If that's too much, I'll take what I can get. But if I had it all in one go, I'd be safe against price rises, and I could also write it off against tax every year as stock.'

'I don't care about your bloody accounting figures,' replied Carton. 'What's my interest in this?'

'What do you want?'

'I can't promise twenty, but I think I can get you ten. If that goes through without any questions, I'll repeat the order. I may have to grease a few wheels, of course.'

'Of course.'

'Well, say a thousand. In one-pound notes. It's easier for me to distribute in oncers.'

'That's all?'

'Not quite,' said Dougie. 'I don't know how things will go for me after the war. I can't face going back to teaching. Not now I've seen what makes the wheels go round.'

Paul said nothing. He always let the go-between name his price, for then he could never claim he had been beaten down. This was especially true with Dougie Carton, who had once been a trade union official, then a lecturer in economics, and finally had found a safe berth in the amorphous ministry that dealt with the myriad permissions and allocations required by industry in war. Carton's position in the ministry shortened otherwise tortuous lines of communication; a wait of months shrank to a delay of days.

There was a price for this, and Paul had been giving Carton regular sums of money within weeks of their first meeting.

'I want a directorship in your company,' said Carton now. 'Not until after the war, of course, but a letter from you now to say you'd like me to join the board. And I would like £2,000 a year, as of now, guaranteed for five years, rather than these odd bundles of notes. With expenses, of course.'

'A lot of money,' said Paul slowly. 'You'd have to pull your weight.'

'Never let you down so far, have I?'

'Agreed.'

Paul held out his hand.

'You'll have a letter by the end of the week,' he promised. 'Now I'll drive you to your meeting.'

'One long round of meetings, committees, sub-committees,' grumbled Carton.

Paul dropped him at the church hall where he was to speak. The hands of the dashboard clock pointed to eight-thirty. He would be late again for supper. Not that it mattered; Clara would have prepared something cold, and there was always enough to drink. Then he remembered that Max was staying. He had forgotten all about Max.

Paul let himself into the house by the side door, and checked that the blackout curtains were in place before he switched on the lights. One dim lamp burned in the sitting room.

'Max? Rachel?'

Clara came out of the kitchen.

'Mrs Harris was poorly, sir,' she said. 'She went to bed.'

'How, poorly? What do you mean?'

'She has a cold, sir.'

'Sorry to hear that. Where's Mr Cornell?'

'He had to go back to camp suddenly, sir, so Mrs Harris said. He left a note for you. I have laid supper in the dining room.'

'Thank you.'

Paul went upstairs quietly and put his head around the open bedroom door. The room was in darkness. He heard her breathing; a faint snore. She was obviously asleep.

He went downstairs again and ate the cold spam and lettuce that Clara had set out for him. Then he fiddled with the wireless for a time, but he was not in the mood for music-hall or dance music. He crossed to the bookshelves, but he rarely read a book and tonight was not the time to start.

At half past ten he went upstairs again, undressed in his dressing room so as not to awaken Rachel, tip-toed into the bedroom, and climbed carefully into the bed. It felt agreeably warm. He had begun to make electric blankets. He was certain there would be an immense market in these after the war. He stretched his legs luxuriously, and Rachel moved against him. He could smell her familiar mixture of scent and gin. He found it not unattractive.

'So you've come to bed, at last,' she said drowsily.

'I thought you were asleep.'

'I *thought* you would think that.' She chuckled. 'Well, now you *are* here, what are you going to do about it?'

# *Three*

While Paul grew steadily richer on cost plus ten, Max enjoyed less rapid promotion.

He became a corporal when the Commando Unit to which he was attached reached the Middle East, and took part in the Sicily and Italian landings. Then, as a sergeant, he returned to England to prepare for the invasion of France.

The end of the war in Europe found Paul in control of four factories in the north of England, producing radio sets, gramophones, electric blankets, and a new style of alarm clock radio which would awaken a sleeper gently with music. He now stood poised for the great jump forward that would lift him into the ranks of the really rich.

Max ended the war in Austria, with less optimism and, it seemed, no prospects. He was twenty-four, a soldier without professional training of any kind whatever.

While Max wondered – and sometimes worried – about the future, he used his position to try and find his parents. Every day, new details arrived of people who had miraculously survived years in concentration camps. Lists and messages were pinned to doors of bombed houses, giving details of the whereabouts of families who had once lived there, or relatives and friends. Max had discovered several people with the same name, but no-one had heard what had happened to his father or his mother. They had simply vanished, like hundreds of thousands of others.

There was always hope, of course, that they might still turn up somewhere, perhaps suffering from loss of memory or having taken other names, but with each day this hope grew fainter, and finally receded altogether, as the truck carrying them away from the Polish frontier had dwindled down that sunlit August road.

Gradually his life before the war, his experiences before

joining the British army, seemed to belong to another almost imagined world, a place of unreality. He had been one person in those days: he was a different person now.

One evening Max was in the sergeants' mess of 36th British Brigade in Southern Austria when an orderly brought him a posting order. He was to report the following day to the company office of the 8th Argylls in Spittal, a small town forty miles east.

A major flagged down his Jeep as he drove into the town square, and handed him a sheet of paper and a megaphone.

'Sergeant Cornell? Good. Stand on the bonnet of your Jeep and read out this notice in German to these men.'

As the major was speaking, several hundred men, some wearing old German uniforms, others in cast-off civilian suits, marched raggedly into the square. An older man detached himself from the head and saluted the major. To Max's surprise he wore Polish uniform with a colonel's insignia. On his tunic were sewn ribbons of Commander of the Bath, the Military Cross and First World War medals. Max began to read, translating as he went.

'Under agreement reached between the victorious Allies, you and your families are to be returned to the areas from which you came. Your original home countries are now in the sphere of influence administered by the Union of Soviet Socialist Republics. You are therefore to be transferred over the border to the Russian sector today for onward transmission to your homes. The Russian authorities have assured us you will be cared for. I can answer no questions. That is all.'

As these words sank in, the men looked at each other in disbelief, wide-eyed with terror. They realised they had just heard sentence of death. The colonel pointed to his medal ribbons in despair.

'Look at these,' he shouted in English to the major. 'His Majesty King George the Fifth personally invested me as a Commander of the Bath. I won your Military Cross, and now – this! You are murdering us! We go back to certain death!'

Others shouted in English and German, 'Why don't you kill us now? We're *not* Russians!'

'Give 'em what assurances you can,' the major told Max hastily. 'We can't have a riot on our hands.'

As Max began to speak, a civilian came from the shadow of a building and stood with his hands in the pockets of his trench coat, watching the parade. Colonel Vasarov.

The memory of Vasarov pacing beside the graves on the Hill of Goats returned to Max with almost overwhelming intensity; he felt physically sick. The major looked at him in concern.

'You all right, sergeant? Having a turn?'

'Bit of gut trouble, sir,' said Max quickly. 'Nothing serious. Tell me, sir, who is that Russian civvy?'

'One of their head secret police wallahs. Bit of a shit in my book. Name of Vasarov. A colonel, though he doesn't wear uniform.'

'You have to deal with him a lot, sir?'

'As little as I possibly can. He's handling this whole transfer. Which makes me weep for these poor devils. Talk about the Germans and their concentration camps! The Reds are just as bad – or worse.'

'Who exactly are these people we are sending to Russia?'

'Poles, Yugoslavs and so on. Most of 'em have nothing to do with Russia at all, but because the Russians have seized their homelands they are apparently technically Soviet citizens. They'll make slave labourers of the men, and kill the officers.'

'Some are wearing German uniforms, though, sir.' Max pointed out.

''Course they bloody well are. What do you expect 'em to wear – fig leaves? They've been in refugee camps for years – poor sods. Towards the end, the Germans gave 'em the only spare clothes they had – uniforms.'

As they spoke, a line of trucks drove into the square and halted; the drivers lowered the tail-boards. The major shouted an order to a British sergeant-major who appeared in a doorway on the edge of the square.

British soldiers carrying rifles now doubled out of houses. As the refugees saw them, a handful moved reluctantly and dejectedly towards the first truck.

'Get a hold of them!' bellowed the sergeant-major. 'Get their bloody arses moving!'

The troops began to push the refugees with the butts of their rifles. When they did not move, they hit them, reluctantly at first, and then with the fury of desperation. When the trucks were filled, they roared away. Within ten minutes, the square was deserted.

'That all I have to do, sir?' Max asked the major.

'Yes, for the time being, I'm glad to say. I'll take you to your mess.'

They drove to a house set back from the road on the edge of the town. Max climbed out stiffly. He felt unclean. His battledress was impregnated with the sweat and tears of other people's fear. An orderly showed him to an attic room, up a staircase, past photographs of a family who had lived in the house before the war. A boy patted the head of a spaniel. A smiling girl and a man with a Meerschaum pipe held tennis rackets. Where were they now?

Max spread out his bedding roll on a spring mattress beneath a crucifix on the wall. Cold water dripped from a brass tap in the bathroom. He washed, and went downstairs. A sergeant was reading a newspaper. He introduced himself as Dick Carpenter.

'You look a bit shagged', he said. 'Have a whisky. Ration's just come up.'

'Thanks.'

The mess corporal poured a large measure. Max drank it neat.

'Where are you from?' Carpenter asked him.

'Brigade. Interpreter. Been giving bad news to those refugees going to Russia.'

'Poor bastards. I was asked to have a go at that, but my German wasn't good enough. Bloody glad, too. Ever been into the Russian sector?'

Max shook his head; this was not the moment to tell of his experiences with the Russians.

'I have a car and a pass,' Carpenter continued. 'Come across tonight, and see for yourself how bloody awful it is.'

'What are you doing there?'

'Private trade'.

'With Russian communists?'

'Sure. Their wide boys are as keen as anyone else to make a bit on the side. I shift silver – coffee pots, spoons, that sort of thing. The Krauts are so desperate, they'll even sell their cars for cigarettes. I've already shipped home two Mercedes and a BMW 320.'

'How?'

'A couple of empty three-tonners go to one of the Channel ports to pick up stores. Right? I slip the driver something for his trouble, shove the cars inside in bloody great crates marked "Enemy equipment for evaluation". The Customs never bother with those. Easy as pissing against a wall.'

'Hardly the best way to build up confidence among a defeated people.'

'Damn good way to build up capital, though. Anyway, if you've done moralising, there's a seat buckshee tonight if you want it.'

'I'll take it.'

A muddy river, the Mur, divided the two sectors: on the Russian side, a few stray dogs prowled the deserted streets. The trucks that had carried the refugees away hours earlier were now parked nose to tail against a high wall topped with broken glass. All the houses in the vicinity appeared deserted.

Carpenter drove to the railway station where a train waited, steam hissing from its engine. Half a dozen Red Army soldiers, rifles piled nearby, sat on ammunition boxes on the platform, playing cards. The two men walked down the line of filthy carriages. Every window had been smashed and barbed wire nailed across the open frames. All doors were padlocked on the outside, and a smell of excrement and stale sweat drifted sourly through the windows. From one open window, a hand waved feebly as they passed. There were sounds of snoring and sobbing. Someone cried out in Polish, 'Hear us, Holy Mother, in our need! Holy Mary, hear us!'

'There's usually an interpreter somewhere about, if I can find him,' said Carpenter. They found him in a waiting room, asleep on a bench, an old man with grey stubble. Carpenter shook him roughly, and he started up in surprise and alarm.

'Calm down,' Carpenter told him soothingly. 'I only want to know when this train is due out.'

The interpreter glanced at a clock on the wall.

'Some time before midnight.'

'Any trouble so far?'

'Four officers killed themselves as soon as they got in the train. Cut their wrists with bits of glass from a window,' said the interpreter, watching the Russian soldiers nervously.

'Any others dead?'

The old man swallowed, but said nothing. The Russian soldiers began an argument among themselves. Carpenter took a packet of twenty Gold Flake from his battledress pocket.

'In the steel warehouse,' the old man whispered, reaching out hastily for the cigarettes. He could trade them for a week's food.

'I've got to meet my contact outside there,' Carpenter told Max. 'Let's have a look-see.'

They drove to a warehouse, several streets away, grim and featureless, without windows. Carpenter stopped the Jeep, lit a cigarette and sat, waiting, hands on the wheel. Max walked to the main door of the building. It was padlocked. A metal staircase led to an upper floor, so he climbed to a small iron landing. He slipped a bolt, opened a door, and walked through onto a gallery

Far beneath him, an oil-stained concrete floor was littered with metal brackets and castings. In a far corner loomed a pyramid of greyish rags. He walked around the gallery until he was directly above the pile. They were not rags, but uniforms. Then he saw that each uniform contained the corpse of its wearer.

Some men had shrunk in death. Faces were bruised or bloodied, arms and legs broken and twisted at unnatural angles. This was not a warehouse; it was a charnel house. These refugees had begun their journey home and ended it here, barely a mile away, and he had willingly connived at their murder.

Max wanted to void his disgust and horror. He ran around the gallery, feet ringing on the metal catwalk – and almost knocked over a man who had just entered from the outside steps.

'What are you doing here?' the man asked him sharply in German.

Max shook his head, only seeing him as a vague blur in the dusk. He leaned on the rail and vomited over it. Sweat rose beneath his scalp, and he held the rail tightly in case he lost his balance and fell.

Then his vision cleared. He turned and found himself face to face with Colonel Vasarov.

'What are you doing here?' Vasarov repeated in English. Max was surprised at his lack of accent.

'Seeing what happened to the refugees who came over in the trucks today', he replied, also in English.

'And are you satisfied?'

'They are dead.'

'They deserved to die,' replied Vasarov quietly. 'They were traitors, turncoats who fought against their mother country.'

'How do you know?'

'We have records. In any case, some of these were shot trying to escape.'

'Escape? From whom? You told them they were going home.'

'They tried to escape the consequences of their treachery. Your face is vaguely familiar, sergeant,' Vasarov continued slowly. 'Have we met before?'

'I was in the square today.'

'Ah. Perhaps that is where I saw you. Yet I could swear I have seen you somewhere else. Have you ever been to Moscow?'

'No, sir. Have you ever been to London?'

'Not yet. But I hope to go eventually. Now, if you have seen enough, sergeant, I will have you escorted back over the bridge to the British Sector.'

'I am with a sergeant who has a pass.'

'Then I will have you both escorted.'

Vasarov padlocked the door behind them. Their boots made the iron staircase boom like a metal gong. Carpenter was still in the Jeep. His cigarette was barely half smoked. To Max's surprise, Carpenter nodded to Vasarov.

'I was wondering where you'd got to,' he said.

'I had to padlock the upper door,' Vasarov explained. He glanced at Max.

'I didn't know you were with this sergeant.'

'Well, I am,' replied Carpenter. 'Now, what have you got for me, Comrade Colonel? I can't hang about all night.'

'Some silver items and share certificates for Siemens and Krupp. And a DKW car.'

'Good. Our trucks will be bringing more prisoners over here tomorrow. You give the driver of the last one some cigarettes. He'll drive round the back of our billet, and we'll unload it.'

'The price is two thousand cigarettes,' said Vasarov.

'Seventeen-fifty.'

Vasarov shrugged.

'Eighteen-fifty. Players.'

They shook hands.

Max climbed into the car beside Carpenter, and they drove back over the bridge.

'You know that character's in the secret police?' Max asked him as soon as they were out of earshot.

'So what? He wants to salt a bit away, like the rest of us.'

'If he's caught, he'll be for the high jump.'

'That's his worry. And if I'm caught, I'll be for the army nick at Northallerton. But we won't be, either of us. Now – a drink before we part?'

Max shook his head.

'Thank you, no. It's an early start for me tomorrow,' he explained.

Max bought his whisky ration from the mess corporal, and in his attic room, he poured a large measure into his tooth mug and drank it neat, sitting on the edge of his bed. The faint sound of accordion music drifted in on the night air.

Carpenter unexpectedly put his head round the door.

'Couple of blokes here to see you, Max,' he said. 'Civvies.'

'Krauts?' Max asked him.

'No. Say they've come out from London. Look like coppers to me. I could understand it if they were on to me – but you've only just arrived!'

Max heard footsteps on the stairs. Two men, incongruous

in tweed jackets and flannel trousers, appeared at the door.

'Sergeant Cornell?' one asked him in a deep booming voice.

'Yes. Who are you?'

'We're here on a private matter. We could discuss it better alone.'

'I can take a hint,' said Carpenter and clattered off down the stairs.

'Now, what do you want?'

The two men sat down in the only two chairs in his room. Max had to sit on the edge of the bed, and instantly felt outmanoeuvred and therefore wary.

'I am Major Blaikie,' the man with the deep voice explained. He only had one arm; his left sleeve was pinned to his jacket. 'This is Captain Reid. We understand you volunteered for X-Troop?'

'That is true.'

'We also believe you would like British citizenship?'

'I was virtually promised it when I joined the Troop.'

'But not in writing?'

'No, sir. Only verbally.'

'Quite so. There is no reason why it should not be granted, but, of course, you will appreciate that the country can only absorb a limited number of new British subjects each year. In your case, there may be a way of accelerating things.'

'What do you mean?'

'We are short of men like you with pre-war European backgrounds.'

'We?'

'What I loosely call the British Security Service. Most of our people in Europe before the war ended up in concentration camps. We have to build a new network virtually from scratch – and fast. I am offering you a job with us as a civilian, with the equivalent rank of army captain, drawing a captain's pay and allowances, and the possibiity of a gratuity when you leave.'

'What about citizenship?'

'That would come automatically. When you finish your tour.'

'How long would I have to serve?'

'Three years minimum. You'd have a good cover, perhaps as a civil servant in the Allied Control Commission.'

'And if I decline?'

'That is entirely up to you, my dear chap,' said Blaikie. 'You would return to Britain and then I understand you are being posted to India.'

'And if I was demobbed after that, what then?'

'Your application for British citizenship would be processed in the usual way through the normal channels.'

'But would it be granted?'

'That is not for me to say,' said Blaikie, shaking his head, as though he wished it were. 'That is entirely out of our court. On the other hand, you play ball with us . . .'

'And you will play ball with me,' Max finished for him.

'You have the idiom perfectly,' said Blaikie approvingly. 'Well, what's it to be, then?'

'There doesn't seem much option.'

'Welcome aboard,' said Blaikie, shaking his hand.

'You don't sound very enthusiastic, old chap,' said Reid reproachfully to Max, speaking for the first time.

'I'm tired. You've caught me at a bad time.'

'Let's drink to better times,' said Blaikie quickly.

He took a silver flask from his pocket, filled the cap with brandy. Max produced his metal tooth mug and a mess tin. Blaikie poured out two further measures, perceptibly less generous than his own.

'To us,' he said grandly. 'Within a couple of days, with luck, you'll be back in England.'

To Max's surprise, a car was waiting for him at the docks at Dover, to take him to the demobilisation centre at Dorking. Here he received a civilian demob suit, a discharge certificate and a gratuity of £110. The same car drove him to a country house between Beaconsfield and Oxford to begin two months' training. Here he learned, among other skills, more ways of killing silently than the army had ever taught him.

At the end of the course, he was driven to Blaikie's flat off the Brompton Road.

'Join the club,' Blaikie said in welcome. 'But now you're a member, don't carry the cares of the world on your shoulders.

There's very little *you* can do to change anything. The sooner you realise that, the better.

'You won't be alone in Germany, of course, though sometimes it may seem like it. We've others working for us out there, too, but you won't know them and they won't know you – unless it's absolutely essential to break cover.

'If you ever had to contact them, you will be given a means of recognition, and other identification checks, which we change from time to time. If you ignore these, or take *anyone* on trust, or believe some excuse that they've forgotten the right recognition word, you do so entirely at your own risk. And the risk, my friend, is death. Yours.'

'It's as bad as that?' Max asked him.

'Of course,' replied Blaikie, surprised at the naive question. 'And getting worse all the time. If you don't believe me, consider the international situation. Five years ago, Britain controlled eighty per cent of the world's trade. Our currency was backed by the largest gold reserves in the world. India was an immense source of raw material. We had rubber in Malaya, tea in Ceylon, teak, rice, oil in Burma, bauxite in Jamaica. You name it, Britain owned it or controlled it.

'When the Japanese humiliated us at Singapore, we lost much more than an Empire outpost. We lost the myth of our supremacy. As a result, we now face trouble in the east. We've already got it in India, which will obviously become independent. India's like the main terminus at the end of a railway line. If you close that, you've much less reason for keeping open all the other stations along the route. So we will no doubt give them all the freedom to run straight into the arms of another country, which really *will* exploit them. America has done all it can to dismantle the British Empire, because they want our markets.'

'Will they get them?'

Blaikie shrugged.

'The Russians also have an interest in dismantling our Empire. Communism thrives on chaos, so there is bound to be a clash between America and Russia over division of the spoils.'

'So you don't see much hope, major?'

'Do you? We sold nearly all our overseas investments to finance a war from which we could not expect to gain anything whatever – not even our original aim of helping Poland.

'Until Japan forced the United States into the war, the Americans insisted that we built new factories for them if we wished them to produce arms for us. Now all those brand-new factories, built with our money, will compete against our bombed-out factories and pre-war equipment.

'We built fighter aircraft, while the Yanks built bombers. Now they can capture world markets for airliners, which are simply converted bombers. I could go on and on, but enough of the gloom. Our job is to help to protect our country's interests – what's left of them. There isn't much we can do, of course. Often there's nothing. But we try. Any questions?'

'The way you spell things out, none seem worth asking.'

'Good,' said Blaikie with satisfaction. 'That's the right frame of mind in which to begin working for me.'

By the end of that week Max was billeted in a house north of Berlin, two miles from the Russian zone, attached to a branch of the Allied Control Commission that traced relatives of survivors from concentration camps.

At first, he was given routine minor tasks. What goods and factory equipment were being moved east by rail? How much did refugees from the Russian zone know of Russian military movements? Then, one evening, Blaikie called him into his office.

'We want you to meet someone who's given us good material so far – perhaps simply to work his way in, perhaps not. You'll have to decide for yourself if he's kosher. Give him whatever he wants for his info – so long as it doesn't cost too much. You know what the Treasury's like.

'The fellow who's been dealing with this man – whom we know as Butcher – has been recalled to London. His code name was Cardinal. The informant will know you as White.'

'When do I meet him?'

'Twenty-two hundred hours tonight. Alone.'

He gave him an eight-figure map reference.

'Is he German?'

'No, Russian. That's what makes him valuable. Listen to everything he has to tell you. Scientific, political and military.'

'Seems a pretty vague assignment.'

'It's a pretty vague career, but it happens to be ours. Little bits of information may mean nothing on their own. Added to other apparently equally useless items, they could add to something valuable. Of course, they can add up to bugger-all. And it's my experience that they mostly do.'

The map reference numbers crossed at a point almost exactly two miles inside a forest off the main Berlin to Oranienburg road. Max felt no enthusiasm at the prospect of meeting a Russian stranger in the darkness, so close to the Russian sector, without any backup whatever. He cleaned his issue Smith and Wesson .38 with particular care, put it in his jacket pocket, then rolled up a pair of socks and placed them inside his hat to provide some protection against a blow to his head. He checked that his torch worked, that he had a notebook and two pencils – in case one broke. Then he changed the registration plates on his car and set off.

When he reached the bend in the road where he had decided to leave the car, he switched out the lights, turned off beneath some overhanging trees, and reversed so that his car faced the way it had come. He locked the door and stuck a spare ignition key behind the rear bumper with adhesive plaster. Then, checking his bearings with an army issue compass, Max set off into the woods.

The looming mass of fir trees stood so close together that it was difficult to find a way between them. Dry twigs cracked like brittle bones beneath his feet.

The rendezvous was a small clearing in the forest, with tracks leading off like spokes from a wheel. The moon had risen, and pale light filtered down through a tracery of high branches. He stood against the bole of a fir tree, to one side of the open space.

As ten o'clock came and went, his unease increased. He would give Butcher another five minutes and then leave. He felt increasingly that someone was watching him – perhaps expecting Cardinal – and therefore wary of making himself known to a stranger. Finally, he heard a slight intake of breath only yards away.

'White – *Weiss*?'

A man whispered the question in English and German.

'Butcher,' replied Max. He could sense fear and distrust only feet away. He tensed himself, right hand in his pocket, gripping his revolver. 'I have a torch,' he said in German. 'I am taking it from my pocket. There is nothing to be alarmed about.'

He shone the light briefly on the ground. Twigs crackled more confidently as the man came into the clearing. In the torchlight Max saw cheap shoes of leather substitute, shoddy grey trousers, uncreased and frayed at the turnups. He raised the torch slowly. A dark blue raincoat, a white round-edged collar, a black tie. Asimir Vasarov was blinking in its unexpected glare.

'We have already met,' said Max carefully. He flashed the torch on his own face, and switched it off.

'So we have,' agreed Vasarov. His voice contained neither surprise nor warmth. Max experienced an almost physical sense of revulsion at his nearness. He had only to reach out and he could have touched him, a gesture that would have meant instant death at Katyn. A slight, trained movement of Max's wrist and his elbow, and he could kill Vasarov without a sound, and avenge all those he had murdered, directly or by proxy, at Katyn and in God alone knew how many other killing grounds. No-one would ever know they had met. He would simply report to Blaikie that Butcher had not kept the appointment. The temptation was great, but he overcame it. He had other orders, and other plans in mind.

'I was expecting someone else,' said Vasarov cautiously.

'Cardinal has gone back to England.'

'You know my name?'

'Butcher.'

'Cardinal,' said Vasarov musingly. 'A religious name. He had once been a monk, apparently, I also studied at a religious seminary. Odd how the priesthood and our profession have so much in common. Both call for considerable acting ability. And we pass on as truth stories we cannot possibly confirm. Cardinal was a Catholic.'

'Like my mother. My father was Jewish,' Max replied, and instantly regretted it. Cornell was not a Jewish name. He did not even look Jewish – so why give away unnecessary information? He saw a faint gleam of interest in Vasarov's eyes.

'What have you for me?' asked Max.

'The Berlin elections this month. The Party is determined to win.'

'But the Party is not very strong in Berlin. And people there know how you treat people in the Soviet zone.

'To show that this is pure capitalist propaganda, we are eradicating many shortages that affect voters. You will make a note?'

'Yes.'

Max took the notebook out of his pocket and waited, pencil poised, like a newspaper reporter.

'One million boxes of matches. 1,555,000 pairs of shoes. A bottle of gin for every male voter, half a bottle for every woman. Sixty thousand pairs of children's shoes. Thousands of bicycle and truck tyres. Tons of cement, steel, paper, glass for building work.'

Vasarov paused.

'Anything else to tell me?' Max asked him.

'Yes. An air force matter. The Tupolev Tu4 and Tu70 are our most modern aircraft. You in the west cannot understand how we developed them so quickly – years ahead of all your expectations?'

Max nodded.

'The reason is simple – and has a lesson for you. They are only larger copies of the American B29. On July 29, 1944, B29 Super fortresses of the twentieth USAAF flew from northern China to attack the Showa Steel Works in Anshan, Manchuria. One of these planes, number 42-5256 – I give you this so your people can check my story – was hit by anti-aircraft fire. One engine failed, and the pilot realised he would never make the fifteen hundred miles return trip, so he decided to head towards Vladivostock, about five hundred miles away.

'As he approached the Soviet airfield, he gave the international radio signal that he was a friendly machine. To his amazement, Yak 9 fighters came up and opened fire on him and forced him away to a tiny airstrip near Tavrichanka. He landed here – and was immediately interned with his crew.

'Shortly afterwards, another B29 was forced down in the same way. Both crews were eventually released, but their aircraft stayed behind. Our engineers dismantled them into their component parts – a total of seventy-six thousand specifications for material and production processes.

'Andrei Tupolev, who designed our Russian bombers, was in charge. Everything was copied – radar, radio, engines. We stole years of American research. We haven't superior technology. But we do make use of *all* our opportunities. Never forget that, Mr White. It is the most important lesson you will ever learn in dealing with us.'

Vasarov paused. Max waited. The forest was so still, it also seemed to be listening.

'One more thing,' Vasarov continued. 'A personal matter. I risked my life every time I met Cardinal. Now I start all over again with you. One hint of our meetings and I am dead.'

Could this nervous man really be the confident colonel whom Max had watched furtively and fearfully through the window of the hut in Katyn? What had happened since then to make him ready to risk his life by selling items of information about aircraft and boxes of matches and half bottles of gin?

'I have accepted these risks,' Vasarov continued, 'but now I find I face greater ones. We have sleepers in every country of the world. Black. White. Brown. Yellow. All patiently await the signal to awake, like the Sleeping Beauty. They are in the British government. In the White House. In the Quai d'Orsay. Men and women in positions of great trust and political sensitivity. I fear these people, because while I do not know who they all are or where they all are, some of them know who I am. It is therefore imperative that nothing I tell you is ever attributed to me by name.'

'You have my word,' said Max. 'Can you give me an example of these sleepers?'

'From the war then, so that you can check what I say. Why did Rudolf Hess, the German Deputy Führer, a prisoner in England since 1941, receive a life sentence at Nuremberg while others of infinitely greater guilt received much milder sentences? Because we in Moscow knew that he flew to Britain to warn Churchill that the Nazis were about to attack Russia – and to offer peace with Germany if Britain would remain neutral during this attack.

'We know this because we received a copy of the transcript of the secret meeting Hess had with Churchill's representative, the Canadian Lord Beaverbrook, *on the day that it was made.* Hess received a life sentence on Soviet insistence – as a warning to others. An example of penetration at a fairly low level. Imagine what secrets are passed on from those more highly placed. Now,' he paused. 'I have a favour to ask you.' Vasarov lifted up one foot. 'Feel that shoe.'

Max ran his fingers over the sodden, shoddy sole and the imitation leather upper.

'I want you to bring me a pair of good shoes when we next meet,' said Vasarov. 'Waterproof. Black. Size nine and a half. Wide fitting.'

Then Vasarov turned, and without a handshake or a backward glance, walked down one of the paths into the forest. Max waited until the sound of his footsteps vanished, and then made his way back to his car. He carried his .38, finger behind the trigger, in case someone jumped him, but the forest was silent, seemingly asleep.

He felt immense relief that the meeting was over. He did not trust Vasarov. More worrying, he admitted to himself as he accelerated along the wide empty road, was the fact that he still feared him.

Blaikie pressed the thick dark shag tobacco into his pipe with the ball of his thumb. Max's report of his meeting lay on his desk.

'Odd,' Blaikie said at last. 'One and a half million pairs of shoes, the man says. And yet he can't get *one* pair for himself! Rings true, though. My brother-in-law, David Graham – just demobbed from the Navy – works in a bank handling thousands of pounds every day. Yet he says he doesn't earn enough to buy a decent car.

'Now, about these sleepers. Keep on to him about their names. Even one would be a start.'

Blaikie nodded a dismissal. Max paused, and Blaikie looked at him enquiringly.

'What can you tell me about Butcher?' asked Max.

Blaikie placed a forefinger against the side of his nose and shook his head.

'Nothing I can pass on,' he said.

'What does he know about me?'

'No more than you tell him. And in our trade, you never tell anyone any more than you have to. You know our motto?'

'Trust no-one?'

'You're learning.'

For some time after Max had left his office, Blaikie sat in his chair, puffing his pipe. Vasarov's warning about infiltrators recalled an incident in Ankara a year earlier, when he had been attached to the British consulate.

Late one afternoon, a stranger came into the building and asked to see the officer for whom Blaikie was deputising. Blaikie saw him in an interview room. The visitor explained nervously that he was Konstantine Volkov, the newly appointed Russian consul. He and his wife had just arrived from Moscow, and his posting was a cover for his real career in the NKVD. Most of his friends in the service had disappeared in Stalin's latest purge and he wanted to quit while he still had the chance. For a safe passage to the West, he could offer full details of sophisticated security systems in NKVD offices throughout the world, the covers particular agents used, even the registration numbers of their cars, plus the names of communist sleepers in British and American government departments.

Volkov urged that his offer should not be sent to London in code, because the NKVD had already broken all British diplomatic codes. He was clearly very nervous, and asked for a reply within three weeks.

Blaikie sent a copy of Volkov's conditions to London in the diplomatic bag, but to his astonishment, twenty days passed without even a routine acknowledgement. Finally, within hours of Volkov's deadline, an emissary arrived from Whitehall. He introduced himself as Harold Philby. He had just been put in charge of the Soviet Section of MI6, and so would personally deal with this matter because of its obvious importance.

'So why did you delay so long before coming out?' Blaikie asked him irritably.

'Couldn't make it any earlier, old man,' Philby replied blandly. 'It would have interfered with leave arrangements.'

Blaikie now tried to contact Volkov urgently, but without success. Philby stayed on in Istanbul for a few days, enjoying the warm weather. Then, chiding Blaikie gently for wasting his time, he returned to London.

Blaikie's own posting to Germany came through on the same day. As he waited for his plane at Istanbul airport, a Russian military aircraft suddenly appeared very low over the trees, and landed in a far corner of the runway. Operators in the control tower tried unsuccessfully to radio the pilot, because he had not received landing clearance, and officials raced to the aircraft in a Jeep to discover the reason for its unscheduled arrival. Blaikie knew one of the controllers and jumped into the Jeep with them.

As they approached the plane, the driver was forced to swerve wildly to avoid a car that suddenly appeared through a gap in the perimeter fence. A body, strapped to a stretcher, was hurried from the car into the aircraft. Only his head was visible. For an instant still etched in Blaikie's mind, his eyes met Volkov's. Then the door slammed and the Russian plane roared down the runway and was gone.

Someone in the British consulate – or someone else in London – had warned the Russians of Volkov's imminent defection. But who?

Reid came into the room, and Blaikie showed him Max's report.

'Think this fellow Cornell's out of his depth?' Reid asked, when he had finished.

'Totally,' Blaikie replied immediately. 'He's only a chicken-hawk, of course.'

'What's that, exactly?'

'You never served in the desert, did you? Well, on the principal that fishermen put out a sprat to catch a mackerel, some desert tribes tie a live chicken to a stake in the hope that it will attract a hawk – which they can then snare.'

'So Max is only bait? Is that why you were so keen on engaging him?'

'We needed someone we could lean on. He needed British citizenship. I also wanted a man who'd had some association with Vasarov before. And there aren't many of them around. The closest I could get was that Cornell had been at Katyn when Vasarov was in command.'

'You know he saw Vasarov over the Mur river? Apparently they were involved in some black-market deal with Sergeant Carpenter.'

'I know,' said Blaikie. 'Another bit of luck for us. Strengthens their contact. Now each knows a secret about the other.'

'There are no real secrets now,' replied Reid bitterly. 'Everything's an open secret. It's everyone for himself.'

# Four

Vasarov paused as he reached the edge of the forest, took a metal flask from his pocket and gulped down four mouthfuls of neat vodka. Despite the coolness of the night, he was sweating and his heart beat like a drum. He hated these secret meetings, but fear for his own survival had finally overcome his fear of discovery. One day, his turn for denunciation must come. His only sure hope of survival lay in somehow fashioning an escape route to the West.

His first opportunity had come in Austria, when he had met the English sergeant, Carpenter, who had been so openly critical of almost everything in which Vasarov was supposed to believe that Vasarov had finally hinted that some things in Russia were not altogether to his liking, either.

Carpenter invited him to a party in the British sector, where he met the man he later knew as Cardinal. He declared that Vasarov had drunk too much to be able to drive himself back over the bridge, and put him up for the night in a requisitioned house. Vasarov was surprised at Cardinal's knowledge of events in Russian politics and guessed that Cardinal worked for some Intelligence organisation. Slowly, Vasarov grew to trust him, and a deal was arranged: so much money deposited in a Geneva bank for each new item of information that Vasarov could supply. This was dangerous, but it was also the only way Vasarov knew of building up capital and goodwill in the West, which one day he might need to save his life. Now Cardinal had gone, and White had taken his place. The payments were still being made; the shoes were simply an urgent requirement and would test White's goodwill.

Vasarov climbed into the requisitioned German Steyr that he shared with two colleagues, thankfully kicked off his soaking shoes and started the engine.

Could he trust White? The fact that he had met him in Austria, and that White knew of his illegal capitalist transactions with Carpenter, made Vasarov uneasy. Added to this was the feeling that he had seen White long before that. Could his photograph be in the NKVD files of foreign spies that he had studied in his office in Lubyanka? Or had he glimpsed him face to face somewhere? But if so, where?

He wound down the window and the scent of firs poured in, recalling other forests faraway, in Tiflis and Katyn.

Three years after that massacre, the German army overran Katyn in their drive for Smolensk, and seized several peasants for interrogation. They suggested to the Germans that they dig in the hillside, where they would find proof of the Soviet mass-killings which had long been rumoured.

When the bodies were exhumed, German Intelligence Officers examined the contents of their pockets. It soon became clear, from dates on letters and newspaper clippings, that the deaths had taken place during the spring of 1941.

Nazi authorities then invited neutral Swedish and Swiss scientists to carry out a full examination of the bodies, for this discovery was of vast propaganda value. These doctors reported that the bodies had either been shot in the back of the head, or beaten to death. Some had struggled before they were shot, some had had their wrists tied together.

Shortly after this announcement, which received world-wide publicity, Vasarov happened to meet the major from Katyn in the lift at Lubyanka.

'What will happen now?' Vasarov asked him. 'The Nazis seem to have pretty conclusive proof of what took place, don't they?'

'The fascist hyenas are lying in their teeth,' replied the major instantly. '*Pravda* prints an article this morning which I strongly recommend to you, comrade, as a masterly statement of the facts. I will have it delivered to your office.'

The cutting arrived within minutes. Vasarov read it with mounting amazement and uneasiness.

> Goebbels' slanderers have been spreading vile fabrications alleging that the Soviet authorities carried out a mass shooting of Polish officers in the spring of 1941, in the

> Smolensk area. In launching this monstrous invention, the German-Fascist scoundrels did not hesitate to spread the most unscrupulous and base lies in their attempts to cover up crimes which, as has now been evident, were *perpetrated by themselves.*
>
> The German-Fascist report on this subject leaves no doubt as to the tragic fate of the former Polish prisoners-of-war who in 1941 were engaged in construction work in areas west of the Smolensk region, and who fell into the hands of German-Fascist hangmen, after the withdrawal of the Soviet troops from the Smolensk area.

When he had finished reading, Vasarov sat for a moment, looking at the obligatory portraits of Lenin and Stalin on the opposite wall. Originally, only a picture of Lenin hung in each office, but this was a new portrait which showed Stalin slightly in front of Lenin, as the increasingly important father figure. When Vasarov took the newspaper back to the major's office, the major did not offer him a seat.

'There is no doubt that this is a foul Nazi lie against our motherland, against workers everywhere, and especially against our beloved leader,' he said categorically.

'But we were there,' replied Vasarov nervously. 'We both know what really happened. The fascists were a thousand miles away at the time.'

'Let me speak to you frankly, Comrade Vasarov,' said the major coldly. 'Unless you cease to spread such lying rumours, you will find yourself in serious trouble, comrade.'

This total denial of what both men knew to be true showed Vasarov how desperate and dangerous his own position could become. No-one was safe. They were all like men on ladders in a strong wind. The higher they climbed, the further they had to fall. Vasarov's only sure hope of survival was to perfect his escape route while he had the chance. If White proved trustworthy, then he would give him his trust.

Nina was dreaming.

She hurried down the crumbling street, past rows of new-made graves, where steel helmets rusted on unpainted wooden crosses, and pyramids of rubble stood like raw burial mounds on each side of the road. This was Berlin in 1945, a return to the caves.

Before dusk she had to reach the Von Seeckt barracks in Spandau, an industrial suburb seven miles out in the Russian Sector. After dark, drunken Red Army soldiers raced through the ruined streets, shooting at anyone they saw.

Nina and her elder sister Anna had been brought up in Hungary, but had moved to Poland before the war. Her mother and father were dead. When the war had ended, the girls had managed to reach Austria with thousands of other refugees, homeless and without any identification papers to prove their nationality. Eventually, they had arrived at the vast tented camp near Spittal.

One morning, as Anna walked into the town in the rain, a Jeep overtook her and stopped. The Russian driver introduced himself as Asimir Vasarov, working in the Commission for the Rehabilitation of Refugees; he would give her a lift.

Vasarov frequently passed the camp gates, and so she accepted several more lifts into the town and back again. Then she became his mistress. She had known that this would happen as soon as she met him – not that he attracted her, but in her situation, without influence, money or papers, she needed a protector. She tried to discover what was going to happen to the refugees, but he was non-committal.

Then one day he told her she and Nina should leave camp early the following morning and keep away until dusk. She was not to mention this to anyone else, and had to swear her sister to secrecy.

The two girls left, and in the evening, they returned, on Vasarov's advice, to the square in Spittal. Here, Vasarov met them. He had arranged for them to share a room in a requisitioned house outside the town. With British help, everyone else in the camp had been forcibly deported to Russia.

Vasarov suggested that they accompanied him on a visit to Berlin. They could work in the kitchens at Spandau barracks for the week or ten days he would be away, and then return to Austria with him. By then, the danger should be over. No-one would challenge them so long as he was with them.

The barracks kitchen in Berlin where Nina was heading was immense. Everything had been designed with the German wish for hygiene and efficiency. But the Russian cooks who now used it had never seen such splendid equipment. These cooks, each wearing three or four looted wrist watches, and chain-smoking American cigarettes, stolidly stirred vast pots of stew, oblivious of the stench and rubbish around them. Nina hurried past a line of rusting and abandoned tanks, a slight, elfin-like girl with large eyes, ringed now by purple shadows because of her constant worry about the future. She owed her freedom to the chance of being Anna's sister. But if Vasarov tired of Anna, what would happen to both of them?

Nina began to overtake the only other person on the road ahead of her, walking in the same direction. He was a tall man wearing a Luftwaffe jacket, with a yellow armband marked by three black dots to show that he had been blinded on active service. He tapped the road ahead carefully with a white stick. In his other hand he carried a grubby white envelope. His eyes were shielded by steel-rimmed spectacles with black lenses.

Hearing Nina's footsteps, he paused and turned slightly, in the way of the blind, so that his head was at an angle, listening.

'Excuse me,' he said as she drew level. 'But it is a long time since I was here in Berlin, and I think I have lost my bearings.'

'You are near the bridge at Stresow,' she explained. 'Where are you going to?'

'Alexander Platz. I have a letter to deliver.'

'It will be dark before you reach Alexander Platz,' Nina told him, falling in step beside him.

'It is always dark when you cannot see.'

'I could deliver the letter for you.'

'You are very kind. But it is vitally important that it is delivered tonight.'

'I could do that.'

'Are you sure? You will not let me down?'

'I promise.'

He handed the letter to her.

'Is there any reply?' she asked him.

'No,' he said. 'No reply at all. God bless you.'

Nina took the letter and hurried on. A hundred metres up the road, she paused to let a truck pass in a section almost blocked by fallen masonry, and glanced at the address. Was the number twenty-seven or thirty-seven? She paused and turned, intending to run back and ask the man, but to her surprise he was now walking the other way, and, not as a blind man, but quickly, with resolute steps, his stick under his arm. Within seconds, he disappeared behind a bombed building. Greatly puzzled, Nina walked on towards the barracks.

As she turned into the main gates, past the Russian sentry, Vasarov climbed out of a parked car. He had come to collect her sister at the end of her shift. Nina explained about the blind man who had suddenly been able to walk quickly without his stick. Vasarov examined the address on the envelope.

'Jump in the car,' he told her, holding open the door. 'We will deliver it together.'

In Alexander Platz a mass of bricks and blocks of concrete had been bulldozed to one side to leave a track wide enough for two cars to pass. Number thirty-seven did not exist and number twenty-seven was derelict, its windows boarded over.

Vasarov knocked on the front door and waited. They both heard the sound of scurrying feet. Vasarov ran to one side of the building as three men raced out of a back door.

'Halt!'

He levelled his revolver. They kept on running. Vasarov fired. One man staggered against a wall and then slowly sank to the ground, arms and legs twitching in death. The other two men stopped reluctantly and turned, hands in the air.

'Who are you?' Vasarov asked them in German. 'Refugees. We thought you were coming to turn us out.'

'Get back into the house,' ordered Vasarov.

He frisked them for arms, prodded them back through the door. It opened on to an empty room, where a strange salty smell hung heavily in the air. A door opened on to a staircase leading to the cellar.

'What's down there?' he asked the men.

'We don't know.'

Vasarov pulled out a pair of handcuffs from his jacket pocket, and handcuffed them together.

'Find out, then,' he ordered brusquely, kicking open the door. He pushed them down the wooden stairs with the snout of his revolver. Nina had remained upstairs, but it was what Vasarov had found in the basement that gave her nightmares.

The walls on either side had been slimy with grease. In the cellar, beneath the glare of a single bulb, six porcelain baths, looted from bombed houses, were propped upright on bricks and wooden blocks. Each was filled to the brim with a raw, reddish bubbling mass of limbs, intestines, muscles, even eyes. Vasarov looked more closely and almost vomited in horror. They were dismembered human bodies.

A hand protruded from the nearest bath, fingers curled like claws, as though in a grotesque, beckoning welcome. A work bench had been dragged in and on this lay several hacksaws and a two-handed woodman's saw. The blades of the saws were spattered with blood and gristle and human hair.

'Who were they?' Vasarov asked the men.

'They were already dead,' one of them answered nervously. 'We did not kill them. I swear it. We are not murderers.'

'Up the stairs,' Vasarov ordered them both. He walked past Nina and out through the front door. A Russian police patrol drove past in a Jeep, rifles at the ready. He waved the vehicle down to a halt. A policeman jumped out and saluted. Vasarov spoke rapidly to him. The policeman bundled the two men into the Jeep which set off at a great pace, horn blaring.

Vasarov lit a cigarette to burn the smell of bodies and blood and bowels from his throat. He knew that cannibalism existed in Berlin because of the desperate food shortage. When a loaf of bread, which should sell at seventy pfennigs – about four pence – cost the equivalent of £2 10s, and butter fetched £30 a pound, the dead also had an inflated value; by weight, as meat.

'What was down there?' Nina asked him curiously.

'Nothing you should bother about.'

'But the letter?'

Vasarov opened the envelope. On the single sheet of paper inside, one line had been typed in capital letters: THIS IS THE LAST ONE I WILL SEND TO YOU TODAY.

He handed the paper to her. Nina read the words uncomprehendingly until Vasarov explained their significance.

Now she woke up screaming, as she always did when she dreamt of this. She climbed out of bed and switched on the light. Anna called anxiously from the next room.

'You all right?'

'Yes,' she called back. 'It's nothing. Are you alone?'

'Yes. He left early.'

Nina went into her sister's bedroom. Anna switched on the bedside light, and Nina sat down on the edge of the bed. She was shivering, although the night was warm.

'I'll make you a hot drink,' said Anna.

'No. I just want to talk.'

'You've been dreaming about Berlin again? That's all in the past now,' Anna assured her sister, stroking her hand.

'So you tell me. But what's in the future? We can't go on living like this. Your Russian will be posted somewhere soon, and then what? We have no job, no proper papers, no country. We can't prove we belong anywhere.'

'We have survived so far,' Anna reminded her. 'That's something.'

'I know. But it's not enough any more,' replied Nina. 'Without papers, we're nothing.'

'I will see you are all right,' Anna promised her. 'Now, go back to bed. You won't have that dream again.'

'Dear Anna.'

Nina's eyes filled with tears as she bent to kiss her sister.

Under the pale sun of northern England, the garden furniture glowed with white and expensive newness. It was the most costly in the shop, so the salesman had told Paul in awed tones, as he gleefully recounted to Rachel. She now sat on a swinging hammock watching her husband and their son Robert play what the little boy called 'two-man cricket'. He held a toy bat and Paul bowled under-arm with a large soft ball.

Rachel's mother sat in one of the adjustable canvas chairs, purposely set in its most upright position. She did not trust the folding mechanism, and suspected that it might suddenly collapse and throw her backwards. Her lips were pursed together as she frowned over her knitting. She glanced up as Robert hit the ball into the shrubbery. One of the gardeners called out that he would find it for him.

'Easy to tell whose son he is,' she said fondly.

'They certainly get on well,' Rachel agreed.

'Just like you and I, when you were that age,' replied her mother with satisfaction. 'When you were growing up, people often mistook us for sisters. How I wish your dear father had lived to see you now. This lovely house and everything.'

'Yes. Paul was only just starting when he died.'

'He's been gone six years this Whitsun,' said her mother in the hushed voice she always used when speaking of the dead, any dead.

How long ago that seemed, thought Rachel. How long every day and night seemed now, despite the increasing wealth with which she was cocooned. Neighbours envied her the Triumph 2000 roadster that Paul had recently bought her. They envied her the clothes she could buy, apparently without any concern for coupons, and, of course, the whole sybaritic style of her life. And yet, sometimes, when she drove the green Triumph to pick Paul up at one or other of his factories, and she saw the girls from the assembly departments cycling home, cheerfully chatting together, scarves around their hair, she would envy them with a deep and terrible longing.

Rachel had everything that money could buy, but there were aspects of her life that were lacking, for which money could never compensate. She had come to dread those mercifully few occasions when all excuses of headaches and migraine finally proved of no avail, and a body she now disliked, almost detested, was pressed, not only against her, but into her. Afterwards, she would lie awake in the dark, remembering other men who had loved her, and some whom she had also briefly loved. How ironic it was that this act of passion and unity should be so different with them, to be warmly recalled, when she dreaded it with the man to whom she owed so much, and who she liked so little!

'He will be going to school soon, will Robert,' her mother was saying. 'Have you decided where you are sending him?'

'We are still talking about it.'

She and Paul could talk about things like that but they never exchanged a word about their own relationship. Everything about their life was outer show, lacquered and bright and expensive, while underneath lay emptiness and, so far as she was concerned, a growing dependence on gin.

Paul and Robert finished their game and came across the lawn towards them, hand in hand, Robert happy and waving his bat.

'Couldn't get me out, could you, Dad?'

'No. You are far too clever for me,' Paul agreed warmly. 'Like your mother.'

'You are very good with the boy,' said Rachel's mother approvingly. 'With all you have on your plate, I am impressed you find so much time to play with him.'

'But he is my son,' Paul pointed out.

'Not all fathers look at things like that.'

'Well, let's have tea,' said Paul, changing the subject.

'I'll see how it's coming on,' said Rachel brightly. She turned to Robert.

'Come in and wash your hands.'

He shook his head.

'I'm staying with my dad,' he said firmly. She smiled and walked up to the house alone, glad that her back was turned so that the others could not see her face.

Rachel had thought the years would diminish the strange jealousy she experienced when she saw Paul and Robert together, but instead it had increased. The boy obviously adored Paul, and as he grew older they would clearly grow even closer together. She could imagine Robert eventually taking over Paul's whole business. There was a bond between them that she could never share. More and more, she felt an onlooker watching a game that only two could play. The reason for her unease was that she alone knew exactly why she felt this way; and she also knew that never could she explain the reason to anyone, anyone at all.

Max parked his Volkswagen off the Oranienburg road, locked both doors, removed the distributor rotor arm and walked into the forest.

He was due to meet Vasarov exactly 1,752 metres inside, on a north-north-east compass bearing. As usual, their meeting place was a small clearing. Some trees around it had died, and their rotting, fungus-covered stumps protruded like bad teeth from a tangled mass of creeper and ferns.

As Blaikie had instructed him after his first meeting with Vasarov, he had concentrated on discovering the identities of possible traitors in government departments. Vasarov would write a name in capital letters on a piece of paper without any details. If he knew these, he would give them verbally to Max. Thus it came about that a scientist working on jet engine development was quietly removed from his post; then a civilian inspector in an underwater naval research establishment; and finally a woman doctor working on germ warfare.

But these, as Blaikie kept telling Max, were only the small people. There must be bigger fish. Vasarov, after much urging, produced the name of another civil servant in the War Office, but the most stringent interrogation and enquiries produced no corroboration. Had Vasarov been deliberately fed false information because Soviet Intelligence suspected him? This was a worry that Blaikie shared with Max. What Blaikie now wanted were the names of anyone who had originally recruited the sleepers; but so far Max had no success.

Now he faced his final meeting with Vasarov, almost three years after their first. A crackle of breaking twigs underfoot indicated that Vasarov was coming. It was too dangerous to smoke, and the two men stood talking in undertones, as at so many different rendezvous points over these years.

Vasarov brought details of Soviet troop movements on the border, and a new purge by Stalin of higher ranks in the army; general items of medium grade information, but nothing startling.

'I have to tell you,' said Max at last, 'that just as Cardinal handed over to me, I am handing over to a colleague. He will keep all future appointments with you. I am giving up this kind of work. Retiring, if you like.'

'We never retire,' replied Vasarov shortly. 'We are not allowed to.'

He thought of colleagues who had wished to leave behind them the tangled and deadly threads of life in the shadows. Ignace Reiss had operated the NKVD network in Poland. When his time came to return to Moscow, he fled to Switzerland. He was followed and murdered on a lonely road. The assassins spared his wife to be a witness to the fate of traitors.

After Reiss's defection, Walter Krivitsky, his chief, the head of all Soviet Military Intelligence in Western Europe, was ordered back to Moscow immediately to explain his failure. Rather than face certain death, Krivitsky defected with his wife and child to the United States.

Here, for three years, he lived as a hunted man. Stalin's assassins finally cornered him on a February afternoon in a fifth-floor room of a seedy Washington hotel. Because of Krivitsky's past services to the state, they were instructed to offer him the option of death at their hands or his own. He blew out his brains – again with his wife as a witness to warn others who might opt for freedom.

Could Vasarov succeed when such skilled spymasters had failed?

'So this will be our last meeting?' he said in a heavy voice. 'I *must* see you one more time.'

'That is impossible. I leave on Friday morning.'

'We have two days. Meet me here, Thursday night, eight o'clock. I beg of you.'

'All right,' Max agreed reluctantly. 'I will be here. Now, what else have you for me tonight?'

'From time to time I have given you the names of various people who work for us in your country. I now have the name of a man who has recruited several others for us.'

Vasarov took a small envelope from his pocket.

'It's in here. I do not know where he lives, but he should not be difficult to find. But you will have to move quickly. Our people are concerned about him. He is ill. He wants to confess.'

'To confess?'

'Yes. He has become religious. A Roman Catholic. Religion is a great cleanser of the soul. To tell a priest everything can be a great release.'

'Psychiatrists perform much the same service for rich Americans.'

'But psychiatrists sometimes write books about their case histories. Priests keep silent on what they hear. I know. I nearly became one myself, remember.'

Vasarov handed the envelope to Max. They shook hands, then the forest swallowed him. Max returned to his car and opened the envelope. It contained a strip of thin card, cream with red lettering, part of the wrapping from a bar of Toblerone chocolate. The last three letters of the name had been cut off. Max read one word: TOBLER.

When Max told Blaikie of Vasarov's insistence that they should meet once more, he said nothing about Tobler. He did not want to cast any aspersions on the man who had befriended him years before.

Instead, he decided that he would visit Tobler as soon as he returned to England, and make his own assessment of the accuracy of Vasarov's information. After all, Vasarov had made a mistake about the man in the War Office. Might he not have made another mistake here? If it was true, Max would act. If it was not, then he would have spared an old man much trouble. This, he felt, would be one way – perhaps the only way – in which he could repay the professor's kindness to him at Aberdovey.

Eight o'clock on that Thursday evening came and went. By

quarter past the hour uneasiness hung over Max like a shroud. Vasarov had never been so late. Something must have gone wrong; he had been a fool to agree to this final rendezvous. Then, just as he was about to leave, he heard the tell-tale crackle of dry twigs. His right hand gripped the comforting Smith and Wesson in his jacket pocket as Vasarov appeared between the trees.

'I am sorry to be so late,' he said. 'But it is the first time.'

And the last, thought Max. Someone else was also approaching, behind Varsarov and still out of sight. Max raised the revolver in his pocket, aiming at Vasarov's stomach, in case of treachery. Then he lowered the gun. A girl was walking through the forest, a girl wearing a dark blue coat and carrying a small attaché case. She had a hood on her coat, and as she came into the clearing she tossed this back and shook her head. Her hair spread like a dark fan about her shoulders. She was young and pretty.

'Who's this?' Max asked. He could not afford to be taken in by a pretty face and seeming innocence. The trade of espionage was rough and deadly; danger wore many disguises.

'Nina. The sister of a friend. I want you to take her with you, and give her a chance to live in freedom.'

'It's impossible,' said Max shortly. 'Things were different just after the war – not so much red tape. But not now.'

'Her father was a professor of ancient history.'

'Was?'

'Yes. He was killed in the war.'

'What is your relationship with this girl?'

'None. As I say, I know her sister. I used my influence to stop them being sent to Russia. Surely you have influence, too? Put this down as a final payment if you like.'

'Is this why you had to see me?'

'Yes. I could not tell a stranger this. But I can trust you.'

'I will take her back,' said Max. 'She can stay in our sector, but only until a decision is taken.'

'If you can't or won't help her, I will not continue my meetings with your successor.'

'But you will if we help Nina?'

'For as long as I am able. I give you my word.'

Vasarov turned to Nina. Her eyes were misty with tears.

'You will be quite safe,' he assured her gently. 'Trust this man. I do.'

Max indicated that she should follow him. In silence, they walked through the silent wood. Still without speaking, they climbed into Max's car.

'I will put you up in my place for the time being,' Max told her. 'But do not go out or speak to anyone else in the house until I have established what is going to happen. This is for your own safety.'

'I understand.'

Max drove to the house he shared with two other officers attached to the Allied Military Government. Both were living with German girls. They saw Nina arrive and made no comment, just as he never remarked on their arrangements. He showed Nina to the spare room. Then he drove on to Blaikie's requisitioned house and explained Vasarov's conditions.

'She's a plant,' said Blaikie instantly. This had all the elements of a blatant chicken-hawk situation. But now who was the hawk?

'We can easily keep an eye on her,' Max answered. 'If she's on the side of the angels, then she may lead us to someone we don't know. It's not as though you are going to employ her.'

'What is she going to do, then?'

'Find a job as a translator or interpreter. She speaks four languages.'

'Can't say I like it,' said Blaikie uneasily. 'But I'll take it up with the powers that be. Keep her under cover for the next day or two.'

'If we don't help her, we lose Vasarov. He's given us a mass of stuff – and there's a hell of a lot more where that came from.'

'What are your feelings in all this? Fancy her at all?'

'I fancy freedom,' Max told him. 'Perhaps she does, too.'

'We'll see.'

Two days later, Blaikie called Max into his office. He had with him a tall thin man with ginger hair and an incongruously black moustache. The man's eyes were pale as Wedgwood china, his skin too white, almost Albino.

'This is Colonel March from London,' Blaikie began. 'About this girl, Nina. We've checked her background so far as we can, and it seems genuine. But then that is only to be expected. It appears Butcher is knocking off her sister, and wants to do the girl a good turn – or get her out of the way.'

'So what are you going to do about it?' asked Max.

'Not what *we* are going to do about it, old man. But *you*,' said Colonel March.

'Me?'

'Yes. There is a wee bit of difficulty over her naturalisation. Pure bureaucracy, of course, but we can get round it quite easily with your help. You must marry her.'

'Must? But I have only just met her. I don't want to marry anyone.'

'Just go through a marriage ceremony. Then, as soon as you like, you can divorce, and that's that. A marriage of convenience.'

'I cannot possibly agree,' said Max vehemently.

'There is, of course, the matter of your own naturalisation,' said Colonel March slowly. 'I hardly like to raise the matter, but . . .'

Max turned to Blaikie.

'When I joined you told me I only had to serve three years with Security for this to be guaranteed. I thought an Englishman's word was his bond.'

'So it is,' said March. 'Always has been. But Nina's a pretty girl.'

'I had your word that I would be given citizenship,' said Max.

'And we will stick to our promise, of course. But things might be delayed. Unless you can help out here, that is.'

Max looked from one to the other, wondering who he distrusted the most.

'And if I agree to marry her?'

'Then you become a British citizen the day before the wedding. After all, you have to be British to make the thing work, so that you can bring her into the country.'

'And I can get a divorce immediately?'

'Of course. If you want one.'

'What is in this for me, besides citizenship?'

'We haven't discussed that. You know how tight we are for funds.'

'I know how tight *I* am for funds. Put five hundred pounds on the table now and a written guarantee of immediate naturalisation, and I'll marry her.'

Colonel March held out his hand.

Max walked back to his billet. How did people propose marriage – if they did not want to marry the person to whom they were proposing?

Nina was in the kitchen making coffee. She was not used to the idea of drinking real coffee. It was still a luxury, like electric light and hot water from a tap.

'I have something to tell you,' Max began slowly. She looked at him enquiringly, holding her cup between her hands like a child.

'You are going to England.'

Her face brightened.

'When?'

'In a matter of days. But it entails a formality I must explain, one that I hadn't expected at all. I want you to marry me.'

'To *marry* you?'

She looked at him in amazement.

'But I don't even know you. We are not, how do you say, in love.'

'Agreed. It won't be a marriage of love, but as we also say, a marriage of convenience. As my wife, you will immediately become a British citizen, with a British passport. You can come and live in England right away.'

Even as he spoke, he realised that he was not a British subject himself, but she must never discover this.

'Marriage is simply a legal device to help you to do this quickly,' he went on. 'As soon as we get to England, you can start proceedings for a divorce, if you wish.'

'Why won't you start them?'

'Because in England it is considered more gentlemanly to allow the lady to do so.'

'Are you doing this to help me – or because Colonel Vasarov asked you?'

Max looked at her young earnest face. He could not bring himself to tell her that it was simply because he desperately needed British citizenship himself; because otherwise he would be like her, a person without papers.

'Not because he asked me, but because I wanted to help you,' he lied.

'You are very kind.'

'And you accept my proposal?'

'I do. In the spirit in which you make it.'

Max looked at her sharply, but she was smiling. Was she laughing at him? Did she – could she – suspect his motives? What the hell did it matter anyway? This was, as Colonel March had said, a business arrangement.

'Now,' he said briskly, 'let's celebrate with another cup of coffee.'

They were married the following week in a south London registry office. It was not a romantic or a happy occasion. The registrar suffered from adenoids and wore a rubber carnation. For Max's occupation he put 'Retired (Army)'.

Afterwards Max took Nina's arm and they walked in silence down the steps into the street. The sun was shining, although the day was cold. A man at a brazier was selling roasted chestnuts in paper bags, and on impulse Max bought a bag and showed Nina how to peel them.

'Now,' he said with a brightness he did not feel, 'let's have a wedding lunch – even if we are the only guests.'

He hailed a taxi, and they drove in embarrassed silence to an Italian restaurant in Soho.

Max had rented furnished rooms in an area that people sensitive to social matters described as Kensington, and others as Earls Court. The furniture was poor and the blankets threadbare, but it was a base, with one welcome luxury: a coin box telephone in the corridor outside.

On their return from Soho, they sat rather awkwardly in

the sitting room, on either side of the gas fire. Here they were, husband and wife, yet total strangers. Max regarded Nina critically, without any stir of admiration or desire. She looked thin and pinched. Her clothes were cheap and shoddy. She was simply someone he had married in order to gain a British passport and five hundred pounds in cash. He was by nature a loner, without the need of friends. On his own, he felt free. Attached to her, he could become a prisoner of her moods and whims. Also, Nina, with her foreign appearance and accent, reminded him of a past he wanted to forget.

Nina was thinking about her sister, about being in a strange, cold country with a strange, cold man. And he was her husband! How different from girlhood dreams of a white wedding to a man she cared for, with family and friends, fun and laughter and love!

And yet she was alive and free, and that was more than could be said for most of her contemporaries, or her parents.

Max spoke and scattered her thoughts.

'Until we know each other better,' he said, 'you sleep in that room, and I will sleep here. I don't want you to feel you owe me anything that you don't wish to give.'

'That is surely very strange?' replied Nina, not entirely understanding him, but grateful all the same.

'I might as well tell you,' Max told her with unexpected directness. 'In English law divorce is easier – for both of us – if the marriage has never been consummated.'

'How could anyone prove that?'

'They would take your word. For a fee, of course.'

'Always with you it comes down to money,' said Nina slowly.

'Doesn't it with everyone?' Max replied.

# Five

Next morning when Max awoke, Nina was still asleep. He dressed quickly and went out to buy breakfast of coffee and toast in a café in the Earls Court Road. Through the wide, steamy indow near the counter, he watched people hurrying to work through the rain.

They wore drab clothes and they lived drab lives. Individually, they were nothing. They had little ambition, less money, and offered no competition whatever to anyone determined to make a fortune. Yet collectively they must represent an enormous market, and could help him make that fortune. What did they want that he could provide with a total capital of around five hundred pounds? What common interests did these men share? Sex? Food? Cars?

A Packard roadster with its hood down pulled into the kerb. The driver jumped out and went into a tobacconist's shop next door. Sunlight gleamed on the car's rich red upholstery and glittering black paint. The sight made his heart beat like a drum. If he felt this way, wouldn't other young men also want a car, even if only as a visible proof to others – or even to themselves – of success and achievement?

They probably could not afford the cars they might really want to own – a Bentley, a Mercedes, a Bugatti, or even a Packard like this. But if he presented cheaper cars attractively at prices they *could* afford, then he might be on his way to wealth. Most young men would have at least their Service gratuity to spend; wives worked now as well, so married men could rake together two or three hundred pounds for a car, if they liked the look of it. His task would be to ensure that they did.

If his ideas proved wrong, then he had only lost his own gratuity. And at the worst, perhaps Blaikie would take him back. At the best, he would make a lot of money. If that happened he would need a bank behind him. He remembered Blaikie's brother-in-law, David Graham.

Suddenly cheerful now that he had made up his mind, Max paid his bill, walked to the telephone at the back of the café, looked up the number of the head office of Graham's bank and dialled it.

'I knew his brother-in-law in Austria and want to open an account at his branch,' Max explained.

Whispering, while Max waited. Then a man came to the telephone; Max repeated his question.

'He's now manager of our Sloane Street branch.'

Max caught a bus to Knightsbridge and walked down Sloane Street until he reached the bank. Five minutes' wait, and he was inside the manager's office.

David Graham was older than Max had anticipated.

'Never quite know what Blaikie does for a living,' he said brightly, after Max had opened an account with his gratuity cheque.

'Perhaps you're not the only one,' Max replied. 'But I'm more concerned about what I am going to do myself.'

'What were you before the war?'

'A student.' This description conveniently absolved him from long and involved explanations.

'What are you going to do now?'

'Buy and sell cars. They're the only thing I know anything at all about.'

'You have a showroom?'

'No. I'll try without at first. Cut down my overheads.'

'Better have a walk down Warren Street, then. I've several clients in the trade, and that's where they go for bargains. No cheques there, of course. No books to keep. Only bundles of pound notes. Certainly makes you think. Well, let me know if I can help in any way.' They shook hands.

Outside the bank, Max bought an *Evening Standard* and studied details of cars for sale in the classified advertisements. As he read, he realised his intuition had been correct; this was where money could be made. Thousands had learned to drive in the Services. Others had grown rich through exploiting wartime shortages, and since no new cars had been made for six years, prices asked for second-hand cars and the premium demanded for new ones had reached ridiculous heights.

He took the underground to Warren Street and walked along the road. Cars stood, half inside open-fronted shops, half out on the pavement. Many traders had no showrooms, but simply parked cars at the kerb and leaned against them, smoking and whistling at passing girls. He watched men working on cars by the roadside, burnishing dull paintwork, painting tyres, even cutting new treads. Half way down Warren Street Max saw a pre-war Austin 10 with black wings, blue body and upholstery.

'How much?' he asked the dealer who was rolling himself a cigarette.

'Three hundred nicker. On the nose.'

'What about two hundred and fifty?'

The man looked at him with narrowed eyes, sensing a buyer.

'Three hundred. But for you – two-seventy-five. Cash. Listen to the motor.'

He switched on the engine.

'Sweet as syrup.'

'Make it two-sixty and you've got a deal.'

'I've got a deal,' said the dealer quickly, turning off the ignition before the tired old bearings began to thump. He had filled the crankcase with sludge, but nothing could conceal the wear once the engine was warm.

'Let's have the readies and you drive off, matey. Here's the log book. Car's taxed and insured for the rest of the month.'

Max climbed behind the wheel and drove back to his rooms. On the way, he stopped at an ironmonger's shop to buy several tins of paint, brushes and sheets of sandpaper. For a pound, he rented a week's space in a mews garage and cleaned and polished the car thoroughly. Then he wound back the mileage indicator to read 15,021 miles – it sounded more genuine than a round figure – painted the wheels blue to match the upholstery, daubed the leather with blue paint, and wiped off most of it with a rag to revive the original colour.

He dealt with the awkward matter of having the names of six previous owners in the registration book by simply pouring a spoonful of ink over the damning section. Then he took the book to the local motor taxation office in the council offices, with a postal order for five shillings, and was given a replacement. Into this he wrote one owner's name – his own.

Finally, he advertised the car in the *Evening Standard* at £350, phrasing the advertisement carefully: 'Reluctant sale . . . superb condition . . . totally overhauled by Austin expert . . . always garaged . . . one careful owner emigrating.'

Max gave the telephone number of his rooms in the advertisement, and waited anxiously for the telephone in the corridor to ring.

Seven people telephoned that evening and three actually came to see the car. One did not like the blue wheels. The second would only afford £250. The third offered £325. Max pocketed the notes and watched the new owner drive away. More than £80 profit for barely two days' work, and he still had five days' use left of his mews garage.

It was half past six, and Nina had been on her own all day. She finished the letter to her sister, read each page through, sealed it carefully in an envelope, and put it in her handbag.

This was the seventeenth letter Nina had sent to Anna since her arrival in London, and so far she had not received one reply. Was Anna still at her old address? Had something terrible happened? Or perhaps letters from overseas were just not being delivered? Nina was careful never to mention any controversial subject that could conceivably interest a communist censor. Neither did she give any hint of her feelings – or her disappointment. She and Max might be brother and sister, or even worse, total strangers thrown together by chance. In Austria, she had believed she spoke English well, perhaps because British people she met spoke slowly, knowing she was a foreigner. Now, when she went shopping, people spoke so quickly that she could scarcely understand them, and was too shy to ask them to repeat what they said. The food was different, the measurements were different, life was different. And where was it all leading her?

She was afraid to ask herself this question, because there seemed no clear answer. At the least, she told herself, she had survived and was in a free country, even if as an alien, and married to a man with whom she had little in common and who seemed uninterested in her.

Nina was not a virgin, and it had seemed reasonable that Max, as her husband, would make some sexual advances however mild or cautious. But instead he had treated her with scrupulous coolness; always civil, always friendly, but never allowing any spark of mutual attraction to light between them. Was Max a homosexual? Or was she physically repulsive to him? She felt she could not ask Max outright without causing offence and she was too vulnerable, too dependent, to risk offending anyone – least of all Max.

She heard the scrape of a key in the lock, then footsteps on the stairs. She stood up and instinctively patted her hair into place in the mirror above the mantelpiece. Max came into the room. He was grinning.

'I've made a deal,' he said excitedly.

'A deal?' What did that mean, exactly? An arrangement? Something in the market place? A compromise of some kind?

'Money,' he explained. 'And here's some for you.'

He took two five pound notes from his jacket pocket and handed them to her. She fingered the large and unfamiliar notes.

'This isn't for food,' Max explained. 'It's for *you*. A present. You can't buy much these days, but money is always useful.'

'You are very kind.'

She crossed the room and kissed him gently on the side of his face, putting her arms around him, hoping he might kiss her on the mouth.

Feeling the warmth of his body through her dress, and the muscles in his arms firm beneath her fingers, Nina believed that he must react, and show that he was at least attracted by her. But, instead, Max only pressed his hands lightly on Nina's shoulders and then gently but firmly he pushed her away.

This movement of rejection, coming on top of her concern about her sister, was too much for her. She burst into tears, sobbing uncontrollably on his shoulder.

In the mirror behind her, he could see the two notes still in her hand. Outside in the square a young couple walked under the plane trees and stopped and kissed and walked on. He thought, how strange that I am here with a woman in my arms, a woman who is lonely and pretty and in every way desirable – and yet she means nothing whatever to me. Not because she is who she is, but because I dread any attachment.

If he had been involved with someone else, someone weaker, he could never have escaped from the Nazis, or survived the miseries of the communist camps. The lesson was plain: life is a long hard race, an obstacle race, and first prize only goes to the man who travels alone.

Where others sought release and relief in sex, Max needed success, for money meant security, independence, power; perhaps even time and opportunity to look for love. Money meant you could buy your way out of almost any catastrophe, political, medical, legal – for everyone had their price. Like death, cash was the ultimate and universal common denominator.

'What's the matter with me?' Nina asked him miserably. 'Do you hate me? Am I repulsive to you?'

'Certainly not,' he answered her, wondering how he could possibly make her understand without hurting her. 'You are very attractive, and very pretty.'

'But we are *married,*' Nina went on. 'Don't you *want* to go to bed with me?'

'It's not simply with you,' he replied gently. 'It's with anyone.'

'Let us be frank. Are you a homosexual?'

'No. But I was a prisoner of the Russians. You don't know anything about that, and I am not going to tell you about it now, except that I suffered. I learned then that I don't want or need any emotional attachments.'

'What is going to happen to me, then?' she asked him. 'I can't go on living with you like this.'

'I'm sorry, but I don't think I can love anyone – not even myself. I just ask you to accept that. One day, Nina, you will meet someone whom you can love, and more important, who loves you.'

'But how can that happen? I never talk to anyone here. Only shopkeepers.'

'You will – when I have more money. I promise you I will do everything I can to help you. You will have a proper marriage then, not like this.'

Max took out his handkerchief, wiped her tears. She blew her nose shakily. He poured two glasses of whisky, handed one to her.

'Let's drink,' he suggested.

'To what?' she asked tremulously.

'To the future. Your future.'

Next morning, he took the tube to Warren Street and found the same trader, now leaning against a Hillman Minx with scuffed tyres and a cracked right headlamp lens.

'What's the matter, then?' he asked Max belligerently, surprised at seeing him again. 'Don't you like the motor?'

'Someone liked it even more, so I sold it. Now I want to buy another.'

'Don't buy it from him, Max, buy it from me,' advised a voice behind him. Max turned. Dick Carpenter was standing in the open front of a salesroom, between an Atalanta and a 3½-litre Jaguar drophead with Grebel headlights.

There was nothing of the army sergeant about Carpenter now. He wore a superbly cut grey suit with a fine chalk stripe, a blue silk polka dot tie, a cream Sulka shirt. Clothing coupons obviously meant little to him.

'Didn't know you were in the car trade,' he said as they shook hands.

'I'm not really,' Max replied. 'I've just sold my first car. But it's a start. You own this firm?'

'Outright,' said Carpenter proudly. 'My good friend Jim' – he indicated the man who had sold the Austin – 'looks after things. I've got my eye on other areas. Antiques. Houses to do up and sell. Anything with a quick turnover.'

Carpenter paused for a moment, reflecting on the gullibility of people, and on something else.

'Doing anything this afternoon?' he asked suddenly.

'I was going to buy another car, tart it up and sell it.'

'And make a hundred quid top whack? Want to make a bit more?'

'Doing what?'

'Come in with me on a deal. I was going to keep it to myself, but I'll cut you in for old time's sake. It's an auction. Ex-army trucks in a field near Newbury.'

'I don't want any old army trucks. Saw enough of them during the war.'

'Possibly. But lots of contractors go mad for 'em. Bit of signwriting thrown in buckshee, with their name and address on the side of the cab. They could do it all themselves, but they haven't the imagination. And there's a bonus, which I'll tell you about later. You on?'

'How much would I have to find in money?' Max asked dubiously. 'I'm not all that flush.'

'Three hundred nicker, top.'

'I'm on.'

They drove down through the Berkshire countryside in Carpenter' Jaguar with the hood folded down, the milometer disconnected, and the sun warm on their faces.

'There's a catalogue in the back,' Carpenter told him, as they glided through Maidenhead. 'I'm bidding for Lot 15. Bedford three-tonner. You bid for Lot 16, another Bedford. You won't lose, I can promise you that.'

Outside Newbury, they turned into a field, muddied and churned by the heavy-treaded tyres of the parked trucks. A notice nailed to a tree announced that on the following day there would be a sale of several hundred motor-cycles.

A seedy man, wearing an oil-stained battledress, detached himself from the shade of a tree and nodded respectfully to Carpenter.

'Everything all right?' Carpenter asked him brusquely.

'Perfect, sir. All laid on.'

'What time do our lots come up?'

'Around two, sir.'

'See you in The Three Compasses afterwards, then. You and your mucker can drive the wagons back to London.'

The man all but saluted Carpenter. Max glanced at the ex-sergeant quizzically. Carpenter winked at him.

'I've put you on to a good thing,' he said. 'You'll go down and thank me on your bended knees, Max.'

At ten past two, Max bid £218 and became the owner of a

Bedford three-ton truck. By three o'clock, it was in the public-house car park. The landlord had obtained a special licence for the sale, and all the bars were full of red-faced men in cloth caps and raincoats drinking whisky. Carpenter ordered two doubles.

'Only for regulars,' replied the landlord gruffly.

'We're regulars,' Max told him. 'Here's a pound to prove it.'

The landlord took the note, bent down beneath the counter, poured out two large whiskies.

Carpenter looked at his watch.

'Come out to the gents.'

'What's out there?'

'The bonus I told you about.'

The seedy man in the battledress followed them into the lavatory.

'How many did you get aboard?' Carpenter asked him, without any preamble.

'Twenty three-fifty side valve Nortons in each truck, sir.'

'Twenty for you here, then.'

Carpenter peeled off twenty pound notes from a gold clip and nodded to Max to do the same.

'Thank you very much, gentlemen,' said the man. 'Next sale is in three weeks' time. Bikes the day after.'

'I'll be here,' Carpenter told him. 'Same again?'

The man nodded agreement and left the lavatory.

'What's going on?' asked Max in bewilderment.

'A deal, that's what. You saw that notice about the motorcycle sale tomorrow? Well, you won't find many people wanting to buy motorcycles here today, now, will you? Which is why I came down last night and saw that bloke, who loaded twenty motorcycles in each of our trucks for us. So you've bought a three-tonner for £218 *and* have a bonus of twenty motorcycles at a nicker each. You'll make a hundred on the truck at least, and damn near eight hundred on the bikes. A bit easier than bashing a barrack square, eh? Now, what about another drink?'

Max saw Carpenter only once more before he heard of his death.

Carpenter had asked to meet him in a public house off

Warren Street late one evening. Over several months, Max had bought a number of nondescript cars from him, repainted wheels in bright colours, cleaned the engines with detergent and sold each one at a good profit. He now rented two mews garages and paid a man ten pounds a week in notes to work with him.

'I'm clearing out of cars and going into property,' Carpenter explained. 'There's far more profit in a house or a shop – or better still, a row of both. Property's going to be very big if this Socialist government gets thrown out. But there's still one motor venture that might be worthwhile – if we did it together. Car auctions.'

'Didn't know they auctioned cars. Thought it was only houses or antique furniture.'

'So it was. But a bloke's started at Erith, in Kent, down on the Thames, and he's doing well. He suddenly wants to sell out. I've a feeling someone is leaning on him – hard. That's the whisper, anyway. He'd get suspicious if I poked my nose in, but he doesn't know you. You go down, have a butcher's at the set-up, and tell me what you think. I must say, *I* like the idea.

'You don't need to carry any stock. Every car entered means a five quid entrance fee, cash. And then you take five per cent commission on sales. Not bad when even a ten-year-old Ford 8 makes £250 – twice what it cost new. If we can take it over, and I don't see why we shouldn't, then we might have a go together on some properties. Small stuff, at first, to feel our way. Then, out for the killing.'

'In what?'

'Can't tell you yet, it's too risky. But if we can pull these small details off together, I'll cut you in on the big one. You'll never need to work again.'

'I haven't worked much so far,' Max reminded him, suddenly recalling the waxy faces of the office workers seen through the café window. 'But why include me in? I'm grateful, but I know sweet FA about property.'

'Most of the buggers in there now know less, so that's no hardship. But we can trust each other – I think. With two, we halve our problems. You can work one side of the street and

I'll take the other. Could be, that way we also double our take.'

'I'm on,' said Max with enthusiasm.

'Good. So you can buy the next round. Auction starts tomorrow. Give me a ring when you get back.'

They spent another hour drinking. Then Carpenter suggested that Max should take home one of his cars – a 14/65 Triumph Dolomite roadster. It had been luxurious once, but now it felt weary. Going down Bayswater Road, at half past eleven, the engine died with a melancholy backfire.

Max cursed under his breath, coasted to the kerb, pressed the starter and jabbed the accelerator. He opened the bonnet, shone his torch over the engine, tapped the cover of the electric pump.

A woman approached, walking slowly. She wore a black fur coat, high heels with ankle straps, and the new nylon stockings, with thick seams. A smell of scent lay like honeysuckle on the warm night air as she paused near him.

'Waiting for a naughty girl?' she asked him.

'Not right now,' Max told her. Bayswater Road was a favourite promenade for prostitutes. They walked poodles on long leads, or stood in pairs at street corners, or, like this one, they prowled on their own.

'When you're ready then, dearie.'

She walked on slowly towards Marble Arch. Max struggled with the engine in the darkness. Unexpectedly, rain began to fall, a summer shower; slowly at first, and then in a torrent. He lowered the bonnet and jumped inside the car. Two whores across the road sheltered under one umbrella. He heard the patter of high heels, and his passenger door opened. The woman who had spoken to him climbed inside.

'I'll only wait until it stops, love,' she promised. 'But I don't want to get soaked before I start work, do I?'

Max offered her a cigarette. He did not smoke himself, but carried a packet for others. The offer of a cigarette could sometimes clinch a sale.

'Live up this way?' she asked him as she lit it.

'Off the Cromwell Road. And you?'

'I've got a place in Notting Hill. Not where I take men to, of course.'

'Why not?'

'Well, I've got a kid and a man. It wouldn't be right.'

Max smiled at this morality. But was it any worse than his, with regard to the stolen motorcycles, or marrying a refugee for five hundred pounds? The only difference was that his profits were higher. Rain drummed impatient fingers on the canvas roof, and then it stopped as suddenly as it began. The prostitute stubbed out her cigarette, smiled at Max.

'How about one for the road?'

'How much?'

'Short time, here, a quid. Proper go, two quid.'

'Where?'

'In the park.'

'Bit damp, isn't it?'

'What about your place, then?'

'No. I've a wife.'

'That's the trouble. All the attractive men are married. What do you say, then?'

Just for a moment, Max wished he could say Yes. The girl was pretty, the night was warm, and their closeness under the taut canvas would have excited almost any other man of his age, but not him. He felt as little desire for this girl as he felt with Nina. Was it really because all his energies had been drawn to the task of becoming rich – or could that blow in the hut at Katyn be partly to blame?

'What do I say?' he repeated. 'I say I'll give you two quid now' – he took two notes out of his jacket pocket – 'if you'll do something else for me.'

'What?' she asked suspiciously.

'Hold my torch while I get this damned engine to start.'

She laughed. The pound notes crinkled in her hand.

'I've done all sorts of things,' she said. 'But never that.'

'There's always a first time,' Max assured her and handed over the torch. Within minutes he had the engine running and offered her a lift.

'Thanks. But I can't go back to my man until I've made twenty quid. So far tonight, I've only made your two.'

'What would he do then?'

'Beat me up, like as not. But not where it shows, of course, or I couldn't make anything tomorrow night.'

'Why did you start on the game?' Max asked her.

'Why did you marry?'

'That would take a long time to answer.'

'Same with me. Leave me here, ducky. It's about the end of my beat.'

'You have a prescribed area?'

'Of course. Everything's organised nowadays. We pay protection. They cruise about in a car just to see we're not poaching on each other's beats.'

'And if you are?'

'A warning the first time. Done up a second.'

'You don't like the game, then?'

'Right. But how else could I make this money? If I worked in a shop I'd be lucky to get four quid a week. My man allows me to keep twenty. And I've got the kid to bring up, remember.'

'Why don't you rent a room or flat with your money? Do things in more comfort?'

'Don't be daft. If you were a landlord, would you rent to me? A girl on the game? No way, dearie.'

She sat for a moment, not speaking, running her fingers along the leather. Then she spoke.

'About that room you said I should rent,' she said finally.

'What about it?'

'You could rent a room anywhere, 'cos you got style. Nice suit, flash car, classy voice. Then I could rent it from you.'

'But if I did that, I'd be had up for running a brothel. Living on immoral earnings.'

'No. You're wrong. I've got a regular every Thursday night, a solicitor. I asked him about my chap and me, how we stood if I took anyone home. He said you got to have at least two girls in a flat to make it a brothel. If there's only one, she's just having friends in. Could be some money in it for you.'

Max felt faintly amused at the proposition; surely this wasn't the type of property Carpenter had in mind?

'You rent a room somewhere off the Bayswater Road here, near my pitch, for say, five quid a week,' the girl continued, seeing that he was interested. 'I pay you ten. So you make five nicker clear. Can't be bad.'

'A very good return,' agreed Max. 'But that's only one room.'

''Course it's only one. You're like all men – greedy. But I know other girls on the game. Some of them have friends I don't know. I reckon I could find thirty – maybe forty – girls willing to pay five quid a week extra for a warm place to take a man. That could mean two hundred quid every week. Better than a drunken sailor, eh?'

'Much better,' Max agreed. 'More profitable, too. But it really isn't for me.'

'What's your line of business, then?'

'Cars. I buy and sell them.'

'You could do this, too. It's only buying and selling rooms. No overheads.'

'You could be right. What's your name, anyhow?'

'Betty Mortimer. And yours?'

'Max Cornell.'

'That your real name?'

'It's the one I use. If I find anyone who's interested, how can I get in touch with you?'

'You'd have to pick me up here. I work from seven every night until I make my twenty quid. Unless the weather is bad, of course. Keep cruising up and down the road, but watch out for coppers. They'll take the number if the same car goes by too often.'

She opened the door, turned and paused, put her hand on his knee.

'Sure you won't change your mind, then?'

He shook his head.

She walked away up the road.

Watching her in his mirror as he drove away, Max saw her saunter back towards Marble Arch. A Hudson coupé slowed and stopped. His last view was of Betty leaning into the front window to proposition the driver.

Erith (Population: 48,270; London 15 miles. Borough. Motto: *Labor Omnia Vincit*. Early Closing: Thursday) was originally a fishing village, on the south bank of the Thames.

William Hickey, the eighteenth-century diarist, visiting a friend's house in Erith, spoke highly of the salmon caught in the river. But with the opening of the London to Chatham railway, other industries were established, mainly engineering and the manufacture of guns and munitions. Gradually, the village became a town and spread from the river to higher ground near the new factories. Streets of terraced houses were hurriedly built for workers. A public house in the middle of one of these estates was called 'The Nordenfeldt', after the locally made machine gun which produced ferocious fire power from five parallel barrels. Others, like 'The Eardley Arms', and 'The Wheatley Arms' were named after old local families.

When Max came out of the station at Erith, a brisk breeze filled the red sails of coal barges moving ponderously up the Thames. He dug his hands deeply into the pockets of his raincoat. He was not used to meagre civilian rations after years of plenty in Germany. A spoonful of dried egg on a piece of butterless toast and a cup of coffee without sugar did not seem the best breakfast on which to start a bleak day in a windy suburb.

Max wished that Dick Carpenter was with him, for he enjoyed his company and enthusiasm, his willingness to take risks, and his readiness to put all profit from one deal into the next.

'I can't win 'em all,' he would admit cheerfully. 'No-one can – or does. But I started with nothing, and I can always go back to that. But not for long, Max, never for long.'

Dick's reaction to Betty Mortimer's proposition had been typical.

'What a bloody marvellous idea,' he said enthusiastically.

'It's living off immoral earnings,' Max pointed out.

'Who the hell cares? Better than not living at all, isn't it? And the girls' earnings don't *have* to be immoral.'

'Betty'll swindle you.'

'I won't give her the chance,' Dick retorted. 'We'll cut her in right from the start. Give her an interest in the action.'

'How?'

'We'll rent rooms to her friends only through her. Say we pay the landlord a fiver a week for each room, and take ten off her. She takes eleven off each of her friends and puts the odd quid up her knicker leg.'

'You're smart,' said Max admiringly.

'I have to be – I've got expensive tastes. Now, you get down to that auction. See what we can do there, while I take a drive along the Bayswater Road and pick up your tart.'

'You'd better use the Triumph,' said Max. 'She'll recognise that car. Otherwise she won't know you.'

'Good thinking,' said Dick approvingly. 'Only one thing I ask from you, since you live nearer Betty's beat than I do. If I find there's mileage in the idea, you fix up the first few rooms. After all, I've done you a couple of favours, or three.'

'Agreed,' Max promised him.

He smiled at the recollection, as he walked towards the auction field. Above the gateway fluttered a canvas banner with two stencilled words: 'Car Auction'. A handful of cars were drawn up in lines in front of a caravan hitched to a 1939 Buick. A fat man in shirtsleeves stood on a wooden box, adjusting a microphone linked to loudspeakers. Three men wearing belted camel-hair overcoats and soft felt hats walked slowly along the cars, kicking tyres reflectively, or leaning heavily on mudguards to see the car move on its springs. As other people began to arrive, the fat man tapped the microphone once more, and now sound bounced like drumbeats through the speakers.

'Welcome to our open-air auction,' he began. 'All cars bought at buyer's risk. No money refunded. No reserves. No cheques. No guarantees. No trouble. Cash only. Right? Right. First, a 1935 Standard 12, three owners. Over to you, Charlie.'

Charlie, a bald-headed man in sports jacket and grey flannels, climbed into the tiny car and drove it slowly up and down in front of the crowd.

'There she goes,' said the fat man approvingly. 'No smoke. No noise. A little beauty. Give the wife and kids a treat. Take 'em to the seaside for a day. Now what am I bid? Shall we say three hundred? No? Then . . .?'

'Two-fifty.'

'Very good, sir.'

He nodded to someone Max could not see at the back of the crowd.

'And again. In bundles of five, if you please.'

'Two-seventy-five.'

The car was finally knocked down at an unexpected three hundred and fifty pounds. At five per cent plus the initial fiver entrance fee, this meant £22 10s for five minutes' talk. Dick Carpenter was quite right. This was money for jam.

By three o'clock every car had been sold. Max calculated that the fat man had made at least £175 – and from a modest site. What if he and Carpenter ran two or three car auctions in different parts of the country? The profits would be enormous – and largely in cash.

He was walking back to the station, thinking about such possibilities, when a new black Mark VI Bentley overtook him, going very slowly, and stopped twenty yards ahead. As Max came level with it, the nearside front window opened and a man smiled out at him. The face was plumper than he remembered, hair not quite so dark, the width of shoulders exaggerated by the cut of his vicuna coat.

'Max!'

A soft and well-massaged hand that had never held a rifle was extended through the window. A heavy gold ring gleamed in the pale sunshine. Paul Harrow was greeting his cousin.

'What a turn up,' he said in amazement. 'How extraordinary that I should see you down here!'

'I could say the same,' agreed Max.

'Well, don't stand about in the cold, saying it, come inside.'

A flood of warmth engulfed Max as Paul opened the door. The radio played Maurice Winnick and his orchestra. Max remembered Jack Hylton and Ambrose and Rachel's slurred voice, and what had happened. Did Paul know? Did he guess?

'After all these years,' said Paul, 'I wondered what had happened to make you rush off.'

'I got posted suddenly,' Max explained. 'I wrote. Probably the army messed up the letters.'

'Ha, very likely. We never heard from you, anyhow – and we hadn't any address to write to, either. Now, what brings you down here?'

'I buy the odd car to sell.'

'You haven't got a regular job, then, since you came out of the army?'

'No.'

'Going back to London?'

'Yes.'

'I'll give you a lift. Then you can claim a refund on your ticket. Waste not, want not, eh?'

'Wouldn't think you wanted for a lot,' said Max appreciatively. The car reeked of wealth; a subtle amalgam of cigar smoke, rich leather, beeswax polish on burr walnut; a travelling token of Paul's success.

Its opulence exaggerated the sad drabness of south London: the jagged gaps in terraced houses where bombs had fallen; weeds sprouting unchecked on mounds of rubble.

Yet from houses such as these had come soldiers with whom Max had served. Now, like him, they were out of uniform, with six years of lost life behind them. Whoever could harness their discontent, their ambition, to some enterprise of his own would make a fortune.

'How's Rachel?' Max asked at last.

'Fine. She *will* be surprised when I tell her I've seen you. Got a little boy now, you know.'

'Congratulations. Business all right?'

'Can't grumble.'

Paul glanced sideways through a haze of cigar smoke.

'You look pretty fit,' he said, almost in admiration. 'Commando, weren't you?'

'Yes.'

'My father might have something for someone like you.'

'Your father? Last time we met you didn't even know if he was dead or alive.'

Paul grinned.

'Oh, he turned up. Like a bad penny. He's a survivor.'

'Aren't we all? How did you get in touch with him?'

'Too long a story to tell now,' said Paul shortly. 'But I

happen to know he's looking for someone like you. I'm on my way to his place now. You wanted to meet him, so here's your chance. Let him tell you all about it.'

They entered and left south London, crossed the river, and finally stopped in Berkeley Square.

'Not many freeholds in this square,' Paul told him proudly. 'But the old man's got one of the few. He's like that. Must have the best.'

Max followed Paul across a carpeted entrance hall. A porter nodded obsequiously. Max saw the Italian Star ribbon on his uniform. Sam Harris's front door had a spy-hole and was protected by three locks. The carpets inside were thick and white; door panels were picked out in gold leaf.

'Got a visitor for you,' Paul called. 'A relation.'

'You joking?'

The voice from another room sounded harsh and guttural. Then Sam Harris came into the hall, face puckered disapprovingly as though expecting a practical joke. He was squat, powerfully built, with grey hair and small mean eyes. He wore crocodile-skin shoes, a dark blue suit, a white silk shirt. He looked enquiringly between Max and Paul.

'I used to be Max Kransky,' Max explained. 'Now I'm Max Cornell.'

Harris stood staring at Max without any sign of recognition.

'Kransky?' He repeated and paused awkwardly. 'I was very fond of your parents,' he said at last. 'Dear people.'

'But you never answered my mother's letters, when she wrote from Prague,' said Max.

'Letters? Your mother wrote to me? I didn't know. Bloody Nazis must have pinched the letters.'

'And you didn't get mine either, I suppose?' Max continued. 'I wrote when I came over here in the war.'

'You did? Never had a letter from you, either, I can tell you. What address did you write to?'

'The only one I had. Golders Green.'

'Oh, I left there early on.'

'The army did get in touch with you, and you said I was an imposter.'

Harris shook his head.

'No-one ever contacted me,' he said. 'I'd have been the first to help, if they had.'

'I ran into Max at Erith,' Paul explained. 'He'd been down looking at the auction. Going into the motor trade, he says. Used to be a commando. Hasn't got a job yet. I told him you might have one.'

'Can you look after yourself?' Harris asked Max.

'I have, so far.'

Max was surprised to discover that he disliked Sam Harris as much as he disliked his son. It was a chemical reaction, compounded of distrust, distaste – and something else? Contempt? Envy?

'Have a drink first,' suggested Harris. He pressed a bell. A manservant in a dark suit appeared in the doorway.

'Three malt whiskies,' Harris told him. 'Trebles. No ice. No soda.'

'Well, you did your bit,' he said when the drinks arrived on a silver tray. 'King and country and all that. A few friends and I have a proposition that could interest you.'

'I've no money to invest,' interrupted Max. What little he had, he must keep for future deals with Carpenter and Betty, for buying more cars in Warren Street. 'All I have is what I learned in the army.'

'That's just what I want,' said Harris. 'My friends own a couple of rather special greyhounds. A lot of suckers bet regularly on the dogs because there's not much else for them to do.

'Well, my friends have brought over these two greyhounds from Ireland to race here. They are unbeatable at short sprints, say two-fifty yards. Another friend of mine owns a track and he announces a very special race, a marathon, over a thousand yards. First prize, two hundred and fifty nicker. Second prize, a hundred nicker. Third prize, whatever you like. Big time stuff.

'Got to have a few short sprints thrown in, of course, as heats, to sort out the duds, but all the big money goes on the marathon. We put the two dogs in for these heats – and bet on them, hard. We stand to win a fortune.'

'What about the marathon?'

'Sod the marathon,' said Harris. 'We've made our killing on the sprints. It's the original double-headed penny. We can't lose.'

'Are you sure?'

'Certain – provided we only bet in small sums. If anyone started putting hundreds on our dogs just to win a minor heat, the bookies might get suspicious. So we put money on them all round the country, in small amounts. Quid here, two quid there, now and then a fiver. The odds will be fantastic, maybe a hundred to one. Maybe even more.'

'But won't anyone suspect anything?'

'Of course not. They're with a trainer – for the marathon. When the touts watch them training, they'll see they're no good for long distances. Of course, they aren't. They'll be last in the marathon, but first for us. A top hundred yard sprinter will always beat a top long distance runner – over a hundred yards.'

Harris paused.

'There is only one thing.'

'And that's where I come in?' Max asked him. 'Correct?'

'Correct. Some bookies have nasty minds. They don't like paying out. They might even suggest there has been a fiddle. You have to persuade them otherwise.'

'How?'

'Surely I don't need to spell it out,' said Harris, frowning. 'Maybe you lean on them a little. Show them where their real interests lie. I leave it to you. With your commando background, you can do a professional job.'

'How much is in this for me?' Max asked him.

'Fifty,' said Harris.

'Too little.'

'Hundred then. For old time's sake.'

'Two.'

'A lot of money.'

Harris suddenly smiled; a plump, middle-aged businessman who simply wanted everyone to be happy.

'OK,' he said genially, 'seeing how you've been to the war, and we're related – even if only by marriage. But one thing.

No betting yourself, eh? If you start putting money on the dogs, you could louse up the market. My friends wouldn't like that. Nor would I.'

Harris crossed the room, moved a Stubbs painting of a racehorse, opened the safe behind it, and took out a sealed brown envelope.

''undred nicker inside. The rest when you've done the job. Count it if you want, or trust me.'

Max counted it.

He took the tube from Green Park to Gloucester Road and walked through almost empty streets to his lodgings. A government power cut to conserve coal was in operation. Only a few street lamps were lit. A feeling of gloom and defeat hung over the streets. Victory had brought no release from shortages. Even bread had recently been rationed, something that had not happened during six years of war. He had seen queues of people, eager to emigrate, waiting every day outside Australia House and South Africa House.

He wondered whether any of the men he had met in Aberdovey were among them. Thinking of Aberdovey, he remembered Professor Tobler. He must get in touch with him. Tobler had befriended him when he was lonely, had taught him how to think through any situation, how to pierce layers of humbug and wishful thought. Max would look him up in *Who's Who* and find out where he lived. Then he would pay him a visit, surprise him, explain how he was putting at least some of his teaching to the test.

As he climbed the steps to the front door, a shadowy figure moved from behind a pillar.

'Max Cornell?' a man asked him hoarsely.

'Who are you?'

'It's Jim. I sold you that first Austin you bought. Remember? I worked for Dick Carpenter.'

'Worked?'

He was back in the army again. Old so-and-so was a good bloke, one of the best. Was? Yes, didn't you know? Bought it on patrol this morning. Now the use of the past tense alerted him instantly.

'Let's get off the street,' said Jim nervously. Max remembered that Nina had told him she was going to the cinema. He opened the front door and led the way up the stairs to his rooms. Jim was trembling, not at all the brash man with whom he had bargained months ago in Warren Street.

'What's the trouble?' Max asked him.

'Dick Carpenter's been killed. Burned to death. His car caught fire.'

Again Max noted the choice of words: killed, not died.

'Where did it happen?'

'On the North Circular. Only a couple of hours ago.'

'Who told you?'

'I had a 'phone call. Man said it should be a warning to me.'

'What man? For God's sake, get a grip on yourself.'

'I don't know what man. But I've heard his voice before. I've picked up the 'phone in the shop, and this guy would ask for Dick.'

'So it wasn't an accident?'

'Doesn't look like one to me.'

'But why should anyone want to murder Dick?'

'I don't say they did. Maybe they only wanted to frighten him, warn him off, and something went wrong.'

'But who are *they*?'

Max could not believe these rambling accusations. They smacked of too many films he had seen, too many thrillers he had read in the army.

'You think I'm making all this up, don't you?' said Jim. 'Well, I'm not. You've been away for too long, Max. I was here in the Fire Service all through the war, and saw what went on when you blokes were overseas. The black market wasn't a few ounces of bacon being sold under the counter. It meant whole truckloads going astray – regularly. Someone inside the bacon factory would drop the hint a truck was leaving. Others would stop the truck on some pretext, knock out the driver or fix him with a fist of fivers. Then off with the load and away. Like a military operation. Organised crime, you see. Been like that in the States since Prohibition, so a Yank told me. But it's still fairly new here.'

'But how would this affect Dick?'

'Only reason I can think of was that car auction idea. It's so smart – and legitimate. The guy who started it off was warned off, remember. Others wanted to take over – by force if persuasion didn't work. Dick was like you. Out of touch. He'd been in the army too long. Didn't believe things had changed so much here. He wouldn't take a hint and keep out, so they gave him a shove.'

'How did his car catch fire?'

'Three tonner came up too close behind him. Driver said his wheels locked on a wet road. Bumped Dick's motor up the arse. Petrol tank blew up. That bit probably *was* an accident.'

'You may be right about all the rough stuff, or you may be a hundred per cent wrong. There's only one way to find out.'

'Which is?'

'Do what I intended to do with Dick. Take over the auction.'

'You must be mad, mate. I'd keep out of that unless you also want to get planted. After all, we've had a warning.'

'So I take it you don't want to come in with me?'

'Too right, I don't.'

'Then I'll have to go it alone. If others think they can make a fortune there, I *know* I can.'

# Six

The front door bell rang in a rented semi-detached house in Edgware when Mrs Cartwright, the tenant, was up in the loft. She frowned at the interruption, and climbed down the folding extension ladder to the landing.

Who could be calling at ten-thirty on a Tuesday evening? Mrs Cartwright cautiously fitted the safety chain, for there had been several recent burglaries in the locality, then she opened the door. A plump woman in tweeds, flowered scarf around her neck, stood in the porch, beaming at her. Her vision was poor without spectacles, and she took a few seconds to realise that the woman lived on the other side of their cul-de-sac.

'Hope I'm not butting in,' the woman began brightly, 'but I saw you'd left a light on in your loft last night and again tonight, and I wondered whether you knew about it? With the price of electricity, that could become expensive.'

Mrs Cartwright looked puzzled for a moment, then she smiled.

'How kind of you,' she said. 'I am having insulation fitted up in the loft to try and cut down on our fuel bills. But thank you very much for calling. Most neighbourly.'

The woman was peering over her shoulder into the hall to try and see how well it was furnished.

'You must come and have tea one afternoon,' said Mrs Cartwright vaguely, not specifying a day.

'I'd love to. Canadian, aren't you?'

'Yes.'

'I have a brother in Vancouver.'

'Lovely city,' said Mrs Cartwright briefly.

The woman smiled, then realising that this conversation could not be prolonged, walked down the path to the gate. Mrs Cartwright closed and locked the door, took a handkerchief from her sleeve and wiped her forehead.

Neighbours knew her as Mrs Cartwright, but that was not her real name, nor was she Canadian, although she held a Canadian passport. She was Russian, and after training at a special spy school in Kiev, she had entered Canada illegally from a Polish cargo ship, and had travelled to Regina, in Saskatchewan, where, shortly after her arrival (as she had checked in advance from local contacts) a mining engineer, Mr Ian Cartwright and his wife, were taking a trip to Toronto to visit relations.

During their absence their house was most unfortunately burned down. All furniture was totally destroyed and no-one wondered whether their passports had survived.

Shortly afterwards, a new Mrs Cartwright crossed the border into the United States, and then flew to England. Mrs Cartwright was a colonel in the NKVD. In espionage terms she was the 'Resident'. She was not a spy herself, and she did not usually meet agents, but maintained close contact with them through go-betweens or cut-outs.

Twice a week, at some varied hour of the day or night, she would monitor a brief Morse broadcast. This was usually a recording played at many times the speed of human speech, possibly backwards, perhaps at varying speeds and in a little known dialect – Pushtu or Gujarati or Swahili – and always in code. Mrs Cartwright would then decipher this and carry out whatever instructions it contained.

Up in the cold, cheerless loft Mrs Cartwright now carefully adjusted the blackout curtain around the skylight, pinned the edges with drawing pins and sat down at a table. On this stood her receiver, the size of a leather suitcase into which it fitted perfectly for quick concealment. At exactly seventeen minutes to eleven, she threw two switches. A green light glowed, and reels of tape began to revolve. At a quarter to the hour, the green light dimmed and went out, and the reels stopped turning. Mrs Cartwright wound back the tape, and taking care to switch off the light, carried the spool downstairs to transcribe. From a locked case she took a small book entitled *German-French Dictionary*. This contained several pages of code-names with numbers. She dialled one number and let the telephone bell ring exactly six times. Then she replaced the receiver, waited for nine seconds by her watch, and dialled again. The telephone was picked up on the seventh ring of the bell.

Mrs Cartwright said, 'Susan here. How is Antoine these days?'

'Not at all well. But he finds comfort in religion,' a man told her, speaking into a cone-shaped mouthpiece to disguise his voice.

'A great sustainer,' agreed Mrs Cartwright. 'Friends tell me he would appreciate a visit.'

'Someone will telephone you to see when that would be convenient.'

As Mrs Cartwright replaced the receiver, she smiled to herself. She was wondering what the woman in tweeds and the flowered scarf would think if she knew that she had just arranged for a man whose name she did not know to murder another man she had never met.

The rain had been heavy that afternoon and traffic in Piccadilly was unusually thick. Blaikie's little car shuddered and jumped as he kept letting in its worn clutch. He had a special extension to the gear lever because of his disability, and this needed readjustment.

Reid sat next to him, puffing his pipe stoically. It had been a depressing day for both of them. The Russians had discovered a tunnel beneath Berlin crammed with listening devices which British and American Intelligence had used to eavesdrop on Russian telephone calls.

Its existence could have been denied easily enough – and probably would have been – but for one unfortunate fact. In an attempt to save expense the British had not used specially made apparatus. Repeaters, transformers, even the telephone sets, were all stamped 'GPO London'.

The discovery of this listening post greatly increased the value of Vasarov's regular meetings with Cornell's successor. But for some reason, the two men did not get on well. On several occasions, Vasarov had asked to be put in touch with White again, but this was, of course, impossible. Cornell was out of the Service.

'Funny bloke, Cornell,' said Reid, as though guessing at Blaikie's thoughts.

'He has to be in this business,' replied Blaikie bitterly. 'Always scrounging, doing things on the cheap, and then wondering why so often it all goes wrong. This bloody car, for instance.'

He glanced with distaste at the shabby imitation leather upholstery seats of his pre-war Morris 10.

'I hear that Cornell's in the used-car trade. Maybe he could find you something better?'

'If he did, I probably couldn't afford it.'

Reid wished he had not made the remark. He knew how tight Blaikie was for money. It showed in Blaikie's flat, with its pre-war decorations, thin curtains and worn carpets, in his wife's dowdy clothes. He felt almost embarrassed about his family's brewing concern, in which he held the controlling shares.

Blaikie jabbed the horn viciously as a motorcyclist tried to cut in ahead of him. The man turned in the saddle and made a 'V' sign at him, and then accelerated away on the wrong side of a bus.

I am sick of my life, thought Blaikie, as he felt pain in his injured arm, as though he still possessed the hand he had lost at Cassino. The doctors said that he would have these strange feelings for some years to come, in moments of stress or irritation. They referred to it as 'the phantom limb'.

Cornell probably makes as much in a few weeks as he did in a year, he thought. Him and that other rogue, Sergeant Carpenter. Two of a kind.

Blaikie glanced irritably at his watch. He would be late for a supper of Spam and lettuce and his wife's complaints about making do on rations for two.

People like Reid, who had money, could not begin to understand what it was like always to be short: to be forced to accept the cheapest option, or none at all; to pretend you didn't mind, that you really liked economy. If you didn't inherit money, then you should be like Cornell and Carpenter and have the God-given gift of making it, creating it from nothing.

He glanced through the narrow windscreen at the hurrying crowds in their utility clothes. They had accepted the dreary sameness of their lives, he thought; they were defeated before the battle began. A handful, like Cornell and Carpenter, never would. He must be like them and make the most of whatever opportunities presented themselves.

It was one thing being loyal and obedient and willing to work all hours when – like Reid – you did not need to do so in order to earn your living. It was totally different when your survival depended on it and promotion on someone else's whim. The car jerked forward awkwardly into the next hold-up.

Vasarov parked off the road outside Spittal and walked back three hundred metres to the wood-framed house where Anna lived. It was late evening; lights glimmered hesitantly behind curtained windows. He tapped lightly three times on the kitchen window, paused, and gave a fourth heavier tap. A bolt slid back, the door opened into a darkened room. Anna closed it behind him before she switched on the light.

The kitchen smelled pleasantly of charcoal and garlic and new-made bread. In once corner a stove, crammed with blazing logs, crackled a welcome. How welcoming was this house, compared with the tiny flat he had shared in Moscow with his wife, her parents and her half-witted brother; two rooms in a damp concrete building that stank perpetually of stale cabbage water and blocked drains! This room reflected the warmth he felt for Anna – who still believed that their original meeting had simply been fortuitous, a lucky chance for her. But Vasarov had engineered it deliberately; he had no room for chance in his closely ordered life.

One morning, a few weeks after that meeting, Anna noticed that his fountain pen had leaked ink over his wallet. She shook out the contents on the kitchen table to dry them. Suddenly, her face stiffened.

'Where did you find this?' she asked him in a strange, tight voice, and held up the photograph of two girls and a woman he had found on the Hill of the Goats at Katyn, years before.

'It belonged to a Polish prisoner-of-war.'

'Is he still alive?'

'I don't know,' Vasarov lied. 'It's a long time ago.'

'My father took that picture. That is my mother with Nina and me. Don't you recognise us?'

Vasarov peered intently at the picture as though he had never really examined it closely before.

'Well, now that you tell me, I do,' he said in simulated surprise. 'But I thought you were Hungarian?'

'Yes. We lived for years in Debrecen, in Hungary. But my father was originally Polish, and as he was on the list of reserve officers, he was called up. He must have been taken prisoner. *Please* find where he is.'

Vasarov dutifully made a note of her father's name, and date of birth, but only to please her. He already knew where he was: under the ground at Katyn.

'In the meantime, you keep this photograph,' he told her. 'And you must stay with me – in case we *can* trace your father.'

'I will, I will.'

Anna kissed him passionately, and he felt her tears on his face. Clearly, she had been devoted to her father and this was not the time – in fact, there never would be a time – for Vasarov to explain that his meeting with her had not been accidental, but arranged.

Her smile had haunted him since the day he had taken the photograph from her dead father's wallet. It seemed to symbolise all he yearned for in the snows of Katyn; warmth, friendship, laughter. Time and again, he had read the name on the back of the picture, and since the end of the war, had used his influence to trace every refugee of the same name. Vasarov had interviewed fifteen before he discovered the two sisters in Speggetz. They had been pointed out to him, so he knew her identity when he had first picked her up on the Spittal road.

Shortly after two o'clock next morning, Vasarov let himself out of the back door, walked quickly to his car, and then drove away. He was back in his requisitioned house just after three. To his surprise, a colleague, a bull-necked colonel with a florid face and mean pig-like eyes, was still downstairs, attempting to read a book by Mikhalkov, a Soviet poet much in favour for his lavish praise of Stalin.

'You've been long enough,' the colonel told Vasarov accusingly. 'Just after you'd gone, a signal came in for you from Moscow. A Most Immediate'.

'What's it about?'

'You're leaving tomorrow. Or rather, today. Train goes at oh-five-hundred.'

'That's in less than a couple of hours,' protested Vasarov.

'When you receive a summons like this, you don't delay. You *go*,' replied the colonel, enjoying Vasarov's discomfort.

Vasarov walked thoughtfully upstairs to his room, sat on the edge of the bed and poured himself a neat vodka. He found that he was trembling with surprise and fear. Someone must have followed him into the forest – someone who knew of his regular meetings with Cardinal and White, and now with White's successor. Yet he had carefully covered all his tracks. Perhaps a Soviet sleeper in the British Intelligence service had discovered his identity and warned Control? He was due to contact White's successor again in three days, and now it would be impossible to tell him that he could not keep the appointment. Wild plans of escape surged through his worried mind. Then he heard the creak of the colonel's boots outside his bedroom.

'I'll wait with you while you pack,' he said, and sat down on Vasarov's bed with his book of poems.

Max struggled up through warm layers of sleep. The telephone was ringing in the corridor outside his room. He glanced at his watch; a quarter to two in the morning. He jumped out of bed, mouth dry, and ran to pick up the receiver. Sam Harris was on the line.

'A bookie down Catford way, name of Rafferty,' he said, without any greeting or preamble. 'Radwell Crescent. Number 47. He refuses to pay out three thousand pounds I won on the dogs. Cheeky bastard says the heats were rigged. Persuade him where his interests lie.'

The receiver whirred emptily in Max's hand.

Nina came to the door of her bedroom, blinking in the light.

'What's the matter?'

A call as early as this aroused uneasy memories of the Gestapo.

'I have to go out. Business. You go back to sleep. Sorry I woke you.'

Max dressed quickly and then, almost as an afterthought, put three pennies in his pocket, something he had learned at Blaikie's training school. Between the knuckles of a clenched fist, they could produce as devastating a result as a knuckle-duster.

He checked the guide to London streets, walked downstairs and out to the mews where he garaged the Triumph that Carpenter had lent him. A few street-cleaners, wearing their quaint Australian-style slouch hats, with turned up brims, were hosing Westminster Bridge. The only vehicles he saw were several taxis, and a few newspaper vans on their way to the stations to catch early morning trains.

Number 47, Radwell Crescent was a mock-Tudor detached house, with phoney black beams set into pebble-dashed walls. Max drove past it without slackening pace, then turned, cut his engine and lights and coasted to the front gate.

He walked up a short path of neatly laid stone slabs, and pressed an illuminated bell push. Chimes boomed in the recesses of the house. Nothing else happened. He pressed again. A light came on in a front upstairs window, and a man's head appeared, hair damp and ruffled with sleep.

'Who is it?' he asked in a strong Irish accent.

'Important personal message for Mr Rafferty.'

'Who from?'

'I don't want to wake the neighbours,' explained Max quietly. 'Please come down. It's very urgent.'

The window slammed shut. A light came on in the hall, and a man about his own size, but fatter, with reddish eyes and a whisky gut and two days' stubble on his chin, stood in the open doorway. He gripped a walking stick belligerently in his right hand.

'Who are you? What do you want?'

'Let me come in. I can't discuss business on the doorstep at this hour.'

'You'll stay where you are.'

'Do you want me to wake your wife and family?'

'They're not here,' said Rafferty. He lifted his stick and prodded it into Max's stomach to make him keep his distance. Until that moment Max had hated his assignment, but now he hated Rafferty, fat, bullying and over-fed, for Rafferty suddenly reminded Max of the German policeman who had ordered his parents into the truck to begin the last journey of their lives.

'It's about money you owe Mr Harris,' he explained as calmly as he could.

'I owe that bastard nothing. The race was fixed. I'm not a bloody fool, you know.'

'That is not for me to decide. Are you going to pay?'

'No. Sod Sam Harris, bloody cheating Yid. If he's so keen on the money, let him sue.'

'People can't sue for gambling debts. As a bookie, you know that.'

'Then let him do what he bloody likes.'

Max shrugged and stepped back, as though admitting defeat.

'That's why I'm here,' he said, almost with regret.

At his movement and the sudden, unexpectedly contrite tone of his voice, Rafferty lowered his stick slightly. As he did so, Max seized it, pulled it sharply towards him and then rammed back the handle into Rafferty's soft belly. The bookmaker fell back, gasping with pain. Max moved swiftly into the hall and closed the door behind him. As Rafferty struggled to rise, Max knocked the stick out of his hand, then forced him up against the wall.

'Now will you pay?'

In that instant, Max heard a sudden slight movement behind him and instinctively swung to one side. A young man with blond hair and full sensual lips, wearing a woman's dressing gown, held a heavy wooden carving like a club above his head. Max side-swiped him across his Adam's apple and as he fell, struck the inside of his wrist with the edge of his hand. The carving clattered to the floor.

'Now, Rafferty.'

The bookmaker did not reply.

Max banged Rafferty's head hard against the wall. An ornamental mirror trembled and fell from its hook. The glass splintered.

'Seven years' bad luck for you,' Max told him. 'It could be starting tonight.'

'All right,' said Rafferty slowly, sobbing for breath. 'I'll pay. But I'll get that bastard Harris for this. Then I'll get you.'

'First of all, get your cheque book.'

'I can cancel a cheque.'

'Not this one, you won't. Not unless you want Mrs Rafferty to know that the moment she and the kids go off for a night, you have your boy friend in here. And you'd get another visit from me.'

Max released him and followed him into the sitting room. Rafferty opened a drawer in a reproduction desk, took out a book of uncrossed cheques and wrote out one for three thousand pounds, Cash to Bearer. Max put it in his back pocket.

'Sleep well,' he told them. 'Both of you.'

He walked out to his car, climbed in behind the wheel, glanced at the dashboard clock. He had been inside the house for exactly eight minutes.

He wondered what he would have done if Rafferty had not prodded him with the stick and triggered those buried memories. Probably nothing, or at the most, simply warned him. Sam Harris would never know, and anyway, Sam Harris didn't need the money.

He drove into his garage and locked the door. Then, hands in pockets, he walked thoughtfully along the cobbles of the mews towards his rooms. It seemed too late to go back to bed, and yet too early to begin the day. He thought about Vasarov. Suddenly, he realised that he was experiencing the same warning sensation of danger that he had felt when he walked through the woods to those meetings. He looked behind him. Two men wearing belted raincoats and trilby hats stood about twenty feet away, watching him.

'We understand you work for Mr Harris,' one of them said. 'We also understand you agreed not to bet on two dogs. But despite this, we understand you did so.'

'You are very understanding people,' replied Max.

'We tailed you to Rafferty's place, in case you decided to ignore your orders again. We want the money. It's Sam Harris's by rights.'

'By what rights? I put my own money on his dogs and what I won is mine.'

The two men did not reply, but began to walk towards him.

'I don't carry that sort of money around.' Max put one hand in his pocket as he spoke, slipped the three pennies between the knuckles of his right hand.

'Sam will take a cheque for it.'

They were very close to him now.

'Then he'll have to come and collect it himself.'

Max jumped forward and kicked the nearest man hard on the left leg, just above his ankle. As he buckled up in pain and surprise, he hit him on the side of the chin and felt the pennies score the bone. The man dropped on the cobbles, screaming, both hands at his shattered jaw.

The other man now leaped at Max, head down, to butt him on the forehead. Max dodged to one side, tried to trip him, but failed.

Max guessed that he was up against a pro, probably an old boxer or wrestler: he could not beat him with blows, but he might trick him.

He began to retreat deliberately, to bring the fight nearer the entrance of the mews, and the man who was still writhing on the ground. Then he turned. His opponent followed him, took a pace back for another charge, trod on his companion's arm, steadied himself, and in that second off balance, Max hit him under his nose. The cartilage snapped like a dry twig. He went down heavily on his back, and his head hit the cobbles like a hammer. Max dusted his hands, smoothed down his coat and walked out into Courtfield Gardens.

He was badly shaken and would have liked to run, but a running man always attracts attention. He hailed a cruising taxi, gave the driver Sam Harris's address in Grosvenor Square.

'Wait for ten minutes,' he told him as he paid him off. 'I want to go back to where you picked me up. There's a five bob tip in it.'

The cabbie grunted in disbelief.

The ornate wrought-iron trellis gate at the entrance was locked. Max pressed the night bell. The porter came out of a booth, yawning.

'What do you want?' he asked him crossly.

'I need to see Mr Harris urgently.'

The porter looked at him suspiciously, 'At this hour?'

'As an old Italy hand, yes.'

The porter peered at him more closely, recognised his face and opened the gate.

'What mob were you with, then?'

'Commandos.'

'I was with the Leicesters. Got chopped up at Cassino.'

'I heard,' said Max, who hadn't, and strode towards the lift. He rode to the fourth floor, examining his face in a mirror in the cage. He straightened his tie carefully, walked across the thick carpet, and pressed the button outside Harris's flat. He held his thumb over the spy-hole so that Harris would have to open the door to see who was calling on him.

'Let me in,' said Max, when Harris opened the door cautiously on its golden safety chain.

'I've a girl here,' replied Harris in a whisper, and winked.

'All the more reason, uncle. You don't want a fuss, do you?'

'What sort of fuss, boy?'

Harris appeared surprised, but not worried. He paid others to worry for him.

'You saw Rafferty?'

'I did. Here's his cheque.'

Max handed over Rafferty's cheque for three thousand pounds. Harris saw cuts on the knuckles.

'You had trouble, then?'

'Not a lot there. But later, a little. In a mews, after I'd put away my car. Two men said you resented me betting on the heats, wanted back my winnings.'

'And you handed them over, I hope? No trouble?'

'Nothing serious. I told them that if you wanted the money you'd better come and collect it.'

'And?'

'They accepted that. The condition I left them in, they couldn't do much else. And here I am. But not with the money.'

'You broke your word, boy,' said Harris harshly. 'No-one does that to me. I told you not to bet.'

'I don't take orders from anyone,' replied Max. 'Not any more. Even from you, uncle. I wagered my own money, and I keep my own winnings.'

'I don't like your attitude,' said Harris slowly. 'I tried to help you and this is what you do. I thought we could have done business, seeing as we're related. If you go on like this, I'll break you before you begin. I know a lot of people.'

'Like the two men who attacked me in the mews? Someone else always does the hard work, and you collect the cash. To refresh your memory, and keep it green, I have written out an account of our little transaction with the races. It is in a bank where the manager's a friend of mine. Then, if I should meet with any accident, like a three tonner going up my backside – however legitimate it may appear – he sends it immediately to the police.'

'You're talking crap,' said Harris. 'I got lawyers. You can't prove anything. I got the paperwork right.'

'Some of those bookies you cheated might send round a few heavies just to see how right.'

'You bastard,' said Harris, but without conviction. Even a rich man's kneecaps could be broken; already, he felt pain by proxy.

'I can ruin you,' he went on. 'If you try to sell cars you'll find paint stripper poured over them, the tyres slashed. You'll be finished before you start.'

'Then I'll pay you another call, like this,' retorted Max. 'Now, less talk, more action. I want the hundred quid you owe me.'

Harris went into a side room, paused for a moment, then unlocked a filing cabinet. He opened a bulging brown envelope and counted out twenty five-pound notes. Max put them in his pocket, let himself out of the flat and took the lift down to the street. He was experiencing the same strange feeling of invulnerability he had known years ago, in the army, when he was out of the landing craft and running up the beach.

Enemy firing, at first so crisp and heavy, had suddenly dwindled and died. Nothing could stop the advance then; nothing would stop him now.

The cabby was dozing behind the wheel, and looked at Max in surprise, shaking sleep from his head.

'Didn't altogether think I'd see you, so bright and chipper,' he said.

'You're not the only one,' Max told him, and sank back thankfully against the camphor-scented seat.

Vasarov had been walking along the Arbat, one of Moscow's busiest streets, crowded at that hour of the evening with people coming out of the Art Cinema and walking to the Metro station under its huge illuminated red M. At the sound of the sirens, the street filled with human statues and all cars and trucks immediately pulled into the side of the road and stopped.

Uniformed police and armed security men appeared in doorways, and shutters clanged across upper windows, as five black cars came through the Borovitsky Gate.

They were identical Zis limousines, based on pre-war American Packards. Their headlights had yellow lenses instead of white, a sign after dark that these were not ordinary cars. None of them carried a registration number. All had windows of bulletproof glass, with side curtains drawn to conceal the passengers.

As they swept past, racing across all the intersections, the drivers overtook each other or fell back to allow a colleague to pass them, so that the order of the cars was constantly changing. This was a security measure, designed to confuse any assassin, for these vehicles formed the special convoy in which Stalin regularly drove the twelve miles from his office in the Kremlin to his country home outside Kuntsevo, south-west of Moscow. The wise and beloved leader travelled in one car, but no-one knew which, for all carried one rear seat passenger whose face was in darkness. Stalin made the journey every week, but for security reasons, on a different night.

Vasarov waited with everyone else until the sirens died away. Then policemen retreated into shadows and doorways; drivers restarted their engines, pedestrians began to walk on. It was absurd to be starting work at nine-thirty in the evening, but for years Stalin had suffered from almost chronic insomnia, and so had initiated the unpopular custom of holding conferences and meetings at midnight or three o'clock in the morning. Vasarov showed his identity pass to the guards on the outer door, gave the password to the second set of guards within, and took the lift to the office where he had been working since his return from Austria several months earlier.

A uniformed captain led him into another, larger room. Here, under a portrait of Stalin, sat Lavrenti Beria behind a desk. He might have been a bank manager or the finance director of a modest commercial company; he had the neat, meticulous appearance of a man to whom figures were important. Vasarov felt his heart jerk with fear. Next to Stalin, Beria was easily the most powerful man in Russia – and the most feared.

'I am told that your father studied with Generalissimo Stalin at Tiflis Seminary,' said Beria, and paused.

'That is so, Comrade Beria. And I was also at the same seminary.'

'I know your work for my ministry, and for our country, and I congratulate you upon it. You have served our cause well, in dealing with agents of the forces of reaction in the West.'

Vasarov inclined his head. He could not trust himself to speak. Did Beria know – or was he hinting? Was he just playing with him?

'I can tell you that the greatest honour open to any officer is to be yours. You will be attached to the general staff of the Generalissimo himself, our wise and beloved leader, Josef Stalin.

'Several other candidates were considered, of course, but none so well qualified – or who attended the same theological college.

'Now, a car will take you tonight to Comrade Stalin's dacha outside Kuntsevo. My wish is that you should continue your career with the loyalty and devotion you have shown so far. You will, as before, report to me personally on the habits, loyalty and opinions of everyone else on the staff there – as, of course, they will be reporting on you.'

Vasarov's car turned off the Mozhask Highway, down a narrow road. An iridescent red disc striped with yellow glowed in its headlights: the way ahead was forbidden to general traffic.

On either side, pine forests stretched, dark and thick and scented. The car drove on, more slowly now, towards the Lenin Hills. Guards opened two barriers in response to a password from the driver. The third opened automatically. They were now on the final avenue that led to Stalin's dacha, a squat, square building in a small clearing. On three sides were verandahs shielded by huge glass panels.

A hundred yards from the dacha stood the guardhouse. Searchlights were fixed on the roof, and other searchlights around the perimeter of the clearing, pointed out into the forest. Beyond the extremity of their beams lay a mine-field, with trip wires attached to explosive charges. Beyond this, again, two more barbed wire fences between which, as in the labour camps, dog-handlers patrolled with alsatians. A radio mast poked up above the trees, and farther still in the forest was a radar installation with a constantly revolving aerial.

Stalin was protected from attack by land or air. But Vasarov knew how old and almost senile he had become. Against the march of years there was no lasting defence.

As the car stopped, two officers came out from the guardhouse. A colonel examined Vasarov's papers minutely while his companion opened his suitcases, shining a torch over their contents. An orderly carried the luggage into the dacha. Vasarov followed him across polished wooden floors, covered by carpets and rugs.

A log fire burned in every room, for Stalin would sometimes move restlessly from room to room throughout the night. Dried herbs were regularly thrown on each fire to give a fragrant, haunting smell, not unlike incense.

Vasarov's bedroom was small and unpleasantly like a prison cell. The curtains were already drawn. On impulse, he pulled them open. To his surprise, there was no window; one had simply been painted on the concrete. He turned the door handle and tried the door, but it had been locked from the outside. He examined the room and found a concealed microphone in the base of a reading lamp. Almost certainly, there would be another, better hidden. As a precaution, he had brought with him in his sponge bag a roll of adhesive plaster. Every night he intended to cut off a two-inch strip and seal his lips, in case he talked in his sleep.

At precisely twenty-five minutes past one next morning a warning bell rang above his head, and the colonel opened the door from the corridor.

They marched along the corridor to a large room that contained two settees, a huge sideboard, and a long table with chairs drawn up around it as for a meeting. On the walls hung idealised portraits of Stalin – young, vigorous and dark-haired, right hand raised, fist clenched. Alongside them were framed cartoons of capitalists in top hats, smoking cigars, and enlarged newspaper photographs of Stalin. The colonel closed the door and Vasarov was alone with a small, round-shouldered old man.

His hair was almost white, his drooping moustache stained with nicotine. His face was coarse and the skin greasy, pitted from smallpox. His left arm was deformed, and he held it close to his body as though to minimise the disfigurement. Vasarov thought he looked like an old and evil carrion bird with a broken wing. This was Stalin, the man of steel.

Stalin nodded to Vasarov with the almost imperceptible movement of the head an old man makes when he is stiff and tired.

'So you are Dimitri Vasarov's son?' he said ruminatively. 'Your father and I were expelled from the seminary in the same month. You know that?'

'He often spoke to me of those days, Comrade Stalin.'

'Then I hear that sadly he fell prey to those false ideologies against which he had once fought so strongly.'

Vasarov bowed at this roundabout way of referring to this father's murder.

'I hear good reports of you from the ministry, comrade,' Stalin continued. 'Your duties will be to assess everyone who comes to see me, and then to give me your frank opinion. When you are young, Comrade Vasarov, and you first drink *mukuzani*, our Caucasian wine, it tastes like champagne. You have a woman for the first time, and she is the most beautiful creature in the world. But as you grow older, wine and women become commonplace. One no longer sees things as one once saw them, in bright, clear colours. That is why I have selected you, to be my young eyes and ears.'

Stalin gave a brief nod of dismissal. Talking had tired him, and he had said enough. Doors opened silently. Stalin walked past Vasarov, stiff-jointed, shoulders stooped, his feet shuffling across the thick carpets.

Each day thereafter, Vasarov arose late, after a night spent talking to Stalin or walking with him from room to room. As he recounted his impressions of each visitor, the realisation of his own danger increased. Every servant in the dacha was a member of the NKVD. He knew no-one with whom he could safely hold a conversation on any but the most trivial level.

Frequently, Stalin slept fully clothed, only removing his boots. Vasarov had been in the dacha for two weeks before he discovered that the dictator had four identical bedrooms, all without windows. Each possessed its own alarm system, separately wired in case of any power failure. Every night, beds in all four rooms would be made ready, and then, at the last moment, as dawn crawled up the sky, Stalin would select at random the bed he would use.

The more Vasarov learned about the workings of the state,

the more uneasy he became. There seemed no continuity, either of policy or of individual careers. The wheel of fortune turned, stopped, and started or reversed at the sudden whim of an old and ailing despot. Molotov, the Foreign Minister, for example, had risen to such eminence that a city had been named in his honour, as well as several mountain peaks and culture parks, and even a range of diesel trucks. But then his Jewish wife, a former factory worker, was suddenly denounced as a Zionist conspirator and banished to a prison camp in North Kazakhstan.

Molotov had been one of Stalin's most faithful supporters since his youth – he even changed his name from Skryabin to Molotov, (from *molot*, meaning a hammer) because he thought that this sounded more in keeping with the aims of the workers. Now he was publicly denounced as a British spy. The charges were ludicrous, but no-one dared to say so. If members of the *soratniki*, described in the official *Great Soviet Encyclopaedia* as 'close comrades-in-arms of J. V. Stalin', could be treated in this way, what hope remained for less important people who fell from Stalin's favour? The question was rhetorical, for Vasarov knew that thousands of men and women were sent every week to work-camps on equally absurd charges.

He also discovered that Beria was growing increasingly concerned for his own safety. The signs had an ominous familiarity. One by one, Beria's supporters in different cities and departments were being systematically denounced. Stalin let no opportunity pass for criticising the work of Beria's ministry. Vasarov was uneasily poised between Stalin, old, cunning, and increasingly suspicious, with his need for continual reports on the loyalty of his colleagues, and Beria, with his agents masquerading as staff in the dacha. If Vasarov's bedroom contained a microphone, was it not also likely that other rooms were similarly equipped? And who held the key to the master copies of such secret transcripts, which could so easily be edited to favour or discredit any speaker? More and more, as Vasarov lay awake in his cell-like room, waiting for the bell to ring, his thoughts turned towards the only person he felt could conceivably help him: the Englishman he knew as White.

# Seven

Sam Harris awoke late in a bad temper. He had been disturbed more than he cared to admit by Max Cornell's visit. Cornell could prove troublesome, perhaps more than troublesome. He'd let him alone for a week or two, then have one or two of his employees teach him a sharp and painful lesson. That was the only way to deal with people like him.

After breakfast he left his flat, hailed a cruising taxi, and told the driver to drop him off at the corner of Kensington Park Road and Westbourne Grove. He was ten minutes early for his appointment, and he walked slowly along the side roads, unimpressed by what he saw. Here and there a shabby car was parked against the pavement. The wind had blown off a dustbin lid and scattered the contents. Through an open window of one house he heard a baby screaming.

All the houses looked seedy; some were almost derelict. Paint peeled from scuffed front doors. The stucco on facings had cracked and split as though the walls were diseased and erupting in giant swellings and sores.

Sam Harris had an appointment with an estate agent, a Mr Goudousky, whose shop was filled with postcards offering bedsitters and flatlets for rent. He read some details without interest:

'Fish shop. W.11 area. Wkly trade: £50. 3 rms, bth. Stott fryer, gdn, lock-up garage. £750 f'hld. Snip.

'Gen. stores. d.f. s.a.v. rent £110. £40 wkly tkngs. Good liv. accm. Exc. prospects. Owner retiring. Long lse. W.14

'Flatlet-hse. 20 rms. Low outgoings. Fully let. Exc return. Gd. liv. accm. Gas, elec. meters. Offers. W.11 area.'

Underneath each set of particulars was typed one line: 'Building Society mortgages arranged.'

It was in connection with this announcement that a friend had suggested he should meet Mr Goudousky. Harris pushed open the door. Above his head, a bell tinkled on a curved spring, and girl typing at a table looked up at him enquiringly. To one side, a gas fire hissed like an angry serpent.

'Mr Goudousky?' Harris asked her.

'He's expecting you?'

'Yes. Mr Harris.'

She opened the door into an inner room.

'Please go straight in.'

Mr Goudousky was a small, thin man, with an extremely large head. He looked so curiously misshapen that he might almost have been a maquette for a full size human being. Someone might have made him from a kit of parts or the pieces left over from other, better formed specimens. He spoke with a strong European accent, and almost unconsciously Harris adopted a cultured English voice. He did not wish this grotesque man to think he could be his social equal, to suspect they might both be aliens and immigrants.

'I am very glad you could come along, Mr Harris,' Mr Goudousky said gravely. 'A busy man like you. Would you have a cup of tea?'

'No, thank you.'

'Something stronger, perhaps?'

He made a movement down to one of the drawers of the desk.

'A bit early,' said Harris.

'Excuse me if I imbibe?'

'Of course.'

Mr Goudousky took a bottle of whisky from the drawer and one glass, which he filled.

'To you, Mr Harris, sir. Good stuff, this. Hard to get. Know a man in the trade.'

'You are very lucky,' said Sam Harris.

What the devil could his friend have in mind, introducing him to a small-time character like this? He was wasting his time.

'Can we discuss your business proposition?' he suggested, and glanced pointedly at his gold wristwatch.

Mr Goudousky nodded. 'Of course. To begin at the start, I deal in properties in this area. We have a strong Polish community here. Refugees and people who came out of the services. Now, they want to start up a business or buy a house, but they can't get a building society mortgage. They are foreigners. No roots. No references. So – no money!'

He paused.

'I can see all that perfectly, but what is your proposition?' Harris asked him, trying to conceal his impatience.

'This, Mr Harris. *We* start a building society, you and I, to meet this large demand. I have the clients, and I am told you have the money.'

'Who has the profit?'

'We split it fifty-fifty. After expenses.'

'But surely the profits are very low in building societies? They only pay say two and a half per cent to depositors. And then they lend at four. That leaves a profit margin of only one and a half per cent – before overheads and expenses.'

'True, Mr Harris. Good thinking. But we would not be depositors, or borrowers. We would be *owners*. Let me explain.

'We form our society, choosing a reliable, solid title, like The British Flag Building Society. Something safe. Solid. Reassuring. We put an advertisement for it in local papers. Places like Cheltenham. Bath. Bournemouth. Where retired people – and widows or maiden ladies – go to live. People with a bit of money, who want a safe return.

'The big companies offer them two and a half per cent, so we offer two and three-quarters. If we offered three, then their old family solicitors would say there's a catch in it.'

'And is there?'

'Of course not. If we find these adverts aren't pulling in enough cash, then we write direct to the solicitors. We offer them one per cent on the money they persuade their clients to invest. Not bad, eh? They advise a little old lady to put in, say, two thousand pounds. She's happy with just over a pound a week interest on her capital. Her solicitor is also happy with ten bob a week as his cut, and we're happiest of all, Mr Harris, for we're making ten times as much on someone else's money. We use it to finance our own deals.'

'I thought you wished to help the immigrants?'

'Of course I do, Mr Harris. But aren't we, as immigrants, equally deserving of help?'

'What is the background to building societies, then?' asked Harris. 'It seems too good to be true.'

'Forgive me if I go into some detail while I explain. We're in the middle of a property revolution, Mr Harris. Before the first war, ninety per cent of people in this country rented their homes. They didn't *want* the responsibility of owning them.

'Then the war breaks out, and almost at once everything changes. The government fears profiteering, so it brings in a Rent Restriction Act. Landlords can't put up their rents, although all their costs – repairs, rates and insurance – soar.

'In 1920, there's another Act. The tenants are now called Statutory Controlled Tenants, "stats". So long as they pay their rent, you can't boot them out. Ever.

'When the last war starts, in comes a third Act. So who wants to own a house let to a tenant if it's costing you more than it brings in? I tell you, Mr Harris; no-one.

'The tenants complain that landlords are allowing houses to fall apart. But what else can they do?'

'Doesn't seem much of a proposition for me so far,' said Harris drily.

'That's what so many people think. That's why these properties are going for absurdly low prices.

'But to go on. Building societies were originally formed to lend money to build houses to let. But then fewer people wanted to build houses to rent to other people, so the societies began to lend money for people to buy their own houses.'

'How can we compete?'

'We don't. We lend over the odds to individuals who can't borrow money elsewhere, but we make our real money out of rooming houses. Say an existing landlord owns a rooming house and he's got barbary tenants. He only has to replace a couple of dustbins, say, or a new lavatory pan, and that's his rent profit gone for a week. Now I suggest we buy these houses – not in ones and twos, but by the dozen, maybe the hundred. I know people who would buy what we don't want

– if they had the money. Our building society will provide the money – for us – and them. At a price.'

'But I still cannot see how, when the original owners are not making any profit, new owners can succeed, and still pay us heavy interest on top?'

'That's the secret of the deal, Mr Harris. Say a client buys twenty houses, and each house has ten letting rooms. You might have twenty rooms unlet out of your total two hundred.'

'I suppose so,' said Harris. 'People move out, get new jobs, die.'

'Exactly. The law allows you to move a tenant if you offer him alternative accommodation. So you move your tenants around. Then out of twenty houses you find you've two or three empty.

'Then you tart them up. Put washbasins into each room. Furniture, carpet. Let each room at four or five quid a week. Furnished flatlets, you call them. One room in the basement you let to an old soldier, retired sergeant-major type, six foot four, won't stand any messing. He collects the rent every week. In cash.'

'You make a strong case,' said Harris. 'How much money do you need?'

'A few thousand. Five or six. No more at the start. Just enough to form a company, rent a room in a good area – the City, Bond Street, to give people confidence. The rest we spend on advertising, with some in reserve. We'll have to put out a few quid for some swanky names for the letterheads to make it sound solid.'

'If I put up this capital, what is your contribution?'

'Expertise. My contacts, my knowledge.'

'Draw up some letter of agreement,' said Harris, 'and I will let my solicitor go over it.'

Mr Goudousky's face lit up like a huge turnip lantern.

'I thought you would be interested, Mr Harris. Your friend told me you have a great head for business. *Now* will you have a drink? Coffee? I'll get Sandra to make two cups.'

He opened the door, giving Harris a clear view of the outer office. The girl was going through a typed list of properties with a young man. As Mr Goudousky called, she turned. Harris saw, with a shock like a physical blow, that the young man was Max Cornell. Quickly, he moved to one side, in case Max should see him.

What the hell was that bastard doing here? Had he followed him? Was this some kind of trap?

'You all right, Mr Harris?' Mr Goudousky asked with concern, for some of Sam Harris's anger showed in his face.

'Yes. Yes. Shut the door.'

He heard the bell tinkle as the shop's outer door opened and closed. The girl came in carrying two mugs of coffee on a tin tray.

'Who was that fellow outside?' Harris asked her as casually as he could.

'Man who wants to rent a room,' replied the girl. 'Gave him a number of possibles.'

'He could be one of our tenants, Mr Harris,' said Mr Goudousky cheerfully.

'Not one of mine,' Harris retorted sharply. 'Never!'

At half past nine that night, Max drove along the Bayswater Road to pick up Betty. He had found five rooms in separate houses from the lists of properties that Mr Goudousky and other local agents had supplied, and had rented under a pseudonym. An ironmonger cut him duplicate keys. Now all that remained was for Betty to see whether the financial equation worked.

'How's trade?' he asked her.

She made a face.

'Been raining. Keeps them away – like the flies!'

'I've got five rooms for you,' he said. 'Should be useful in the rain.'

He handed the keys to her.

'You trust me, then?' she asked shyly, obviously pleased.

'Trust no-one is a good enough motto,' retorted Max with a smile. 'But let's say I'm not worried.'

'How can I get in touch with you?'

'You can't. I'll find you here. Say the day after tomorrow? Same time?'

'But I might not be able to fix anything up by then.'

'No matter. Do your best. God made the world in six days and rested on the seventh. So you shouldn't have such a difficult task.'

Max drove up towards Baker Street. He had read an article in the *Evening Standard* the previous evening about people who had carried out secret jobs during the war – under 'Now it can be told,' or some such title. One of the men mentioned was Professor Tobler, who had been interviewed in his Marylebone flat. Max looked up his address in the telephone book. He thought he would pay him a surprise visit. Ten minutes later he was walking along an empty corridor on the eighth floor. From behind the cream painted front doors, he heard radios, but Flat 818 was silent. He tapped lightly on the door. A quavering voice called out suspiciously:

'Who is it? Not another reporter, I hope?'

'No. An old comrade from Aberdovey. Max Cornell. Formerly Kransky.'

Tobler's voice cracked with pleasure and surprise.

'Goodness me! Wait till I reach the door, dear boy. I'm a bit slow on my feet these days.'

A shuffling of slippers, the slide of a safety chain, the door opened.

Tobler shook him warmly by the hand.

'Come inside, dear boy. My, you look fit! It must be nearly ten years since we met.' He shook his head in disbelief.

'Now, tell me all your news. You served abroad, of course?'

'Middle East, Sicily and Italy. And you, sir?'

'I've had a few trips. Casablanca. The Tehran Conference. Things like that. A backroom boy, as that newspaper fellow described me. You read it, I suppose? All sorts of people seem to have seen it and rung me. Very nice of them. But when you live alone it's even better to have a visitor – especially you! Now, a drink.'

Tobler poured two large whiskies, added soda. The glasses trembled in his hands.

'A toast,' he said brightly.

'To what? A better world? A communist Utopia?'

'Shall we way, *some* Utopia? As one grows older, dear boy, solutions seem less simple. Nothing is black or white any more, as it seems when you are young, but grey. Like my future.'

'Nonsense. You're looking fine.'

But Max was lying, and his assurance sounded false and hollow. Tobler seemed to have shrunk physically. Flesh that had once been plump now hung in loose, sallow folds. His hair was white and thin. He sat down heavily in an armchair with threadbare arms.

Max glanced around the room: dust lay thick on bookshelves. Tobler's drive and charisma had totally disappeared. Max was not sitting with an intellectual whose mind he could admire, but with an old man, failed and frightened.

'You've kept up the good work?' Tobler asked him, looking at Max quizzically.

'I've kept myself as fit as I could,' replied Max carefully.

'The fact is I've not been very well, you know.'

Tobler spoke conspiratorially, as though this explained his vagueness, the shabbiness of his surroundings. 'I had to leave Cambridge because of my health.'

'Is there any treatment?'

'You know what Sir Thomas Browne wrote? "Death is the cure of all diseases." That will be my cure – the ultimate one. The truth is, dear boy, I have cancer. The crab. Sometimes its iron claws grip as though they would never let go.'

'You have pills, though, to ease the pain?'

'My doctor here has been very kind. But pills only conceal the pain, they can't cure it. There's not a lot of hope.'

'Is there for any of us?'

'I don't know. But I am being instructed in the Catholic faith. It's a great consolation to know that over the edge of darkness I have something to look forward to. I can be forgiven for my sins. And, my God, I value that knowledge, when I think of the harm I have done in the past.'

'Think of all the young people you've taught to think for themselves – to form their own conclusions. People like me.'

'You're very kind. I'd like to look back on my life in those terms. But I've also corrupted a number of people.'

'You mean sexually?'

'No, I mean politically. I helped to instigate something terrible in Austria at the end of the war – and then covered it up afterwards. Hundreds of thousands of innocent people, and their wives and families, were sent to Russia to face certain torture or death as traitors. Not something anyone wants to shout about now. You didn't read about that in the paper yesterday!'

'You did what seemed best at the time.'

Tobler shook his head.

'I didn't, dear boy. I did what was best for the Party. What I was told to do. I also influenced young men and women – undergraduates who admired me. I believed in communism then and converted them like a missionary. Now I feel that communism is totally incompatible with human dignity or happiness. The priest who is instructing me in the Catholic faith told me how the Jesuits used to send out what they called "penetration agents" in the service of the Catholic church. I sent out many such agents in the service of communism. I mean to make a confession of everything.'

'Everything?' Max sounded puzzled.

'Yes. Dates, times, places, people. I cannot purge my body of these monstrous cells. But I can at least ease my mind.'

'Will that really help you?'

'It will give me peace,' said Tobler simply. 'I cannot hope to go to the Kingdom of Heaven if I am less than honest. Mind you, they may not want me, even then.'

'How can you recall all you wish to confess?'

'I kept notes. I should not have done, of course, but all academics like to keep records of their work. I was no exception.'

'Won't this be very damaging for you?'

'What does that matter now? The doctors won't give me more than months – which probably means weeks. When you're in that position, dear boy, what happens when you leave is of no concern. But let us not be morbid. This is a reunion, not a requiem. Have another whisky.'

Tobler stood up to reach the bottle.

'I wouldn't like to think of your name being blackened,' said Max gently.

'Let the dead bury the dead,' replied Tobler. 'The worst thing for me is that dying will be very long drawn-out. The doctors can only promise me increasing pain and final indignities on which I do not want to dwell. Not a very pretty way to go, dear boy. Sometimes, I even wish I knew someone who could bear me away swiftly from this world to the next as Aeneas carried old Anchises from the ruins of Troy.'

Suddenly, as he spoke, Tobler jerked forward, head down.

'What's the matter?' Max asked him anxiously.

Tobler shook his head, biting his lower lip. A thin trickle of blood dribbled down his pale chin. He crouched farther forward, as though in a foetal position he could better cushion the agony that scored his bowels. Then he voided. The sharp stench of cancered faeces made Max choke. He flung open the window.

'The pills,' gasped Tobler. 'The top drawer! Round pack!'

Max opened the drawer of the desk. Inside, lay notepaper and envelopes of various sizes, two small circular white boxes of pills, and, at the back, several large diaries bound in red leather.

'For God's sake! The pills!'

As he had said, pills could only mask his pain, they could never cure the cause. But Max could – and no-one would ever know.

Tobler's head was now tucked down between his thighs. He began to sob in a rasping, choking way, as Max leaned over, moving his hands expertly behind and below Tobler's ears. He pressed gently as he had learned in Blaikie's training camp.

Tobler gave a faint moan and his whole body relaxed. He collapsed, falling forward clumsily on the floor. Max stood up, waited for five minutes by his watch and then felt Tobler's pulse. He was quite dead.

He wiped the sides of Tobler's neck with his handkerchief to remove any fingerprints. Then he took the diaries from the drawer, put them in a large envelope. He dialled 999 and asked the operator for ambulance service. An old man had apparently suffered a heart attack. The ambulance men arrived and lifted Tobler on to a stretcher, wrinkling their noses at the foul smell in the tiny room.

'He's dead, you know,' one told him.

'I thought so. I rang as soon as he collapsed.'

'Better come down to the hospital, then. You'll have to make a statement.'

At the hospital, Max explained he had been visiting the professor when he had collapsed.

'There may be an inquest,' an official told him. 'The police may wish for a statement. Nothing to worry about, though. He's probably got a medical history.'

'I think you will find he had cancer.'

'Then it's a blessing he went out so quickly.'

'You are absolutely right,' Max agreed.

On the way out of the hospital he saw a rubbish chute marked: INCINERATOR. He tossed the envelope containing Tobler's diaries down this, and then drove back to Courtfield Gardens.

It was several years since he had killed a man, and that had been in war. By putting on a uniform and killing a stranger similarly dressed, murder was elevated to a noble deed. In a sense, he told himself, what he had just done was not ignoble. It had been an act of mercy, and something more. He had ensured that a man who had befriended him years ago would be remembered as someone who – in the words of the newspaper article – had served his country well. Whether he had also served any other country was now a question that could never be answered.

Usually, Nina was sitting in the front room overlooking the square, listening to the wireless or reading when Max returned, and there would be an appetising smell of continental cooking from the kitchen. Now, the room was empty, and smelled damp with that chilliness of an old house in a cold climate. He turned on the electric fire to bring some warmth, drank a large neat whisky, then another to drown memories of what he had done.

He called out, 'Nina?'

There was no answer. Where the devil could she be? A quarter past ten. If she had been to the pictures, she should be back soon. He searched through the kitchen cupboard, made himself a cup of coffee and sat in the sitting room, looking out over the central darkening garden from which the square took its name.

A taxi stopped outside the house. Nina climbed out. The room was very dark now, and she did not realise Max was there until he called out: 'Want a drink?'

'I'd love one.'

He poured her a whisky and switched on the ceiling light. Nina blinked in its sudden glare. She seemed very pale, and her eyes were wide and frightened.

'You look as though you've seen a ghost,' Max told her. 'What's happened? Where have you been?'

'Out. Shopping.'

'At this hour?'

'No. I went to the pictures.'

'On your own?'

Something had upset her, but was that any concern of his? Nina drank the whisky thankfully, flopped down in an easy chair and ran a hand through her long hair. He looked at her closely.

'Are you *sure* you're all right?'

She nodded, and held out the glass for another whisky, an unusual gesture for her.

'Well, what is the matter, then? Because something *is* wrong.'

'I am afraid,' she said simply.

'What of?'

'I was followed this afternoon. That's why I went to the cinema, and took a taxi. To shake him off.'

'Shake who off?'

'I was out shopping and I saw an odd-looking man across the road. He kept looking at me. I walked up Dean Street, and he followed me on the other side of the road. I went on to Oxford Street, and he was still there. I went into Selfridges by one entrance and out by another. There he was, across the road, reading a paper.'

'Did he speak to you?'

'No.'

'He was probably waiting for someone,' said Max reassuringly.

Nina shook her head.

'This is not the first time. Last week the same thing happened. The same man, with a smaller companion. They're from Moscow.'

'All the way from Russia? Next you'll say they have snow on their boots. You are British now.'

'That is just a matter of altering a passport.'

'What do you want me to do? Tell the police?'

'They'd think I was making it up. They wouldn't understand, either.'

'I will try to understand,' said Max patiently.

'I'm scared, Max. You know how these people work. They will force me to do something here, or else my sister will be arrested. You're never free of them.'

'What you need is a holiday. I have a relation in the north of England, a rich man. He'll put you up for a week or two, if I ask him.'

Nina's relief showed in her face.

'Would he really?'

'Of course, I'll ring him now while you get some supper.'

He took a handful of coins, went out into the corridor, and dialled Paul's number on the coinbox telephone.

'Where are you speaking from?' Paul asked him.

'London.'

'I was there yesterday. If I'd known, we could have met. Well, what can I do for you?'

'There is something, Paul. I'd like my wife to come and stay with you – if you could put her up for a few days. She is from Austria, and the strange language and rationing and so on over here are a bit difficult for her. I am away a lot, which doesn't help things.'

'I'd be delighted. Rachel and my son are away, too, so I'm on my own. Put her on the train, and I will meet her personally at the station. What is her name, by the way?'

'Nina. And thank you.'

Max replaced the receiver, and went into the kitchen.

'It's all fixed,' he told Nina. 'No-one will follow you up there. Paul will meet you at Stockport. I'll ring him with the time of the train. You'll be all right, there.'

'I hope so.'

'I know so,' Max assured her cheerfully. 'We'll both be all right, then.'

When Paul collected any visitor from the station for the first time he generally drove them past his factories with the huge sign, 'Harrow Radio' incongruously garish against sooty brick buildings erected eighty years earlier during the cotton boom.

Paul found further satisfaction in viewing the source of his success from the back seat of the Rolls he had recently bought. And the house which his chauffeur now approached by its long gravel drive was further proof that Paul Harrow was not the equal of other men, but richer than most.

'Is *this* where you live?' Nina asked him in amazement.

'Yes,' agreed Paul. He patted her hand. She looked very small and defenceless with her head resting against the silk-covered corner cushion.

The car stopped outside the house. A manservant in black jacket, striped trousers and white gloves was already walking down the front steps towards them.

'Money buys many things,' said Paul reflectively, 'but to me the most important is freedom. From chores and worries, in particular.'

Although it was not yet noon, huge candelabras glittered like frozen stars in the hall. Hidden lights illuminated paintings of men in rich ermine robes and women with demure oval faces. Nina had seen such paintings before, but only in museums.

'Are they ancestors?' she asked.

'Of course,' said Paul. 'But not mine. I bought a job lot from an artist who needed the money. Quite a trade in England, painting ancestors for people like me who haven't got any of their own. Another thing money can buy, you see!'

'Your grandchildren will be more fortunate,' said Nina. 'They can look back on you as their ancestor.'

'Possibly,' agreed Paul. 'At present I feel like Napoleon. When Josephine's family asked who his ancestors were, he replied: "I am my own ancestor."'

A maid appeared from a side door.

'She will show you to your room,' said Paul. 'Then do come down and join us for a drink.'

He crossed the hall into the sitting room. Two men were standing by the fireplace. One was Douglas Carton, red in the face, wearing a grey suit too tight for him, and looking as he imagined the Right Honourable Douglas Carton, Minister for Redevelopment in the second post-war Labour Government, should look: grave and ponderous and smug.

His companion was taller, with grey curly hair. He wore gold rings on the little fingers of both hands. This was Colonel Richard Liddle, the Conservative MP for Paul's constituency.

Paul thought, not for the first time, that they looked like actors playing the parts of politicians; in a sense they were. He despised them both, but he needed them.

'Sorry I had to leave you,' he said. 'But I see you have wisely helped yourself to drinks.'

'You are always a good host,' said Carton. 'And this malt stuff is in very short supply down south, you know. You have to come north to live well.'

Liddle had served in the army with the former MP for this constituency, who had been killed in Normandy. Liddle broke the news to the MP's widow, whose father had built up a chain of grocery shops. They became friendly. She suggested to the local constituency office that 'to keep the continuity', as she put it, Liddle should stand for her husband's seat. To his surprise, he was elected. He then married the widow. He wasn't a 'real' colonel; only a colonel in the local cadet force.

'Who's that gel?' Liddle now asked Paul. He called young women gels or fillies, because he believed that this sounded aristocratic, as indeed a stage colonel might describe them. He was ever careful lest by anything he said or did or wore he might give away the fact that far from being educated at Eton, the closest he had been to the College was to drive past it in the car his wife had bought him.

'A relation by marriage,' Paul explained carefully. 'Here from London for a few days.'

'I wish my relations by marriage looked like that,' said Carton. 'Who's she married to?'

'Fellow who was in the army.'

'What rank?' asked Liddle quickly.

'Sergeant.'

'Ah, not commissioned, then? What does he do now?'

'Sells cars, I believe.'

'Damned fine taste in gels.'

'You're staying for lunch?' Paul asked them. They accepted.

Nina came into the room.

'We were just talking about you,' said Paul. 'They were saying how lucky I was to have such a pretty relative.'

Nina smiled nervously. She was not sure whether they were making fun of her. Paul introduced his two guests and poured her a large sherry.

'Now tell me about Max,' he said. 'I saw him not too long ago, quite by chance. But before that, not for years. The middle of the war, in fact.'

'He's very well.'

'What exactly does he do?' asked the colonel.

'He is trying to buy an auction to sell second-hand motor cars.'

'Lot of money in that,' said Carton approvingly. 'Cash trade.'

After lunch, Paul took Nina for a walk around the garden, while the other two men drank his brandy and dozed in front of the fire.

'Max told me you weren't quite used to England and our ways?'

'That's so,' agreed Nina. 'It's all so strange. Also I felt lonely. I have a sister in Austria. She promised to write to me every week, but I haven't heard from her.'

'What Zone is she in?'

'The Russian.'

'That explains it. I've got Polish refugees – we call them Displaced Persons up here – working for me in my factory.

They haven't heard from their families since the day they left. They're uneasy, too.'

'About their relatives back home?'

'And about themselves. They get visits from other Poles who they think are communist agents, checking on them. We had a Polish priest near here, and he said as much publicly.'

Paul paused.

'And what happened to him?'

'He was found dead. Floating in the canal.'

Nina shivered. This well-ordered English garden, with lawns freshly cut, trees and bushes trimmed, roses growing in neat rows, recalled another open space: the field outside Speggetz, trucks filled with desperate refugees weeping as they crossed the bridge to the station.

'You can't understand what it is like there,' she told Paul. 'You've had safety and security all your life.'

'You're wrong,' he retorted. 'Even so, we all feel insecure at times. But now you are with friends.'

To prove this, Paul gave a cocktail party so that she could meet his friends. He took her to the theatre and to dinner in restaurants. Sometimes he or the chauffeur would drive her into Manchester so that she could spend a morning looking at the shops. They would meet for lunch and he would drive her home.

One day, about a fortnight after her arrival, they met for lunch in the Palace Hotel, Buxton. Nina was very quiet and only picked at her meal – although when Paul had dropped her in Buxton that morning, she had appeared extremely cheerful.

'Are you feeling ill?' he asked her. 'Or still lonely?'

She shook her head. All around her, women with bright hard faces were sharing tables with older men in expensive suits. She sat in the centre of wealth and privilege and felt more afraid than she had ever been. She had no-one in whom she could confide, for who would believe her story – and who could she trust?

'There must be *something* the matter,' Paul persisted. 'I wish I had a pretty girl moping for me.'

'You have a wife and son.'

'Ah. Rachel. I have had one letter from her since she's been in Paris. She's going on to Prague, of all places.'

'But how can she afford it when you can only take twenty-five pounds out of this country?'

'Simple. I put up a foreign buyer here, pay all his expenses, and when I go over to the continent, he looks after me.'

'Isn't it risky for your wife and child to go there? Politically, I mean?'

'No. I asked Dougie Carton. He has contacts in the Foreign Office. He assured me they would be perfectly safe. Anyhow, what could happen? They are both British subjects.'

'But that doesn't really mean anything, does it?'

Paul looked at her more closely now.

'You *are* worried about something.'

Nina glanced down at her plate. She could continue denying it, or she could tell him. She made up her mind.

'I'll explain all about it back home,' she said. 'But not here.'

'In that case, we had better finish our lunch quickly and go.'

Paul stood looking out of the window, his back to Nina: she found it easier to talk if he was not looking at her directly, rather as penitents reveal sins in a confessional, where they do not have to face the priest.

She had explained how Max had agreed to marry her and bring her to England for a fee of five hundred pounds. They had never consummated their marriage, for he had assured her that she could then obtain a divorce more easily whenever she wanted.

She told of the two men who had followed her, and how Max had suggested that she came to stay with Paul. But that morning she had seen one of these men again in Buxton. Obviously, he had followed her there. She had not been able to escape from them after all. What could she do to be free?

Paul sat down by her side on the sofa, where, years earlier, Max had sat beside his wife. He put an arm protectively around Nina's shoulder.

'Let me have a word with one or two people about this,' he suggested. 'Dougie Carton is a minister in the government. A word from him, and the Special Branch could sort this out in no time.'

'No. I am so afraid. These people never give up.'

His hand rested on her shoulder, and in her longing for human contact, Nina instinctively moved towards him. Paul felt the warmth of her body through her silk blouse. With his other hand he gently stroked her hair. Nina leaned against him, comforted by his presence. He pulled her more closely to him and she did not resist. His arm tightened around her shoulders and the tips of his fingers caressed her breast. They brushed her right nipple and he felt it harden. In that instant, pity turned to need. From comforting Max's wife, he wanted her.

Desire moved like a tide through him, as he looked down at her. He allowed his cheek to rest against hers, then his lips to touch her forehead, her face, her mouth. This was not the routine, boring lovemaking experienced with Rachel; the minimum a cold and selfish woman grudgingly gave as a duty regretted, because it was with the wrong man. This was what sex should be, could be, and now would be.

Without a word, he lifted Nina and carried her up the wide staircase, to his bedroom. He locked the door. She leaned against it as he kissed her, undressing her slowly as he did so.

'But I am married to your cousin,' she protested weakly.

'Only in name,' he said. 'You have said so yourself.'

'But your wife?'

For an answer, he carried her to the bed and placed her on its golden silk coverlet. Then, naked, the hair on his chest dark against his pale skin, he lay down beside her. She lay tense and a little frightened, but he was unhurried and expert in his lovemaking. Nina's cry when it came was part pain, part exultation, part thankfulness.

Not only had she found a friend and a protector; she had found a man.

Blaikie had moved offices several times since Max had last seen him. He now occupied three rooms above the shop of a soft-fruit merchant in Covent Garden, near Inigo Jones's church. The strange hours worked in the market, with heavy lorries arriving early and late to load and unload crates of apples and oranges and bananas, provided a useful cloak for the arrivals and departures of other more silent visitors. Nothing in the bleak outer reception room gave any indication whatever of the activities conducted in the rooms beyond.

Visitors who came up these stairs by accident, mistakenly believing that they led to the fruit merchant's private office, would have been amazed to learn that in each tread of the staircase was a switch operating concealed cameras that photographed them in front view and profile. A button beneath the carpet under the desk of the receptionist could close the street door instantly. The ceiling, walls and floor of Blaikie's office were also armoured by concealed steel plate. His office, Blaikie liked to say, was safe as a bank vault – but not a lot more comfortable. Now, if he were in the City or in any other business, he would have at his age a fine office, with panelled walls and fitted carpets. He would have leather arm chairs for visitors and a huge desk with a red leather top edged in gold instead of the issue Ministry of Works furniture he had to endure.

He sat, rather disgruntled, his arm aching and his swivel chair uncomfortable, and read *The Times*. Obituaries always attracted his attention, especially those of people he knew or about whose life he had a professional interest.

Professor J. K. Tobler, who had been awarded the CBE for his work during the war, much of which was still of a classified nature, had died in his London flat.

'With his death,' declared the writer of his obituary sonorously, 'another link with wartime Intelligence has been severed. Joe Tobler was a rich man. His family had been mill owners in Lancashire for several generations. Yet, apart from a love of travel, good food and wines, the professor lived a quiet life. He brought to every task, however difficult, a clear analytical mind, a selfless dedication, and a willingness to help all members of his staff, however junior.'

Especially if they were young, slim, male and had blue eyes, thought Blaikie unkindly. Tobler was apparently sixty-two; Blaikie had thought he was older. He had failed by eight years to reach his allotted span. But how many, because of his activities, had failed by thirty or forty years to reach theirs?

Blaikie refilled his pipe thoughtfully, and was about to relight it when Reid came into his office and sat down in the hard-backed chair provided for visitors.

'He died conveniently, I would think, for a number of people,' he said, when he saw what Blaikie was reading. 'Special Branch intended to pull him in – in a discreet and dignified way, of course, as befitted a traitor of his wealth and eminence – the following afternoon.'

'How was he found?' asked Blaikie.

'When Burgess and Maclean cleared off, Five did a check on all their known associates. Threw up a few odd names, I can tell you. One was Tobler's. That seemed so unlikely in view of his war work, and his own money, that we did a bit of work on him ourselves. Strictly unofficial, of course.'

'Of course. Never do to ruffle Five's feathers.'

'Quite. Vasarov tipped us off, said he'd warned Cornell about it way back, but either he was lying or Cornell never passed it on. Five were quite right. Tobler *was* working for the other side. Had been for years.'

'Was he really a big wheel?'

'My own view is that he wasn't – as a recruiter. But he was important to the other side as a chicken-hawk, to use your phrase. If we pulled in a wealthy left-wing professor who'd obviously preached the gospel according to St Marx to generations of students at Cambridge, we'd think he was the main recruiter of all those young men from Oxford and Cambridge who went over to the angels. He probably thought he was himself – gave importance to a rather lonely life. And we'd leave alone the real recruiters.'

'It's possible,' agreed Blaikie. 'But then why would they kill him – if they did?'

'Maybe because they thought that since he was ill, he might break down under questioning. Or leave incriminating papers behind. Oddly, he was known to keep a diary, but nothing was found in his flat or in the bank.'

'Who found him?' asked Blaikie.

'That's what I came in to tell you. Cornell.'

'What the devil was he doing in Tobler's flat?'

'Paying a social call, apparently. Saw that article about him in the paper. Tobler used to give lectures to his commando in the army, so he thought he'd look him up. They were having a drink together, and apparently Tobler just collapsed. Cornell rang for an ambulance, but it was too late.'

'Lucky.'

'For whom?'

'Tobler, I suppose. Pretty miserable to die alone. And for the other side as well. The whole thing seems just a little too trite for my money.'

Reid nodded, but said nothing.

'Now listen to what *I* think happened,' said Blaikie.

# Eight

On this particular Monday, Max rose late and went downstairs to see whether there were any letters. One lay on the mat behind the front door; he recognised Nina's round handwriting, and slit open the envelope.

> Dear Max [he read] I am feeling so much better already, and am enjoying life up here. Now that I am on my own and have gathered my thoughts, I have come to the conclusion, which I think you will agree is the right one, that since ours would always be a marriage of convenience and not of love, I think I should go ahead with divorce proceedings, which you have told me could be started whenever I wished.
>
> I will always be grateful for all you have done for me, and will always think of you as a friend.
>
> I hope that you may regard me so, and that one day you will find the woman who will give you the happiness and love you so greatly deserve.
>
> Yours, Nina.
>
> P.S. Your cousin, Paul, has been most sympathetic, and has introduced me to a lawyer to help speed up the divorce.

Max put down the letter, and tried to analyse his feelings. He had not been attracted to Nina, but even so he felt deflated and rejected. Nevertheless, he had told her often enough that she could leave him whenever she wished; so how could he now be surprised that she had done so?

He walked slowly upstairs. As he reached his landing the telephone rang. He picked it up. A familiar voice said, 'Hel-*lo*!'

'Dick!' Max exclaimed in amazement. 'But . . .'

'Don't say anything over the 'phone. Come to 25 Shooters Hill Gardens at seven tonight. It's south of the river, past Blackheath. Park in the next street. The back door of the house will be open. Walk straight in. See you.'

The telephone went dead.

Max recognised Dick Carpenter's voice – but Dick was supposed to have been killed in a car crash. All day, he wondered about it, glad of something to take his mind off Nina's decision.

Carpenter was waiting for him in the kitchen as Max pushed open the back door. Carpenter was grinning, and held out a whisky in greeting. His hair was dyed blond and cut much shorter. He wore horn-rimmed spectacles, which he took off when he saw the amazement in Max's face.

'I wouldn't have recognised you,' said Max.

'Good. I hope no-one else does, either. Now – meet Manuela.'

A dark-haired woman smiled at him.

'She's Spanish,' Carpenter explained unnecessarily.

They shook hands.

'What happened to you, then?' asked Max.

'I had word on the drums that some hard men were out to teach me a lesson. Nothing more than a beating, I thought, but I've had too many of those in my time. I felt I could do without one more. So I told a fellow who did a few odd jobs for me I was having it off with a tart up Finchley way, and my wife had put a private detective on my tail. I paid him a fiver to put on my hat and to take a three-hour drive around north London one evening in my car.'

'So he died instead of you?'

'Got killed, you mean.'

'Didn't he have any relations?'

'None,' said Carpenter. 'I only thought he might get a going over. And I'd have seen him right if that had happened. Never imagined it would be a terminal job. And he was a toughie himself, you know.'

'Why were they after you? To warn you off the car auction?'

'Could be. I never thought of that. I thought it was because of some other deals I've been doing. Tanks. Bren-gun carriers. The big one I told you about – and promised you a share.'

'So what are you going to do now?'

'I'm leaving the country, that's what. Probably for good. On the dead man's passport. I may even take his name. Amazing how easy it is to change your looks.'

'I see that. But why call me here? To say goodbye?'

'No. To say hello. To offer you the chance of making some real money – like I promised.'

'This opportunity come up suddenly?' Max asked him.

Carpenter nodded. 'You read the papers much?'

'Not a lot.'

'But do you know there's a war between Israelis and Arabs, and both sides are short of arms? Trucks, tanks, planes, and all that?'

'Of course.'

'Then you'll have read of people buying up old aircraft from dumps and flying them off to France?'

'In the stories I've read, the Air Ministry says that all the planes are quite harmless, for the guns have been removed.'

Carpenter shook his head at the naivety of anyone who would believe such an official explanation.

'But they don't add that other men have bought those guns and are shipping them out in crates marked "Tractor Spares", do they? Then both parties meet up in Corsica – and Bob's your uncle. Another fighter's ready to fly.'

'Where do I come in?'

'With me. But not here. In Corsica.'

'What the devil's out there, then?'

'The biggest collection of American armoured vehicles, trucks and Jeeps left behind in Europe, that's what. All war surplus, and most have never been used. Brand spanking new. When the Yanks went home, they just left them. No-one wanted to buy them, and they weren't worth transporting back to the States, so they dumped the lot in Corsica.'

'Haven't the locals looted them?'

'Sure, quite a number. But there's a limit to the amount of tyres, batteries or Jeeps even Corsicans can use. I am negotiating to ship out several hundred vehicles from Bastia, the main port.'

'How do you get them out of Corsica?'

'I won't. That's the buyer's affair.'

'What is my part in this?'

'I need help, a second outside opinion to cover snags I may have missed. The main risk is that I do my part and they just don't pay.'

'How do you collect the money?'

'It's already in a Swiss bank. In an account with two numbers. I know my number. The other party knows theirs. Our arrangement is that when they've loaded the trucks, they cable the bank to delete their number from the account. Then the money's all mine.'

'And if they don't do that?'

'That's why I need you. To stop them swindling me, maybe even killing me.'

'Pretty tall order.'

'Pretty good fee, too. Two thousand pounds in any currency, up your shirt. Cash, of course.'

'How much down?'

'Hundred. Because at the moment it's my money I'm using, not theirs. Your air fare to Corsica via Paris and Nice and return, of course.'

'They won't cable the bank until everything is loaded on the ship?'

'That's right. And that's what is worrying me. I tried to make them pay before, but no luck.'

'But once they have the trucks on board and the ship's at sea, you can whistle for your share? I have to find a way to stop that?'

'Yes. If you can.'

'I'll try. But for three thousand, not two.'

Carpenter smiled.

'Done,' he said, and they shook hands.

Max drove home slowly, turning over the problem in his mind. Back in his rooms, he poured himself a whisky and sat considering several possibilities. He wrote down each one on a piece of paper and then listed its weak points. By midnight, he had reached his decision.

Early that morning, he rang Paul at his office. Since Paul was advising Nina about her divorce, Max felt that Paul owed him a good turn . . .

As the Air France Languedoc from Nice came in over Bastia airport, Max had a sudden view beyond the harbour of purple hills shrouded in mist, milky as pastis, the national aniseed drink.

The aircraft taxied across a crumbling wartime runway to a row of camouflaged hangars with French fighter aircraft lined up outside them wings folded like bats' ears.

Max followed Carpenter down the shaky aluminium ladder into the afternoon sunshine. After the stale, processed air of the cabin, the fresh scent of eucalyptus trees and the sharp tang of wild sage and lavender seemed overwhelming. Two French customs officers sitting behind a trestle table waved them through to the only taxi, a shabby Renault with a glass flower vase on its dashboard.

'Ile de Beauté Hotel,' Carpenter told the driver. In a reek of Gauloise cigarettes, petrol and exhaust fumes, they bumped over unmade roads, through a vineyard, to the Bastia highway.

They passed a Corsican cemetery jammed with white marble monuments shaped like huge chests of drawers. Each drawer contained a coffin; a filing cabinet for the dead. Carpenter squeezed Max's arm and nodded to the other window. Jeeps stretched to infinity, each bonnet still bearing its wartime marking of a white five-pointed star.

'And that's only one lot,' said Carpenter.

The Ile de Beauté was near the railway station, surrounded by yellow-washed houses with red tiled roofs. Workmen were regilding the huge Napoleonic 'N' on its wall.

Carpenter paid off the driver, walked purposefully into the hotel, paused to let the taxi driver leave, then led Max out again.

'We're not staying here,' he explained. 'It's too obvious. I've booked in elsewhere.'

This turned out to be a small hotel in the Boulevard Paoli. Its upper windows were shuttered, and the entrance hall smelled damp and musty.

'Never mind,' said Carpenter cheerfully. 'After this, it's the Ritz.'

Max had a headache from the bumpy flight to Nice, where he waited for two hours in the sun for the Corsica connection. He had flown to Nice by way of Geneva, where, with a letter of introduction from Carpenter, he had opened a numbered account at the Banque d'Otztaler.

Into this he paid the hundred pounds Carpenter had given him. British travellers were only allowed to take twenty-five pounds out of the country, so Max carried the single hundred-pound note in his left sock. Neither was he allowed to have a bank account overseas, out of the sterling area. But as Carpenter explained, this was only a law of man, not a law of God.

They walked down the hill to the Café des Sports, and ordered two pastis. Several customers sat reading newspapers and smoking Gauloises. A man of about forty, wearing lightweight trousers and a faded blue shirt, came up the hill and joined them at their table.

'This is Mr Cann,' said Carpenter.

He did not introduce Max.

'Can also be Cohen – or Khan. According to which side he is working for at the time.'

Mr Cann smiled, but only with his mouth. His eyes were cold, unfriendly, watchful.

'When you have finished your drinks, gentlemen?' he said in a voice a little above a whisper. They followed him up the hill, where a Citroën was parked in a side street. He drove them back along the airport road. Twelve miles south of Bastia, they bumped off along a cart-track between cactus plants, past a sleepy farmyard. Beyond the barns stretched acres of six-wheeled Studebaker trucks, parked neatly side by side, in rows.

'My friend here is the mechanic,' said Carpenter. 'Have you got everything he asked for?'

Mr Cann rolled up the canvas cover of the nearest truck. Inside, Max saw a portable fast-rate battery charger with a generator driven by a small petrol engine.

'Jerry cans of petrol are in the one behind it,' said Mr Cann.

Max climbed into the cabin of the nearest truck, turned the ignition switch. The ammeter needle did not even flicker.

He connected the charger, started the motor, waited for a few minutes and tried again. This time the engine turned over sluggishly, but still did not start.

The two other men exchanged glances. Max tried again. The engine spun furiously, fired, caught and went on running.

'It's taken you ten minutes to start one truck,' said Carpenter. 'I timed you.'

'It should only take two if I put double voltage through each one. Who's going to drive them?'

'I have hired twenty men.' Mr Cann explained. 'Locals.'

'When do we start?'

'Five o'clock tomorrow morning. I'll pick you up here.'

'How many trucks do we have to get out?'

'A hundred, including ten water and petrol bowsers and four communication wagons. Day after tomorrow we shift some of the Jeeps opposite the cemetery and then a dozen Sherman tanks.'

'We'll never start those,' said Max.

'We don't need to. There's a tank transporter dumped with them. We simply winch them on to that, one by one.'

'What if they don't work when they reach wherever they're going?'

'That's the buyer's problem, not ours. We've only got to ship them out.'

Max nodded, thinking of unknown young soldiers fighting a war he did not care about, in untried vehicles left to rot in the sun, so that men like Mr Cann and Dick Carpenter – and he himself – could make their profit. He shrugged away the uneasy images. He was not concerned with the rights or wrongs of either side, nor was he in the deal for patriotism or loyalty. Like the others, he was in it for money.

All the next day, he worked with the charger. Some engines had seized, others had parts looted, or batteries split after years in the open air. If a truck did not start within five minutes, he went on to the next one. The wireless trucks and petrol bowsers he drove out himself to the main road. He wanted to check that their equipment worked.

Four days later, the three men stood on Bastia Docks and

watched the last rusty steamer move sluggishly out into the Mediterranean.

'Now, to business,' said Mr Cann briskly. They walked back to the hotel. 'Let's talk in your room,' he said and led the way up the stone staircase. He appeared cheerful and was humming the Tennessee Waltz. Carpenter followed, with Max behind him.

As Cann and Carpenter went into the bedroom first, Max bent down in the corridor and took from his pocket a length of thin wire. He tied this across the second step of the stairs, a few inches above the tread.

Inside the bedroom, Carpenter produced a bottle of pastis from a bedside cupboard and three tooth glasses. They toasted each other.

Cann pulled a sheet of paper from his pocket.

'Here's a copy of the telegram I sent today to the Banque d'Otztaler in Geneva.'

Max read:

'MANDRAKE PRO-MANAGER STOP ON RECEIPT THIS TELEGRAM PLEASE WITHDRAW 652850 LIEN REGISTERED ON DUAL NUMBERED ACCOUNT STOP CABLE CONFIRMATION RECEIPT THESE INSTRUCTIONS CARPENTER HOTEL DES AMIS BASTIA CORSICA SIGNED CANN ENDIT'

'When did you send this?' Max asked him.

'Eight o'clock this morning. The reply is probably waiting downstairs in the office.'

Max went down to see. The reception cubicle was empty. Behind the desk was a row of pigeon holes with keys on hooks. One envelope was in the hole for Room 15, addressed to Carpenter, and one in the hole for Room 14, addressed to himself. He did not open his own cable, but put it in his pocket. He took Carpenter's telegram up to the bedroom.

Carpenter read it aloud:

'CARPENTER HOTEL DES AMIS BASTIA CORSICA REFERENCE YOUR CABLE ADDRESSED MANDRAKE PRO-MANAGER STOP THIS REPLY CONFIRMS THAT YOUR LIEN 652850 RELEASED AS PER EARLIER INSTRUCTIONS STOP HOLDER OF SECOND NUMBER THIS

ACCOUNT NOW ASSUMES SOLE AUTHORITY OVER ACCOUNT STOP SIGNED MANDRAKE PRO-MANAGER BANQUE D'OTZTALER'

'Well, that seems satisfactory,' said Mr Cann, smiling at them both. He poured another drink for himself.

Max now opened hs envelope.

'EXPRESS CORNELL HOTEL DES AMIS BASTIA CORSICA STOP NO REPEAT NO COMMUNICATION RECEIVED REGARDING ACCOUNT 712519 UP TO CLOSE BANKING BUSINESS TODAY STOP SIGNED MANAGER BANQUE D'OTZTALER'

'I don't understand it,' protested Mr Cann, frowning in perplexity. 'They must have sent that before they received my cable.'

'The time is stamped on both cables,' Max pointed out. 'This telegram was filed two hours after yours.'

'Well, it's an office error. Some bloody clerk's fault.'

'I wish it were, Mr Cann. But I don't think so.'

Mr Cann made to stand up. Carpenter pulled him down in his chair.

'Someone may have made a mistake,' he said, 'but it's unlikely. Maybe you sent the wrong account number. I don't know yours – only mine. Seven-one-two-five-one-nine.'

'That *is* the right number, I'm positive. But I've left my briefcase at the reception desk. The number's on a sheet of paper in there. I'll check just in case I did get it wrong.'

Mr Cann stood up, walked to the bedroom door, then paused as though to say something. He half turned away and then swung round to face them, a gun in his hand.

'Back across the room,' he ordered.

'Wait a minute,' Carpenter protested.

'Do as the man says,' said Max gently. Carpenter stared at him in amazement.

Mr Cann slipped out through the door, locked it, and ran towards the stairs. Carpenter charged at the door. Max pulled him back.

'Listen,' he told him urgently.

Both heard Mr Cann's cry of surprise as he tripped over the stretched wire, and the bump, bump of his body down the stairs.

'Now!' shouted Max, and he and Carpenter smashed down the door.

Mr Cann had fallen head first and lay stunned, but apparently otherwise uninjured. Max retrieved his gun and then helped Carpenter to carry Mr Cann up the stairs to the bedroom. He paused in the doorway, but no-one appeared to have heard thc commotion. He jammed a chair against the back of the door just in case it was not quite so empty as it seemed, and anyone tried to join them. Then he sat Mr Cann down in another chair and poured him a pastis.

'Now,' he said briskly. 'Let's have the right number.'

'I've sent it,' said Mr Cann wearily.

Max toyed with the pistol in his hand. He looked up at Carpenter.

'I want to get something from my bedroom,' he said. He went out and returned with a small suitcase, opened it. Inside were two metal boxes with a crackle grey finish. He began to unwind a long aerial wire, with four rubber suckers. He stuck one on each corner of the room, and then lifted the lid on one of the boxes, and busied himself with the dials inside.

'I have two transmitters here,' he explained. 'One is an ordinary radio-telephone which can reach the ship we saw off at the docks. That old tub can barely make six knots an hour, and she's not been gone thirty minutes, so we're well in range. The other transmitter is rather more sophisticated.'

He turned to Mr Cann.

'We've put aboard several trucks fitted with wireless transmitters and receivers. I drove those out of the field myself to check that the equipment worked. It does. I tuned each of the receivers to a different wavelength. The sets are all connected to the truck batteries. I turn this tuning dial, press this key and one picks up the signal. I change the wavelength and the second sets picks it up, and so on. Each set is wired to an explosive charge. The first one is just enough to blow up the truck. The charge on the next is a bit more powerful. The last will blow a bloody great hole in the ship. Now are you going to give us the correct number?'

'I've told you. I have,' said Cann stubbornly.

'Here goes, then,' said Max and pressed the key. A needle trembled on a hairspring, a green light flickered and died. He released the key, and Max waited for five minutes, opened the other box, took out a telephone hand set and began to tune to the ship's wavelength.

A voice boomed metallically from a loudspeaker in the suitcase.

'*SS Himalaya* here. *SS Himalaya* here. Over to you. Over.'

Max pressed a button in the hand receiver.

'Corsican coastguard calling. Explosion reported in your ship. Kindly advise any damage and location of source of explosion. Over.'

A voice replied: 'You're right. On A deck. A truck suddenly blew up. Small fire now under control. Any further details required? Over.'

Max pressed the button.

'Thank you. None. Over and out.'

He turned to Mr Cann.

'Want the second one to go?'

'You won't risk it.'

'I have nothing to risk,' said Max. 'You've everything. Those trucks are going to the Israelis, aren't they?'

Mr Cann nodded.

'So you'll have the fellows who blew up the King David Hotel on your tail. They won't like paying for goods they don't receive, or that don't arrive in working condition. I'll give you only days before they visit you, wanting an explanation.'

Mr Cann said nothing.

Max shrugged, returned the dials and again pressed the key. Carpenter watched, fascinated, as he picked up the receiver. This time there had been a more serious explosion on B deck. Several trucks had been totally destroyed and a fire had broken out, for the petrol tank on one had exploded.

'Want me to go through with it?' Max asked.

Mr Cann shook his head. He wrote a number on a piece of paper.

Carpenter went downstairs to cable the bank with it. Max poured himself another pastis.

'I hope you're not playing silly buggers,' he said. 'You won't get another chance. We may not get our money, but you certainly won't live to spend yours. Now, any second thoughts on that number?'

Cann shook his head.

'No. It's correct.'

They waited in the room until an urgent-rate reply came from the bank. The money was theirs.

They paid their hotel bill, drove out to the airport with Mr Cann. It wouldn't do to let him free too soon. They waited, Max gripping Mr Cann's revolver in his jacket pocket.

Finally, when the Languedoc was airborne and Corsica was shrinking beneath them, they relaxed.

'Where did you get all that kit?' asked Carpenter.

'I've a relation in the radio business,' said Max. 'He owed me a favour.'

Vasarov waited in his room in Stalin's dacha for the alarm bell to ring. It was a quarter past two in the morning, and he was reading *Pravda*.

In his time attached to Stalin's staff he had learned the significance of each nuance of editorial opinion. By counting the number of lines given to the activities of politicians and soldiers – or more sinister, how many days passed without any mention of them – he could assess the degree of favour or displeasure in which Stalin held them. Now Vasarov read a headline and report with mounting unease:

> MISERABLE SPIES AND ASSASSINS MASKING AS PROFESSORS OF MEDICINE.
>
> In the U.S.S.R., the exploiting classes have for a long time been vanquished and liquidated, but there are still some survivors; spokesmen for bourgeois opinions and bourgeois customs, LIVING MEN, hidden enemies of our people.
>
> Some time ago, the organs of State Security discovered a terrorist group of doctors whose aim was to shorten the lives of leading figures in the Soviet Union by means of harmful treatment . . .

Western newspapers might trivialise items of news, but any reader could understand them. In Russia, only readers who appreciated certain typographical nuances could guess at the real meaning of any article. Capital letters were used in mid-sentence to warn that a new purge was about to start.

Every year since the war, campaigns had been launched against engineers, poets, academics and factory managers. Now, it was the turn of the doctors. He turned the page and read the next clue, a Tass report, recalling the deaths, some months earlier, of Andrei Zhdanov and Aleksandr Shcherbakov, two powerful members of the Politburo. For many years both men, known as heavy smokers and drinkers, had suffered from severe heart trouble; eventually they died from heart attacks. The article now claimed that 'new evidence' had emerged to prove that 'doctor assassins' had murdered them by deliberately prescribing a course of harmful treatment. Nine doctors were apparently involved – six of them Jews, and members of the Academy of Medicine. All had been arrested. The article ended with the sombre remark that 'some others' were also involved.

Vasarov turned the pages until he found a final reference crucial to the doctors.

> Most of the participants in the terrorist group – M. S. Vovsi, B. B. Kogan, A. I. Feldman, A. M. Grinshtein, Y. G. Ettinger, and others – were connected with 'Joint', an international Jewish bourgeois nationalist organisation set up by the US Intelligence Service, allegedly to render material aid to the Jews in other countries.
>
> This organisation, under the guidance of the US Intelligence Service, conducts large-scale espionage, terrorist and other subversive activities in a number of countries, including the Soviet Union . . . Vovsi stated during interrogation that he had received a directive from the United States 'to exterminate the leading cadres of the USSR' from the 'Joint' organisation through a Moscow doctor, Shimelyovich, and the well-known Jewish bourgeois nationalist Mikhoels.

The naming of these prominent Jewish doctors was a warning that all Jews must expect to be regarded as potential targets of official displeasure.

As Vasarov pondered on this prospect, the alarm bell clanged over his head. After years of living in windowless rooms, surrounded by watchers and guards, sleeping fitfully by day and working through each night, Vasarov was in poor physical shape. He smoked too much, and frequently found himself sipping a tumbler of neat vodka to steady his nerves.

Stalin had also changed markedly. His hair was now much whiter, but he refused to dye it, as several of his colleagues had done. His skin was rougher and more wrinkled, and he appeared almost a caricature of his picture on the posters. For public appearances, a younger double was now used.

Vasarov found him in front of the fire in his huge room, holding a glass of pale brown liquid. Stalin did not trust any doctor, and believed he could cure all his infirmities by homely peasant remedies. Every night, he would drink a glass of warm water into which he personally decanted a few drops of tincture of iodine. This he drank now, grimaced at its taste, and turned to Vasarov.

'You have seen *Pravda*, of course?' he began.

'I have, Comrade Stalin.'

'Comrade Beria has uncovered a fiendish plot by Jewish doctors, suborned, as always, by American Jewish capitalists and bankers. And in the background, as ever, the British hover like hyenas, waiting to pick up any little pieces.'

Vasarov bowed his head in acquiescence.

'You notice that Mikhoels is also mentioned?'

'I read his name, Comrade Stalin.'

When Mikhoels had been director of the Moscow Jewish Theatre, he had somehow offended Stalin in his delivery of a speech from *Julius Caesar*. He had been immediately arrested and beaten to death. It was later announced that he had died in a motor accident.

A disturbing thought now crossed Vasarov's mind. Mikhoels had been dead for several years. If he had really been among the plotters, why had Beria's investigations not discovered this at the time? Stalin could have included his name as an excuse to attack Beria, even to exterminate him. In the overheated room, Vasarov sweated with fear for his own prospects.

'Comrade Beria will have these treacherous physicians tried,' said Stalin. 'They will pay for their deeds with their lives.'

Already, he had pronounced them guilty. But of course they would be guilty, otherwise why would they have been arrested? No-one arrested on political charges was innocent.

'When I was a boy in Gori, Comrade Vasarov,' said Stalin ruminatively. 'We would sometimes find a rat beneath a stone in a barn. I learned that a rat is never alone. Where you find one, there are always others. So we would lift another stone and, suddenly, the place would be alive with vermin. It is the same with these Jewish traitors.'

Within days, the purge spread, as Vasarov feared it would. The Jewish head of the official Tass news agency – who had put out the original story – was arrested as a traitor to the state. He simply disappeared with doctors, surgeons, lawyers and academics.

One night, at the height of these mass arrests, Vasarov drove to Lubyanka to check some details in a secret dossier and Beria summoned him to his office.

'I have to tell you, Comrade Vasarov,' Beria began, 'I have received information from usually trusted sources that our Beloved Leader's health is not as good as we would wish. You have the honour to be in close and constant contact with him. What is your opinion, comrade?'

For a moment, Vasarov did not reply.

Beria recognised his dilemma and smiled.

'You can speak freely, comrade,' he said. 'The microphones are switched off.'

'Do you think any of the treacherous doctors now awaiting trial can have poisoned him, Comrade Beria?' Vasarov asked cautiously.

'What I think, what you think, is immaterial. We need facts. In Germany, did you hear of any Western specialist in diseases of the circulatory system, whose impartial opinion you could trust?'

'There are several such American and British specialists in military hospitals.'

'I would prefer a civilian,' said Beria. 'And not an American or British subject.'

Vasarov thought for a moment.

'Have you approached any doctor in our sector of Germany?'

'That is too risky,' said Beria. 'If word should leak to our enemies, the damage could be incalculable.'

'I will approach my contacts in Germany. We shall have to furnish the specialist with a full report of any relevant symptoms, so that he can make his assessment at a distance.'

'That can be done. But no names will be mentioned under any pretext whatever.'

'Money must also be made available. These Western specialists command considerable sums for their services.'

'That I am aware of. Whatever is needed will be at your disposal in any currency you require.'

'Give me twenty-four hours and I will endeavour to provide an answer.'

Late on the following night, the bedside telephone rang in the home of Dr Fritz Heese in a suburb of West Berlin. Dr Heese was a heart specialist whose rise to eminence had been halted by the war and its aftermath. He was thus anxious to make up for years lost in his career, and had recently published a paper in an American medical magazine about a new treatment for arteriosclerosis, for which he claimed a high rate of success. His work was extremely well regarded by his colleagues and it was generally believed that this article was a major step towards international recognition.

The caller explained that he was the Tass correspondent in Berlin. 'My editor has asked me to contact you urgently – hence my call at this hour – because of the impact that publication of your paper in the United States has made on the thinking of many Russian specialists in your field of study.'

Dr Heese was surprised, but pleased. This interest from a communist country was extremely encouraging.

'I have the pleasure to inform you, doctor, in strict confidence, that your name has been put forward for a special award by the Moscow Academy of Sciences. Since formal announcement can be expected within the next few days, I would greatly appreciate an interview with you in advance. I must, of course, ask you to observe the strictest secrecy about the forthcoming award.'

'But of course,' replied Heese, greatly gratified. 'What about tomorrow? Ten, in my surgery?'

'I will be there,' the caller assured him.

The following morning, when Vasarov arrived at Dr Heese's surgery, he wore horn-rimmed glasses and a small moustache, and with his bow tie, loose raincoat and green felt hat, he appeared as people imagine a journalist to be. Certainly, Dr Heese had seen his like time and again on screen and stage, and glanced only casually at his press card.

Vasarov conducted an obsequious interview with the doctor, and finally took a small buff folder from his briefcase.

'To conclude, Doctor Heese – and naturally for a full professional fee – I would be obliged if I could ask you to comment on the case history of someone very dear to me – my own father.'

He handed the folder to him.

'I attach copies of reports from his specialist, and would be interested to see whether you agree with what he says.'

'I am not a quack practitioner,' replied Dr Heese sharply. 'You will appreciate that I need to meet your father and study his background, and then carry out a number of tests before I could give any considered opinion about his health.'

'You will find everything that I know about the patient, including his age, weight, height; and background in these papers,' said Vasarov. 'I realise that the question is unusual, but my father is very dear to my widowed sister and to me, and we are anxious to do anything we can to help him. I hope I may have your co-operation.'

Dr Heese reluctantly opened the folder. Every medical detail was there in German for him to study; pulse and respiratory rates, results of blood examinations and other tests. He read through each page slowly, then handed the folder back to Vasarov.

'On the evidence you provide, I have to tell you there is nothing I can do to help this patient,' he said. 'If these details are accurate, you are consulting me too late. His habit of constant smoking, over possibly sixty years, despite warnings that this was endangering his health; his strange life-style of working by night and sleeping by day; his almost total lack, for decades, of outdoor exercise – lead me to tell you that the prognosis is not optimistic.'

'Is there any treatment whatever you could recommend, doctor?'

'Nothing, without examining your father myself, as I have said. There might have been, even as recently as a year ago. But on what I read here, I would be raising your hopes in a totally inadmissible fashion if I made any claims now for his recovery. On the basis of the facts you give me, I regret to tell you that, in my opinion, your father's decline is irreversible.'

'How long would you give him, doctor?'

'Only months. Probably less.'

'And then?'

'Then he is a dead man.'

# *Nine*

The auction was all but over. Successful bidders had already collected their vehicles, and only half a dozen unsold cars stood in a forlorn row on the far side of the field. The fat auctioneer was dismantling his microphone when Max strolled across the tufty grass towards him. He looked up sharply as Max approached.

'Well?' he asked almost aggressively.

'You knew a friend of mine, Dick Carpenter?'

'What about it?'

'We were in the army together,' Max went on. 'He told me he wanted to make a bid for this pitch.'

'Damned sorry he didn't. But he had a car crash, got himself killed.'

'Why do you want to sell? Doesn't it make money?'

'Too much. That's the trouble. Others want it.'

'I want it,' said Max simply. 'I was going in with Dick. Now I'm interested on my own.'

'Come into the caravan,' said the fat man. He closed the door, opened a cupboard beneath the tiny sink and took out a brown bottle labelled, 'Paint Thinners: Not To Be Taken.' He poured out two whiskies into tea cups.

'You on the level?'

'Absolutely.'

'Funny do, that accident.'

'In many ways. Dick mentioned that some people were also making life hard for you.'

'They still are. This is becoming a hard way to make an easy living. I've had paint scratched, tyres slashed.'

'How much are you asking for the whole shooting match?'

'I'm not asking anything. But Carpenter was talking about three thousand clear. I'd still take that. These other people won't name any figure at all.'

'You own the freehold of the field?'

'No. But the owner has offered it to me for two thousand. Including this caravan.'

'I'll give you three thousand,' said Max. 'But the lawyers will take weeks to sort things out. I'd like to get going as soon as possible.'

'I've got two months' lease left to run at fifteen nicker a week. Sign a contract, and pay me a tenner a week on top in notes until it's all tied up.'

They shook hands.

'But I'm warning you. You may have trouble.'

'Why didn't these people go to the owner and buy the land?'

'They have. Several times. But he won't sell to anyone. He is a stubborn old sod.'

The fat man smiled almost affectionately.

'So why will he sell to me?'

'He won't,' the fat man corrected him. 'He will only sell to *me*, and *I* will sell to you.'

'Why?'

'Because, my friend, I happen to be his only son.'

Max arranged with David Graham at the bank for an overdraft against the deeds of the auction field, and immediately placed advertisements in local papers: 'Cornell Car Auctions sell – without reserve – the best cars in the business. 2.30 every Thursday and Saturday. Why wait for a new car, when you can buy a genuinely *pre-owned* model now?'

'Pre-owned' sounded better than 'used'.

On the first Thursday, he sold fourteen cars, and made £115 clear profit after paying his rent and two helpers; Charlie, whom he inherited from the fat man, and Keith, a sixteen-year-old youth who washed and polished the better cars in his school holidays.

Max put his Triumph in the auction and bought a small Ford van. It was already taxed and only fetched thirty pounds without a reserve, a bargain too good to miss. As he parked this van near the caravan on the following Saturday, Keith came up to him.

'Mr Cornell,' he began nervously. 'Some rough-looking men are hanging around. One told me to get out of it if I knew what was good for me. The man who warned me is over in the corner.'

This man was standing with one hand on the roof of a grey Ford Ten. He wore shabby flannel trousers, ex-army boots, a shirt without a collar, and an oil-stained sports jacket. Max walked towards him.

'I understand you have warned off one of my people?'

The man spat on the ground.

'I'll say the same to you, mate. Beat it. While you can.'

'But why?'

'Because I'm giving you advance notice that you're in for a rough time if you don't.'

'From whom?' Max asked him, but the man did not answer. He simply climbed into his car and drove out of the gate. Max walked back to his caravan, searching for a piece of paper to note the registration number. All he could find was a letter he had received a few days earlier inviting him to a commando reunion in London.

He wrote down the number on the envelope and, after adjusting the microphone, began to speak with a confidence he did not feel: 'Welcome, ladies and gentlemen, to our second car auction . . .'

The first car was a Singer Bantam, a tiny car, which, except for its overhead cam engine, was almost a carbon copy of the Morris 8, that in turn owed much to the baby Ford.

It would be expensive at two hundred pounds. A dark-skinned man in a roll-top sweater quickly bid against a man with a beard in jumps of twenty pounds. The car was knocked down to him at four hundred pounds. He came into the caravan, and handed over two twenty-pound notes as a deposit.

Every car in the sale went for around double its worth with four men bidding recklessly in twenties, while other bidders cautiously offered rises of a pound, or, at the most, a fiver.

By half past four Max had sold every car to these men for sums so far above their true value that he felt uneasy. The crowd began to drift away, surprised at the prices. Charlie came into the caravan to collect his jacket.

'Can you stay on for half an hour?' Max asked him. 'I'll pay you double if you will.'

'Sorry. No can do. Got to drive the wife over to our daughter's place. She'll give me hell if I'm late.'

'Ring her. Tell her you've been delayed.'

'We're not on the 'phone, Max, or I would.'

Max watched him walk out of the gate. Keith had already gone. Max was now alone in the caravan in the centre of an empty field. The four men started to walk towards him. They were all smiling in a way that told Max they meant trouble.

The auctioneer had told him he always kept a crowbar in the caravan, but now he could not find it. The four men reached the caravan steps and stood in a line, looking up at him.

'You can drive the cars away,' Max told them. 'as soon as you pay the rest of the money. Cash only.'

'You're paying *us*, mate,' replied the dark-skinned man. 'We don't want your bloody cars. Just our deposits back.'

'A deal's a deal,' replied Max. 'You bought the cars under the hammer, and you've paid your deposits.'

The men laughed.

'Are you going to give us our money back?' asked the bearded man. 'Or do we have to come and take it – with a little interest in kind?'

It was clear what they intended to do; nothing he said now could make them change their minds. This was obviously a stage along the road that had begun with slashing car tyres. Where would it lead? To an 'accident' like the one on the North Circular?

The first man leaped up the stairs into the caravan. Max stepped back and tripped him as he came through the doorway. Then the second man was inside the caravan. After that, Max remembered nothing but the hammer of boots, knees, fists and elbows. He fought with every trick he knew, but he was hopelessly outnumbered. Finally, he sank down into merciful darkness. Vaguely, as from an immeasurable distance of time and space, he saw the men rifling through the table drawer for their deposits. Then they ran and left him on his own.

The air felt chill, and tall thistles trembled in the evening wind by the time he felt able to stand up shakily and lean against the table. Blood spattered the front of his shirt; more was splashed on the caravan walls. His left eye was difficult to focus, and several teeth were loose.

A voice spoke from yards away – or was it from miles? Max turned his head slowly and painfully towards the sound. The man he had spoken to near the Ford was in the doorway, picking his teeth with a match.

'Just a message,' he said. 'You'll get hurt if you go on like this. But you're a sensible feller. You can take a hint, eh?'

'Next auction's Thursday,' replied Max thickly, through split and swollen lips. He did not understand what he was saying. His brain seemed unable to comprehend what had happened, what was happening. The man spat on the floor, and then walked away slowly, across the darkening field.

Max sat down on the caravan steps, head in hands, and then unsteadily opened the panel beneath the wash basin and pulled out the bottle of whisky. He drank greedily. Then he washed the blood off his face. It was dark by the time he was well enough to lock up the caravan, climb slowly into his van, and drive back towards London.

Next morning, he consulted his AA handbook to discover which county registered cars with the letters on the number plate of the grey Ford. Kent. He telephoned the motor taxation office in Maidstone, and asked how he could discover its owner. He explained that it had been involved in an accident, which was not entirely untrue. A clerk rang him back within the hour. The car was owned by Beechwood Garages, a company controlling several garages, with a registered office in Leadenhall Street.

In the afternoon, Max visited Companies' House, and looked through the files. He was not greatly surprised to learn that the major shareholder and managing director of this particular company was Mr Samuel Harris, of Berkeley Square, Mayfair, London W1.

The commando reunion was held in London in an upper room of the Albert Tavern, near Victoria Station. Muscular young men in tweed sports jackets drank pints of beer, and kept looking expectantly over the rim of their tankards, hoping to see someone they had known in the army.

There were many stories to exchange: the sergeant-major who had committed suicide because he could not adjust to Civvy Street; the corporal who had made a fortune; the captain, down on his luck, about to emigrate.

Max gravitated to half a dozen former Austrians and Hungarians he had known in Aberdovey. All, like him, now had British names, but some still spoke with heavy accents that could scarcely pass as British.

'How did you get that black eye, Max?' someone asked him. 'Did her husband catch you, then?'

Max remembered the company office clerk asking him the same question when he returned early from leave after his experience with Rachel. How long ago that seemed now! He joined in the general laughter, although it still hurt him even to smile.

Half an hour before the Thursday auction was due to start, Max drove past the field in his van. He stopped beyond the corner and looked cautiously over the fence. The four men who had disrupted the Saturday sale had just arrived, and were climbing out of their grey Ford. So he had been right. There was going to be more trouble, with more cars unsold. And this could go on until he was ruined. He drove on thoughtfully until he came to a telephone call box. Then he dialled Sam Harris's number in London.

'Max here,' he began. 'Had a bit of trouble at the last car auction.'

'Sorry to hear that,' said Sam Harris, as though he meant it. 'But then, life is full of trouble, boy.'

'Seems so. But I don't want any more, Uncle. You're the only man I know in the car trade who might make me an offer for the whole thing. Are you interested?'

'I'm above those little deals now, boy,' replied Harris grandly. 'However, I might just use the field for storing second-hand cars I can't get into other depots.'

'That's an idea,' agreed Max brightly. 'Anyway, the

auction usually finishes just after four. But there's double the number to sell today because we didn't shift a single car last time, so we may run a bit late. Can you come down around four fifteen?'

'I wouldn't offer much more than three grand for everything, freehold and all,' warned Harris.

'Well, we'll see,' said Max. 'I may have to accept. Anyhow, bring an open bank draft so we can settle up right away for whatever is agreed.'

Charlie and Keith were waiting for him as he climbed the steps into the caravan, and began to set up the microphone.

'What happened to your face?' Charlie asked him. Max shrugged.

'Why are all these cars from Saturday's sale still here?' Charlie went on. 'I don't believe *every* buyer welshed?'

'Yes they did. Those four men over there were the only bidders. They came over after you had gone, and took back their deposits. By force!'

'Why didn't you call the police?'

'No names, no witnesses. I thought there might be trouble when the bids went so high. That's why I asked you to stay. I hope you can stay today?'

'If only you'd asked me earlier,' said Charlie quickly. 'Matter of fact, I promised to take the wife into Woolwich, shopping.'

'Today's early closing, Charlie,' replied Max drily. 'If we have much more trouble here, we may have to close ourselves.'

He turned to Keith.

'If you don't want to get involved, either,' he told him, 'say so now. I want to know where I stand.'

'I'll stay,' Keith told him firmly.

'Good. I hope you won't regret it.'

Max turned up the volume control and began.

'Welcome to England's fastest growing car auction. A lot of fine cars to sell. Many without reserve.'

'Bollocks!' shouted the bearded man from the back of the crowd. Several people turned uneasily to look at him. Wives moved perceptibly closer to their husbands.

'Now, now, we don't want any boasting,' said Max, trying to turn away the remark.

'You're the boaster, mate. Just rubbish you're selling!' The dark-skinned man was calling now.

'Didn't sell a single motor last time, did you? Know why? 'Cos it's junk you're flogging! Tat and junk!'

The heckling went on as Charlie drove each car in front of the crowd, and again the bids came in, every one absurdly high. No other bidder could approach the sums that these four men offered. The crowd began to drift away, sensing trouble. When only about twenty people were left, the microphone suddenly went dead. The bearded man came out from behind the caravan, showing the blade of his pocket-knife.

'That's enough of your chat,' he shouted. 'Shut your mouth and give your arse a chance!'

'We have some badly behaved visitors here, ladies and gentlemen,' declared Max. 'We will call it a day. But we will be back here again on Saturday, same time, same place. Without, I hope, these interruptions.'

'I'd call the police, mister,' a middle-aged man shouted from the crowd.

'He ain't got no 'phone,' retorted one of the four. 'Ain't got no bloody sense, either. Neither have you, if you stick your nose in, matey!'

The middle-aged man looked nervously around him. Everyone seemed to be leaving. The bearded man shook a fist at him. As quickly as he could, without actually running, he also made for the gate.

'I'll have to go now, Max,' Charlie explained hastily. 'The wife will be asking for me.'

Keith and Max were on their own.

'Keep close and we'll see what happens,' Max told him. 'If there's any rough stuff, stay in the caravan.

He glanced at his watch. Five minutes past four. Sam Harris should be here within ten minutes, and probably not a moment too soon. He quickly disconnected the microphone, and carried it into the caravan in case it should be broken.

'Don't lock up,' ordered the dark-skinned man warningly. 'We want our deposits back. Like last time. You got to learn the hard way, haven't you, buster?'

They began to walk towards the caravan, obviously enjoying the prospect of another fight, four to one. Max put his hand into his pocket, took out a whistle and blew on it twice.

'No good doing that,' shouted the bearded man. 'No coppers about here. Just you and us.'

At that moment, the back doors of Max's van burst open. Out jumped six former commandos who had served with him in Aberdovey. Each one gripped a home-made club attached to his wrist by a leather bootlace. They raced across the grass towards the four men, who turned towards them, bewildered by this unexpected turn of events.

'What the bloody hell?' cried the dark-skinned man in amazement. And then the commandos were on them. The fight was short but fierce. Within minutes, all four men were out on the ground.

Max and his colleagues tied their hands behind their backs with lengths of rope. Then they dragged them out of sight on the far side of the caravan.

Max opened the caravan door. Keith was inside, his face pale.

'Run along, kid,' Max told him, and gave him a pound note. 'That's for being brave enough to stay. Back here on Saturday, though. We'll have no more trouble. It'll even be safe enough for Charlie, too.'

As the boy ran through the gateway, Sam Harris drove in. He glanced at the mass of unsold cars from two auctions, and was smiling as he approached Max, cigar in mouth.

'Not much trade today,' he said. 'More trouble?'

'A bit,' Max agreed. 'But I think you are going to do a deal that will surprise you.'

'I could do with a surprise,' agreed Sam Harris. 'I've been thinking. Three thousand's a bit steep.'

'Come into the caravan and I'll tell you what I've worked out for you.'

They climbed the steps. Harris blew cigar smoke into Max's face as they walked through the door.

Max closed the door behind him. Then he ripped the cigar from Sam Harris's mouth and threw it out of the window.

'What the hell?' began Sam Harris angrily.

'I don't like cigars, and I don't like you,' Max told him shortly. 'When I did that dirty work for you about the greyhounds I warned you about causing me any trouble.'

Sam Harris looked nervously around the caravan. There was no way out.

'Saturday, you sent four thugs down here. They blocked every bid and then set about me. They came back today.'

'I don't know what the hell you're talking about,' Harris assured him.

'Surprised that your four men aren't here to meet you? Well, they are.'

Max pushed open the door and took Harris round to the far side of the caravan. The commandos had lit cigarettes and stood, arms folded, regarding their captives, who had now regained consciousness.

'Here's the man who hired you,' Max told them. 'So don't get any ideas of coming back to see me again. That would mean a hard time for Mr Harris here, as well as for you.'

He turned to Sam Harris.

'We just have two matters to discuss, Uncle,' he said. 'Then, as you keep telling me, since we are related – if only by marriage – I suggest you may care to leave. But first, business. Your employees here paid deposits last week on all the cars they bought, and then took the money back by force. They owe me a lot of cash.'

'That's nothing to do with me,' said Harris quickly.

Max nodded to the ex-commandos; each one took a step closer to Sam Harris.

'These friends of mine think differently. So do I. You're outvoted, Uncle.'

A pause. The bearded man groaned.

'My jaw,' he said thickly, through clenched teeth. 'They've broken my jaw.'

Max looked at Harris, and stroked his own jaw.

'I'll give you a cheque,' said Harris hurriedly.

'No, you won't. You will give me that bank draft. You can't cancel that. Twenty-eight cars for which they bid a total of £10,581 17s. Add another £200 for my friends' trouble and expenses.'

Harris wrote out the draft with a trembling hand.

'Now,' said Max. 'I want to draw you all closer together.'

He pulled Harris towards the men on the ground. One of the former commandos produced a camera and photographed them together. Then he took individual photographs of each man's face from several angles.

'Just in case we meet again,' Max explained. 'I should think the police can put a name to every face. Perhaps even yours, Uncle.'

Max turned to his companions. The ex-commandos climbed back into his van. He drove slowly out of the field. Harris watched them go, hatred in his eyes.

Vasarov slept badly and awoke before midnight, and switched on the radio. Exactly on the hour, Radio Moscow broadcast the familiar hymn relayed every night at this time: 'The great Lenin has illuminated our path. Stalin has formed us. He has inspired us with his loyalty to the people, its work and deeds . . .'

The recorded male voices boomed back from the cold, sweating walls. Vasarov checked his watch automatically. At this hour the trains also left Moscow for the Siberian camps.

An orderly knocked on the door.

'Comrade Beria wishes to see you,' he announced.

Vasarov followed the man past the empty rooms with their bright fires, to a small office near the main hall. Beria was still wearing his overcoat; he had just arrived from Moscow. He nodded dismissal to the orderly.

'I have read the medical report on the patient. Clearly, his condition is very grave. I want you to realise that, in blunt terms, enemies will attempt to seize the moment of confusion to be rid of me. They know I have incriminating files on all of them.'

'What have you specifically in mind, comrade?' Vasarov asked him.

'Certain dangerous rivals will have to be eliminated before they can cause further trouble. It will be a time for loyalty – to persons as well as to the party.'

The two men looked at each other in the drab room. Vasarov saw a worried, unattractive mass murderer in middle age, with bad teeth and weak eyes, uneasy for his own future.

Beria saw a young man whose father he had murdered, but who was still said to be politically reliable. Neither could like or trust the other, but both realised that they shared areas of personal danger. Beria needed a loyal lieutenant, just as Vasarov would need a protector.

'I will follow you loyally, comrade,' Vasarov assured him. 'As I have from the day I came under your authority.'

'You will not regret your decision,' replied Beria earnestly. Then he smiled, as though at a secret joke.

'You have been visiting Austria after your trip to Berlin, comrade?' he asked gently, still smiling.

Vasarov paused, forcing himself to meet Beria's eyes, hugely magnified by the thick spectacles he wore.

'I went to see a woman I used to know, comrade. A loyal Party member.'

'I know you did. Name of Anna. But whether she is loyal is a matter we are now investigating.'

'Investigating? You mean . . .?'

Vasarov could not bring himself to finish the sentence. Beria did it for him.

'I mean we are interrogating her. So far, she has admitted that her sister has gone to live in England. No doubt she will have other matters of interest to reveal.'

'You will not harm her, Comrade Beria?'

'I do not harm anyone, Comrade Vasarov. But sometimes people harm themselves by being unco-operative and devious. And then unfortunate incidents can occur. It is really up to you. Prove your complete loyalty to me and I will see that this woman comes to no harm. But should events go against me, then I would not be in any position to guarantee her life – or even yours.'

When Max banked Harris's draft, David Graham put his head

round the door of his office and beckoned him inside.

'Haven't seen you here for some time,' he said almost reproachfully. 'I meant to send you a letter, but then I thought I'd wait until I saw you. You have paid off the two thousand pounds you borrowed for that field in Kent, plus all interest.'

'Good. So now I can borrow some more? Property seems the best bet these days. Know anything about it?'

'Not personally. I have a number of customers who have done very well at it, but I also see the other side. Men, sitting facing me across my desk, who tried – and failed.'

'Well, you won't see me. What would my field be worth if I had planning permission?'

'I'd say, at a guess, ten thousand. But put up an office and it's ten times that because of the rent it brings in.'

'So could I borrow ten from you, then?'

'No. Say seven and a half. We'd hold the deeds, of course. Short term loan.'

'How does one get this permission?'

'See the local town planning people. Engage an architect to draw up plans. Have a solicitor make formal application on your behalf.'

'There must be an easier, quicker way. The sort of short cut your successful clients would use.'

'You find it, then,' retorted Graham. 'But don't come to me to get you out of trouble if you trip yourself up.'

'I won't,' Max assured him. 'All I'll ever come to you for is money.'

Max motored down to Erith early on Thursday morning, several hours before the auction was due to start. He was driving a Lagonda V12 Rapide, with the rare two-seater body. The car could have made a good price at his auction, but he had bought it himself, paying the owner more than it was worth, because again the black paintwork and red leather had attracted him. The twelve-cylinder engine hummed like a turbine as he came into the town down the main Bexley Road, past a row of large Edwardian houses that stood on his right, each in stately isolation. When they had been built, their windows had looked over sandy cliffs towards the Thames. Now, red trolley buses ran along the top of those cliffs, and at their foot, a huge engineering works had been built with a vast yard littered with rusting metal castings.

These houses, like their counterparts in Bayswater and Paddington, had gone down in the world. Some had already been divided into flats or furnished rooms to let to apprentices at this factory. Outside others, 'For Sale' boards were nailed to gate posts.

Max parked behind The Wheatley Arms, opposite the local council offices. As he climbed out of his car, he saw the borough's motto above the main entrance: *Labor omnia vincit*. Work might conquer all things, but a little shrewdness could also save a lot of labour. As he had learned in the army, sweat saves blood, and brain saves both.

After the last auction, Max had asked Keith to stay behind: he wanted to discuss his future. If he was leaving school shortly, then Max would give him a permanent job instead of a part-time one. On the other hand, he might wish to be apprenticed to a garage and learn the mechanics of the trade and then join him. Max appreciated his loyalty in staying behind with him when he could have gone.

Max asked Keith whether he knew anyone who could help him with introductions to members of the local council or planning committee. Keith looked blank for a moment and then his face brightened.

'Only one I can think of is the chap on the local paper. He bought an MG last week. He must know everyone in his job.'

Max walked down Pier Road until he came to the office of the local newspaper in a converted private house. A warning bell clanged over the door as he went in. A young man came out from the back premises and looked at him enquiringly.

'Want to put an advert in the paper?' he asked Max hopefully.

'No. I already advertise every week,' said Max. 'I want to see the local reporter.'

'He's on holiday. I'm standing in for him.'

'Then I want to buy you lunch,' Max told him.

'Me? Why? Who are you?'

The young man looked at him in amazement.

'I run the car auction up the road.'

'I bought an MG J2 there last week. Red body and green wings.'

'So I understand. I took your money then, so now let me take you out in return. Not entirely an act of reciprocity. I want your advice over a local matter. Where do you recommend we eat?'

'The Running Horses. By the river.'

They lunched in the upstairs restaurant, with a view over the Thames.

'You must know everyone of consequence in this town?' Max remarked after they had ordered.

'Most of 'em,' the reporter agreed.

'Well, here's my problem. A friend owns one of those big houses in Bexley Road. Far too large for him as an old man, but he can't get planning permission to build something smaller for himself in his garden. Who should he see on the council to help him?'

The reporter smiled knowingly.

'There's only one man,' he said immediately. 'And he's not even on the council. Mr Bentley.'

'Like the car?'

'The way he's going, he'll have one soon.'

'What is he? Town Planning Officer?'

'Nothing so grand. In that department, though. He's a lot of influence, has Mr Bentley. What he backs goes through without any trouble. Know what I mean?'

'Exactly. How can I find him – apart from in his office?'

'Sometimes here at night, after work. Or maybe The Wheatley, or The Prince of Wales. Saloon bar. He only drinks doubles, Mr Bentley. Scotch.'

'A man of rich tastes?'

'He can afford them, too.'

'What's his background?'

'Married, three kids. Wife's a bit difficult.'

'In what way, difficult?'

'Like you'd be difficult if you were married to Mr Bentley. He's never at home. Always got some girl or other in tow. Buying her gins. Dancing at the Embassy Ballroom in

Welling. Got a flash car. A Graham. Supercharged.'

'I remember the car. It went through my auction. Who's his current girl friend?'

'Someone my sister knows slightly. Name of Olive. Works in the council's costing department. She's only about nineteen. Bentley's old enough to be her father, dirty old sod. She's meeting him tonight, actually.'

'That is very helpful. Now I have a suggestion to make. *You* take Olive and your sister out to dinner tonight at my expense, somewhere as far away from Erith as you can. Get her to break her date, but not to tell Mr Bentley.'

'You mean, stand him up?'

'Tell her that's how to make an older man keener than ever on her.'

'But why?'

'That's my business. Here's a tenner to help with yours.'

Max put a ten pound note on the table.

'A meal won't cost anything like that,' protested the reporter, looking at the note. He had never seen a ten pound note before; he liked what he saw.

'Who says it's only a meal?' asked Max grandly. 'You may have other expenses. Now, say no more about it. On another subject altogether, could you help me punish another bottle of Beaune?'

At six o'clock that evening, a black Graham, the rare supercharged model with the radiator grille like a fencer's mask, was the only car in the public house car park. Max parked alongside it.

Four middle-aged men stood drinking morosely in the saloon bar. The barman looked up expectantly as Max entered, recognising him from lunch-time. He had deliberately left an unusually generous tip.

'A Scotch,' said Max. 'Single, with water.'

The other men looked at him critically, as regulars view any stranger in any bar. Three appeared to be together. The fourth stood on his own, a little distance apart, glancing from time to time at his wrist watch as though impatiently waiting for someone who was already late.

'Two shillings and sixpence,' said the barman. Max put

down a ten shilling note. The barman brought back three half crowns. Max pushed two towards him. The barman looked surprised.

'When I order any more whisky for myself,' he whispered, 'charge me, but serve me ginger ale.'

He wanted a clear head.

'That man on his own, Mr Bentley?'

The barman nodded.

'Thank you.'

'Thank *you*, sir.'

The three men drank up and went out through the swing doors. Bentley glanced towards Max.

'Late, is she?' Max asked him sympathetically.

Bentley nodded, but did not reply. He had no wish to be drawn into pointless conversation with someone he did not know. He was waiting for that pert little bit from the costing department. The chemistry between them was right; of that he felt convinced. All he needed now was an opportunity to prove it.

Bentley had danced with her twice at the local council dance, and taken the opportunity to press himself to her as closely as he dared. Olive had not pulled away; that was always a good test – and a safe one. If she had said, 'Hang on, let me breathe,' or something like that, Bentley would have instantly dismissed all further action from his mind as being unwelcome to her, and more important, since he was married, potentially dangerous to him.

He had seen her several times since then in the council offices, and they had chatted, but this was the first time he had asked her out. Now the little bitch was late. Who the hell did she think she was? Bentley ordered another drink. He was forty and running to fat and easily irritated, especially when he felt that he was not being treated with the respect due to a man in his position. He'd give her five minutes, then go, and to hell with her. Plenty of other tail about. That new redhead in the surveyor's department, for one. Good pair of tits, too. Probably better than Olive's, actually.

Max moved along the bar towards him.

'Mr Bentley?'

'That's right. Who are you?'

'Max Cornell. I run the car auction here. Not often I meet a man who is actually named after a famous car. Any relation of W.O.?'

'Unfortunately not. How do you know my name, anyway?'

'Everyone knows you,' replied Max easily. 'You're a man of power around here.'

'Wish more thought the same.'

The barman served the whisky that Bentley had ordered.

'I'm in the chair,' Max slid three half crowns across the counter.

'And another one for me.'

He turned to Bentley.

'I was coming to see you tomorrow.'

'Cheers. Know where the office is, I suppose?'

'I do indeed. And you know where my car auction is, for I believe you bought that Graham from me.'

'Correct. I did. Very fine car. Bit heavy on the juice, though.'

'But think of the performance. If you ever want a car for anyone else, we can sometimes find you one at a good price.'

'How? It's an auction, isn't it?'

'Certainly. But some stuff just doesn't sell.'

'Ah,' said Bentley knowingly. 'A fiddle, eh?'

'Not at all,' Max answered. 'Simply the acceptance of a fact of life. What are you doing this evening, by the way?'

'Waiting for a friend of my wife's.'

'Marriage is like insurance. You have to die to beat it.'

'You single, then?'

'No.'

'You don't look like a married man.'

'How does a married man look?'

'Like me,' said Bentley bitterly, and gulped down his whisky. He had already drunk three doubles and his hand was shaking. That bloody girl. Where was she? Could she be standing him up? *Him*? In his position, with all the important people he knew? Je-sus.

'Tell you what,' said Max, as though he had just thought of the idea. 'If your wife's friend doesn't arrive in five minutes, be my guest for dinner? My wife's up north. I have to get back to London tonight and if we could combine a bit of business with dinner it would save me a drive all the way back here to see you again in your office tomorrow.'

'Thanks. But she'll be here,' said Bentley confidently.

Half an hour later, when Olive had still not arrived, they were sitting opposite each other at the same table where Max had sat with the reporter. Another double whisky was in front of Bentley; a ginger ale for Max.

'Now,' said Bentley. 'What did you want to see me about tomorrow, Mr Cornell?'

'I want planning permission for my auction field.'

'What do you want to put up there? Houses? I can tell you straight away, you won't get it. That land's not zoned for residential development. Never has been. The bloke who owned it originally tried that and was turned down. Twice. In the end he was allowed to use it for selling cars. Couldn't very well stop that, I suppose.'

'I am not interested in building houses, Mr Bentley. I want to put up an office block. With room on the ground floor for me to run the auction under cover.'

'Offices? But that's impossible. You can't put up houses, you can't put up offices. No trade use on land out there.'

'But it's already being used for trade purposes, as you yourself say. Selling cars.'

'There's no permanent building on it, though. Only a caravan.'

'That's why I want your advice. I could remove the caravan wheels and put it on bricks. Then add a portable hut or a tent or some such thing, seeking permission at every stage until, finally, the planning people might allow me to build a brick office. But that would take time. Maybe years. And I don't want to wait that long. Can you help me.'

Bentley looked at him reflectively. 'Wouldn't have any noisy machinery, that kind of nuisance?' he asked.

'Nothing whatever. Only a few typewriters. With a pretty girl behind each one."

'Ah,' said Bentley reflectively. His eyes misted over for a moment. 'A novel idea. I suppose that a change of use for trading purposes has already been agreed – in principle, at least. You *could* argue along the lines you propose. And commercial property there *could* help with the rates. Might be able to push it through the council on that basis.'

'Naturally, you would have expenses to meet, people to see.'

'You offering me a bribe?'

'Good God, no. I'm not a bloody fool. Man in your position – a bribe? Heavens, no. But you may have to see some of these old councillors right.'

'A load of hypocrites,' replied Bentley sourly. 'Spouting about the fight against corruption, and all the while taking backhanders right and left.'

Max shook his head sadly at the thought.

'A terrible world we live in, Mr Bentley. Standards aren't what they were. What would you need, say?'

'It'll cost me five hundred,' declared Bentley instantly, 'if it costs me a penny.'

'Is that enough?' Max asked him solicitously. 'I want this to go through smoothly. We might be able to work together in the future. I always say that both parties should walk away from a deal as they would from a good dinner – satisfied.'

'You're bloody right,' replied Bentley. 'By the way, did you see that waitress's arse? Skirt as tight as a drum. Bet she'd go like a train.'

'Very likely,' Max agreed. 'Very possibly, an express. But how's our deal going?'

'Ah, you and your bloody deal. Six hundred, then. That should cover it. Won't need to come back to you.'

'Right. When and how?'

'Three hundred now, said Bentley. 'Have to see one or two people about it before it's discussed officially.'

Max shook his head sorrowfully.

'I don't carry that sort of money about with me, Mr Bentley. When's your next planning meeting?'

'Tuesday. Seven o'clock.'

'I'll come down Tuesday morning, not with three hundred, but four. Give you that at lunch, here. The rest afterwards, in the bar – if you get it through. So at the worst, you'll have four hundred nicker up your shirt.'

'How do you know I'll even try to push it through? I might just take the money and run.'

'You're not that sort of chap,' said Max shaking his head. 'I'm a good judge of character. Now, what about another whisky?'

'You're in the chair,' said Bentley. 'Excuse me while I go to turn the bicycle round.'

He left, walking rather unsteadily towards the men's cloakroom. It had not been an entirely wasted evening. Out of the six hundred, he'd keep at least two for himself. What had the lesson been about at the civic church service they'd held last Sunday? The labourer is worthy of his hire. Pity about Olive, though.

'Can't understand about Olive,' he said regretfully when he returned.

'You never will understand about any woman,' Max told him.

'What do you mean?' Bentley asked him belligerently.

'Simply what I say. No man ever does. So far as we're concerned, women aren't a different sex. They're a different race.'

# Ten

Seven ageing men who hated and distrusted each other, and who between them controlled the lives and destinies of 670 million people in Russia and its communist empire, sat around the horse-shoe table in Stalin's conference room in the Kremlin. Stalin, wearing his usual brown jacket, buttoned to the neck, sat at their head.

These meetings might last through a night and for much of the following day, or, on Stalin's whim, they might break up after half an hour. Vasarov, glancing cautiously at the heavy and deliberately expressionless faces of the members of the Praesidium, wondered whether he and Beria were the only ones who knew that Stalin was a dying man.

In front of each man was a black blotter to minimise the chance of any unauthorised eyes reading what they might blot out.

Molotov sat on Stalin's right hand, plump and impassive as a malign Buddha. He would not meet anyone else's eyes, for, as one of Stalin's longest surviving colleagues and now in disgrace, he knew how vital it was never to react to anything until Stalin had first given his opinion. Had the man Lenin once contemptuously described as 'the best filing clerk in Russia' the strength and spirit to seize his chance after a lifetime of servitude when the Leader died?

Beria sat on Stalin's left, also careful never to look anyone in the eye or to give an opinion until Stalin had spoken. In Moscow, where several families would be crowded into a two-room apartment, Beria owned a two-storey house in Katchalov Street. He had a country house outside Tiflis, a summer home at Sochi, near Sukhumi, and another near Kuntsevo, close to Stalin's dacha. Here he kept a large collection of pornographic books and films.

Malenkov sat farther away, wearing the curiously old-fashioned jacket of the style Stalin had adopted in the early days of the Revolution. All references to Malenkov's youth had been expunged from his NKVD dossier. No-one knew for certain who his parents were, nor whether any of his relatives were still living. He was always embarrassed by any suggestion that he might have been born into a higher social class than Stalin, for in the Praesidium's world of intrigue and fear it was unsafe to have such links with the past.

Stalin liked Malenkov; he would be his own choice as successor. But how could he ensure this if he died? Malenkov was as ruthless as Stalin; perhaps that was the main link between them. During the war, he decreed that factory managers whose factories did not reach their quota should be shot as saboteurs and that factory workers absent from their jobs too often should be transported without further discussion to exile in Siberia. His own life style was in sharp contrast to the harsh hours of work he advocated for others. Beria's dossier on him listed the enormous number of servants he employed in his dacha, and referred to his inordinate love of French pastries and cream eclairs.

Farther down the table sat little Anastas Mikoyan – recently branded by Stalin as a Turkish spy, insulted, humiliated – and then more recently brought back into favour. Like Stalin and Vasarov, Mikoyan had studied for the priesthood at Tiflis Seminary. Unlike them, however, he finished his training and became a priest in the Nestorian Order before joining the Bolsheviks. He was a sharp man with bright watchful eyes, always on the alert to safeguard his own position.

As a pilot-fish to the powerful he had backed Stalin against Trotsky in the 1920s because he felt instinctively that Stalin would win. Vasarov wondered who he was backing now to succeed Stalin.

Nikita Khrushchev, another with the gift of choosing potential winners, sat next to Mikoyan. While Malenkov suppressed all details of his background, Khrushchev continually stressed his lowly beginnings. 'My grandfather was a serf,' he would say. 'His landlord owned him, and could have traded him if he wished for a hunting dog.'

When Khrushchev became political overlord concerned with constructing the Moscow Metro, he insisted that each station must be designed as a tribute to Stalin. As a result, giant portraits of the dictator in stained glass and mosaic smiled down benignly on thousands of commuters.

Khrushchev owned a hunting lodge at Zavidovo on the Volga River, four hours drive from Moscow, and another house on Cape Pitsunda. Here he would invite foreign diplomats, and delight in their surprise at the total opulence which a man of the people could enjoy in a communist country. An electrically controlled sliding glass wall overlooked a private bay. On warm days Khrushchev, a cautious swimmer, would float in the water, wearing the inner tube of a car tyre round his waist. The house and grounds were remarkable for the number of telephones he had installed in water-proof boxes in trees, by the swimming pool, on the beach, all of them linked to the Kremlin's private switchboard.

Every man around the table had his own personal directory, for telephone directories were not available to the public. When somebody important was due to be denounced as a traitor or imperialist agent, the telephone numbers of his immediate colleagues were secretly changed. Thus, when he frantically tried to telephone friends to rally support, their numbers were as unobtainable as their help.

Kaganovich, a Jew born in Kabassy (renamed Kaganovich in his honour), was one of Stalin's oldest colleagues and less venal than the rest. Stalin had conducted a long affair with his niece, Rosa, a physician. For many months, however, her photograph had not appeared in any Russian newspaper, and it was generally supposed that she had fallen from favour and been removed to a work camp.

In a room farther along the corridor sat more junior members of the Praesidium, permitted to listen to the debate through a loudspeaker but unable to take any part in it. In a third room, relays of stenographers wearing headphones sat in front of typewriters. They knew who was speaking at any time because everyone declared his name as he entered the discussion.

'Any other matters, comrades?' Stalin asked at last. They

had discussed last year's harvest (poor), and this year's prospects for the state-owned tractor factories (even worse), without reaching any conclusion, except that deviationists and Trotskyites must have wilfully ignored Stalin's orders to increase crops and production. Stalin looked at each man in turn with yellowed, distrustful eyes. Kaganovich cleared his throat nervously.

'Kaganovich,' he announced, for the benefit of the unseen stenographers, with the air of one who has an unpleasant subject to raise.

'Knowing how you value frankness, Comrade Stalin, I feel that something not as yet mentioned may hold the key to what we have discussed so far.'

He paused and wet his lips with his tongue. No-one looked at him, or even in his direction.

'Pray proceed, Comrade Kaganovich,' said Stalin. His eyes were almost closed now. Only a glint of moisture beneath their lids betrayed his watchfulness.

'I propose we cease the mass arrests of our professional men and women. We are sending to Siberia surveyors, engineers, surgeons, physicians. Many are Jews, Comrade Stalin. We have seen how the Nazis decimated those of my faith. Not only did they alienate the world by this persecution, but they denied to Germany the great talents and loyalty of millions of people. We cannot risk this result ourselves.

'Comrade Beria's Ministry has done wonders in ridding our land of saboteurs and bourgeois fascist hyenas, and to him and his vigilance we are forever in debt. But, to my knowledge – doubtless through the over-enthusiasm of minions – men and women now being transported every night are innocent of any political offence whatever against our beloved country.'

'I do not understand you aright, Comrade Kaganovich,' said Stalin slowly. Vasarov thought of the stenographers listening breathlessly. Kaganovich's next sentence could be crucial to his survival.

'Every day and every night for the past few months we have been sending people with Jewish blood – and some only with Jewish names – to Siberian camps,' Kaganovich replied passionately. 'We are using the hands of our best surgeons to dig latrines. Engineers, trained for years at state expense – who could be devising new ways to increase tractor production, or speed the building of great roads and bridges – are instead chopping wood in a climate of thirty degrees below zero.

'This haemorrhage of talent is not only unnecessary, but it is bleeding us of our best brains. I propose therefore that everyone transported to the camps as from the beginning of this year should have his or her case re-examined as a matter or urgency. Everyone found to be innocent of definite and proven political crimes should be brought back at once to take their rightful place in helping us to rebuild our country after the ravages of war.'

Vasarov saw sweat shining on Kaganovich's forehead. He had put his life at risk, and he knew it.

'You astound me, Comrade,' said Stalin hoarsely. 'I have irrefutable evidence from Comrade Beria that Jewish lackeys of the imperialists have been masquerading as doctors while they are actually in the pay of British Intelligence. We would indeed be failing in our duty if we let such criminals go unpunished.'

'Lavrenti Beria,' announced the head of the NKVD, and went on, 'I agree whole-heartedly with Comrade Stalin. It is imperative that we purge our country completely of dissidents and subversive agents of our fascist imperialist enemies.'

'Molotov. No-one here would disagree, Comrade Beria. But who in fact says that these medical specialists *are* all foreign agents?'

'Beria. We have unassailable evidence of their guilt. In most cases, we also have their own confessions. They have been working against us for years.'

Molotov looked up for the first time, and smiled at the naivety of Beria's reply.

'If that is so, Comrade Beria – and you of all men must know that it is – how can you claim that your security service is efficient? If these people have been such dedicated traitors for years, why have you only now discovered their treachery?'

He smiled at each of the other members of the Praesidium in

turn, but no-one would meet his gaze. To score debating points off Beria was a deadly course to follow.

'Malenkov speaking. Let us not waste time criticising each other, Comrades. What numbers are we discussing, Comrade Vasarov?'

Vasarov took a file from his briefcase.

'During the past three weeks we have deported 3,578 live bodies, Comrade Malenkov,' he replied.

'How many more are due to leave?'

'It is impossible to give a firm figure, Comrade Malenkov. But as new evidence against individuals becomes available, more arrests are made every night.'

'Kaganovich. Evidence, you say? Just what evidence? Someone with a grudge – or who fancies someone else's wife – or husband?'

Before Vasarov could reply, Stalin interrupted in his harsh, rough voice.

'Comrades,' he said, 'I speak as the oldest and most trusted disciple of Lenin, and I assure you that no-one in the Soviet Union is ever arrested unless they constitute a real or potential danger to socialism and our Motherland.'

'Kaganovich speaking. I am sure, Comrade Stalin, that this is your firm belief. But since more than two million political prisoners are already incarcerated in camps on the flimsiest of so-called evidence, I submit that they cannot surely *all* be a danger to our security.'

Vasarov watched Stalin's right hand move towards a push button by the side of his blotter. If Stalin pressed it, armed guards would immediately occupy the room. How many – or how few – of the men around the table would survive?

'Are you saying, Comrade, that I am in error?' Stalin asked him gently.

'Kaganovich. Of course not, Comrade Stalin. But as a man of the countryside, you know that if a farmer has a bowl of milk, he may skim off some cream. If he removes *all* the cream, the milk remaining is thin and weak. That will be the eventual condition of our country, if this policy persists.'

Everyone watched Stalin's puffy, nicotine-stained fingers jerking as they crept nearer to the button.

'And if I refuse to release criminals and Jewish plotters, who have all readily confessed their guilt?'

Stalin's lips had drawn back from his yellow, uneven teeth.

'If you refuse, Comrade Stalin, then I will seek the opinion of others here in this room.'

'Comrades,' said Molotov earnestly, neglecting, like Kaganovich, to announce his name in the urgency of the moment. 'Do not let any of us make decisions that are irrevocable. There may have been isolated cases of misplaced zeal. Let us look into each case in a detached, dispassionate way.'

'Perhaps you have in mind a reappraisal of the arrest and punishment of your Jewish wife?' Stalin asked him bluntly.

Molotov stood up angrily. Instantly, Stalin's hand moved nearer to the button. He had only to flex his wrist now and the alarm would sound.

'Before you press that,' Mikoyan said, not addressing Stalin as Comrade, and without announcing his own name, 'I must tell you that if any of us does not leave this room freely at the end of this meeting, the Red Army has orders to occupy the Kremlin.'

'Orders? Whose orders?'

Stalin stared at him in amazement. He stood up slowly, like a man in a trance, trembling with incomprehension and rage, and put out one hand to steady himself.

'I cannot agree with your proposition, Comrade Kaganovich,' Stalin said stiffly. 'We must rid our country of the cancer of treachery before it spreads beyond any control.'

Kaganovich pulled a card from an inner pocket and angrily waved it above his head.

'You see this card, Comrade Stalin?' he shouted. 'Its number proves that I was one of the Party's earliest members. This is what I think of Party membership now!'

He ripped the card into pieces and threw them contemptuously on the table. Stalin swayed on his feet, overcome. Then his fingers prodded at the bell push.

'Wait!' cried Molotov sharply.

Stalin turned and stared at Molotov in disbelief.

'Stop him!' shouted Mikoyan.

Molotov seized Stalin's arm while Mikoyan ran to help from the other side of the table. Stalin struck out wildly at them with one hand, still keeping his other on the table to steady himself. His hasty, awkward movement threw him off balance. He took a pace backwards, lost his footing on the polished floor, slipped and fell forwards across the table.

Stalin's head struck the polished wood with the force of a hammer. He groaned and then, eyes upturned, rolled gently backwards over the chair, and collapsed limply on the thick carpet.

'Cut the wire,' said Beria. With a pocket-knife Vasarov snipped the thin cable that led to the Kremlin guardroom. Then he knelt down by the dictator's side. Stalin's face was sweaty and diffused, an unhealthy purplish colour. Vasarov loosened the two metal clips on the collar of the dictator's jacket.

Beria, kneeling on the other side of Stalin's body, looked across at him. His pince-nez dropped from the bridge of his nose, and swung at the end of their black silk cord.

'We are free,' he said in a whisper. 'At last. He's dead!'

He turned to the others and repeated, *'He's dead!'*

'He's not,' said Vasarov quietly. Stalin opened one eye, and glared balefully at Beria. Immediately, the smile left Beria's face. He began to wring his hands in an extremity of simulated grief and concern.

'A miracle,' he declared in a harsh, strained voice. 'He lives. Our beloved leader lives.'

He bent down to kiss Stalin's forehead. Kaganovich pulled him away roughly.

'Get him a drink,' he ordered. Someone picked up Stalin's bottle of water and started to fill the glass.

'That's no good,' said Molotov sharply. 'He needs something stronger.' He crossed the room to one of the wooden panelled walls and pressed a concealed catch. A panel sprang open. Inside, on shelves set against a mirror, diffused lights reflected from rows of polished glasses and bottles: vodka, brandy, whisky.

Molotov opened a brandy bottle, hurried back with a half-filled glass and knelt down by his side.

'Drink!'

It was a command, not an invitation.

Stalin's mouth opened automatically. He gulped greedily, choking as the fiery spirit ran down his throat. A little trickled from the side of his mouth, staining his jacket. His eyelids fluttered.

'He's coming round,' said Vasarov. 'Help me lift him into the chair.'

But Stalin appeared to have lost control of his muscles. His head lolled backwards, his jaw hung loose. Panting with his weight and their inability to get a firm grip on the tight uniform he wore, they lifted him up clumsily and lowered him into his chair. Vasarov straightened out the old man's legs. He lolled, head against the back rest, arms and legs stretched out stiffly.

Molotov carried the glass into a small ante-room which contained a lavatory and wash basin. There was the sound of a running tap. Mikoyan felt Stalin's pulse. It was beating feebly. The old man's lips began to tremble.

'He is saying something,' said Mikoyan excitedly. 'Call a doctor.'

'No doctor,' said Stalin weakly. 'I do not trust doctors. I have had a fall, Comrades. Nothing serious. Please go about your duties. You can stay with me, Comrade,' he told Malenkov. Laboriously, he turned to Vasarov, moving his whole body as though he could no longer turn his head independently of his trunk.

'You wait as well.'

'So will I, Comrade Stalin,' said Beria, afraid of what might happen in his absence if Stalin had heard the joy in his voice when he thought he was dead.

Colour was returning to Stalin's face, but his forehead still glistened with sweat. His lips were encrusted by a white salty rime of dried saliva. The others bowed to him, and as though already in the presence of death, tip-toed over the carpet towards the main doors.

Stalin licked his lips, and frowned.

'Brandy,' he said. 'Who gave me brandy?'

'Comrade Molotov.'

'I thought as much. Show me the glass.'

He waved a hand weakly in the direction of the concealed cupboard.

'There is no glass, Comrade,' replied Beria. 'He washed it.'

'Get it for me!' commanded Stalin.

Vasarov went into the washroom. The basin was wet, the hot tap still felt warm, and a hand towel had recently been used. But there was no sign of any glass.

'Where is it?' Stalin called to him.

'I am looking for it, Comrade.'

Vasarov came back into the room. Molotov must have replaced the glass without any of them seeing him do so. Vasarov knew the location of the hidden catch, and ran his fingers along the beading on the panel until the door clicked open. Fifty identical glasses reflected the light. From which one had Stalin drunk? It was impossible to say. They all looked alike, polished, unused.

'I cannot say which glass he used, Comrade Stalin. They are all clean, all in place.'

'I have been poisoned,' said Stalin simply, stating a fact, not giving an opinion, but with total detachment, as though he was not personally involved.

'No, Comrade. He gave you brandy,' Beria assured him. 'I saw the bottle.'

'I know what is in those bottles,' replied Stalin simply. 'So does our Comrade. I will be dead within days.'

'*Dead*?'

At the sound of the word, the three other men looked at each other nervously. Was Stalin rambling – or did he speak the truth, because in the past he too had poured poisoned drinks for others from these bottles?

'We must consult a doctor, Comrade,' said Beria firmly. 'I have a trusted physician in my ministry.'

'I will not have a doctor,' repeated Stalin firmly. 'It is too late. There is no antidote. Nothing.'

He began to breath through his mouth, snoring slightly. Sweat shone like varnish on his forehead.

'Let's take him to a hospital.'

'Take the Generalissimo on a stretcher to a hospital – where dozens of people will see him?' asked Beria in amazement.

'But he cannot remain here like this,' protested Malenkov.

'Call our cars,' Beria ordered Vasarov. 'We can carry him out concealed in rugs, and drive him to his dacha. I will bring my own doctor to him there, whatever he says.'

Vasarov opened a side door, intending to reach a telephone with which he could speak to the officer in charge of all Kremlin transport. He had forgotten that this room was filled with other junior members of the Praesidium.

'We heard everything', said Marshal Bulganin, pointing to the loudspeakers. 'Everything.'

He stroked his goatee beard nervously.

'Then you know how serious the situation is, Comrades,' replied Vasarov. 'Please take up residence in your dachas around Comrade Stalin's in case he – or we – have need of you.'

Bulganin and the others filed silently out of the room.

At a rear entrance of the building, used for bringing in supplies and removing rubbish, five identical black Zis limousines waited, curtains drawn across their side and rear windows. All lights around this doorway were now extinguished, except for weak blue emergency lights on the staircase.

Beria, Malenkov and Vasarov carried Stalin to the third car in line. They had wrapped him so closely in a grey blanket, bordered with red, that it was impossible for anyone to recognise him. He might be any member of the Praesidium who had become unwell, or who had drunk too much and was incapable of walking. At a signal from Vasarov the drivers started their engines.

'You ride with him,' Beria told Vasarov. 'I'll be in the car behind, in radio contact. If you have to speak *en clair*, refer to him as Uncle Vanya.'

The convoy set off.

The figure in the grey blanket lay still. Once, Vasarov drew back the blanket from his face to allow him air. Stalin's skin was pale and waxy beneath the fleeting glare of street lamps. His jaw had sagged open, and he was breathing noisily through his mouth. Occasionally, phlegm bubbled in his throat.

In the dacha, Beria's personal doctor waited while Stalin was undressed, placed on a bed, and sheets and blankets were reverently pulled over his soft, flabby body.

'He is in a very serious condition, Comrade Beria,' the doctor said cautiously after he had examined the patient. 'All the signs are of arteriosclerosis. I think he has also suffered a stroke, which accounts for his stertorous breathing and the partial paralysis on one side of his body. But there are other symptoms that do not fall into the category of his condition. I would like a second opinion.'

'What other symptoms do you refer to?'

'His pupils are dilated. His pulse rate is abnormally high –120 beats a minute. His breathing is uneven, and there is a look about him which would suggest complications.'

'Of what kind? Be specific. Perhaps something he has eaten has disagreed with him?'

'Until we examine the contents of his stomach I can do no more than say that is a possibility.'

'Something he drank, perhaps?'

'Alcohol would not bring on these symptoms.'

'Would poison?' Vasarov asked him bluntly.

'*Poison*?'

The doctor repeated the word in horror.

'If Comrade Stalin has been poisoned – by something he ate or drank – would these symptoms be present?'

'It is possible,' the doctor agreed cautiously.

'Is there any antidote?'

'I cannot give an opinion until we have examined the contents of his stomach.'

'Our beloved leader is no longer young,' said Beria. 'He has been a very heavy smoker all his adult life, and his hours of work have been long and harsh. None of these habits is conducive to a long and healthy life, doctor. Nicotine is itself a strong poison, is it not?'

'That is so, Comrade. But he has none of the symptoms of nicotine poisoning.'

'Then do not allude to that or to any other possible accidental poisoning of his system. If, unhappily, our beloved leader does not recover, stress that complications of the circulatory system have arisen from years of selfless toil. Men can die for their country in peace as well as in war, Comrade doctor.'

At ten o'clock the following morning, the warning bell above Vasarov's head pealed imperiously. Beria was standing on his own, in what had been Stalin's room, warming his hands at the fire.

'He is failing. The Praesidium has issued a bulletin. They are reading it on the wireless every few minutes.'

Beria switched on a radio as he spoke. An orchestra was playing. Slowly, the music faded. An announcer began to speak. His voice sounded high and nervous.

'The Central Committee of the Communist Party of the Soviet Union, and the Council of Ministers of the USSR, announce the grave misfortune which has been inflicted on our Party and our people: Comrade Stalin's serious illness.

'During the night, between the first and second of March, Comrade Stalin, while in his apartment in Moscow, was struck by a cerebral haemorrhage which attacked the vital areas of the brain. Comrade Stalin has lost consciousness. His right arm and right leg are paralysed. He has lost his power of speech. Serious cardiac and respiratory complications have set in.'

By that evening, nine doctors were in attendance. Relays of stenographers from Beria's ministry, dressed as nurses and medical attendants, made shorthand notes of every suggestion and proposal that was made, every nuance of the muttered consultations.

One doctor injected Stalin with glucose for nourishment. Another fixed a saline drip into the back of his left hand. A third administered caffeine in an attempt to stimulate his sluggish body, while others gave him regular sessions with an oxygen mask. In desperation, one even tried the eighteenth-century treatment of using leeches to suck blood from the old man's veins, but all without effect. Stalin was dying, and no medicine or surgery, no sorcery or magic could now hold him back from the grave.

Beria called Vasarov to his room.

'When he goes, Comrade,' he said, 'there will be a fight for succession.'

'I believe that his wish is for Comrade Malenkov,' Vasarov replied.

'When Lenin died, he left a will naming Trotsky as the most capable member of the Central Committee to succeed him. Stalin he called rude, capricious, and a brute. Who took over? There is a saying "Let the dead bury the dead". Our leader is as good as dead already. We must now concern ourselves with the living – more particularly with ourselves and our future.

'In the meantime, inform the great Soviet people that their father's health is weakening. Draft a message to put out on the radio in the morning. Follow it with subsequent bulletins throughout the day. In each one, hint at the increasing gravity of the situation. I will approve the final wording of each bulletin.'

'And if he dies?' asked Vasarov.

'We withhold the news until the Praesidium decides on his successor.'

'It would be prudent, Comrade Beria, for at least two senior members of the Praesidium to be available at all times, in case urgent decisions need to be made.'

'I agree, Comrade Vasarov,' said Beria approvingly. 'Anything else?'

'One last thing, Comrade. We know that others overheard the latter part of the discussion in the Kremlin. It is unlikely that they will dare to repeat what they heard, but in case malicious rumours spread and are elaborated by imperialist hyenas and their lackeys in the lickspittle press, I propose that a more accurate version of events be circulated. Our revered leader invited you and Comrades Malenkov, Bulganin and Khrushchev to dinner here. You discussed matters of state, and then returned to your own dachas. Next day, an officer of the private guard reported that he had not seen our leader all day.

'It is well known, even abroad, that when Comrade Stalin is asleep, no-one is allowed to disturb him, but usually during the day he will summon orderlies to his room. You therefore communicated with your colleagues. You all came here, and feeling that the importance of the matter overrode all protocol, you entered Stalin's private apartments and found him unwell.'

'Excellent,' said Beria. 'A most accurate account of these sad events. I could not have put it better myself. We will feed it through Disinformation for foreign consumption. We must make it appear to be a clandestine report so that our enemies will be more willing to accept its veracity.'

Every few hours during the rest of that day, Vasarov drafted a new and fictitious official communiqué for publication in *Pravda* and *Isvestia*. One spoke of Stalin's 'temporary absence from affairs for a more or less long period'. Another reported that Stalin's pulse was irregular, his breathing uneven. A third announced that 'the rupture of the cerebral functions has worsened'. By then, Stalin was already dead.

On the Thursday morning when he died, the weather was bitterly cold. All members of the Praesidium were called to his dacha, where they waited in an ante-room. They did not speak to each other, but stood in silence, concerned with their own uneasy thoughts. Watching them, Vasarov noted how they had reverted to type. They were no longer ministers and generals, but peasants, gathered at the death-bed of a harsh father. They had all feared him, but without his authority and confidence they feared their future even more. Who would now advise how best to deal with truculent neighbours, or which seeds to sow for next year's harvest?

It seemed incredible that these dull, careful, cruel and now frightened men controlled an empire greater than any envisaged by Ghengis Khan, Tamberlaine or the Tsar.

Vasarov followed the doctors into Stalin's bedroom. Stalin was propped up in bed, eyes closed, his breathing heavy and laboured.

As they gathered around his bed, Stalin suddenly choked. A little yellow bile dribbled down the greyish stubble on his chin. He opened his eyes, neither seeing them nor recognising his surroundings. His lips suddenly drew back, exposing the stumps of his nicotine-stained teeth as though he had seen, through the eternal mists, a sight too terrible to contemplate. His left hand plucked furiously at the open collar of his pyjamas as though he was choking. His body arched and trembled.

'Oxygen!' cried a doctor. Two nurses wheeled an oxygen trolley to his bed. A third held the rubber mask to his face. Stalin raised his arm suddenly and clenched his fist. The nurse removed the mask as his face became contorted, either with the paroxysms of death or from some burning inner hatred. His appearance was momentarily so malevolent that those nearest to him drew back in horror and revulsion.

In that split second, Vasarov recalled Latin words learned as a student at Tiflis Seminary, part of a Roman song composed in honour of the Emperor Aurelian. Like Stalin, Aurelian had been the most powerful leader of his age – and the most feared. Like Stalin, too, Aurelian had repelled a German invasion of his country – but finally his officers, fearful for their own safety, had combined to murder him.

'A thousand, thousand, thousand men, I alone, a single man, have slain.' The words could serve as an epitaph for the old man in front of him. Stalin's hand dropped on to the coverlet and he fell back against his pillows. Oxygen hissed uselessly through the rubber mask. A doctor signalled to the nurse to turn off the valves. The hissing stopped and the room fell silent. Stalin was dead.

# *Eleven*

David Graham was about to leave the bank for an early morning appointment, when his assistant told him that Max Cornell was on the line.

'You should have received a letter from me this morning.' Max began.

'I did,' Graham replied. 'It contained the outline planning permission you've been given to build offices above a covered car auction room on your field. Now how on earth did you manage to get that through so quickly?'

'Put it down to charm – and something I learned in the army. Time spent in reconnaissance is seldom wasted. There's another paragraph to the letter. You read that, too?'

'Of course. You want an overdraft of seven and a half thousand pounds against the deeds and this planning permission. That's what I promised you.'

'You'll stick by that?'

'Naturally.'

'Good. That's all I wanted to know.'

For the past few evenings Max had been studying the Town and Country Planning Act of 1947, which he had bought at His Majesty's Stationery Office shop in London. One section dealt with blocks of flats which had been requisitioned as offices during the war. They could now continue to be used as offices without payment of the crippling development charge introduced by the Socialist Government. Max could not afford to buy a block of flats, but he intended to try his luck with the best he could afford, a single large house in London before others found this loophole and it was closed.

For the past week, he had been collecting details from estate agents of extremely large and elegant private houses, that had been used as temporary offices during the war.

He felt that he must make more capital before he became used to affluence. He wanted to open other car auctions around the country, and possibly on the continent, but this would have to wait until he was financially independent. Once his gift for making money had been proved beyond doubt, he would never have to ask Graham for another loan; the bank would deluge him with offers.

The house he liked best was off Queen Anne's Gate, near Birdcage Walk, and a few minutes from the Albert Tavern where he had attended the Commando reunion. With several others adjoining, it had been requisitioned for government offices. Now it was empty, and in the words of the estate agent's details, 'awaited a discriminating buyer'. He drove to the estate agent's office, and a young man, hair brilliantined, and wearing a suit with extravagantly padded shoulders to give him a breadth that nature had denied him, turned up the particulars in a file.

'Here we are, sir. A very fine property indeed,' he said. 'Under the terms of the government lease, all damage will be repaired and the whole house decorated inside and out to the buyer's reasonable choice. Accommodation is on four floors. Total of twenty-five rooms, three bathrooms, very good staff quarters.'

'How much is it? There was no figure in the particulars you sent me.'

'Our client is asking fifty thousand pounds for the freehold, sir.'

'A very high price indeed. What have you been offered?'

'I am not at liberty to disclose exact sums, sir, but we have had expressions of interest around that figure.'

'Let's have a look at it. Then maybe I'll express my interest at that figure.'

Max had already inspected the house from the outside, but he saw no reason to admit this to the young man.

It had the forlorn, betrayed, unwanted look of any empty and once-beautiful building. Pale squares on walls showed where pictures had been removed; floorboards, stained black around the skirting, revealed naked areas of unpainted wood in the centre, once concealed by carpets. Max jumped up and down to test the strength of the joists. They seemed firm enough. The staircase was wide with carved bannisters of polished rosewood. Doors were beautifully panelled, with eighteenth-century brass fingerplates and handles. The ceilings had moulded cornices and centre pieces.

Max made up his mind on the spot. If his equation did not work over this property, it simply would not work at all.

'I'll buy it,' he said. 'Full price, subject to contract – and two small conditions.'

'What are they, sir?'

'Ordinarily, I would pay you a ten-per-cent deposit, five thousand pounds. But because I accept your asking price, although I consider it high, I propose to pay you five-per-cent deposit, £2,500 – nonreturnable to me – for one month's firm option against *any* other offer you may receive during that time.'

'I think our client would agree to that, sir. And the other condition?'

'That I redecorate one room. I will have a carpet laid in it, and chairs, hang a few pictures and so on. I am buying this property for someone special. I want them to see how it could look when it's redecorated.'

Max did not add that he had not yet met this special person, and indeed, had no idea who they might be. He would meet them. He had to, or he would lose £2,500.

'Our client wouldn't wish for anything bizarre, sir, in case you did not take up the option?'

'I would suggest we paint the walls Wedgwood blue. Ceilings slightly darker. Cornice and carvings, off white. The very highest quality of paint and workmanship, of course.'

'That should present no problem, sir. Come back to the office, and I will telephone our client, and if he agrees we could draw up an agreement on those lines. An exchange of letters would probably be sufficient. And your full name and address, sir?'

'Max Cornell. I have no firm address in London at present, but write to me care of the Dorchester. That will always find me.'

The young man looked impressed, as Max had guessed he would. His real address, in a rooming house in Courtfield Gardens, would have produced a totally different reaction.

When Max had signed his letter of intent, he drove on to the Dorchester and walked through the swing doors as though he did indeed live there.

In the centre of the lounge were several ornate writing desks with racks of notepaper and envelopes. Max sat down at the nearest as though to write a letter, appeared to think better of it, and stood up. As he did so, he casually picked up a handful of envelopes and sheets of note paper headed The Dorchester Hotel, London, then walked on through the lounge, and out through the other entrance into Park Lane.

Back in Courtfield Gardens, he drafted out a basic letter, had this typed on twelve sheets of Dorchester Hotel notepaper by a small typing agency that he found through an advertisement on a postcard in a confectionary shop window. He addressed each letter to the chairman of a large public company – engineering firms, motor car manufacturers, oil refineries, and insurance concerns. To each, he offered the unique opportunity of renting a prestigious office in London's most exclusive residential area, at a fixed rental, with no reviews or increases whatever for the next twenty-five years. He pointed out the advantages compared with an office designed simply as a work place.

Next day, he called at Grosvenor House Hotel, in Park Lane, removed several sheets of writing paper and envelopes, and sent out twelve similar letters to twelve more chairmen. For the rest of the week, he concentrated on the car auctions, and collecting Betty's rents. On the following Monday, he again visited the Dorchester, and approached the porter's desk.

'I am Mr Max Cornell,' he explained. 'Any mail for me?'

'Your room, sir?'

'I've not booked in yet.'

He waved towards three or four new arrivals who stood in line at the reception desk.

'Very good, sir.'

The porter sifted through a pile of letters.

'Four for you, sir.'

Max thanked the porter, walked back through the lounge, and out into Park Lane and opened the letters. The chairmen of four companies to whom he had written thanked him for his offer, but were not interested in discussing it further.

Max called at Grosvenor House. Here, five letters awaited him. Twenty-four letters out and nine replies back. All negative.

Two days later, he again called at the Dorchester. Six replies this time; five negative and one from an American oil company official whose president, Mr Jasper Mulheim, had arrived unexpectedly from Texas that week. He would like to see the property personally before he reached any decision. Max made an appointment with him for noon the next day.

In the intervening time he tried to find out some details about Mr Mulheim and his company, but the local public library reference section could not help. He took a bus to Fleet Street, and went into El Vino's, where journalists drink at lunchtime.

He ordered a glass of Sauterne, soda and ice and then deliberately knocked the elbow of another customer, who was holding a full glass of red wine. He glared angrily at Max.

'My apologies,' said Max at once. 'I didn't see you. Here, let me buy you another glass.'

'No need for that.'

'I think there's every need.' He ordered another glass of red wine and handed it to the man. They introduced themselves; he was a reporter on the *Daily Sketch*.

'How do you find all the details about people's pasts when you write up a story?' Max asked him innocently after they had gone on to gins.

'Cuttings,' the reporter explained. 'We've a library where people sit all day, cutting out every item in every paper. Then they're filled away.'

'Ever get beaten?'

'Very rarely. Why?'

'I'll take a bet you can't give me any details on an American oil man.'

'How much are you betting?'

'Dinner in Soho tonight. Eight o'clock.'

'You're on. Now let's have the fella's name.'

So for the price of three glasses of red wine, two gins and a plate of spaghetti, Max discovered that Jasper Mulheim's father, a widower, had owned a very small ranch on which oil had been discovered just before the war. He had speedily drunk himself to death, leaving the majority interest in his company to Jasper, his only son, who had since spent much time persuading himself that he did not owe his wealth to this but to his own sagacity and business acumen.

He dressed and acted as he had seen tycoons act in films; the man at the top who alone could take the big decisions.

'Pretty shabby old place,' he said disparagingly, wrinkling up his nose and shaking his head, as he followed Max up the wide staircase in the empty house.

'You're right,' Max agreed. 'But of course it will be totally redecorated free to the tenant's choice'.

'Yeah. But it's difficult to see how it would look then. All this dirt and faded paintwork. I'm not an interior decorator, Mr Cornell, I'm a businessman.'

'Exactly. So I've had one room done out to show how all the house could look. I figure it should then appeal to a company, or rather, to a company president, of impeccable taste. You would be carrying on a long tradition, Mr Mulheim. Do you know that one of the early owners was a love child of King George the Third?

'Is that right?' asked Mulheim, impressed.

'Absolutely.'

Max had made up the story on impulse, but if the man insisted, he could no doubt fake up some facsimile papers – so long as he rented the damned place.

'Let's see this room, then,' said Mulheim.

Max opened the door, and stood back to allow his guest to enter. He had hired a Turkish carpet and heavy brocaded curtains, rows of leather bound books and reproduction antique furniture from a firm that supplied film studios. The room looked lie a set for a country house library.

'See what I mean?' said Max.

'You really do have something here,' admitted Mulheim appreciatively. 'A bit of old England.'

'Exactly. A president could have a superb private flat on the top floor, Mr Mulheim, where he could entertain his guests privately. Save the bother of booking hotel rooms and eating out in restaurants.'

Mulheim nodded.

'Better than hotels with their impersonal service – and, of course, the possibility of unwanted publicity for people coming and going,' Max added as an afterthought.

'I get your point,' said Mulheim. 'What rent are you asking?'

'Twelve thousand pounds sterling a year.'

'That's one hell of a lot of money.'

'Agreed,' said Max. 'But remember this is a fixed rent for twenty-five years – a quarter of a century. No increases whatever during that time.'

'Check,' said Mulheim.

'Now, Mr Mulheim, your profits will have increased over the last ten years, I'm sure?'

'Trebled,' said Mulheim with pride. 'Last year was our best ever.'

'So, if you take this at twelve thousand it will be very cheap indeed in another ten years' time, in 1961. And by 1976 – twenty-five years on – this rent will be laughable. If the lease had a revision clause, your company might then be paying four or five times as much.'

'Still too high,' said Mulheim, shaking his head. He wanted to show this Limey he was a man of quick decision, who could make up his mind on the spot, and would not be bullied just because he was American and rich. But he liked the idea of renting a private house of this size in such a select part of London. The fact that he could have his own flat here also had attractions. He had heard interesting reports about the capabilities of young girls in this strange shabby capital. He could foresee pleasant liaisons conducted with total discretion.

Max assessed his man.

'Well,' he said in a resigned tone of voice, 'I am sorry you won't take it.'

'I didn't say that,' replied Mulheim quickly. 'I just won't pay twelve for it.'

'So what would you pay? I have to redecorate the whole place, remember. It will cost me thousands. Shall we say ten?'

Mulheim stroked his chin.

'*And* I'll buy you lunch,' said Max with a smile. 'At my hotel. The Dorchester.'

'You're on,' said Mulheim. Max's response appealed to his sense of the theatrical; it was exactly the sort of thing a tycoon would say on the screen. 'Ten thousand pounds sterling. My company will need a survey, of course, but subject to that I'll give your agents a letter of intent.'

Max took this letter to David Graham.

'What do you want me to do about it?' Graham asked him, puzzled. 'You have let a property you don't own, and which you can't possibly afford to buy, but which if you *did* own, would now be bringing you in about twenty per cent on a purchase price you can't pay.'

'You agree that it is an unusually large return for a commercial property?'

'I most certainly do. Can't see how you brought if off.'

'Let's just say you gave me a hint that I followed. Time spent in reconnaisance is seldom wasted. Now what could I sell the property for, once it *is* mine and bringing in that amount?'

'The usual ratio is ten per cent. But as there are no rent reviews, it would probably be rather less. Say, eighty thousand pounds.'

'Know anyone who would pay that for it?'

'Not a private buyer. Like yourself, they are after more adventurous things. But I do have various contacts with insurance companies, pension funds and so on. They might like something safe and solid like this.'

'And in twenty-five years,' said Max, 'think how they could jack up the rents.'

'I am thinking,' said Graham, and reached for the telephone.

Before Max's option ended, he had sold the house for seventy-five thousand pounds to the Midland Widows' Insurance Company. This meant that after legal expenses he had made a tax free profit of nearly twenty-five thousand pounds. But, most important, he had proved that his theory worked, for what he had done once, he could – and would – do again.

As Sam Harris would have said, he had got his paperwork right.

Early in 1955, the estate agent who sold Max the property near Queen Anne's Gate told him that a house in Eaton Place, divided into three flats and occupied for some years by a European government in exile, was about to be derequisitioned. He could arrange a ninety-nine year lease on the top flat at an unusually low rent. Max agreed at once. When he moved in from Courtfield Gardens, he invited the young man to dinner, to show him how the flat looked after it had been completely redecorated.

'In a few years,' the estate agent assured him, much impressed, 'you will be able to sell your lease here for a lot of money – if you want to, that is. Lots of young married couples would rather have a flat than a house, but understandably they don't like the idea of paying rent forever. I don't myself. They'd rather own it – and who can blame them? We can sometimes give them hundred per cent mortgages – over thirty years.'

'Who puts up money for deals like that?'

'Smaller building societies. Like this one.'

He took a folder from his jacket pocket.

'The Union Flag. Never heard of it, I imagine? It's one of several that have mushroomed – they aren't as fussy as the big boys.'

'Who runs it?'

'Estate agent named Goudousky in Bayswater is involved. He's got a couple of deadbeat peers on the board, and a broken down judge and that financial fellow, who has a finger in a lot of pies, Sam Harris. He's a sharp, hard bastard. And tight with his money as a fish's arse – water tight!

'Anyway, Harris put up some money, so I'm told, just to

start it off, and the rest comes from private investors who want a little bit more interest than proper building societies will pay. Plenty of people like that about, so it's self-perpetuating.'

When the young man had gone, Max sat down in the room he had decided to call his study, and began to work out some figures on the back of an envelope. Half an hour and several brandies later, he realised that he had been making totally unnecessary complications for himself. The sum was so simple that he had to smile at his slowness in realising this. He tore the envelope into pieces and went to bed.

Next morning, he telephoned Mr Goudousky and made an appointment for that afternoon. Sandra hovered nearby with two cups of tea on a tray, as Mr Goudousky ran his fingertips across Max's card, to measure the depth, and therefore the expense, of the engraving.

'Eaton Place,' he said reflectively. 'And what sort of house are you looking for in this area, Mr Cornell?'

'A flatlet house,' said Max.

'We have plenty of those. You can find one in good repair for fifteen hundred. One a lot better, two thousand. Low return, of course. Lot of statutory tenants at that price.'

'What sort of mortgage can you offer?'

'It depends on your status.'

'I would be buying through limited companies.'

'Several companies for one house?' Mr Goudousky looked at him quizzically.

'Who said I was only interested in one?' replied Max. 'I am after dozens. Hundreds, if you have them.'

'Are you serious?'

'I never joke about money,' Max told him severely.

'Ah,' said Mr Goudousky, smiling. 'I like that. I really do.'

'I'm glad. Now let's get down to business.'

Max bought fifty houses that afternoon. He checked the first five inside and out, but the next five outside only. The day was wet, and he soon grew weary of climbing rickety staircases, avoiding loose banisters and peering into sordid rooms with cracked plaster and peeling wallpaper. He bought the rest on trust at a total cost of seventy-five thousand pounds, of which he borrowed seventy thousand pounds from the Union Flag Building Society, over an unusually short five-year period.

'What about surveys?' Mr Goudousky asked him.

'You do them,' Max replied at once. 'You're a surveyor, aren't you? Who better could I choose? Fifty houses at, say, ten quid each survey fee. Five hundred nicker in your back pocket for doing nothing at all except signing your name. Can't be bad.'

'It's very good indeed. Thank you, Mr Cornell. And the name of your solicitor?'

'Who do you use?'

'Well, there's Mr O'Flaherty, who is cheap.'

'Doesn't he have a scale of fees?'

'Oh, yes, regular solicitors do. But Mr O'Flaherty was struck off the rolls, so that doesn't apply to him. It will, of course, when he gets back on.'

'So meantime he's got to be honest in case he never makes that journey? Fair enough. Engage him, Mr Goudousky. But have him use a printed form of contract, same for every one. You know how lawyers love to draw out one conveyancing – let alone fifty.'

When the transaction was finished, Max took Mr Goudousky out to dinner. Over their second bottle of wine, he came to the reason for this invitation.

'I want to go on buying,' he explained. 'But before I do so, I want to make a little adjustment. I see from your letter-head you are also agents for the Golden Star Building Society?'

'Well, yes. It's rather like the Union Flag. Helps first-time buyers mostly. Cheap properties. Stuff the big boys look down their noses at.'

'As I thought. Well, I want to re-mortgage those properties I've bought not over five years but over thirty – and for one hundred and fifty thousand pounds.'

'A long time, Mr Cornell, *and* a very high value, which I would find extremely difficult to justify.'

'Then do another survey and justify it. This time, charge fifteen a house. Seven fifty up your shirt.'

'This is a very large sum of money, Mr Cornell. On five thousand pounds deposit, you have already borrowed seventy thousand.'

'Short term. Very short term,' Max interrupted, and smiled inwardly. He had nearly said 'short time'. It must be Betty's influence.

'Now, if the Society advances you a hundred and fifty thousand, you are making a profit of eighty thousand, minus legal fees and mine. And in a matter of weeks.'

'Mr Goudousky, your arithmetic is as correct as your surveys. Both do you credit. You will also have made twelve hundred and fifty pounds for two signatures. That's more than an autograph of the Queen would fetch. Then I will buy another fifty houses through you next week.'

'And do the same thing again?'

'You and I together. As I make money, so will you. Now I want to make an appointment for you to meet the person who will be looking after the day-to-day running of these houses – in association with you, of course. She is already a sub-tenant of some of your clients. A Mrs Mortimer. Mrs Betty Mortimer.

# *Twelve*

Jamaica Rosa sat sipping a mug of rum in a top floor room of a house off the Bayswater Road. She missed the fresh saltiness of the Doctor' Wind from the sea every morning. London's thick stale air reminded her more of the Undertaker's Wind that blew out from the Blue Mountains each evening.

Her forbears had been runaway slaves, Cimarrones, who had fled into these mountains, where early Spanish settlers did not dare to follow. When the British came and drove out the Spaniards, they could not pronounce the word and called them Maroons. They had their own king in their own territory, known now as Cockpit Country. Of the thousands of slaves shipped to the island – Mandingoes from Sierra Leone, Joliffs from the Gambia, Ashanti and Fanti from the Gold Coast, Yoruba and Ibo from Nigeria – the Maroons were the first black people to be freed. Rosa claimed descent from Quao, the great Maroon leader, who had forced white men to admit that they could never subdue them.

She finished her rum, and went downstairs to see her son, Joseph, the last of Quao's line – now living with an English whore.

Rosa was not against prostitution; she had shares in several coloured girls herself, but she did not like this white girl, because she knew that Betty did not like her, and because Betty was in a position of strength – she was white in a white person's world.

Rosa had lived for years with a Portuguese sailor outside Kingston in a tin-roofed hut the size of a chicken coop, where Joseph was conceived and born. The boy was ugly, with dark skin and reddish hair. His father disliked him on sight, and took off; she had not seen him since. She then lived with a docker addicted to rum, for whom she felt nothing but contempt and whom she left to follow Joseph to England, for she doted on her son. At her insistence he had attended the local Catholic school. She admired Catholics. They had discipline and unity and she believed that this was a white man's religion. She wanted Joseph to have a white man's chance in life, not a black man's.

Joseph, however, had no use for his mother or her aspirations; he despised them as much as he despised her. He wanted money. What did it matter what colour your skin was, so long as you were rich? And what did it matter how you made your money – so long as you made it? Joseph wanted to show not that he was other men's equal, but that he was their superior. For this purpose money was the only yardstick of a man's success.

By ten, Joseph was a successful petty thief; by fourteen, although an altar boy at his local church, he was organising girls for American soldiers who arrived in the war. To augment his earnings he stole from soldiers' jackets and trouser pockets; money, a watch, gold rings.

In his teens, a homosexual first mate picked him up on Kingston dockside and smuggled him aboard a Welsh cargo ship. On the voyage across the Atlantic, Joseph was buggered by most of the crew. He did not complain about this, nor did he enjoy it, but when he jumped ship at Cardiff he stole as much of their paying-off money as he could find, and then drifted naturally into the lawlessness of Tiger Bay.

Here, with others of different races and colours, he stole from ships, from cars, from houses. If anyone resisted, he would slam them in the face with his right hand – a fearful blow, for he wore three jewelled rings on each finger. These rings were not simply for defence; they were also instant collateral, should he ever need to convert them into cash to buy a stolen camera or portable radio that a recognised fence thought too risky to handle.

Joseph pushed drugs, dealt in stolen goods, and organised half a dozen prostitutes. This he found the easiest and most agreeable way to make money; he decided to stay with it.

In spite of Joseph's slight stature, his fuzzy red hair, his thick negroid lips and vicious face, he possessed an animal attraction for women – a fact he discovered at the age of thirteen. Boys would examine and compare each other's private parts – ('You show me yours and I'll show you mine') – and he realised then that he was better endowed than any boy, and most men. His friends enviously nicknamed him Iron Bar.

News of Joseph's noble proportions spread rapidly among girls, reaching even their mothers' ears. At first some were sceptical of the rumours, then interested, and, finally, entranced. The knowledge of his power over women gave him confidence. He always lived with the prettiest prostitute. No girl ever left him, unless he wished to be rid of her. If she attempted to do so, a beating-up would follow. If she still refused to return, she would receive a ritual carving of her face with a razor blade inside a potato.

Rosa knew how her son lived, and in a curious way was proud of his sexual ability, but of little else about him. He was a disappointment; he could have done great things – been an entertainer, a politician, perhaps even a priest. Instead, he was a ponce. Now she knocked at his door with caution, because Joseph shared her uncertain temper, and to back it up carried a flick knife tied by an elastic band to his right forearm beneath his sleeve. He also smoked ganja, the Jamaican equivalent of Indian hemp, and was sometimes confused as to people's identities or intentions; better to be safe than slashed.

'Come in,' he called and she entered the room. A naked bulb hung from the ceiling with a fly paper encrusted with dead flies tied to its flex. A tumbler of whisky was on the table, among old milk bottles and dirty dishes crawling with blue-bottles. Joseph lay stretched fully clothed on his bed; he had not even removed his shoes. Even under his clothes, the bulge in his trousers was of remarkable size. She envied his women and hated them, but none with the intensity she reserved for Betty.

'How long are you on your own here?' she asked.

'Till Betty comes back. She'll be early. It's raining.'

'I don't know how you can live off a woman like that,' she began.

'I'm following my father's example,' he retorted.

'You make me sick. All you got is a big dong and big talk. No pride. No job. And you can't find any better way of making money than living off an English tart.'

'Do you expect me to work on the Underground for five pound a week?'

A timid knocking on the door interrupted them: Rosa looked at her son enquiringly.

'That your English whore?'

Iron Bar shook his head.

'She has a key,' he said.

The door opened. A white youth, thin, with long hair and a narrow, vole-like face, came in. He was puffing busily on a cigarette.

Rosa sniffed.

'You'll have us all arrested, smoking that stuff. Who are you?'

'He works for me,' said Iron Bar. 'Keeps an eye on some of my girls.'

'You asked about Betty,' said the youth, pointedly ignoring Rosa. 'I told you she'd been meeting a regular every week. Man who comes in a flashy car. Now, each time, she gives him a parcel or an envelope.'

'Do you know where this man lives?'

'Yes, Bar. I followed him. Eaton Place.

He gave the number.

'You've done well.' Iron Bar nodded a dismissal, and the youth crept away.

Iron Bar considered the situation for a moment. Clearly, Betty must have been holding out on him. He would have to investigate the matter, or, rather, have someone else look into it for him.

A struck-off solicitor, Mr O'Flaherty, who lived on the top floor, and whose legal opinion he sometimes sought, had advised him against involvement in anything that could conceivably lead to trouble.

'Always let others do the hard stuff,' Mr O'Flaherty told him. 'Then, if anything goes wrong, they go down and not you. You've a perfect alibi elsewhere.'

'What if I haven't?'

'Call on me, dear boy. I'll always speak up for you.'

'But you mightn't know where I'd been?'

'Then you'd tell me, so I would know.'

'So your whore has another friend?' said Rosa mockingly.

'Get out,' said Iron Bar, 'before you make me angry.'

Next morning, Iron Bar went to work at Waterloo. Sometimes, he worked there or at London Airport, depending on where the next group of West Indian immigrants were due.

They arrived full of hope, remembering the false promises of touts in their home villages who had sold them steamship tickets at inflated prices. They wore bright clothes which had seemed fashionable in Jamaica or Trinidad, but which in the grey grime of Waterloo station looked pathetically symbolic of their total lack of preparedness for a new life in a cold country.

They piled their luggage in the centre of the platform and set off in search of relatives and friends who had promised to meet them. Everything was strange, and they might be away for ten or fifteen minutes. During this time, Iron Bar and his team went to work.

Each bought a platform ticket, and, carrying a huge suitcase in each hand, they walked slowly along the platform as though trying to find friends among the new arrivals. In fact, they were looking for quick profit, which they always found. Not only were their suitcases empty, but they had cut out the bottoms, with another long slit near the handles. When they saw another slightly smaller suitcase, the more expensive the better, they would drop their empty shell over it, grip the handle through the hole and saunter off the platform.

Back in Bar's room they would sift over the contents of each case. Frequently, they found a family's life savings wrapped up for security inside a shirt. They might make two or three forays during the day to Waterloo or the airport. Each brought in at least fifty pounds, sometimes two or three times as much.

On this particular morning, however, Iron Bar rose late and so had only time for one trip. Betty had not come to see him and he felt concerned, although sometimes she went back from her beat to her room in Earls Court. It seemed that she had recently been doing this more frequently than in the past, and in the light of what he had been told, these absences became sinister. In the afternoon, Iron Bar went to a dimly lit basement club in Notting Hill. Off-duty whores sat on bench seats around the walls, smoking and chatting. Men, mostly West Indians, gambled at small card tables. A record player blared 'Lemon Tree'. There was plenty of rum to drink and ganja to smoke, and in the heat and darkness the exiles were briefly transported to earlier, warmer lands and lives.

Iron Bar sought out two men he sometimes used to bring a prostitute into line.

One was large, just beginning to run to fat; a former fairground wrestler. The other was smaller, but broad in the shoulders. He made some money playing gangsters in low budget films at Elstree and Shepperton Studios, and rather more by persuading bookmakers' clients that it would be less painful to pay their gambling debts than to suffer a broken arm.

Now Iron Bar took them into the third room of the club, generally reserved for discussions of a confidential nature, and poured out three tumblers of rum.

'A frightening,' he began. 'I want you to find out who a girl is seeing every Friday.'

'Who's the girl?'

'My woman. Betty.'

'You breaking with her then, Bar?'

'Possibly. She's giving something – a parcel – to the man, a whitey. I want to know what it is and who he is. If she won't tell you, persuade her. No permanent damage to her face, though.'

'Where is she now?'

Iron Bar glanced at his watch.

'On the game. The north side of Bayswater Road. Take a car. Safer than risking a scene in the street.'

'How much?'

'Thirty between you.'

He peeled off six five-pound notes, gave three to each man.

'See you back at the house tonight?'

'Tomorrow,' said the big man. 'We got another job after this. Peter Rachman. Owns a lot of houses over our way. Wants one cleared. Worth a grand more if it's empty.'

Betty sauntered along the Bayswater Road, from Queensway Terrace towards Lancaster Gate. She wore a black costume, high-heeled ankle-strap shoes and carried a handbag. She allowed herself exactly two hundred paces in each direction. If a policeman stopped her, she would say she was waiting for her husband, who had gone to fetch their car which was parked in Leinster Terrace.

She took her two hundred steps, paused and turned. At that moment, a grey Humber pulled up alongside her. The wrestler wound down the side window.

'I am looking for a naughty girl,' he said with an exaggerated Oxford accent.

Betty smiled automatically, and then her face tightened when she recognised them. It was not wise to go with them when they knew Iron Bar.

'Well, you're not looking at one now, dearie,' she replied briskly. 'I'm waiting for two friends.'

'We're two friends. Both of us. Get in.'

He opened the rear door. Betty glanced along Bayswater Road. Almost incredibly, it was totally empty, except for a kerb-crawler two hundred yards away, moving west on the wrong side of the street.

'Well, short time only,' she said reluctantly.

The car accelerated away and swung through Victoria Gate into Hyde Park, and on towards the Serpentine. Here, several cars were usually parked after dark, but it was a risky place for a pro to work, for policemen had the habit of shining a torch suddenly through a window.

Half a dozen cars were parked now, side by side in the darkness, lights off, bonnets facing the shining expanse of water. The driver stopped about a hundred yards short of them, under the trees.

'I'll do it here, in the back, 'said Betty. 'A pound, short time.'

'Not for me, it isn't,' said the wrestler, leaning across her. She could smell his sweat, soaked into his clothes, and sugary rum on his breath. She hated him and all men who had bullied and insulted her, forced themselves on her.

'What do you want, then?'

'A talk.'

'Iron Bar know you're here?'

'He sent us. He feels you are tiring of him, love,' said the film man. 'Wants to know who else you got you give money to.'

'No-one. He knows that. I give him all I make, except twenty a week.'

'What about that man you meet every Friday?'

'I have several regulars on Friday,' said Betty stoutly. 'It's pay day.'

'But who pays who? You give this man a parcel every time you meet him.'

'That is a private thing. Nothing to do with the game. Or Iron Bar.'

'So you *are* giving him money?'

'Only what he's entitled to. What the hell is it to do with you, anyway – or Iron Bar?'

'Because you're his woman, and he's hired us. That's what.'

'I'm not his woman. I don't belong to anyone.'

'He thinks differently, Betty. He's put out, and you know how he gets when he's put out. You going to tell us what all this is about, or do we have to persuade you?'

'I'll tell you,' said Betty.

This gave her the chance to open her handbag. She searched carefully for a nail file.

In the darkness of the car they did not see it concealed in her palm.

'Well,' said the big man impatiently. 'We're waiting.'

'There's nothing to tell,' she said flatly.

'What?'

The wrestler gripped her arm. Betty shook him free, grabbed the handle of the door, pushed it down and out. The door opened. Before she could jump, the man grabbed her roughly and heaved her back.

Betty jabbed the sharp point of the metal file up towards his face. He instinctively jerked back his head, and took the point beneath his jaw. It dug deep into the soft flesh like a dagger blade.

He screamed in pain and surprise. The driver watched them anxiously in the mirror, at the same time keeping a look-out for any cruising police car.

The wrestler knocked away Betty's hand and pulled out the file. Blood streamed down the front of his shirt. He hit her across the face with the back of his hand, ripped her blouse in a fury. Then he seized her hair and slammed her head against the side window of the car.

'Now, talk, you bitch!'

The lights of an approaching car suddenly lit up the scene; blood-splattered upholstery, the wrestler holding a folded handkerchief against his chin, still shaking Betty furiously with the other hand.

The driver held up one hand to shield his eyes from the blaze.

'Get her out, for Christ's sake!' he cried, recognising the car as a Wolseley. 'It's the fuzz!'

The wrestler seized Betty by the back of her jacket, and threw her out on the grass. The driver raced away, back towards Bayswater Road. The other car came on slowly, then passed. It was not a police car. The driver was only looking for a place to park.

She crawled beneath a bush and lay on the grass, sobbing and trembling. Then she saw the Humber return, also travelling slowly, headlights on, while the two men searched for her. She lay still. They would never think she was still where she had fallen. The car passed by without stopping.

She stood up, and, still trembling, began to run across the bridge over the Serpentine. On the other side, she left the road and walked across beneath the trees towards Prince of Wales Gate and the lights of Kensington Road.

She had lost the heel from one of her shoes, but she still had her handbag. Her blouse was ripped and stained with blood, her hair dishevelled. Under the street lights she would look like the victim of a car accident. Perhaps that was what she should tell any policeman who stopped her?

It was obviously impossible to go to Iron Bar's place now.

She would take a taxi to her own rooms in Earls Court. Then tomorrow she would decide what she had to do; nothing ever seemed so bad in daylight.

Carton hailed a taxi. He and Nina climbed inside and he closed the sliding window that separated them from the driver, so she guessed he was going to make a pass. As he leaned across her, she smelled the mingled and unattractive odours of hot sweat and cigar smoke she associated with him. In her mind, one represented his humble background, and the other the rich expense-account life to which he aspired so desperately. To her surprise, Carton did not make a pass at all. Instead, he grabbed her hand and held it tightly. His palm, as always, felt damp and soft.

'That man at the party,' he said excitedly, 'the one I introduced you to. In the grey suit, with the pipe. If Labour wins the election, he'll be Prime Minister.'

'Are you likely to win?'

'If I didn't think there was a chance, now that Churchill has finally resigned, I'd give up.'

'To do what?'

'I'd go into business, I suppose. I'm already on the board of two of Paul's companies. He tells me I have an eye for wheeling and dealing. And if I can be elected on to two boards, then I can get on to ten. It's like being a rich man's girl friend. Once you're in that league, you go from one to another.'

She drew away from him slightly.

'Like me?'

'Of course not like you. I wasn't thinking of you at all.'

Carton kissed her clumsily. His lips were sticky and tasted of a non-vintage sweet champagne. Surreptitiously, she put up her hand to wipe her mouth. In his clothes, his tastes, his whole life, Carton was cheap and shoddy and he disgusted her. But he was useful; he was her card of entry into a world of politics and power.

'Staying the night?' he asked her.

Nina did not reply. She usually spent Wednesday and Thursday nights with him, then drove down to stay in Hove with the heir to a brewery fortune, who lived alone in splendid style. A peer, who had invested a few hundred pounds in Paul's firm when it first started, would entertain her in the early part of the week at his country house in Dorset.

What Carton had said was quite true; once you were on the right social level you could move from one rich lover to the other. And he had introduced her to both these other lovers. Of course, there was the danger that, like a trapeze artist, you could fall. It was imperative therefore for a girl like her to marry somebody rich or to make enough money to secure her independence. Neither was easy to achieve. She could never forget that she was only a whore on a high level, and younger, prettier girls were always close behind her. How different life had turned out to be in England from her innocent imaginings in Austria!

Originally, Paul set Nina up in a flat in Southport, and took her onto the pay-roll of his company. He saw her most weekends, an arrangement that lasted for nearly a year, until Rachel discovered it. A friend of hers saw them walking down Lord Street in Southport one Saturday morning when Paul was supposed to be in London for a conference about the new commercial television broadcasts on Channel Nine.

Two weeks later, Paul telephoned Nina and asked her to meet him in a wood off the main Southport to Manchester road. Early in their relationship they had agreed on this meeting place equidistant between their two homes in case of any emergency, for it was virtually impossible for anyone to follow them.

Nina parked alongside Paul's Bentley and climbed in beside him.

'Rachel knows about us,' he said at once, in a dull, flat voice. 'Someone saw us in Southport and told her. She hired a private detective. He soon found out your address. If we go on, she'll divorce me.'

Nina said nothing. This was the moment she had known must come one day. But now that it had arrived, she felt hurt, unsure of herself and her future. She could see tears on Paul's face.

'If she does that, I lose my son,' he went on.

'How do you mean, lose him?'

'She will get custody. English courts always give custody to the mother when the father's to blame. As it is, her people hate me. They've done all they could to turn the boy against me.'

'But when he is older, Robert will realise that you and his mother just didn't get on, and that there are always two sides to every question.'

'Maybe. But he's only ten. If he goes, he's gone for ever, and I couldn't bear that.'

She was not going to make it easy for him, for she felt a smouldering resentment that he had not taken her feelings into consideration.

'If I stop seeing you, Rachel says she'll forget all about the affair. But of course she won't. Women don't.'

'Why should they?' asked Nina. 'I won't forget.'

'So I have to stop seeing you. I have no alternative, really. You do see that, don't you?'

Paul looked at Nina pathetically, trying to will her to answer in the affirmative.

'I see your point of view,' she agreed. 'But what about me? Did you never think that I might love you, genuinely love you?'

She didn't, of course. She never had, she never would, but she knew she had to salvage as much as possible while she could.

'I will keep you on the payroll for as long as I can,' Paul said, not answering her question, hoping to buy her off. 'I may have to get rid of you – only technically – for Rachel is a major shareholder and can check on all employees. But I'll take you back. You might have to change your name, though, to fool her.'

He tried to laugh at the suggestion.

'I had hoped to change my name to yours,' Nina said coldly.

He put out his hand and touched her face. She drew back instinctively. She wanted no maudlin fumblings and weepings now.

'What about the flat in Southport?'

'Keep it on for, say, six months, until you know what you're going to do.'

'At thirty pounds rent a month, that's £180 you would save if I left now.'

'Well, I suppose so.'

'Give me the money instead. I'll find something else cheaper.'

'I'm not paying you off,' Paul protested.

'You are certainly not pensioning me off,' she retorted.

'You will keep in touch?' he asked her anxiously. 'How will we know where to send your salary?'

'I will write,' she said. 'Care of the main Post Office in Manchester. It's goodbye, then?'

'For the time being.'

He reached towards her once more and again she drew back.

'Don't kiss me. Don't touch me. I know your son means so much to you, but surely you could have found a different way to do this, a kinder way?'

'What would you have done? Tell me.'

'It is too late now. It is all too late now.'

Suddenly Nina felt that she would burst into tears if she stayed for another minute, and she could not bear to let Paul see her cry. She ran to her car and accelerated away wildly, showering his Bentley with a fusillade of stones from her spinning tyres.

By the time she had reached Southport she was calmer, and next morning she telephoned Douglas Carton and explained her predicament. He was married, but his wife was insane and in an asylum. Nina moved in with him at the end of that week, ostensibly as a political researcher. Carton introduced her to several other men. There were discreet lunches in private rooms at hotels or in town houses. Then, weekends in London, in the country, in Paris. Some of her liaisons died very swiftly; three had lasted. But all could easily end as quickly as her affair with Paul. Nina was determined that this would never happen again; she had not escaped from the prospect of slavery to be paid off by rich men, and then by the less rich, and finally to end up on her own, without money, resources, looks or hope.

The taxi stopped outside Carton's house in Chester Square. They would go out to dinner later, but first there was the ritual love-making in his big four-poster bed in the second storey bedroom, overlooking the square. Carton was vigorous and greedy as ever, but he was never a disappointment. Afterwards, they lay naked under a single silk sheet.

Suddenly, Carton glanced at his watch, bounded out of bed and switched on the television that faced them. On the black and white screen, wearing a business suit, he sat facing an earnest young interviewer. This was not the Carton she knew, sweaty and lustful like a middle-aged satyr, but calm, sincere, idealistic, a man who eschewed wealth and luxury, whose heart was with the people. As he talked, the camera moved in so that his face filled the screen.

'. . . And in the next Labour government, of course, while we would welcome and encourage enterprise of all kinds, we would clamp down most strongly on the get-rich-quick merchants and property developers. Why should one man labour with his hands or brain for a few pounds a week, while his neighbour makes – and keeps – thousands, by what is simply a knack with figures?'

'I like that phrase,' said Carton. 'A knack with figures.'

His hand moved down from Nina's breasts. She wriggled away.

'I'm listening,' she said, frowning. 'Don't interrupt.'

'What are your views on the proposed commercial television channel?' the reporter asked obsequiously.

'Quite honestly,' replied Carton earnestly, 'commercial TV – or as its backers like to call it – independent televison – is a total non-requirement. It is absolutely inessential. We have in the BBC one of the finest television services in the world. Why should we now put money into the pockets of advertising agencies and advertisers to produce something which *must* be inferior? There is not a thinking man or woman on either side of the House who is one hundred per cent in favour of it. I personally am totally against it. So are my friends in the trade union movement, and the Parliamentary Labour Party.'

Carton switched off the set.

'So that's where I stand.'

'That's where you lie,' she said, running her toes along his ankle.

'Do you like me?' he asked suddenly.

'Of course,' she replied mechanically. Why did men seek this absurd reassurance? Was it likely that a woman naked and in bed with the questioner would reply other than as he expected?

'There is a reason for asking,' Carton went on. 'I want you to do me a favour. Simply a business deal.'

'For whom?'

'Well, me actually. But of course I would give you a very nice present if it comes off.'

'Go on.'

'You heard my views about commercial television? Well, despite the fact that a lot of people are against it, it is going to start, you know. And it *is* quite a good idea – it must help firms to sell more goods, if they are advertising right in your home, with moving pictures.'

'So why are you against it?'

'Party policy. I have to follow the line. But to go back to my proposition. These people are having a hell of a job getting it off the ground. There are less than a dozen of them beavering away. They have written to the chairmen of companies and to all kinds of businessmen, to show business people, in fact to anyone they think might be interested, because they want a sub.'

'What for?'

'To finance the companies that are going to bid for the franchises. If they are successful, then they will have to find offices, studios, buy equipment, hire staff.'

'Won't the banks back them?'

'You would be amazed how hard it is to raise what the City calls risk capital. There is no security whatsoever here. Nothing the investor can exchange for cash – yet. No property, no freeholds, only the possibility that we will make a profit.'

'*We?*'

'Well, I have been asked to invest. I'm putting in two thousand pounds.'

'Despite what you have just said in that interview?'

'That is the favour I'm asking you. I can't very well invest in my own name, can I? But I could in yours. I would give you the money, and you would send a letter with your cheque for the same amount, for forty-thousand one-shilling fully paid-up shares.'

'I have a hundred or two saved,' said Nina. 'Could I buy some in my own right?'

'No way,' Carton replied emphatically. 'You could have done, even a week or two ago, but now it is too late. The thing is closed. Will you do this for me?'

'Of course.'

'Then if the company succeeds and goes public, you simply let me have back the shares, and Bob's your uncle. I'm rich.'

'You talk too much,' Nina said dreamily, and drew him down on top of her.

Max coasted his Phantom III Rolls Royce to a standstill in the Bayswater Road, switched off the engine and sat, waiting for Betty to appear.

He was using the Rolls for a few weeks because he had bought it at a knock-down price. It was one of several older, larger cars that had not reached their reserve at his last auction. Cars like these were becoming difficult to sell now that smaller new ones were available.

Just after the war, prospective buyers had to wait two or three years for a new car, depending on the popularity of the model they wanted. Now, most cars could be bought off the showroom floor, and pre-war cars decreased in value at every sale.

Earlier that morning, Keith – who had recently finished a course in mechanical engineering at the local technical college, and worked full-time for Max – pointed out that in the last three auctions an eight-litre Bentley, a V12 Hispano-Suiza, two sleeve-valve Daimlers and an Isotta-Fraschini had not attracted a single bid. All their owners had asked Keith afterwards whether he knew anyone who would buy these cars privately for only thirty or forty pounds. New, they had cost two or three thousand pounds, but now, with spares expensive or impossible to find, they were a liability, and only fit for the scrapyard.

'We should buy these big, old, aristocratic cars ourselves,' Keith proposed to Max. 'In their way, they are antiques. One day they will be as rare as old paintings or furniture – and as valuable.'

'What if they aren't?' Max asked him.

'Then we can always sell them for scrap or parts. We can't possibly get less than we'll pay for them now.'

'Storage is the problem. If we let a lot of old cars lie out in fields, they'll just rot away or be looted.'

Max remembered Dick Carpenter and the lines of trucks in Corsica. What had happened to him? He had not seen or heard from Carpenter since they parted at London Airport after the trip from Bastia. How long ago that seemed now!

'My father is working as a civilian on RAF airfield maintenance,' said Keith, breaking into his thoughts. 'A man he knows has bought a disused airfield in Kent, and intends to adapt the runway for car and motorcycle racing. He doesn't need the hangars, though, and would be glad to rent a couple for twenty pounds a week. We could store a lot of cars in each one.'

'This man would pay tax on the rent?'

'Of course.'

'Then offer him fifteen a week – in notes. He'll then have money in his back pocket, but his books will show he's still carrying a number of hangars at a loss. So he'll make a cash profit and a tax loss. Meanwhile, any car of character that doesn't sell, you buy – up to a limit of thirty pounds a time. But no rubbish, mind. Go for the blue-chip names. Rolls. Bentley. Mercedes. Hispano. Delage. When we've bought up the cream, we can look at the others.

'Now, you thought of the idea, Keith, and I'd like you to share in its success – or failure. I put up the money, and you ferret out the cars; a divison of capital and labour. I also like your description of these cars as aristocratic. We'll form a firm, Aristo Autos, to handle them. Fifty per cent equity to you, and fifty to me. Agreed?'

'Marvellous,' said Keith warmly. 'I never expected that,

Mr Cornell.'

'Blessed is he who expecteth nothing, for he is never disappointed. And sometimes – only sometimes, mark you – he has a pleasant surprise.'

Betty climbed into the seat beside Max, and sank back thankfully.

'Let's get out of here,' she said nervously, glancing over her shoulder through the rear window.

'Trouble?'

She nodded, but said nothing until they were in Max's flat in Eaton Place.

Max poured her a large brandy.

'Tell me,' he said simply.

'The man I live with, name of Joseph Diaz, calls himself Iron Bar. Someone told him we were meeting every Friday, and that I would give you an envelope each time. He had me beaten up because he thought I was two-timing and not giving him all my money.'

'Ours is a totally different arrangement. Nothing to do with him.'

'He won't see it like that. I'm so scared, Max. I've moved from Earls Court.'

'He's bound to find you eventually. Can't you explain?'

She shook her head.

'He's not rational. Sometimes I think he is mad.'

'Give me his address. I'll see him and explain.'

'You're asking for trouble,' she said anxiously.

'No, I'll ask him for a business deal.'

'About the houses?'

'Well, other developers are already in Notting Hill doing up properties as they become vacant, and gradually the girls on the game will get the message. Once the properties are clear, we will do them up, split them into flats or sell them as family houses. Splitting profits down the middle, of course.'

'But why do this to me? Those houses are worth thousands.'

'I owe you a good turn, that's why. You had the idea in the first place. Anyhow, it's not entirely altruistic, for I still own the leases. Now, give me Iron Bar's address.'

# Thirteen

Four o'clock on an April afternoon in 1956, in the Brompton Oratory, London. The domed ceiling soared into an infinity of silence. Stone saints watched the only person there, a middle-aged man kneeling in a pew.

He wore a grey suit, a white shirt with starched collar and a slightly frayed Royal Navy Reserve tie. At last he stood up, bowed to the altar, made the sign of the cross mechanically with his right hand, and walked down the aisle, his walking stick tapping on the herringbone parquet floor. Near the memorial to commemorate those killed during the First World War, he paused to light a candle, and read the carved words: 'Dulce et Decorum est Pro Patria Mori'.

Maybe, he thought. But what happens to those who don't die? How does their country treat them then?

He paused for a moment in the porch, as a man does when he has too much time to kill. He was of medium height, slimly built, in his late forties: Commander Lionel Crabb, lately retired from the Navy, partly on grounds of age, partly as a result of government defence cuts. During the war, Crabb had been one of the first Navy frogmen, and for his remarkable dives to remove enemy limpet mines from Allied ships in the Mediterranean he had been awarded the George Medal. But now the war and warm seas were far away, and he walked slowly along the Brompton Road, oblivious of traffic and shoppers.

Usually, Crabb was cheerful, but today he was worried, and, unusually for him, he felt short of hope. In the past, someone or something had always turned up at the right moment.

As a young man he had served briefly in the Merchant Navy, then sold petrol from a Pennsylvania roadside garage, and later worked in a London advertising agency. When war broke out, Crabb joined the navy, and became one of their first divers. Equipment was primitive and improvised. There were no rubber suits, so he dived in swimming trunks. To give Crabb and his fellow divers added weight when under water, they fixed slugs of lead to the gym shoes they wore. Only later, by trial and error, did they wear weights around their belts instead of on their feet. When the war ended, Crabb finally had to retire, and once more began a series of odd and unsatisfactory jobs. He helped to produce a handbook on football pools. He worked for the owner of a fishing fleet calculating the size of shoals of fish reported by echo-sounders. Then he found temporary work in the Admiralty Research Laboratory at Teddington. When this ended, he was hired by a group searching for a sunken Spanish Armada galleon off the Isle of Mull. Then, for a secret government department, he examined the hull of the Russian warship *Sverdlov*, paying a courtesy visit to Portsmouth.

Now his savings had dwindled, and with them his faith in his future, and, saddest of all, in himself. A brief marriage had broken up some years earlier, and on that spring afternoon he felt particularly conscious of the fact that he was on his own, and growing older. A friend in the furniture trade had found him an office job, but that life was not for him.

As he entered the small bed-and-breakfast hotel in Knightsbridge where he rented a room, he looked in his pigeon-hole behind the reception desk, but the pigeon-hole was empty. He collected his key from the cuphook above it and began to climb the staircase to his room.

'Commander Crabb?'

He turned. A man had come into the hotel, and was smiling up at him. He was red-faced but younger than Crabb. He wore a double-breasted blue blazer and grey flannels. Crabb had last seen him in a basement office in the Old Admiralty Building more than a year earlier, when he had briefed Crabb about the assignment on the *Sverdlov*. He was a commander, name of Bates.

'Been waiting for you for half an hour,' Bates said almost accusingly. 'Where can we talk?'

'I've half a bottle of gin in my room, and no-one will disturb us.'

As Crabb led the way upstairs, he thought more cheerfully: it's an answer to my prayer. God works in a mysterious way, but He has received my signal. Message received and understood.

Crabb poured out two half tumblers of neat gin.

'Sorry I've no tonic,' he said. 'I was going to buy some this afternoon.'

'Never drink tonic,' Bates assured him breezily. 'Spoils the taste of the gin.'

He sat down in the only chair the room possessed. They clinked glasses in an unspoken toast.

'How are you fixed?' Bates asked him.

'Haven't done a bloody thing for nearly a year.' Crabb admitted freely.

'I have something that might interest you. Secret job.'

'Like the *Sverdlov*?'

'In that area.'

'Risky?'

'Crossing the road is risky,' replied Bates shortly. 'Keep your wits about you on this, and you will end up a couple of hundred quid to the good.'

'In this country?'

'Yes. A one-off thing.'

'What about getting in on the strength? I'm only forty-six. A lot of life left yet, you know.'

'Staff things are always difficult,' said Bates evasively, 'but I will put in a good word.'

'What does it involve?'

'I can't tell you here, but I have a car outside. We can go to someone who will fill you in.'

'I need a hundred now if I agree. Things are a bit rough when you've nothing coming in.'

'I see no problem there.'

They finished their drinks, and Crabb followed him down to his car. They drove to Covent Garden, almost deserted now, with the market closed. The wind blew sheets of newspaper along empty pavements. A tortoiseshell cat on an empty orange box watched them go into a building and climb the stairs to Blaikie's office.

To Blaikie, Crabb seemed smaller and older than expected. However, two other younger divers had already declined the assignment, and time was very short, so it was Crabb or no-one.

'You've signed the Act?' he began, meaning the Official Secrets Act.

Crabb nodded. 'Who exactly are you?'

'Never mind,' said Blaikie smiling, 'put me down as a member of a government department. Here's the proposition we have to make, on the absolute understanding that nothing *whatever* is ever revealed to *any* third party.'

'Go on,' Crabb told him. 'I've done secret jobs before.'

'I know, and splendidly. But never one like this. You will have read in the papers that the Russian leaders Khrushchev and Bulganin are on their way here for a state visit? They are coming in their latest cruiser, *Ordzhonikidze*, docking in Portsmouth. We understand they have a new gadget to confuse our sonar. Some part that sticks out into the water. We want you to have a look at it.'

'Easier said than done,' said Crabb. 'I will have to do it at night, and the water is so filthy in Portsmouth harbour that I'll have to do it virtually by feel. *Ordzhonikidze* is a hell of a big ship for one man to cover. During the war, when we searched for Italian limpet mines off Gib. or Malta, we had two or three divers for quite small ships.'

'That was then and this is now,' replied Blaikie. 'There is less risk of one diver being discovered than several.'

'There is also much less chance of one man finding anything.'

'Not necesssarily. We understand this gadget is fitted aft, near the propellers. To someone of your experience it's an in-and-out job. You know the fee. And now you know the task. What do you say?'

'I'd say it's bloody risky,' said Crabb.

The three men sat in silence, not meeting each other's eyes. Crabb was trying to calculate the risks, wondering how he could off-set them – if he could. Blaikie and Bates wished they had another, younger candidate for the job. No-one wanted to be the first to speak. Finally, Blaikie glanced ostentatiously at his watch.

'Well, there it is, Crabb. Take it or leave it. You will be doing a good job for us if you accept. But if you decline, I quite understand.'

'All right,' said Crabb in a resigned tone. 'I'm on. I've told the commander here I need a hundred down.'

'One hundred pounds in notes, now,' agreed Blaikie briskly, as though he had expected this request, or even already knew it. He opened a drawer, and from a cigar box counted out twenty five-pound notes.

'The rest when you finish the job. You know Portsmouth?'

'Pretty well.'

'We will book a room for you at the Sallyport Hotel in your own name, and another in the name of Smith, for someone else who is coming down with you.'

'An original name, Smith,' said Crabb drily.

'Well, there you are. Smith has a car. He'll pick you up in London at your hotel, day after tomorrow. Sixteen hundred hours.'

'What about the equipment?'

'That will be deposited in your hotel tonight in two suitcases. Give you time to see whether the wet suit and flippers fit and so on.'

'And if they don't?'

'Bates will be on hand if you have any problems.'

'I just hope to God this helps me get a job,' said Crabb fervently.

'Well, gentlemen,' said Blaikie hurriedly, 'that covers just about everything. I suggest we have a celebration dinner at my club when it's all over.'

Crabb and Bates stood up and left the room. Blaikie pressed a button. A middle-aged woman with grey hair put her head round the door.

'Find out where Max Cornell lives these days,' he told her. 'I want to buy him a drink.'

Max leaned back in his chair at his corner table in the

restaurant in Charlotte Street, exuding a confidence he did not entirely feel.

Across the table sat David Graham, the bank manager. He held a Ramon Allones cigar in one hand and a Hine brandy in the other. His expression was of enjoyment tinged with regret; he might have been a guardian about to admonish a profligate undergraduate ward over his unnecessarily expensive tastes.

'I don't want to be difficult, Max,' he said in the tone of voice which made Max realise that this was exactly what he was about to be, 'but your company, Quendon Construction, is overdrawn by nearly thirty thousand pounds. I am not worried myself, of course, but head office has suddenly become restive. They think you may have bitten off more than you can chew. The property market isn't very active right now. They'd like to see a bit of movement on the account.'

'They'll see it move like a rat up a drainpipe, within the next few weeks.'

'That is what I told them, if not quite in those terms. But you know how they are, still putting pre-war values on things.'

'When did they mention this?'

'This morning, actually. I was on to them about something else, happened to mention I was seeing you, and they brought it up.'

'Did you ring them?'

Graham drew on his cigar to conceal his embarrassment.

'As a matter of fact, no. They rang me.'

Max nodded. This meant that the bank was becoming anxious; that was always dangerous when you owed them a lot of money. If they foreclosed now, he could be finished.

'My security's good,' he pointed out. 'I have the money from Mulheim and the property at Erith and all this stuff in Notting Hill.'

He did not add that the bank did not hold all his securities; the danger about keeping all one's eggs in a single basket was that they could all be broken.

'There are those houses in Fulham, too.'

'But nobody lives in Fulham,' said Graham.

'Well, Fulham's cheap now. Two thousand quid a house, freehold. Less, if it's tenanted. Within five years it'll be ten thousand a house, and in ten years, who knows?'

'The future sounds very promising, the way you tell it,' Graham admitted grudgingly. 'But what worries head office is what is happening *now*. This development of yours down in Kent, for example. Katyn Nominees developing Goatshill Park. Nothing seems to be happening at all. Not a single brick laid. I know, for I asked our local manager to have a look. And what odd names.'

'I chose them for sentimental reasons.'

'Well, what's in a name, eh, as the poet said? What concerns the bank is, what's the profit potential?'

The development was a fifty-acre country estate Max had bought cheaply outside Maidstone. During the war, the army had used it, and a rash of Nissen huts sprang up around the old Georgian manor house, with two concrete roads to carry army trucks. Max had bought the whole estate on money borrowed from the bank on the assurance of an official in a local planning department that permission would be given for the house to be split into flats and the grounds redeveloped. An envelope containing a hundred five-pound notes had changed hands with a view to accelerating this authority, but the promise had only been verbal, and unfortunately the helpful official died next day in a car crash on the Rochester by-pass.

'We'll get action on it.' Max reassured Graham now with a confidence he did not really feel.

'So you keep saying. But when?'

'Soon. Very soon.'

They were the last two customers in the restaurant. Max paid the bill and led the way to the door. The Bentley Continental he was using waited outside.

'Drive you back to Sloane Street?' he asked Graham.

The bank manager shook his head.

'Thank you, no.'

The huge car's metallic red paint work glowed like rich wine in the early afternoon sun.

'You don't *need* a car that size,' he said irritably. 'If you want to borrow more money, you should cut down a bit.'

'The car's not mine,' Max explained. 'It was in the auction and didn't reach the reserve, so I'm using it meanwhile. Now, when is the deadline for this movement you keep on about?'

'The end of this month. About ten days. I've never queried your judgement so far, and I don't now. But remember, it's not my bank.'

'Stay with me,' Max told him. 'Then one day it may be.'

He climbed in behind the wheel of his car and drove back towards Eaton Place. He had intended to visit Iron Bar later in the day, but that would have to wait. Instead, he turned south towards the river. He would drive to Kent and have a look at Goatshill himself. For reasons he could not comprehend, he felt uneasy. The bank had never been on his back before. Why should they suddenly have become so concerned?

The stone posts at the gateway to the original drive were battered where countless army drivers in three-ton trucks had cut the corner too closely, and weeds sprouted out of cracks in the concrete roadway. In the distance, hump-backed roofs of Nissen huts loomed like tarred burial mounds. Max stopped in front of the house. Several workmen, who had been leaning on their shovels when he approached, now began to hack at the ground in a frenzy of simulated effort. Just for a second, their movement brought back a memory of other men digging the long graves at Katyn. What would these labourers think if he told them? A man came out of a hut: Max's foreman on the site.

'Any news?' Max asked him.

'Nothing good, sir. I've just heard on the grapevine that the application was turned down at last night's committee meeting. But they're allowing us to keep the internal roads in order.'

'Kind of them.'

'I'm going to risk putting in a section of new road on to the old, sir, so it's ready when permission finally does come through. If there are any questions we'll simply say we're repairing what is already there.'

'Good.'

'If you could come back in a day or so, sir, just to check the line?'

'If I can, I will. But I think it's doubtful. Ring me if there are any snags.'

He nodded farewell, climbed into his car and drove back to his flat. He now employed a part-time secretary and she had gone home, leaving a note on his desk. Mr Blaikie would like him to join him for a drink in Claridges that evening. Any time up to seven-thirty.

Blaikie was in the lounge, reading the *Financial Times*, a large whisky and soda at his elbow.

'Must be years since we met,' he said in greeting. 'You look prosperous.'

'I cover my losses,' Max agreed cautiously. 'And you? Still in the same business?'

Blaikie sighed and shook his head in self-deprecation, as though he really must make a change, but somehow simply could not bring himself to leave a life he loved.

'Is this meeting business or pleasure?' asked Max, looking at him quizzically.

'Pleasure to see you again after so long, old boy,' Blaikie assured him warmly.

'What about the business?'

'We can discuss that if you are free for dinner tonight.'

'Where?'

'My flat.'

Over a meagre meal of cold ham and salad, Blaikie outlined his proposal.

'You'll have read that Bulganin and Khruschev are on their way here in a Russian cruiser? An old friend of yours is with them. Vasarov. Butcher, you used to call him. He's virtually running the KGB, you know. We used to call it the NKVD. Now it's the KGB or the GB as we pros call it. Stands for *Gosudarstvennoj Besopasnosti*, meaning state security.'

'I thought that General Ivan Serov – Ivan the Terrible, according to the press – was in charge.'

'Serov may be the head so far as the outside world is concerned. But Vasarov is the neck that moves the head.'

Max nodded without much interest. Thankfully those meetings after dark two miles inside German or Austrian forests were all behind him.

'We still keep in contact with Butcher. Off and on.'

'How?'

'You can't expect me to tell you that. But it's very difficult now that he's mostly in Moscow. That's what makes the chance of seeing him so valuable. He always liked you, you know. He trusted you. Now he wants to meet you again.'

'Where?'

'Aboard this cruiser, for a start. All kinds of people will be welcoming the party officially to Britain. Then Bulganin and Khrushchev come up to London to meet the Prime Minister, and for junketings of various kinds. We can get you aboard the ship easily enough with a press card.'

'What would I do then?'

'Listen to whatever he has to say.'

'Surely Butcher won't say anything much when he is surrounded by his own people?'

'He may suggest another meeting. Or you could. There might be a chance to show him Windsor Castle or the Tower of London. Anything to get him on his own. We'll fix all that for you.'

'What's in this for me?'

'The crucial question, my dear chap. What do you want?'

'Not to get involved,' Max replied at once.

'I thought you might say that. And, naturally, the decision is yours, entirely and absolutely. But we could help you – obliquely, of course, and very, very discreetly, over this planning permission that's causing you some headaches in Kent.'

'I'll get that in the end.'

'No doubt. But it could take time. These things can. And the bank, so I'm told, is growing restive.'

'I'm beginning to see the light,' said Max.

Blaikie was smiling; Max knew his guess was right. Blaikie must need his services badly.

'And if I agree to help?'

'Then I think that you will find that planning permission is granted at the next committee meeting, after which I believe the bank will be more reasonable.'

'Only believe?'

'Within these four walls, I can put it more strongly. I know.'

'In that case, I haven't any option, have I?'

'I'm glad you are going to be co-operative.'

'But why me? Why not one of your pros? I've been out of this for years.'

'Which is what makes you so valuable now. We never know for certain who's been compromised among the pros – if any have. But we're pretty confident the other side isn't on to you. Oh, I nearly forgot. One other thing. We'd like you to give a lift to Portsmouth to a retired naval officer, name of Crabb.'

Next day, events moved swiftly. Blaikie produced a nondescript Hillman Minx car for Max, with a driving licence in the name of Smith. He also came to Crabb's hotel to introduce the two men. While Crabb loaded the suitcases of diving gear into the car boot, Blaikie briefly explained Crabb's assignment to Max.

'But why should I be involved in what he's doing?' Max asked him. 'It seems ridiculous to risk my cover as well. Are you trying to save two rail fares to Portsmouth, or what?'

'Surely the reason's obvious,' Blaikie retorted. 'If Butcher's people make enquiries – and be sure they'll have contacts in Portsmouth – they will check you out, and find you are staying with an old naval friend in a quiet hotel, because, as a free-lance journalist accredited to a couple of small magazines and a Scottish weekly newspaper, you are unable to throw money about as you might if you were on the *Express*, say.'

After Blaikie left Max, he walked thoughtfully along Knightsbridge to the Hyde Park Hotel, where he ordered a large whisky, and sat, looking out over the Park and the trees with spring foliage. He wished he was young again –

young and rich. Then he thought of the risk that Crabb was willing to face for two hundred pounds.

How ironic, he thought, that he and I have achieved so little financially, and Max has achieved so much – and from nothing. He felt an almost physical wave of bitterness at the constant economies he was forced to practise while Max drove a Bentley, lived in Eaton Place, had his suits made in Savile Row, and shirts in Jermyn Street.

He knew all this because he had checked him out thoroughly when he sought for a lever to use to persuade him to see Vasarov. He also knew about the houses in Notting Hill and the deal with Mr Mulheim. With each new revelation his envy grew, and with envy grew the feeling of frustration and resentment. Here he was, middle-aged, with only one arm, and passed over for preferment. Others had overtaken him, moved up through the shadowy echelons of Intelligence to become ambassadors, or out to join the boards of important companies. He would stay where he was now until retirement. And then, what? He would not be rewarded with a K, the knighthood that marked the end of a successful career. He might get a CBE, although an OBE was probably all he could count on. That, and his pension – about enough to pay the petrol bill for Max's car!

He had the authority to send a man on a dangerous mission to any part of the world; he knew sordid secrets about nearly every head of state, but this power and knowledge had little market value in the real world. They still only paid for a shabby car, ready-made suits, and serviced an overdraft that nagged him like a stomach ulcer.

Blaikie finished the whisky and ordered another. He put it down to expenses. He crossed to a telephone. While he dialled the number he thought of the final irony of his situation. While Max could probably afford to buy a distillery, he had to cheat to pay for a second drink.

Max and Crabb drove in silence through the suburbs, south-west towards Portsmouth. Max wore a dark blue suit and a trilby, and carried a notebook and press card in his raincoat pocket. Crabb wore a dark blue blazer, grey trousers and a white roll-neck sweater. He smoked constantly. For some time, neither spoke, and then Crabb turned to Max.

'You know what I have to do?' he asked awkwardly.

'Only in the most general terms. Know what *I'm* doing?'

Crabb shook his head.

'Only that you've someone to see in Pompey.'

'Just as well,' said Max thankfully. But an uneasy thought crossed his mind. If he knew about Crabb, was it not also possible – even probable – that Blaikie had also told Crabb more about him than Crabb thought prudent to admit?

'As I understand it,' he went on, 'we are old friends from way back.'

'Like an hour back,' said Crabb with a grin.

They drove in silence for a few more miles, then Crabb said, 'The more I think about this, the less I like it.'

'I am not so wild, either,' Max admitted.

'I am not usually superstitious,' Crabb went on. 'But I hate the thirteenth.'

'But today isn't the thirteenth. It's the sixteenth.'

'Agreed. But I got offered this job on the thirteenth. I was also one of the divers who went down to the *Truculent* when she sank six years ago. That was Friday the thirteenth, of all days. Everyone aboard her was lost. Then my marriage broke up on the thirteenth. And I got involved in an abortive hunt for a sunken Spanish galleon off Tobermory on another thirteenth. I just don't like the number. It's bad news for me. Always.'

'But not this time,' Max assured him cheerfully. 'Do you have a lucky talisman?'

'I did have a piece of jade I bought in Singapore before the war. Then a friend let me down over a debt, and I had to sell it. Thought it must be worth hundreds, but all I got for it was seven quid. Now I have this old swordstick.'

He tapped his walking stick.

'You won't need that in Portsmouth Harbour.'

'No,' agreed Crabb slowly. 'What I will need in that harbour more than anything else is some very good luck.'

They booked into the Sallyport Hotel, and went to their separate rooms. Crabb had brought half a bottle of gin with him in his case, wrapped in a shirt. During the war – as he told Max – he never drank before diving, but as Blaikie had unnecessarily reminded him, that was then and this was now. He poured three fingers of gin into his toothglass and sipped slowly. Such was his unease, he did not even taste the spirit. He then emptied his pockets of his driving licence, cigarettes and wallet, put them in a suitcase and locked it. Like most sailors, years of living in a confined space aboard ship had made him very tidy in his habits.

He had removed name tabs from the corner of his handkerchiefs and the inside pocket of his jacket before he left London. Nothing could identify him if anything went wrong. His diving equipment was civilian, and nothing about it or his clothes could in any way associate him with the navy. He was simply an unidentifiable, middle-aged man.

Crabb lit a cigarette, and blew smoke at his reflection, comforting himself with the recollection of wartime dives undertaken successfully in far more dangerous conditions. But then he had been one of a team, with friends aboard a launch or in the submarine. There had been a joke, a pat on the back, rum when he returned. Now, he was on his own. And he was older.

Crabb removed his watch. He stubbed out his half-smoked cigarette, ran both hands through his thinning hair, then carried his diving gear downstairs in its suitcase. The time was exactly nine-fifteen. As Bates had promised, a taxi was waiting outside the hotel, engine running, 'For Hire' sign unlit. Crabb climbed in without a word. He guessed that the taxi was as phoney as Smith's name. If not, why hadn't the driver asked him for his destination?

In silence, they drove up behind the city, towards the nineteenth-century forts, now deserted, and somehow menacing in old red brick, streaked with ivy. Shuttered windows stared blindly towards the darkening sea where toy warships lay at anchor. The driver turned into a cobbled yard off the road and stopped. He opened the boot, lifted out Crabb's suitcase and crossed to a dark blue Royal Navy pickup van. A petty officer put the suitcase in the back of the van. Still no-one spoke. They might have been mummers acting out a play in dumb show.

The taxi driver switched on his 'For Hire' sign and cruised away. Crabb climbed into the van beside the petty officer, and drove down to the dockyard. Over the roofs of the houses he could see the great bulk of the *Ordzhonikidze*. Her enormous superstructure, masts and radio antennae were ablaze in a brilliance of searchlights. No-one had mentioned that the ship would be floodlit. He would never have accepted if he had known, for it increased the risk of discovery enormously. How had he ever become involved in this farce? If anything went wrong, Blaikie, Bates and Smith, whoever he really was, would carefully melt away, and he would be on his own. And all for a hundred pounds down, and most of that already spent on settling his debts. He had been an idiot.

A dockyard sentry peered through the window at driver and passenger, then the red and white striped boom went up. In the dockyard, criss-crossed by railway lines, they drove out to the farthest corner of the perimeter, and stopped behind a huge shed with a saw-tooth roof.

'Here we are, sir,' said the driver, speaking for the first time.

'Do you do much of this?' Crabb asked him, suddenly anxious to make human contact, for someone to joke with, someone to wish him good luck.

'Quite a bit, sir. A lot of underwater tests going on all the time, sir. You'd better change in the back of the van. I have a rope ladder to let you down.'

Crabb undressed quickly. The sooner he was in the water, the sooner he would be back. He put on his wet suit and his flippers, trying to reassure himself. No doubt Blaikie had been quite right; this would be an in-and-out job. Be back in the hotel in an hour to finish that gin.

Crabb climbed out of the van and walked clumsily in flippered feet across cobbles and the sunken railway lines. The petty officer had secured one end of the rope ladder to a giant bollard. Crabb adjusted his mouthpiece and mask, checked the valves on the two oxygen bottles, and began to climb down the wooden rungs into the water. The ladder swayed slightly under his weight. His stomach muscles tightened; he tasted gin again in his mouth.

Spars of wood and floating orange peel nudged green beards of seaweed. The tide was low. He should have checked high water time before he had agreed to dive, for this again made his task more dangerous. He would have at least six feet less water above his head. Six feet. The depth of a coffin in a grave.

Crabb took a deep breath, released his hold on the ladder and sank gently beneath the oil-streaked, scummy water. The petty officer sat smoking behind the wheel of his van. His orders were to wait for precisely thirty-five minutes. Then, if his passenger had not reappeared, he was to leave and drive back to barracks.

Beneath the filthy water, it was both darker and colder than Crabb had expected – or perhaps he had forgotten the loneliness of his work. He checked his luminous wrist compass, and then set out for the Russian ship. He always experienced a sense of timelessness under the water's surface. The slow, deliberate rhythm of swimming produced in him an almost soporific feeling. Periodically, he stopped, gently trod water, and checked his bearings.

Soon, he sensed rather than saw the enormous bulk, the deeper darkness of a ship. This must be the *Ordzhonikidze*. He moved more slowly now, until, raising one hand, he touched the smooth domes of a line of rivet heads. He had arrived.

He swam carefully along one side until he could make out the dim outline of the starboard propeller, high as a house, incongruous as a gigantic undersea carving. It seemed impossible that any engine could be powerful enough to make these huge blades revolve. He began to feel his way along the hull towards the starboard propeller tube. He would start his search here and then slowly move across to the port propeller.

The two Russian frogmen, who had been waiting patiently for the past twenty minutes on the blind side of the great rudder, saw the trail of small bubbles, then the shadowy outlines of Crabb's legs as he trod water.

One frogman switched on a portable underwater searchlight. Its beam bored through the murky sea. A propeller stood out in enormous silhouette. Crabb saw the light, but only dimly. To him it seemed diffused, like the headlamp of a slow-moving car in an old-fashioned London peasoup fog. So someone else was down here, too, he thought with surprise. He wasn't alone, after all.

When he left Crabb in the Sallyport Max walked to the dockyard, presented his Press pass to the naval security guards on the gate, and to an interpreter from the Russian embassy, who accompanied him up the gangway.

'You are late,' the interpreter said regretfully, almost accusingly. 'The Lord Mayor of Portsmouth and his party have already been received by Marshal Bulganin and Mr Khrushchev. Your colleagues were all on time.'

'The journey took longer than I expected,' Max explained.

'You should live in Russia,' the interpreter told him with a smile. 'We have distances of thousands of miles, yet our trains always run on time.'

Some to Siberia, thought Max, as he followed him to the quarterdeck. A Russian naval band played music beneath a scrubbed canvas awning. Their brass instruments gleamed gold under the unshaded bulbs. A generator hummed somewhere in the depths of the huge vessel, and they passed the open window of a radio room from which static squealed and spat. Two Russian sailors opened the swing doors of what Max took to be the wardroom. The interpreter indicated that he should enter.

'You will find your colleagues in here,' he explained. There was a sudden burst of light from photographers' flash bulbs and a haze of smoke. Stewards in white jackets carried trays of vodka and champagne, and plates with squares of toast covered with black caviare. Max took a glass and waved aside the plates. He could never see caviare without remembering the leaking casks in the Russian train; to taste it again would have made him physically sick.

Khrushchev, bland and beaming, Bulganin with his goatee beard, stood surrounded by security men, local dignitaries and reporters. Max kept well away; he did not want to increase the risk of being photographed by a concealed camera. Then he saw Vasarov, also a little apart from the rest, chatting to a British naval officer. An interpreter was with them, looking at each man in turn as they spoke.

'Excuse me,' Max said deferentially. Vasarov looked at him enquiringly, no hint of recognition in his eyes.

'I represent the *Scottish Weekly Review*. If you have any free time available, my editor – who served in the British Royal Navy on convoys to Russia during the war – wishes you to be our guest, to show you anything, either in England – or Scotland, of course – that you might wish to see.'

'I am sure there are others with me who would welcome such an opportunity,' replied Vasarov.

'Unfortunately, sir, very few speak English.'

'Of course, I forgot. You are an island race and so you only know your own language! It is a kind and comradely gesture of your editor, but unfortunately my schedule is very tight. We travel to London tomorrow, to meet your Prime Minister. Members of the ship's company will also see the Tower of London, where I believe, you shortened by a head many of those who disagreed with your politics years ago!

'On the following day I pay a private visit to the tomb of Karl Marx at Highgate, where I am told one of your Lord Mayors of London, Dick Whittington, heard the bells ring out a message, "Turn again, Whittington". Perhaps a place where communists and capitalists have something in common? But I cannot allow your editor's invitation to go unanswered. Come with me a moment to my cabin. I have a book in English translation about some of the glories of my country. I would like to inscribe it for him.'

The interpreter spoke quickly in Russian. Vasarov smiled and shook his head.

'He said he will get it for me,' he told Max. 'But it will only take a moment. Come with me.'

They went along a corridor, climbed down a companionway. Vasarov took a bunch of keys from his pocket and unlocked a steel door. Max followed him into the cabin. Vasarov locked the door behind him, immediately picked up a note pad and wrote: 'Highgate Cemetery 1600 hours'.

Max nodded. Vasarov burned the page with a cigarette lighter. He picked up a book.

'Here is the book,' he announced. 'Tell me your editor's name and I will make it out to him personally.'

The reception desk at the Sallyport was empty when Max returned. As he removed his bedroom key from the hook, he noticed that Crabb's key was still hanging there. He sat down to read the *Portsmouth Evening News.*

The Lord Mayor of Portsmouth had issued invitations for his annual ball to the Russian officers. Directors of Portsmouth Football Club had invited two hundred and fifty Russians to watch the match between Portsmouth Reserves and Fulham Reserves. A cocktail party for the Russians would be held in Portsmouth City Council Chamber and a dance for five hundred at the Savoy. Certainly, the local welcome for the visitors was sincere enough. But what sort of treatment could Crabb expect if the Russians discovered him?

At exactly half past midnight, Max put down the newspaper, walked to the telephone booth in the hall, and dialled the number that Blaikie had given him to ring.

Bates answered immediately.

'Smith here,' said Max. 'My cousin seems to have been delayed. Is he staying with your relations?'

'No,' replied Bates uneasily. 'I haven't heard a word. I will be over to see you in any case at ten tomorrow morning.'

Max replaced the receiver. Bates arrived on time and went up to see Max in his bedroom. There was still no sign of Crabb.

'One of our people picked him up from here in a taxi,' Bates explained. 'Then a petty officer took him in a naval truck to the harbour. A pleasure launch took a lot of rubber-necks round the cruiser this morning. We put a man aboard, but he reported no sign of any body or gear floating. There are no reports of anyone being washed ashore either. Half an hour ago, though, a fatigue party of Russian sailors were seen in a ship's boat around the *Ordzhonikidze*'s stern, and a Russian diver went down.'

'You don't send a diver down in harbour on a state visit unless there's trouble, surely?'

'It might have been a routine check.'

'And it might have not. Are you monitoring their radio?'

'Yes. No increase in signals. We've tapped the land line to the telephone exchange, but nothing except arrangements for the journey to London.'

'Crabb was too old for this sort of thing,' said Max. 'If he had a stroke under water, his weights would pull him down. It might be weeks before a body comes up. Or maybe the Russians had divers guarding the hull, and they captured him – alive or dead.'

'Only you, Blaikie, Crabb and I know a damned thing about this job,' said Bates accusingly.

'What about whoever thought it up in the beginning? Or your taxi-driver?'

'The driver only had to pick Crabb up here. I'll have to report to Blaikie there's been a balls.'

'I'll wait here until afternoon. If there's no news by then, I can give you a lift back, if you like.'

'Thanks,' said Bates. 'That gives us a bit more time. If he doesn't show up, you pay the bill and take his bag. Now, what about a drink?'

'Bit early, isn't it?'

'If we were in the South China Sea, it would already be too bloody late,' retorted Bates aggressively, and pulled out a hip flask.

At half past five Max was back in his room. There was still no sign of Crabb.

Max searched his room closely, stripped the bed and examined the wardrobe, but Crabb had left no clues as to his intentions.

'I'll pay for us both,' Max told the manager. 'I'm taking my friend's stuff back. He has been called away unexpectedly.'

He and Bates drove slowly out of Portsmouth to join the London road.

'Nothing?' Max asked him at last.

Bates shook his head. He had run into some former naval colleagues, now based ashore, and they had held a heavy drinking session for most of the afternoon. He leaned back thankfully in his seat. Whirling images fumed through his clouded mind. Someone must have split on Crabb; that was the only explanation. Crabb was no chicken, agreed, but he was fit. The job was nothing for a man of his experience. Why, he would only need to be near the bloody ship for ten or fifteen minutes. His equipment was the best that could be found. His oxygen cylinders had been tested and were spot-on. His wet suit, flippers and mask fitted perfectly. His snorkel had the latest double valve. Bates had personally checked Crabb's medical history, and knew that his heart was good, blood pressure low for his age, physical condition excellent. Crabb had been killed, or captured, or both.

Bates shuddered, thinking of death deep below the filthy harbour water. He spoke, almost without meaning to.

'Crabb's a goner,' he announced thickly, alcohol slurring his voice.

'How do you know?' Max asked him sharply.

'Well, he isn't here, is he? I suppose there is a chance he's come ashore somewhere with loss of memory or injured, but that's pretty remote. And if he had, it must have been reported by now. Of course, I rule out Blaikie entirely.'

'Rule him out? What do you mean?'

'As a stool-pigeon. A double – who told the Russians.'

'But that's absurd.'

'What is? To rule him out?'

'Why rule out Blaikie specifically? After all, he asked him to do the job. Or rather, you did.'

'Agreed. But he didn't know where Crabb would actually get into the water. Nor did I. All we knew was that it must obviously be somewhere near the ship.'

'I didn't know, either,' Max pointed out.

'But you knew he was bloody well going to the cruiser.'

'Obviously. We all did. Even the petty officer must have thought it odd, this chap carrying out underwater tests last night, of all nights.'

'They do it all the year round,' replied Bates. 'Nothing odd in that.'

He sat in silence for a minute, remembering another name,

another reference in the secret files he had examined before he left London.

'You were with that pansy professor, Tobler, when he died, too, weren't you?' he went on.

'Yes.'

'Convenient, wasn't it?'

'Not for me, particularly.'

'You knew him well?'

'Not at all. During the war, he lectured my commando. I just thought I'd look him up.'

'Hadn't you seen him since the war, then?'

'No.'

'So what made you suddenly visit him after a gap of eleven or twelve years?'

'I'd been meaning to do so for years, but then I read an article about him, with his address, so I decided to drop in on him. That's all. Nothing sinister, as you seem to infer.'

'Haven't said so, have I?'

'Your tone of voice speaks for you.'

'Well, he's dead, isn't he?'

'That's right.'

'Maybe for you, Mr Smith, but not for me. And another thing, your name isn't Smith or Cornell. It's Kransky. I checked it out. You're a foreigner, a German Jew.'

'Czech, actually,' said Max easily.

'One's allegiance is to the country of one's birth.'

'In many cases, yes. But this is my country now. After all, I served in the British army, and then did three more years working for Blaikie in Germany. That should prove something.'

'Only that for some reason you wanted to work your passage. And yesterday you went aboard the Russian cruiser and told them what Crabb was up to. We had a bloke hidden in the back of a van photographing everyone who came and went. I saw his pictures this morning.'

'Tell Blaikie about it. then. That's his department. I only carry out orders.'

'Whose bloody orders?'

'You're pissed,' said Max in disgust.

'No. Just pissed off with people like you, who claim to be one thing but are actually another. There is no-one else so well placed who could have blown Crabb's cover – just as there was no-one else on the spot who could silence Tobler.'

'Silence him?'

'Yes. Special Branch were going to pull him in for a chat. My view is the other side got wind of it – and got you to shut his mouth for ever.'

'You're mad,' retorted Max angrily. 'Drunk and bloody mad.'

He looked at Bates with contempt.

'See what Blaikie says.'

'I've already been on the blower to him, don't worry. Told him I had a very good idea what had gone wrong. And who was to blame. And why.'

'But you didn't tell him what you are telling me, now?'

'Not on an open line, I didn't. But, my God, I will as soon as I see him.'

'I'll come with you,' Max promised. 'It should be an interesting meeting.'

Bates did not reply. Max looked at him sharply. The commander had fallen asleep, head back against the seat. His mouth hung open. Soon, he began to snore.

Max glanced at his watch. He could easily make a detour and have a look at that road his foreman was concerned about, before this idiot woke up. That would save a special journey from London. The moon was nearly full and he should be able to see all he wanted. So, with Bates snoring loudly by his side, Max turned off the London road, along the A25 towards Maidstone.

Once inside the estate, Max stopped the car gently. He had no wish to hear any further accusations: Bates' theory about Tobler's death was too close to the truth for comfort. He climbed out of the car and stood looking at the newly laid concrete. The pit for the drainpipes was half full of cement. A truck of ready-mixed stood nearby. The men had done well to lay so much so quickly. Next morning they would finish the whole road. Then all Max needed was permission to begin building.

Bates suddenly shouted from the car: 'Where the hell are you?'

Then he saw Max standing by the edge of the new road and lurched towards him. His shirt collar was undone and his tie loose.

'What are we doing here in this bloody place?' he asked belligerently, his voice still thickened by alcohol. 'What's going on? You were going to drop me off at my home in Sevenoaks, not out here.'

'I'll take you on, don't worry,' Max assured him. 'Get back in the car.'

'Don't you damn well order me about!' shouted Bates. He came unsteadily towards Max and thrust his red, sweaty face into his.

'Come on.' Max took his arm.

Bates shrugged himself free and then aimed a blow at Max's jaw. Max dodged to one side, but slipped and took the blow on the side of his head.

'Bloody Red,' grunted Bates and followed his advantage with a left hook. Max jumped back out of range and then seized Bates' arm and pulled with all his strength. Bates did not expect this defence and fell forwards. He regained his balance, took a pace to one side, and slipped on loose earth at the edge of the pit. For a second, he wavered, then dropped full length into the cement. He thrashed about in agony and panic as the soft mass clung to him, closing over him like a grey quicksand. Max searched for a ladder or a pole to put into the pit, but everything had been removed.

He stood at the side, meaning to jump in. Then he paused. Once in, he could not possibly get out again, for the sides of the pit were sheer and deep. If only Bates would turn over, his face would be out of the cement and he could breathe and stay afloat until Max could break into the foreman's hut and find a ladder or a length of rope. But already Bates had stopped moving. He had landed with tremendous force and face down. Almost immediately, the cement would fill his mouth and nostrils and he would choke to death.

Bates' arms suddenly ceased to move. The back of his blazer disappeared beneath the surface. Within seconds the cement lay smooth and shining and still beneath the moon.

Max walked back to the car, climbed in behind the wheel, and sat, aghast and wondering what he should do. This had been a disastrous assignment. Crabb disappeared, probably dead; Bates drunk and certainly dead. Now someone would surely point out that his presence was the only common denominator in the disappearance of three men, not two.

Max decided to dump Bates's suitcase in a quarry he had seen earlier, off the main road near West Malling. Eventually, someone would be bound to find it. They might steal the contents, of course, but if they did he had lost nothing. And if they did not, but reported their discovery to the police, he could gain a great deal.

Max started the engine, and drove onto the road before he switched on his lights. Only when his car had been gone for nearly ten minutes, did a solitary figure detach itself stealthily from the darkness of the overgrown trees. The figure moved like a shadow and then was gone, leaving the estate empty under the moon and stars, its secret secure beneath the setting cement.

# Fourteen

Max drove slowly down Swain's Lane in Highgate, between high brick walls, to the cemetery. Three black Zis saloons, with diplomatic registration plates, were already parked on a patch of gravel opposite wrought-iron gates. Half a dozen broad-shouldered men in blue serge suits stood near them, apparently watching nothing, seeing everyone. Vasarov called from the back seat of the first car. The security men drew back and bowed deferentially as he climbed out.

'I will show you the grave of the man on whose teachings our great communist empire has been built. Karl Marx,' he announced importantly.

They entered the gates, past a red granite mausoleum with the carved inscription 'Dalziel of Wooler', opposite two other huge granite tombs on the left, with the names Strathcona and Mountroyal and Pocklington; on along the weedy path towards the centre of the cemetery. The afternoon felt unusually hot; the air filled with the drone of bees.

Vasarov took out a silk handkerchief as though to blow his nose, but instead held it loosely over his mouth.

'Do the same,' he told Max. 'It prevents any lipreader with binoculars picking up our conversation.'

Max put up his hand as though stroking his upper lip when he replied.

'Do they suspect anything?'

'I am not sure. I hope not. But all the old guard are going. I am the only one left. First, Beria. Then Molotov. After him, Malenkov. Then Voroshilov. Kaganovich will be next to go. Mikoyan was the first to denounce Stalin – and now I wouldn't give much for his chances.'

'Who will come out on top?'

'Khrushchev for the moment. He loathes Bulganin, and will get rid of him as soon as it is safe to do so.'

'And after Khrushchev?'

'God knows. But I have survived a long time, and no lucky streak lasts for ever. Everyone who knew too much has met a violent end. It is a tradition going back to the Revolution. I want to break from it while I can.'

They reached the huge grey stone head of Karl Marx, bearded and sombre, towering above the other tombs. Vasarov wiped his eyes, as though moved by the sight.

'After this amateurish business of the British frogman around our ship, security is much tighter. We have had all kinds of gifts from well-wishers – books, chocolates, dolls for the crew's families, and so on. They are all opened, and cut into pieces in case any of them contain anything sinister.'

'In my car I have a bottle of whisky for you, unwrapped. Nothing sinister in that, I assure you. Wet the label. Then you'll be able to see an emergency number to ring in Paris, and two recognition words for you to give and receive.'

'But I cannot possibly telephone from Russia. You must know that.'

'You will have to go to some other capital, then. On a trade delegation, with a touring ballet company. Something like that.'

'I hope someone picks up what I am going to say. It may help to show my loyalty.'

Vasarov blew his nose, put his handkerchief in his pocket.

Then he read the inscription, written in gold letters on the tombstone: '"Workers of all lands, unite. The philosophers have only interpreted the world in various ways. The point, however, is to change it."'

'How true that is,' said Max, speaking slowly for the benefit of any lipreader. 'I would like you to come and have dinner with me so that you could tell me about this thinker. Could you manage tonight?'

'It would have to be late. I already have two official appointments this evening.'

'Say ten o'clock, then. At my flat. It is the custom in this country to entertain guests at home. You can leave your chauffeur outside.'

He gave Vasarov his address in Eaton Place, and his telephone number as they walked back to the parked cars.

The security men sprang to attention. Max watched Vasarov drive away.

At ten o'clock he was waiting in his study. The heavy curtains were drawn, and the room had a pleasantly masculine aroma of cigar smoke and leather and furniture polish, the scent of money. Between the curtains and the windows, Blaikie's men had hung temporary curtains of thin metal foil energised through a transformer so that the room was totally screened from any known eavesdropping equipment.

The front door bell rang. Max took his guest's coat.

'You will leave your driver outside?' Max asked.

'He is content. He has the car radio, and plenty of your English cigarettes. I must tell you that I have already eaten one dinner.'

'Then I will give you food for the mind rather than the body,' Max told him. 'You are quite secure, by the way. The whole apartment is sealed.'

He led the way across the hall, and opened the double doors to a sitting room. It was in total darkness. He pressed a switch, and the room erupted in a blaze of light.

Vasarov gasped in amazement at what he saw. Fifteen men of various ages were seated in a semi-circle facing the doorway. All were smiling; several stood up to greet him.

'I can't believe it,' whispered Vasarov. 'It is a trick.'

For here, coming forward to shake his hand, was General Brodin, a deputy chief of the army staff, who had been killed in a plane crash outside Kiev.

Next to him was a smiling Professor Borinsky, the atomic scientist and winner of a Stalin Peace Prize, whose funeral Vasarov had attended only weeks before. There were aircraft designers, doctors, commissars, and even a colleague from his own ministry, who had been killed in a car accident in Gdansk.

Was he imagining this? Was this some phantasmagoric nightmare induced by tiredness, dope or brandy?

He turned to Max, seizing his arm in alarm.

'It's all right,' said Max reassuringly. 'The deaths were simply to hide from the public that these men had all come over to the West. Some now live in America. Others in Australia and Canada. Some are living here. My people wanted to reassure you that when the time comes for you to leave there will also be a safe harbour for you.'

'And a state funeral, too, I hope,' said Vasarov drily.

Mr Goudousky closed the trellis door of the lift as quietly as he could. The impressively impersonal opulence of the building in Berkeley Square, its thick carpets, heavy curtains and huge bowls of flowers in the entrance hall, combined to encourage such deliberately delicate movements. Silently, scarcely breathing, Mr Goudousky crossed the corridor to Sam Harris's flat.

A Spanish maid opened the door. He had never visited Harris at home before, and his auctioneer's eye hung price tags on everything he saw. An eighteenth-century gate-leg table, Chinese vases, an early French bronze, an ormulu clock on a mantlepiece; no rubbish here. But then, of course, he wouldn't expect to find any. Sam Harris was a very rich man.

Frosted double glass doors edged in gold opened from another room. Sam Harris came through, a goblet of whisky in one hand. Even the glass was cut, Mr Goudousky noted with admiration.

'Bit early, isn't it?' he asked Harris jovially. The visible signs of wealth lifted his usually cautious heart.

Harris shook his head. His face was grey, and he looked as Mr Goudousky imagined that he might look in ten years' time, but not now; not when he was doing so well.

'What's the matter, Sam?' he asked, concerned by his appearance. 'You ill?'

Harris shook his head. He waved Mr Goudousky to a chair and sat down heavily himself.

'Just had bad news,' he explained. 'My son. He's dead.'

'I'm sorry,' said Mr Goudousky, and meant it, because he hoped that this news would not affect the purpose of his visit. 'What was it? Car accident? So many maniacs on the roads these days.'

'No. I am sorry to say he took his own life. Climbed into his car with a bottle of whisky, shut the garage door and started the engine.'

Mr Goudousky shook his head sympathetically.

'What a terrible thing. I mean, why did he do it? Money worries?'

'No. He was all right financially. Came over here before the war with me, changed his name to Harrow after the school, and started up Harrow Radio. One of the big five in the business now. Or he was.'

'I've got a Harrow television set,' said Mr Goudousky as though this was important. 'Marvellous reception, beautiful tone. In a genuine wooden cabinet.'

'His wife was the real trouble,' said Harris, as though Mr Goudousky had not spoken. 'They never got on. She discovered he'd got a girl friend and said she'd leave him unless he dropped the other woman, and take the boy with her. His only son. He worshipped that boy. So, of course, he stopped seeing this woman. Then he discovered his wife was two-timing him.'

'He put the button on her, I hope? Bought some law?'

'He wanted to. I think he'd have married the other woman if he could, and this time he thought he'd have a chance to keep the boy. Then his wife sprang the news that made him take his own life – the boy wasn't his!'

'Did he look like him?' Mr Goudousky asked curiously.

'He bloody well ought to,' said Harris bitterly. 'Father was his only relation. His cousin.'

'No?'

'Yes! Fellow called Max Cornell.'

'Cornell? Name rings a bell,' said Mr Goudousky evasively. 'But about your son. I had no idea. Best if I go, I think.'

Harris shook his head, took a swig of whisky.

'You came here to talk business?'

'But at this time?'

'Why not? Take my mind off it. Have a drink, will you?'

'Not so early, thanks.'

'What's your proposition, then?'

Mr Goudousky paused before replying. He had rehearsed this scene in his mind so many times that now he was about to play it, he did not wish to muff his lines.

'It's a killing, Sam,' he said simply. 'The big one. After this, we can both get out.'

'Why do you want to get out?'

'Well, the Registrar of Friendly Societies is poking his nose a bit deeply into our building societies. Wants to check they're being run on the right lines and all that. I can still stall him for a while, of course, but it only wants one of those Labour MPs to get wind of things and stand up in the House and start shooting his mouth off, and we're for it.'

'May never happen,' said Harris briefly. 'And if your idea's so good, you won't give a damn if it does. What have you in mind?'

'You know Dolphin Square is the biggest block of flats in Europe? Well, there's a complex of flats in South London – Lesney Park – that runs it a close second. Built in the mid-thirties, and never shown a profit.'

'Why not?'

'Because the flats are let unfurnished and the tenants are rent-controlled stats paying bugger all.'

'So what's in it for us?'

'A fortune,' replied Mr Goudousky simply. 'The owners have got themselves over-extended in some overseas deal and need money – fast, otherwise they're down the hole. The block brings in about two hundred thousand pounds a year. I reckon we could buy the whole issue for under two million.'

Harris snorted. 'If the owners are short, they can't expect to sell on a ten per cent return. Offer them one, top whack. The whole place is probably very run down, anyhow. Take us a year's profit to do it up.'

'I've thought of that. I said, under two. At first we'd only tart up the outside, repaint corridors, put down new carpet in the entrance hall. Nothing more, Then we approach each tenant and ask them the one question no tenant can ever answer satisfactorily. Why pay rent? Why not buy their flat? We'll offer them a ninety-nine year lease each, at say two thousand five hundred pounds.'

Sam Harris nodded approvingly.

'We buy the building through the Union Flag – and lend the tenants hundred per cent mortgages on the Golden Star,' explained Mr Goudousky.

'Over as long a time as we can,' said Harris. 'So they'll be paying no more than they're paying already in rent. It's an offer impossible to beat.'

'On these figures we break even when we've sold around four hundred flats. We then pay off our debt before anyone starts asking questions – and are left holding sixteen hundred flats worth four million quid – clear.'

'We must form a company to do this, you and me,' said Harris.

'That was my intention,' agreed Mr Goudousky. 'If you weren't interested, of course, I'd go elsewhere.'

'Go no further,' urged Harris earnestly. 'I'm more than interested. I'm on.'

'This is, of course, against all the rules of running a building society,' said Mr Goudousky.

'So who's to worry?'

'No-one. But we will have a very dodgy few months when we'll be absolutely nailed to the wall, until we can start shifting the flats. Then we're over the hump and home.'

'That's the way I read it, too,' agreed Harris. 'But so long as you get the paperwork right, we can't lose. It's the double-headed penny. Now, if you will excuse me, I have to go north to clear up my son's affairs.'

At that moment Sam Harris was not a very happy man. He was gravely concerned about Paul Harrow's suicide; not over the death itself, but as to whether Paul had left a note behind him. A death in God's time, by accident, age or illness, was one thing; taking one's life, another. Suicides tended to leave letters of explanation for their decision, making excuses for themselves, blaming others.

Paul Harrow could say what he wanted in such a note, of course, but nothing that would involve him. For Sam Harris had a secret that only Paul Harrow knew, something so dangerous that it must never be revealed. Made public, it would not only lay bare the innermost and most devious recesses of his soul; far more important, it would destroy his credit and credibility, and ruin him for ever.

Max stood bareheaded by the side of Paul's grave and watched the clergyman throw a handful of dust on his cousin's coffin.

'We therefore commit his body to the ground. Earth to earth, ashes to ashes, dust to dust. In sure and certain hope of the resurrection to eternal life.'

Max glanced across at Rachel in her black costume, her face covered by a veil, who, also looked down at the scattered earth on the polished oak coffin lid. She raised her head slowly, as though she felt his gaze. Her son Robert was with her. He wore a grey suit, with neatly pressed short trousers. His shoes were highly polished, his hair well-brushed. Max had never seen the boy before, and smiled at him. Robert did not smile back. Max was a stranger; his mother had taught him never to acknowledge any greeting from a stranger.

Some mourners dropped roses on the coffin until they obscured the brass name-plate. Rachel walked away, hand in hand with her son. Others, mostly business acquaintances, members of Paul's firm, let her go. After all, hadn't she helped to precipitate her husbnd's suicide by threatening to leave him?

Max parked his Rolls next to Rachel's Sunbeam-Talbot. They shook hands formally. She turned to her son.

'Robert, I want you to meet your father's cousin, Max.'

The man and the boy shook hands gravely and walked into the house.

'It seems odd, me being hostess,' said Rachel. 'I was leaving him, you know.'

'I know.'

'Poor Paul,' said Rachel. 'It's all very sad and pointless to end like this. We were never right for each other, not from the start.'

'I guessed that.'

'He had someone else. You knew that, too?'

'I did. My former wife.'

A hired waiter presented a tray with glasses of champagne. They took one each.

'To better times,' said Rachel.

Max raised his glass obediently.

'We have only one life,' she went on, 'and so many options we could take. Why do we always choose the wrong one?'

'Not always,' he corrected her. 'Only sometimes.'

'Speak for yourself,' she said.

'Always, then. Where are you living now?' he asked her, to change the subject, to drive images of death from his mind.

'I have a flat in Romiley. But I think I'll sell up and move to London.'

'Won't you be lonely there?'

'Not really. I have Robert. And lots of friends.'

'Perhaps you'll marry again?'

'Maybe. But not for money. I have been left the majority of the shares, you know.'

'So you're a rich widow?'

'If not a merry one.'

Rachel put out her hand, lifted a second glass of champagne. Her lacquered nails were reflected in the silver tray.

Max looked with distaste at faces sweating and flushed with free drink. A woman wolfed two smoked salmon sandwiches and licked her fingers inelegantly. A man furtively pocketed a handful of Turkish cigarettes from an alabaster box. Across the heads and shoulders of these strangers he suddenly saw Sam Harris. Harris saw him too and turned away deliberately. Then Max recognised Clara, standing in a doorway. As their eyes met, she also turned. He followed her into the kitchen.

'I came here once during the war,' he reminded her.

'I remember, sir. You are Mr Cornell.'

She looked around nervously, as though fearful in case anyone should overhear their conversation, or even see them together.

'I have a message for you.'

'For me?'

Max looked at her in surprise.

'From your wife, sir. Will you ring her at this number?'

Clara pressed into Max's hand a piece of paper on which she had scribbled a telephone number. He put it in his pocket without looking at it.

Clara turned away to pick up a tray of chicken vol-au-vents. Max went back into the sitting room. Rachel was standing on her own, of the crowd but not with them.

'I wish I had known him better,' Max said.

'No-one knew Paul really well. He was like you, from what

I hear. Only really interested in building up his business, in getting richer all the time. Brought him security, I suppose. He was a very insecure person.'

'Did he have any money worries?'

'No. I do know that. But when I found out about his affair, a solicitor told me I could divorce him, get a huge settlement and the custody of my son.'

'So he dropped Nina?'

'At once. He loved the boy above everyone and everything. They simply doted on each other. He was so afraid of losing him. It was very wrong of me to trade on this.'

Rachel paused, examining the bubbles in the champagne as though making up her mind about something.

'We can't talk here,' she said suddenly, and led him into an ante-room and closed the door. Then, 'You don't know why he killed himself?' she asked rhetorically.

Max shook his head.

'It was because of Robert. I told Paul he wasn't his son.'

'Was he?'

'No. You of all people must know that.'

'Me? Why?'

'You're the father, that's why. Didn't that ever strike you as possible, when you think how old Robert is?'

Max smiled, not in amusement, but almost sadly.

'No. I never thought of it.'

'My God! How like a man. I can't believe it.'

'But Paul and Robert got on well together, didn't they?'

'Splendidly. People used to remark how close they were, how like Paul the boy was, and so on. I couldn't stand it, because I knew the truth. Finally, Paul and I had that row and I wanted to hurt him. So I told him.'

'You're wrong, you know. Quite wrong.'

'In telling him?'

'In what you told him. Medically, I can never be a father. I was a prisoner of the Russians as well as of the Germans. They beat me up far too badly.'

'But you *must* be!'

She looked at him with agony in her eyes.

Max shook his head.

'If you don't believe me, I will undergo any medical tests you like. It is absolutely impossible for me to father a child.'

Rachel sat down shakily, put her hand across her eyes. Champagne slopped from her glass across the arm of her chair.

'So I've been wrong all these years,' she murmured. 'My God. Poor, poor Paul.'

'Poor you,' said Max gently.

She shook her head.

'Please,' she said. 'Please go. I'll be all right in a few minutes.'

Max came out into the sitting room and the babble of conversation hit him like a blow. He picked up another glass of champagne from a passing waiter's tray, waited a few minutes and then left.

He drove slowly out of the gates. A Ford Consul was parked two hundred yards down the road. The driver flashed his lights twice as Max approached. Max stopped. The driver crossed the road and handed him a brown envelope.

'Any trouble?' Max asked him.

'None at all. The lock was child's play, and the safe about a hundred years old.'

'What did you find?'

'The will of Paul Harrow, deceased, and a note he had left for his solicitor. I photographed them both with a Minox camera. Here's the film.'

'Thank you.'

Max took a smaller brown envelope from the car door pocket.

'Five hundred pounds,' he said. 'In used notes. Count it if you want.'

'I trust you,' said the man.

'Trust no-one,' replied Max, and, smiling, drove on. He stopped at the next telephone box, dialled the number that Clara had given him: the Midland Hotel, Manchester. A page brought Nina to the telephone.

'I must see you,' she said.

'Why?'

'A business matter,' she explained. 'Something you should know about. It could be very profitable.'

He glanced at his watch; it was only four o'clock. He could meet her for tea and still be back in London for dinner.

'I'm on my way,' he told her.

Nina's appearance had changed since he had last seen her. Charles Jourdan shoes, hair by John of Knightsbridge, Kutchinsky jewellery and a Piaget watch could transform the plainest woman, and Nina had never been plain. Now she looked smooth, urbane, sophisticated – and disturbingly attractive.

They sat in a corner of the huge lounge.

'What was it like, the funeral?' she asked him.

'Better than a wedding,' he replied. 'At least it was final. Did you love him?'

'No. But I liked him. He was gentle and successful. A rare combination in a man. I think maybe he loved me, or thought he did.'

'That's often the same thing. Sometimes better.'

A waiter brought them tea and cakes.

'Do you live up north still?' Max asked her.

'No. I have a flat off the King's Road. I only came north to say goodbye to Paul – and then I lost my nerve. I couldn't face seeing Rachel and wondering how many of the other guests knew about Paul and me. But I thought you would be there, so I telephoned Clara. She was always kind to me – she hates Rachel, you know. And I asked her to give you the message to ring me.'

'Are you staying the night here?'

'I may. I don't know yet.'

'Now, about this profitable deal.'

'It's in commercial television.'

Max made a face.

After years of lobbying, a commercial television service had finally started in London that September. Other companies were due to start broadcasting over the coming months. But so far the prospects for commercial television looked bleak. Advertising revenue was low, for while newspapers such as *The Daily Express* had sales of more than four million copies a day and could command a readership of at least four times as many, by the end of the first twelve months barely one and a half million sets in London, the Midlands and the North would be able to receive ITV programmes. This represented less than a quarter of BBC viewers. In addition, the new commercial television companies had faced formidable development costs.

'Not much hope of profit in commercial TV,' said Max. 'I read that Associated-Rediffusion have already lost £3,250,000. Other companies are losing at the rate of three hundred pounds *an hour*, whether they are transmitting or not.'

Nina nodded.

'That's what Paul thought. He mortgaged his factories to invest in Pennine Television – under a holding company's name, of course. Principally, because he hoped to get a contract for much of the electronic work. And recently the banks have been getting worried about their money.'

'How do you know? You haven't been close to him for years.'

'He still came to see me when he desperately wanted someone to talk to. Someone who wouldn't use whatever he said against him.'

'Did he die owing money?'

'No. He cut his losses, and remortgaged the factories.'

'So who is paying Pennine TV's bills?'

'At the moment, the banks are frantically looking for someone. I thought of you.'

'How much is owing?'

'Two million for an eighty-five per cent stake.'

'I haven't got two million,' said Max instantly.

'You don't have to have it in cash, you know.'

'Agreed. But you still have to show you can raise it if the chips are down. What are Pennine's prospects?'

'A gold mine,' she said. 'The viewing figures are just starting to climb. Very slowly, agreed. But when millions have sets that can pick up Channel Nine, advertisers will be fighting for space.'

'How long until that happens?'

'I think two years at the most. Possibly less.'

'Where can I see the figures?'

'Paul gave me the latest balance sheet when I last saw him.'

She opened a briefcase. Max ignored the huge list of losses, and glanced at the list of fixed assets: studios, offices, concreted car parks, fifty acres of land with planning permission for studios or expansion of ancillary buildings, all on a thirty-year mortgage at four per cent fixed.

'Two million,' he said thoughtfully. 'That's the asking price. What do you think the banks would take to get out?'

'If you take over the debts, a lot less, I'd say.'

'Never mind what you say, Nina. What do they say?'

'Ask the head man.'

'Where is he?'

'At the end of this lounge.'

'Clever girl. You thought I'd be interested?'

She smiled.

'It did cross my mind.'

They walked down the long lounge on the thick carpet, past tables set for afternoon tea, reflected in rococco mirrors. An oldish man was reading *The Evening Chronicle*. He lowered it as they approached.

'Mr Cornell?' he asked, standing up.

'This is Lord Mallett, head of the bank consortium,' said Nina.

'You have a proposition to make?' Max asked him.

'Hardly a proposition, Mr Cornell, but as you know, we wish to dispose of our shareholding in Pennine Television as discreetly as possible. We would prefer to find a single buyer.'

'Having read your balance sheet, that may be difficult.'

'A matter of opinion, Mr Cornell. But to challenge that view, we would have to declare our situation publicly.'

'And let everyone know that Pennine is down the pan, and that the banks made a bad investment?'

'I would not put it as crudely as that, Mr Cornell.'

'I'm not asking you to. But those are the facts.'

'For the sake of private discussion between ourselves, yes.'

'How much are you down?'

'We would take half price for the shilling shares. Sixpence a share. And the buyer would, of course, assume full responsibility for all existing debts.'

'For how long?'

'Until the enterprise is profitable, Mr Cornell.'

'Which may never happen.'

'Quite so. Our statistics branch, however, thinks that it will and perhaps sooner than later. But we have invested a great deal of money for no return whatever and some of our colleagues are becoming uneasy at increasing our investment.'

'How much to get you off the hook?'

'Something in the order of two million pounds.'

'I don't have that sort of money lying loose. You'd take a guarantee?'

'Of course. I take it you are interested?'

'Yes. But not at that figure. Subject to scrutiny of the books, I would say one and a half million, top whack.'

Lord Mallett's face tightened.

'Not a very generous offer, Mr Cornell.'

'And not a very attractive proposition, Lord Mallett. If you are losing what the other contractors are losing, several hundreds an hour, you have already lost a hundred quid while we've been standing here!'

'Quite true. Subject to accountants' approval, and your status, I think we might work out something. Where is your office?'

'I usually work from home,' said Max, and handed him his card. 'Eaton Place. Come and have dinner with me there, say the middle of next week?'

'I would like to bring a lawyer and accountant.'

'Bring whoever you like,' said Max, 'But make sure you also bring all the figures.'

He walked back through the lounge with Nina.

'You think you can pull it off?' she asked him.

'I don't know,' he reflected. 'But I have hopes.'

'How? When they've failed? You know nothing about entertainment.'

'Agreed. But I think I know something about people. They're basically interested in three things. Sex, money and food. By food I also mean good living, fine clothes, smart houses, fast cars. And Mallett and his consortium haven't failed, as you say. They were the pioneers. They planted the seed. Now others reap the harvest.'

'And then what?'

'We go public and I sell out. For cash. No tax, for it would be a capital gain.'

'You seem very confident, then?'

'As I said, I have hopes,' he corrected. 'Now, are you coming back with me to London?'

She shook her head.

'I think I will stay here.'

'I thought you might.'

They exchanged smiles of understanding. Max climbed into his Rolls. Nina watched him out of sight, stood for a moment, and then slowly turned back into the hotel and went up the stairs. Max had been correct in listing the main interests in most people's lives, she thought. Slowly, she walked along the carpeted corridor to Lord Mallett's suite. He was already in bed waiting for her, the silk coverlet turned down to show his naked, sun-burned body.

Max took the film the cat burglar had given to him to a Mayfair chemist who specialised in quick developing and printing. Then he carried the photocopies back to his flat, poured himself a brandy and sat down to read them. The will had been drawn up, signed and dated two years earlier and had not been altered. All Paul's shares in his companies were left in trust for his son, Robert. Rachel was to have the income from these shares, unless or until she married again. Some small sums were to be given to friends, business associates, to Clara and to his gardener. Max was not mentioned, but then he did not expect to be. It was better to make your own money than to rely on the chance of wealth from the grave.

He replaced the will in its envelope and read Paul's letter.

> 'I have decided to end a life which has been a sham from the day I came here in the 1930s. I am supposed to be the son of a Czechoslovakian Jew, Samuel Harschmann, who took the English name of Sam Harris. I have never met him, or his son. I am not his son. Nor am I a Jew, although since my arrival in Britain I have pretended to be one. I am a German and a former member of the Hitler Youth. Certain privileges were promised to my familyand to me, if, with a much older man, a

member of the Abwehr, their secret service, I would travel to England apparently as his son.

'I agreed. The opportunities of advancement seemed much better than in National Socialist Germany. We travelled together on the passports of Samuel and Paul Harschmann. On the journey across the Channel, my companion, who now called himself Sam Harris, explained that we had taken the place of the real Harschmanns. They had been given passports and exit papers but they did not live to use them. My companion had personally supervised their removal from the train and the stealing of their papers, and then they were sent to Dachau.

'As Jewish refugees, we would be sympathetically treated, not only by the Jewish community in England, but by others. This would be our strength.

'I lived briefly in North London with Harris and then started my business in Manchester, using money that the Nazis had provided. As we had been assured, people were friendly. Some invested in my project, and all wanted me to succeed. Then I met Rachel and married her. Her parents were the only people who distrusted me from the start. They felt, as the English say, in their bones, that I was not all I seemed to be.

'Sam Harris ran a spy net from Golders Green. He used young German girls of good family, who, on the pretext of learning English, worked as nursemaids or children's helps in the homes of politicians, businessmen with companies involved in defence contracts, and senior serving officers.

'At the outbreak of war, the girls were all sent home. Harris relieved them of their English currency before they left, and with a secret sum the Abwehr had provided him with in case of dire emergency, he bought a number of houses in different parts of London. With husbands in the services, many wives forgot to keep up building society repayments on their mortgages or were unable to do so. They might only owe ten or fifteen pounds, but the building societies simply wanted to clear their debts, and offered these empty houses for what was owing on them. Oddly, the houses were difficult to sell, even at these absurd prices, for potential buyers feared a German invasion – a prospect that obviously encouraged Sam Harris to buy as many as he could.

'British Intelligence authorities had their suspicions about Harris, but never about me. They arrested him and forced him to become a turncoat, sending back totally false information to his original controller in Hamburg. During this time he received several letters from a young man, Max Kransky, who arrived in this country and who assumed that Harris was his uncle by marriage. Of course, Harris could not answer these letters. I met Kransky, now called Cornell, on several occasions.

'I knew about him, of course, from my briefing as to my supposed background. I also knew something he did not know. The real Sam Harschmann was not his uncle, but his father. He had an affair with Mrs Kransky, but whether her husband, Dr Kransky, knew this or not, it is impossible to say.

'Sam Harris was greatly concerned about Cornell's appearance after the war. He feared that he might discover that he had helped to arrange his father's arrest and death. He is, of course, equally concerned lest the basis of his own fortune – money stolen from the Nazis – and his own background is discovered.

'I kept these secrets for years. Then my wife, Rachel, told me that she was put in child by Cornell when he visited our home on leave from the army. The only worthwhile thing in all my life has been Robert, whom I have always thought of as my son. Now I learn that even this is false. He is not my son, and I helped to murder his grandfather. I have no-one to call my own. All zest, all purpose has left my life. For this reason, I can no longer face the prospect of a future of utter loneliness and the possibility at any time of denunciation and ruin. I leave it to my solicitor to make this information public or to preserve my secret. Either way, it will no longer concern me.'

Max poured himself another brandy. He understood now why the solicitor had not revealed the existence of this letter, and for the first time he felt pity for Paul. Max also understood the otherwise inexplicable antipathy he had for Sam Harris.

His first instinct was to charge him with embezzlement, espionage, murder. But proof would be impossible to provide after all these years. The note of a dead man, written on the eve of his own suicide, could be quickly brushed aside by a competent counsel.

Max thought of his mother, and her frequent affectionate remarks about the real Sam Harris. He thought about her husband, gentle and ineffectual. Had he known the truth, and in knowing it accepted it, because he loved his wife? Did any of this really matter now? The dead had buried the dead; nothing could bring them back.

But while his business lay with the living, he would not fail those no longer able to speak for themselves.

# Fifteen

Mr Goudousky was in his greenhouse, potting out tomatoes when the front door bell rang. He frowned at the interruption, removed his gardening gloves, and walked in through the narrow hall. Beyond the multi-coloured glass panel in the front door he saw the outline of a Bentley Continental; blue, red, purple.

Who the devil could this be? He opened the door. Max Cornell stood on the doorstep.

'Mr Cornell! I didn't know you knew my home address.'

'No-one is in their office on a Sunday, so I thought I'd drive out and see you. I have a business proposition that simply can't wait.'

'Come in,' said Mr Goudousky immediately.

He showed Max into a tiny front room, damp from lack of use, and looked at Max enquiringly.

'I want to borrow one and a half million pounds from the Union Flag.'

'One and a half *million*, Mr Cornell? For a single property?' Mr Goudousky's voice grew shrill with surprise.

'For a company that owns office property, and fifty acres of land with planning permission.'

'A very large sum indeed. You know that a building society is only supposed to lend for residential purposes?'

'If we developed the land for houses, then that would be a residential purpose, wouldn't it? This would also be a very short-term loan. Two years maximum.'

'I would have to consult my directors.'

'Of course. But for your private ear there could be a one-per-cent introductory fee to you personally. Mr Goudousky. So long as you keep my name out of it. If my name is involved, the deal is off.'

'What is the company?'

'I cannot tell you at this stage: the sale is a highly confidential matter. But I can say that it is in the north of England. I have seen the buildings and the land and, of course, the planning permission documents. I don't wish to appear secretive, but any publicity whatever could destroy the whole deal. And one last thing. I need an answer by noon tomorrow. Then, if it is No, I still have time to try elsewhere. But I very much hope it will be Yes.'

'I will do my utmost, I promise you,' Mr Goudousky assured him, much impressed. As soon as Max left, Mr Goudousky rang Sam Harris.

'I have the opportunity to lend one and a half million short term on commercial property,' he said importantly.

'We haven't got a million and a half, and you know it. We're stretched like catskins out to dry. That block of flats you suggested to me, we still haven't completed there. Other side's solicitors are dragging their feet like their boots are full of mud. Who wants this money, anyway?'

'A big company that doesn't want to go through their usual brokers. No names. But it's kosher.'

'Sounds odd,' said Harris. 'What rate will they offer?'

'We haven't discussed that, but I would ask a lot. Say, seven per cent on the total loan, not decreasing.'

'Makes it about nine per cent?'

'If they want the money, they'll have to pay. The law of supply and demand.'

'But how can we supply the demand if we haven't the money ourselves?'

'I would suggest advancing it in hundred thousand pound instalments. This gives us time to increase our advertising and approach more solicitors who control trust funds.'

'What if the Registrar of Friendly Societies hears about this? What's our case then?'

'We haven't got one. Any more than we have for Lesney Park. But why should he hear? If he pokes his nose in, we can keep him stalling until most of the debt's cleared. After all, it's only two years.'

'You feel strongly about this?'

'A double-headed penny,' Mr Goudousky assured him. 'I would put my own savings in on it.'

'Your own money?' said Sam Harris, impressed in his turn. 'All right, then. If you feel that way – and can raise a million and a half – go ahead.'

The Prime Minister had been on to the Home Secretary urgently. The Home Secretary immediately telephoned the head of the security service, who made several curt and increasingly angry telephone calls before Blaikie's telephone rang in his office in Covent Garden. What the hell had happened down in Portsmouth? Who the devil had authorised this ludicrous dive, almost bound to be discovered? If it had been intentionally arranged to ruin a Russian official visit, it could not have been better achieved. Only a D Notice had prevented the Press from publishing damaging rumours about the disappearance of a Royal Navy frogman.

But the government could not stop publication of exaggerated accounts in foreign newspapers. An official explanation would have to be made soon, for this escapade could easily provoke a diplomatic incident of the worst possible kind between the British and Soviet governments, just when there was hope that the coolness between them could thaw.

Blaikie, in turn, showed his anger. Where was Bates, whom he had personally ordered to use the utmost discretion and tact? His grey-haired woman assistant appeared at the door. She had weathered many crises; another did not disturb her.

'We have tried his home,' she said calmly, 'but his wife hasn't seen him since he left for Portsmouth. He hasn't returned. The hotel in Portsmouth says he paid his bill personally. The Sallyport say that a man of his description left with Mr Smith in Mr Smith's Hillman Minx.'

'Get Cornell here. Tell him it's absolutely vital, but don't let him know why. Then ask Colonel Reid to come over as soon as possible.'

Half an hour later, Max was sitting opposite Blaikie and Colonel Reid in Blaikie's office. Max had rehearsed what he would say many times. He now spoke clearly and without concern. He had intended to drop Bates at his home in Sevenoaks, but Bates asked to be set down near a quarry outside West Malling.

'A lonely place?' asked Reid.

'Fairly, I suppose.'

'Do you know why he wanted to be left there?'

'No idea. He had been drinking, you know.'

'I know he liked a dram. But you should have taken him home.'

'Why? He's of age. He particularly asked me to drop him there. So I did.'

'What did you do then?'

'Came back to London. Left the car unlocked with the key under the driver's seat, as instructed, in Upper Cumberland Place.'

'Heads will roll over this,' prophesied Reid bleakly.

'Before any decapitations start,' said Max, 'don't forget you promised to ring the bank for me.'

'That's the least of my worries,' said Blaikie.

'It's not the least of mine,' replied Max, thinking about his meeting with Lord Mallett that evening.

'Tell me,' said Reid confidentially, leaning towards Max. 'What do *you* think happened to Crabb and Bates?'

'I have absolutely no idea. At a guess, Crabb either blacked out or he had a seizure of some kind. Or else someone tipped off the Russians to expect an uninvited caller. That's what Bates thought had happened.'

'You think Bates did it himself?'

'Of course not. Why should he? Is he on our side or theirs?' Max realised that he had almost said 'was' instead of 'is'; a narrow escape. He must be more careful.

'Perhaps Bates heard something,' suggested Blaikie. 'He told me on the phone he had a theory about Crabb's disappearance. Did he mention it to you?'

'Only that he had rung you.'

'I'll ask the police to search around that quarry, and all along the south coast, in case Crabb's body comes ashore,' said Reid. 'In the meantime, we must do all we can to kill Press speculation. I will ask the Admiralty to put out a statement explaining that Crabb was on a test dive in connection with underwater trials.'

This statement only aroused further interest and controversy. In Parliament, Mr John Drysdale, the Labour member for West Bromwich and a former Financial Secretary to the Admiralty, asked a question about the circumstances of his disappearance. Bit by bit, small biographical items about Commander Crabb appeared in the newspapers. After a police officer was reported to have removed the page of the Sallyport Hotel register that contained his name, and that of a Mr Smith, more speculation, hints and innuendo fuelled public interest. Finally, the Prime Minister Sir Anthony Eden rose in the House of Commons to read a prepared statement.

'It would not be in the public interest to disclose the circumstances in which Commander Crabb is presumed to have met his death,' he said. 'I think it is necessary in the special circumstances of this case to make it clear that what was done was without the authority or knowledge of Her Majesty's Ministers. Appropriate disciplinary steps are being taken.'

The Leader of the Opposition, Mr Hugh Gaitskell, was unimpressed.

'Is the Prime Minister aware,' he asked, 'that, while we would all wish to protect public security, the suspicion must inevitably arise that his refusal to make a statement on this subject is not so much in the interests of public security but to hide a very grave blunder?'

Later, after Mr Gaitskell had been privately informed of the circumstances, he paid tribute to Crabb when he opened a debate in the House on the incident.

'All of us will agree that this country would be the poorer if it were not for men like Commander Crabb.'

When public interest subsided, Max invited Blaikie to dinner; he wanted to discover whether he had any news of Bates. But Blaikie had heard nothing.

'The police found his belongings in a suitcase in the quarry where you say you dropped him off. Nothing missing, according to his wife. Clothes neatly folded. Looked as if he'd dumped the case and meant to come back for it. But, why? No money worries, no other woman, so far as we can find out. One little daughter. It was her ninth birthday the following day. He had a present for her in his case.'

Max sat thinking of that humped blazer sinking beneath the cement. Houses would now grow up on either side. Short of a bomb, Bates's body would never be discovered.

'I feel in some way responsible. After all, I drove him back. I feel I should do something for his wife.'

'You mean, money?'

'Not as such. Put a couple of houses in her name. She can find a local estate agent to run them if she doesn't want to do so herself. Bring in an income.'

'That's damned generous of you.'

'Not at all. I agree with what Hugh Gaitskell said in the House. We all owe people like Crabb and Bates a debt.'

'But only when they're dead,' said Blaikie bitterly, his good hand unconsciously clasping the stump of his arm. 'When they're alive, they soldier on with overdrafts, unpaid bills and wives who complain they're never at home. Do you know that a fellow like Bates, in the Navy, in his first command, say, and making a courtesy call to some bloody port, has to pay the entertainment of all the local freeloaders who come aboard? Socialist mayors wearing gold chains, and corrupt councillors with backhanders from property developers like you. They could buy and sell Bates and his kind a hundred times, but he still pays out of his pocket for their gins and whiskies, and that makes me bloody mad. None of us are in it for the money, but fair's fair.'

'Just why are you in it?'

'Because, when I was young, I was idealistic. Wanted to serve my country. Thought I owed a debt to all those who had died for England in the past.'

'A romantic ideal?'

'Possibly. But you weren't fool enough to follow it,' retorted Blaikie. 'That's the difference.'

They sat in silence for a moment. Max poured more brandy.

'Not kept in touch with your former wife, I suppose?' Blaikie asked conversationally. He did not want Max to think that he was bitter or failed or passed-over for promotion. He could not bear pity or condescending concern from a man like Max.

'I have seen her, but that's all.'

'Didn't mention her sister, by any chance?'

'No. Why?'

'The Russians picked her up for questioning some years ago, in the days of Beria. You know what that meant then.'

'How did you hear?'

'Comrade Vasarov.'

'So you had someone else talking to him over here as well as me?'

'The fellow who took over from you met him once, yes.'

'Does Nina know?'

'I haven't told her,' said Blaikie. 'She's probably writing and assumes her sister's letters aren't reaching her.'

'Can't you do anything to help?'

'How? Anna's not a British citizen.'

Max sipped his brandy.

'Nina was followed when she first arrived here,' he said. 'That scared her, so I sent her up north. Would that have anything to do with her sister being taken in?'

Blaikie looked embarrassed.

'Nothing. Nothing whatever.'

He drew on his cigar.

'I feel I owe you a belated explanation about that.'

'Why?'

'You remember when you did your training with us you had to follow various people, make drops in dead letter boxes and so on, until you could do it all without being spotted? Well, when you came over here, we put a couple of trainee agents to follow Nina.'

'Why, in God's name? Couldn't you have told me?'

'Obviously, we couldn't. They must have made a bad job of it. We told them there was this foreign girl married to a British subject, and we wanted her checked out.'

'And you call yourselves professionals?'

'At times like this I call myself a bloody fool,' said Blaikie, and held out his glass for another brandy.

Max was parking his Rolls outside the Ritz when someone tapped on the window. Dick Carpenter smiled at him through the glass. Max climbed out, delighted to see him after so many years.

'I was thinking of you only the other day,' he told Carpenter as they went into the hotel together.

'I live in Spain now.'

'How are the deals going?'

'Very little nowadays,' said Carpenter. He seemed quieter than Max remembered him. They joined Manuela at a side table. Max ordered a bottle of champagne to celebrate their meeting. Carpenter asked the waiter to bring him a Perrier water.

'Unlike you,' said Max, surprised.

'Times change,' replied Carpenter briefly. 'Excuse me one minute. I've left my pills in the bedroom. I have to take one four times a day. Also unlike me, eh?'

He stood up, walked towards the lift. Manuela waited until he was out of earshot and then leaned towards Max.

'He's not well,' she explained quickly. 'We're over here to see a specialist.'

'What's wrong with him?'

She glanced down at the bubbles rising in her glass.

'Cancer of the stomach. But don't let him know I've told you. He's had several operations, but he still has the pain. That's why he has to take so many pills. I don't think there's much anyone can do for him now, but he's very brave.'

'He did me many good turns,' said Max.

'He's like that with everyone. And he's still full of ideas. His latest one is about holidays. Soon, it won't take people much longer to fly to Spain, say, where they can be sure of sunshine, than to take a train to Clacton or Margate.

'He's bought up miles of land along the coast in Southern Spain and wants to put up hotels and apartment buildings. Then he'll charter aircraft to bring people in for two or three weeks at a time, from the cold countries of Europe. You can charter planes surprisingly cheaply. If he owns the hotels, too, he can offer holidays at very low prices, all in. What he calls a package.'

'A good idea,' said Max, impressed. 'How did he raise the money?'

'He's bought and sold a number of things since he saw you last. The biggest one was a block of flats in South London, Lesney Park. He finally sold that some weeks ago.'

'Difficult to raise money for that, surely?'

'Very. Finally, a dubious building society helped him out. Something called the Union Flag Building Society. He gave them the idea that they should sell the flats to the tenants, and make a capital gain. Their head man thought it a great idea.'

Max was thinking about this as he came down the steps into the basement. Instead of threatening Iron Bar he had originally intended to buy him off. But what Manuela had told him gave him a better idea. He would placate Iron Bar – and at the same time ruin Sam Harris.

The basement smelled of sweat and ganja. On a Harrow record player, a steel band played 'Lemon Tree'. Dim red and blue lights flickered on the painted ceiling. A West Indian in sweat shirt and jeans blocked his way.

'Looking for someone? This is a private club, man.'

'Iron Bar,' said Max. 'I've called at his house. His mother told me he'd be here.'

'He know you?'

'He will do.'

The man eyed Max speculatively, taking in the breadth of his shoulders, his hard cold eyes, and decided not to push his luck. Bar had been seeing a number of influential white visitors recently, mostly local Liberal and Labour councillors. He was up to something, and wouldn't thank anyone for being rude to a guest.

'Over there. In the corner.'

Max crossed the room. Iron Bar was sitting at the table with two men, drinking rum. He looked up as Max approached.

'Mr Diaz? Iron Bar? I'm Max Cornell. I'd like to speak to you privately.'

'Who are you, man?'

Max made an impatient gesture of dismissal. Iron Bar turned to his companions.

'Be with you in a minute,' he said. They stood up sullenly, and slouched across the room.

'I have a business proposition to make,' said Max, sitting down at the table. 'But first, I understand you object to Betty Mortimer seeing a man every Friday evening and giving him a parcel?'

'She's my woman,' said Iron Bar shortly, glancing over Max's shoulder. Max moved around the table and sat at Iron Bar's side. If he was going to be attacked, he wanted it to be from the front, where he could see and not from the rear, where he couldn't.

'Just for your private ear, then, I am the man she meets.'

'You moving in on her?'

'Not in the sense you mean. We have a purely business arrangement, nothing to do with your agreement. I own some property. Her friends rent rooms. When I see her, she hands me the rent. That's all. Satisfied?'

Iron Bar looked at Max uneasily, wondering how he should react. He could not be certain, so he said nothing, following Mr O'Flaherty's advice.

'Now, my proposition,' Max continued. 'I don't know what your ambition is, but I hear stories that it's political. You want to put the rackets behind you and become a spokesman for the immigrants around here.'

'What of it?' asked Iron Bar sullenly.

'This. I can offer you help of a kind you won't get anywhere else. I will write you a cheque now for two thousand pounds on condition that you invest it in the Union Flag Building Society. The main agent's just up the road. Mr Goudousky.'

'I pay him rent,' said Iron Bar.

'So you know him. One week after you put the money in, write and ask him for your money back. Do not visit him. Put it in writing.'

'Why?'

'Because that's the condition on which I give you the money in the first place. You won't get it back – then. So keep on writing. You'll still not get it back. You will find that someone of liberal views will raise this matter in Parliament, or the newspapers. You may or may not get the money back, but what you will get is a lot of absolutely priceless publicity.'

'Why do this for me? What's in this for you, man?'

'You lay off Betty Mortimer.'

'All right. If what you say is true, man.'

Max took out his cheque book. He began to write the cheque.

'Only one thing,' he said. 'Make sure you do invest it.'

'You threatening me?' asked Iron Bar belligerently, now that he thought the moment of danger was past.

'I never make threats,' said Max mildly. 'Only promises. You understand me?'

Iron Bar looked at the cheque and nodded.

Max stood up, walked across the floor. A crowd of West Indians at a pinball table near the door parted to let him go through and up the stairs.

Sam Harris sat alone in the double-glazed silence of his study, high above Berkeley Square.

On his huge desk lay two open folders, one for the Union Flag Building Society, the other for the Golden Star. In theory – and, after all, accounting dealt with theoretical figures – he had no problems whatsoever. In a very short time he would be very rich. To convince himself, he reduced the equation to its simplest form, as his maths master in Berlin had instructed him long years ago.

He was borrowing from investors at, say, three per cent, allowing for all commissions to solicitors and bank managers. He then invested this money in cheap run-down properties at five, six, or seven per cent, largely to newly arrived immigrants from the West Indies and Pakistan. No problem about the profit margin there.

On a higher level, he had agreed to pay one million pounds, in ten equal monthly instalments of one hundred thousand pounds, to the owners of Lesney Park. Here, he faced his first setback, unforeseen in Mr Goudousky's original optimistic appreciation.

As soon as contracts had been exchanged for the complex, Sam Harris wrote to every tenant, offering each one a ninety-nine year lease on their flat for no more than the rent they were already paying, with a hundred per cent mortgage. Some had agreed at once. Others had asked for time to consider the offer, but most had not even bothered to reply. In time they might possibly be persuaded of the value of the proposal, but not as quickly as Mr Goudousky had assumed.

Time was his enemy, not his ally, and this was made more acute by the further loan of one and a half million pounds that Mr Goudousky had proposed, and to which he had agreed. He had since discovered that this involved the assets of Pennine Television, but he did not know the identity of the principals behind it, although their bank gave them the highest recommendation.

Again, time would see him through, but how to find the time? Letters to savers with both building societies, to solicitors and bank managers who advised clients on investments, were already producing an encouraging response, but not nearly fast enough. Assets were pouring out at a rate of two hundred thousand pounds a month, with deposits totalling at most a thousand or two every day. This realisation brought him to the contents of the third folder, which troubled him most of all. About them, Harris felt an animal instinct of approaching danger, possibly disaster, last experienced with such intensity when two men in raincoats and trilby hats called at his house in Golders Green shortly after war had been declared.

'We're from the Special Branch,' the first had explained. 'We understand you are in communication with a country with which we are now at war.'

It turned out that they had been watching him for months and he had never known, never even suspected. What if some rival, some enemy, had done the same here, and this was part of a complex plan to bring him down?

Yet why should he suddenly feel like this simply because of four letters written by some damned West Indian immigrant?

The first was dated more than a month earlier, from a Mr Joseph Diaz, in Notting Hill, and was written in pencil in a semi-literate hand on lined paper. Mr Diaz explained that he had recently invested two thousand pounds, his total life savings, in the Union Flag Building Society, and now he wished to withdraw this money as soon as possible. A copy of the reply from Mr Goudousky assured Mr Diaz of the society's best endeavours to accede to his request speedily, but added that there seemed no trace in their books of a deposit account in this name, and therefore could he please kindly confirm his account number? This was, of course, simply a stalling reply.

A week later, Mr Diaz wrote a further letter. This time it was typed, and possessed what Harris regarded as ominously legal undertones. Obviously, the bugger had taken advice somewhere; legal aid was free now to anyone who wanted to make trouble.

'Dear Sir,' he read. 'Under the terms of your advertisements, money in deposit accounts is payable on demand. I would therefore appreciate it if this money is repaid immediately.'

Ten days elapsed before Mr Goudousky's next reply, in which he said that a cheque was already being processed, and should be in Mr Diaz's hands very shortly. This cheque had not reached him for another fortnight, however, and now Mr Diaz threatened to raise the matter with his MP unless he received his deposit plus interest by return. In itself, in isolation, two thousand pounds was nothing. Sam Harris had paid more for the desk at which he sat. Unfortunately, he could not sell the desk or even borrow against it, because, like all the contents of his flat, and even his Rolls, it had been itemised and valued, and the list sealed and deposited with his bank against money which he had been forced to borrow to help with the Lesney Park transaction.

Goudousky, he knew, had had to take out two mortgages on his house. They had nothing whatever in the kitty until the Lesney Park flats started to move, or the unknown buyer of Pennine Television repaid his loan, or some huge (and extremely unlikely) deposits were made by private investors.

Yet he had to settle with Mr Diaz quickly, for if the man did complain to his MP, and a question was asked in the House, all those wealthy widows and spinsters in Cheltenham and Bournemouth and Hove, who had trusted the advice of family solicitors, would immediately become agitated and seek to withdraw their savings.

This would spell instant ruin of both societies, and infinitely more important, of himself. An official investigation would be ordered; this would reveal that the directors had been borrowing money to finance their own property ventures, and Harris would be finished. With luck, he might avoid jail, but his credibility would be totally destroyed.

Harris poured himself a whisky and pondered the situation. Two thousand pounds. If he could borrow this amount somewhere, he would gladly pay it back five times over – in time. But who would lend money on such ridiculous terms? Even to offer these terms was to invite instant disbelief. Another letter to Mr Diaz could only precipitate his reaction. Perhaps he should visit him; explain that there had been an office upheaval, a senior accountant had died, a bank account changed, any plausible excuse he could produce to secure more time in the hope that, from somewhere, more money would come in? In the meantime, he might be able to sell off some of the shoddy property in Notting Hill that Cornell had bought.

But why not try Cornell? That business of the car auction was a long time ago; he must have forgotten all about it by now. No time to stand on ceremony. Again that fearful word obtruded. Time. He remembered the story of the little Dutch boy with his finger in the dyke. So long as the flow could be stemmed, the whole edifice would hold. But once a trickle became a flood, all would be destroyed. On the impulse, he telephoned Max.

'Haven't seen you for some time,' he began as genially as he could.

'You ringing at this hour to tell me that?' Max asked him coldly.

'Only a friendly call.'

'You're no friend of mine.'

'Wait a minute,' said Harris in an aggrieved voice. 'I'm more than a friend, I'm a relation. Your uncle. Have you forgotten?'

'No. I have remembered. My uncle is dead.'

'What do you mean? Dead?'

'Don't waste time discussing the matter. What do you want?'

'Money,' said Harris simply. 'The two building societies I'm involved with are a tiny bit stretched. Nothing serious, of course, but actually I think Goudousky was probably a mite generous when he remortgaged those houses for you. Not that I'm objecting, mind. A deal's a deal. It's only that deposits are down. Other societies say the same, of course. A sign of the times, I suppose. I was wondering whether you'd care to consider selling off any of your houses – or, say, shortening the length of repayments?'

'No to both. But I could be interested in buying the garage chain you own. Beechwood Garages.'

This was the firm that had owned the grey Ford 10 that had given Max the first clue that Harris wanted to muscle in on the car auction business.

'A number of sites, there,' said Harris. 'All freehold, too. But they're down against loans to the Union Flag. Sorry.'

'Well, another time, then. I could still be interested. Nothing else?'

'No.'

'Well, I can only suggest you do what you used to tell me to do. Get the paperwork right!'

Harris shook his head miserably. He could not bear to continue this sterile conversation.

The telephone died in his hand.

He poured himself another drink. How had Max got hold of the idea that his uncle was dead? Who could have told him? Only Paul had known, and Paul was dead. Anyhow, Cornell couldn't prove a bloody thing, whoever had told him. All that happened years ago, in another country, almost another life. What was happening now was the important thing and there was no mileage in asking Max for help. He would have to see Mr Diaz himself.

Midnight was too late for a business call, yet by all accounts these West Indians kept odd hours. He could say he was driving past, and suddenly thought he would drop in.

He finished the whisky, put Mr Diaz's letter in his jacket pocket and went out to find a taxi.

They cruised past Diaz's house, for Harris had deliberately given the cabbie the wrong number. A hundred yards up the road, he stopped. Harris paid him off, added ten shillings to the fare.

'The other half on top if you wait until I return.'

'Don't be too long, guv'nor. I don't like this area. I'll give you ten minutes. No more.'

Harris walked up the road, scattered with blown-about newspaper pages. Empty cornflake packets and tin cans spilled from overflowing dustbins. A radio blared in a basement.

He climbed the crumbling concrete steps to Mr Diaz's front door, shone a pencil torch on the five bell pushes; Rosa, Obeah, French Lessons, one for a Mr Singh and the last for Mr Diaz. He pressed this button and waited.

The door opened a few inches. A small dark-skinned man stood peering out at him.

'What do you want, man?' he asked impatiently.

'Mr Diaz?'

'What if I am?'

'I may be able to help you. I'm from the Union Flag Building Society.'

'At this hour, man? Half past bloody midnight?'

'Happened to be passing,' Harris continued unconvincingly. 'Thought I would call in. Could come back tomorrow easily enough.'

'No. Now you're here, come up,' said Mr Diaz.

He opened the door wider. Harris stepped into the hall, accidentally brushing one wall with his hand. The plaster felt damp, cold as a corpse. He followed Iron Bar up the carpetless stairs to his room. The smell of hemp was strong. Iron Bar sat down on the edge of the bed. He did not offer Sam Harris a seat.

'About your letters withdrawing your money,' Harris began tentatively.

'I've waited long enough. If I was a white man, you would have replied immediately.'

'We did reply immediately. I assure you Mr Diaz, your colour has nothing whatever to do with things. It was simply a matter of tracing your account number.'

'Well, you've done that, so where's the money? Got it with you?'

'I don't carry sums like that about at this time of night.'

'Your last letter said you were sending it to me.'

'It's on the way. We have to get several signatures.'

'For a cheque that size?'

'Purely office routine,' Harris assured him quickly. 'You will have the money by the end of this week.'

'You know what I will do if I don't?' said Mr Diaz.

He stood up menacingly. He was a foot shorter than Harris. He resented this difference in their height, as he resented Harris's expensive suit, and what he considered his supercilious attitude.

'I will go to my MP. You know about Black Power?'

'Only in the papers.'

'Well, my friend Michael X runs that. We've got all kinds of important people on the committee, man. Councillors. Members of Parliament. Trade union leaders. I tell you, they won't stand by and see a black man done down by a big company.'

'I assure you, Mr Diaz, there is no intention of doing you or anyone else down. I just paid you a casual social call as I was passing through.'

'Where the hell were you passing through to, in this area? Something's frightened you, Mr Harris. Or someone. And I think that someone is me. Unless I get my money tomorrow, there will be trouble, man. I tell you that,'

'If I had thought you would adopt this attitude I would not have called to see you.'

'I didn't ask you to, so bugger off. Remember, tomorrow.'

'It may take a day or two in the post.'

'Why post it? Bring it. Next time you are just passing through – like tomorrow. Now get out.'

Harris went down the stairs, through the damp hall, into the street. The taxi driver was still waiting.

'Almost gave you up, guv'nor,' he said.

Harris did not reply; he had almost given himself up. He had either to find two thousand or go down for millions.

Iron Bar put down his mug of rum as the two men came into the club and waved excitedly to him.

'What you doing in here, Bar?' one shouted. 'You should be out at the protest meeting.'

'What you protesting about, man?'

'Those riots in Nottingham. Didn't you read about them? White Teddy boys beat our people up. When we fought back, *we* were arrested – not them! I got this.'

He pointed proudly to a black eye and a cut on his forehead.

'Afraid the same thing is going to happen here, are you?' Iron Bar asked him. 'I'll tell you, *I*'m not afraid. Come on!'

He led them up the stairs and out into the street. This was the moment for which he had been waiting. Cornell had been quite right. His days of pimping were about to end; his mother could handle that business. Politics was where his future lay.

At the far end of the square, on that hot August evening, more than a hundred black youths had already gathered. Mothers and wives and girl friends stood in doorways, arms akimbo, curlers under bright bandanas. There was a strong whiff of ganja and the sharp scent of male bodies tensed for violence.

Fifty yards away, the Teddy boys were also assembling in their curious Edwardian style jackets and narrow trousers.

'Down with niggers! Back to the bush!'

Iron Bar saw the glint of a cut-throat razor, the dull metal of an axe blade. He jumped up onto the bonnet of a parked car. Never mind who owned it, he'd never dare to complain.

'We're waiting for Michael X!' shouted a Bahamian on the edge of the crowd.

'Well, you got *me*! And I want to tell *you* something. So long as we allow ourselves to be beaten up by this white trash, we will *never* be free! We know this is a white man's country – but we're going to change it. You and me together!'

The West Indians began to cheer. This was the talk they liked, part of folklore from the past; echoes from Runaway Bay and Maroon Country. Some waved pieces of wood, spanners, tyre levers; a few, their fists.

'I am a man of peace, as you know,' Iron Bar went on, 'but I have just had an experience that makes me willing to fight. Not for you, not for me, but for *justice*.

'All my savings – all my widowed mother's savings – I invested in a building society run by a white man. The Union Flag. Everything we had saved over many many years, I put into that building society because I believed what they told me. I could have this money back with interest *on demand*.

'But, friends, I didn't *demand* that which was my own. I only asked. And when I asked, they refused to give me my own money!

'At midnight – not in office hours – a white man comes to see me, saying it's on the way. That was a week ago, *five* weeks after I first asked for them to give me back my life's savings.

'If I had a white skin, comrades, if I spoke with a posh English accent, if I wore a Savile Row suit, they would have paid me immediately. But I have none of these things. I am black, friends, black! I don't ask for other men's money. I only seek my own. *And it is denied me* – just as freedom to walk the streets without being insulted, attacked, humiliated, is denied to you!'

A tremendous roar of approval echoed back from the shabby houses. Some women began to scream encouragement. Others, more fearful and unwilling to become involved, retreated into their homes and locked front doors. A few frightened faces, black and white, peered apprehensively from upper windows; elderly tenants who feared violence, but had nowhere to go.

Iron Bar pointed towards the Teddy boys who now stood in two ranks across the road, those in front holding razors and hammers.

'There lie your targets!' he shouted. 'The Teds who beat us up, as their bosses seize our savings. Crush them! Crush oppression *everywhere*! For freedom!'

Iron Bar jumped down, as the West Indians surged forward past him. He took care not to be in the first or second rank, for they would take the hardest blows. The wisest generals always led from behind.

Doors in other streets now opened, and out poured men of all ages and colours. Some carried broom handles or spades. A photographer's flashlight exploded in a flare of magnesium. A police whistle blew. Broken glass tinkled and splintered. Windows caved in, and black and white looters swarmed into houses and shops. In the distance, Iron Bar heard the urgent wail of police car sirens.

He prudently withdrew into the safety of a doorway as the mob screamed past him. He did not wish to be arrested until the press photographers and television crews were there to see him being taken. He found he was sweating, not from fear or anger, but with exhilaration. At last he had found his niche. All his early bitter years were but a necessary training for this hour. He was a leader of men, born to command. And this realisation was not the end; it was only the beginning.

As Douglas Carton was speaking in the House of Commons he surveyed the faces of the government ministers opposite him. One appeared to be asleep. Two were whispering to each other. Others looked bored as he droned on.

'No doubt you will have read in this morning's newspapers the reports of sentences passed on instigators of disturbances in August in Nottingham and Notting Hill, the clashes between hundreds of coloured immigrants and white people, mostly youths.

'Thousands and thousands of pounds of damage was done to property. Scores of people were injured by stones, clubs, knives, some very seriously, including many not involved in any way. It is impossible to set a value in monetary terms on the grave and lasting damage these riots have inflicted on British credibility in the emerging countries of our Commonwealth.

'And what are the punishments? Five men are sentenced at the Central Criminal Court to terms of imprisonment from eighteen months to two years.

'I put it to this House that the real criminals are those who deliberately exploit the wretchedness and misery of hard-working coloured immigrants who only seek a modest home and the right to be treated as equals with their white neighbours.

'This House will already have heard of the exploits of Peter Rachman, who, as landlord of unknown numbers of houses in the Notting Hill area, has given his name to the foul custom of demanding extortionate rents, largely from coloured people. It is well known – but again little seems to be done – how he has driven out harmless tenants, with the use of dogs in some cases, so that he could re-let their rooms at even higher rents.

'No doubt, at the proper time and in the proper place, others will have much to say about Mr Rachman's activities. What I want to say today is that he is by no means alone. There is another figure, whose empire sprawls not only in the rundown slums of Notting Hill, but has tentacles reaching out into many other highly lucrative commercial concerns.

'Is it right that one man, by investing a relatively paltry sum, can suddenly find it transformed – I would say, transmuted, as the philosopher's stone of the ancients could turn dross into gold – into thousands, perhaps millions, of pounds without any exertion whatever on his part?

'Surely in a country and under a government that speaks so much of caring for the weak and helpless, steps should be taken forthwith to protect humble and decent people from vile predators like this?'

'Name him!' shouted someone as Carton sat down. 'Name him!'

# Sixteen

Next morning, Nina was still in bed when the telephone rang. It was twenty-five to ten. She had overslept.

'Dougie here,' announced Carton loudly in her ear. 'Seen the papers?'

'No. I haven't been down to collect them yet.'

'I'm rich,' he said proudly. 'At last. Half a million pounds. I'm half a millionaire.'

'*What*? But how?'

'Those TV shares. Pennine Television. Don't you remember?'

Nina struggled into wakefulness. She had almost forgotten the transaction two years earlier with what had since seemed to be worthless shares. Debts had piled up against the company, revenue had fallen. She had not dared to contact Max in case he blamed her for suggesting he bought out the bankers.

'I will buy you the best present you have ever had. Fur coat, car, anything,' Carton was saying.

'But I thought that Pennine was broke. Where's all this money come from?'

'The shares are going on the market, that's where. It's on every front page this morning. My shilling shares are worth nearly twelve pounds – *each*! Think of that! And it's all tax free. Like having your own gold mine.'

He paused as a thought suddenly struck him.

'You've still got the share certificate, of course?'

'Of course. I wouldn't lose those.'

'I thought not. Just for a moment, though, I wondered. Well, I'm on my way over.'

He rang off.

Nina jumped out of bed, had a quick shower, dressed and checked that the certificate was in the locked drawer in her dining table where she had pushed them all that time ago. Now she put it in an envelope, addressed this to herself, and ran with it to the nearest post box. She had just time to pick up the newspaper from the front step when Carton arrived.

'Isn't it wonderful?' he said excitedly. He was carrying a bunch of flowers.

'Come in and calm down,' she said. 'I've not had breakfast yet.'

'Never mind about breakfast, what about those shares? I must get them transferred to my name this morning.'

'But they are in my name, Dougie.'

'Of course they are. But they had to be. You know that.'

'But if they are in my name, they are my shares. Surely *I* collect any profit?'

Carton looked at Nina sharply, then relaxed. Of course, she was having her bit of fun. Her friendly smile reassured him.

'Don't be silly, darling. That was our arrangement. I gave you two thousand pounds for you to buy the shares, and then you promised to let me have them back when I wanted them.'

'I never agreed to that.'

'What? But you know you did.'

'I know I didn't. All I know is that you gave me two thousand pounds and I bought forty thousand one shilling fully paid-up shares in Pennine Television. Now you tell me they are worth twelve pounds each. The papers agree.' She pointed the headlines on the front page of *The Daily Express*.

'Here's Norman Collins, who had £2,250 worth of shares in Associated-Rediffusion. It says here, they are now worth £501,750. Lew Grade had £1,250 worth – now worth £278,000. And I am worth half a million. Out of which I would like to pay back the two thousand you gave me.'

'*I* am worth half a million,' shouted Carton, his face contorting with horror at what she said. 'I don't want your bloody two thousand. I want it all. After all, it's *mine*. We had an *agreement*.'

'You gave me two thousand pounds, agreed,' replied Nina calmly. 'I would say it was payment for services rendered.

For putting up with your perversions, being whipped, humiliated, all those disgusting practices you wouldn't want your constituents to know about. You didn't have the guts to invest in the company yourself, and now you can't begin to prove that I owe you one penny, Douglas Carton. And you would not dare to try.'

Carton turned away from her, pulled open drawers in her desk in the sitting room, then ran into the bedroom and burrowed into the dressing table drawers.

'You're wasting your time,' Nina said calmly. 'The certificate isn't here. Anyway, it's in my name. So even if it were, it's still useless to you.'

'You bitch! You bloody bitch! You *know* the arrangement!'

Carton lunged at her, striking a clumsy blow across her face. Nina jumped behind the table. He pushed it roughly to one side. A glass vase crashed, and the flowers were scattered. Water poured across the carpet.

'If you go on like this, I'll ring the police,' she warned.

'I'll kill you,' he said through clenched teeth. 'If it's the last thing I do, I'll bloody kill you.'

He came slowly round the side of the table, eyes narrow, lips drawn back over his yellowing teeth. He saw her smiling at him, taunting him, it seemed, and then suddenly the image grew fainter. Nina dwindled to a dark shadow, then became a pin-point of blinding light. Carton fell forwards over the table. His nails gored the polished wood as he slid back slowly and collapsed onto the carpet.

He lay, eyes open, breathing heavily, as though he had been running uphill. Nina stared down at him in horror, her heart trembling. Then, with distaste, not wishing to touch his flesh more than she must, she lifted his right sleeve and felt his pulse. It was feeble and irregular. She telephoned her doctor.

'Poor fellow,' he said, when he had examined Carton. 'A heart attack. We'll get him to hospital. Lucky I was in when you rang. It's amazing what they can do now in cases like this.'

He paused, looking at Carton's waxy face, his open, drooling mouth.

'Isn't he the politician?'

'Yes.'

'Thought I'd seen him on the box. Very much against this commercial television, wasn't he? Must have had a very bad shock. Did you see in the paper today about all those people who have made fortunes?'

'Yes. So did he.'

'Ah. That could have brought on the attack. All against his principles.'

'I think the news probably did upset him,' Nina agreed gently.

Blaikie was half way through his morning coffee when Reid came into his office without knocking.

'Seen the papers?' he asked him.

'Only glanced at the *Times*. Been too busy over this ballet dancer who's defected in New York.'

Reid put a copy of *The Daily Express* on the desk.

'Oh. Those new television fortunes?' said Blaikie. 'I did see something about that in the *Times*. Doesn't affect me, though. I don't own a single share in anything. Unfortunately.'

'It affects Max Cornell.'

'How? Is he involved?'

'Apparently, he bloody well *owns* a company. Borrowed money somewhere and took over Pennine Television when it seemed it was out for the count. Now the whole thing is up and running. Estimated profits next year could be a million – possibly more. City editor says that he's worth millions overnight.'

'Bastard,' said Blaikie, and meant it.

'Oh, well, good luck to him. Shouldn't think money's brought him happiness. Always seemed a lonely sort of cove to me. Changing the subject a bit, this defector is shooting his mouth off, isn't he?'

'They usually do,' said Blaikie. 'Frightens our regulars, this sort of thing. We've just had a message about Vasarov. He wants out.'

'As a result of this?'

'Possibly. The ballet dancer was a KGB colonel, too, of course. Left it a bit late to jump, though. Just hours before the others flew back to Moscow.'

'Sounds like Vasarov's got the wind up?'

'Very likely. He's done us well for years. Wouldn't like to be in his shoes. He's due to visit Paris next Tuesday, with a trade delegation. We could lift him then, I suppose. Won't get a better opportunity.'

'Who can we use?'

'I propose the richest agent in the business. Who else? Max Cornell.'

'You're joking?'

'No. He's one man Vasarov trusts. And so far as I know, he hasn't been blown.'

'If what the paper says is true, he should have another advantage,' said Reid philosophically. 'He won't charge expenses.'

Reid turned to go, but Blaikie called after him.

'By the way, seen the Special Branch report on Bates?'

'No. I didn't know there was one.'

'I keep forgetting, you've been away for a fortnight. We managed to keep it out of the papers here with a D Notice, but Bates's body has been discovered.'

'Where? What happened to him?'

'He got himself buried under six feet of concrete on a new housing estate in Kent.'

'You mean he was pissed and fell in?'

'Not exactly. Hell of a lot of pilfering goes on around these estates, you know. Somehow seems fair game. Anyhow, this character is on the estate looking for some bricks when suddenly a car drives in. He dives for cover, and sees two men get out. They have a fight. He wasn't sure of the details, but it seems to have been pretty violent. One man is knocked into a newly dug pit or drain, half full of liquid concrete. The other fellow just stands watching him drown. Then he gets in the car and drives off, cool as you like. Our thief scarpers as soon as he can, and tries to forget the whole thing.'

'So why does he come forward now, after all this time?'

'He didn't want to admit he was thieving. Sidesman in the local church, or some such thing, and it would look bad. However, in his agitation, he'd dropped a handkerchief with his initials on it. So much stuff had been going missing that the contractor handed this over to the police, who contacted local laundries and so on. Finally, the police caught up with him and when he saw them on his doorstep, he thought they'd come about this chap in the cement – and told them what he'd seen, that he'd had no part in it, and so forth.

'They hired a pneumatic drill and dug up the pit. And there's Bates's body, still with his driving licence in his pocket.'

'Who owns the site?' asked Reid.

'Firm called Quendon Construction. Majority shareholder, Max Cornell.'

Reid pursed his lips in surprise.

'And who was Bates fighting?'

'Impossible to say for *certain*,' replied Blaikie slowly. 'But since he arrived in a Hillman Minx of the colour we lent to Cornell, who admitted driving him back from Portsmouth –who do *you* think?'

Reid stroked his chin.

'Is he going to be pulled in?'

'No. We're giving him more rope. I've had the SB check into his background. He's involved with several fairly big deals –property, car auctions, and a lot of rubbish down in Notting Hill. Full of blacks and whores.'

'Like that character Peter Rachman. Do they know each other?'

'Must do, I would think. They're in the same line of country. Rachman's been having an affair with those two girls SB told us about who're too friendly with the War Minister. *And* they're involved with Captain Ivanov, the Russian naval attaché!'

'And what about Max?'

'Not involved with girls or boys, yet he's got a whore with a record running his houses in Notting Hill.'

'You think he's on the side of the angels, then?'

'He has always seemed straight to me,' admitted Blaikie. 'On the other hand, he does seem to be in odd places at odd times.'

'What do you mean, exactly?'

'Professor Tobler. Max was alone with him when he died. He hadn't seen him for years. That was their first meeting – and their last. Did he somehow kill Tobler – either on orders, or to keep his mouth shut about himself?'

'Go on.'

'Crabb. An easy, open-and-shut job. But Crabb didn't make it – and it was all over. The wrong way. Now, Bates. And how did Cornell make all this money? Comes here with nothing. Is only naturalised because we vouch for him, and in no time at all he's a millionaire, while we still sit on our arses here, grateful for our annual increment of two hundred a year.'

'So far, that's all circumstantial,' said Reid. 'But if you ask him to jump Vasarov, it wouldn't be too surprising if Vasarov never gets here alive.'

'Save us a lot of trouble and money if he didn't,' said Blaikie shortly.

'He's served us well, of course, but now his usefulness is over. His nerve is obviously going – and no wonder. And, we've got others better placed and more with us in spirit than he ever was. Colonel Penkovsky, for one.'

'Well, if Vasarov doesn't make the distance, we'll know who to blame, and nab him. No mistake this time.'

'My thinking entirely. Two birds with one stone. Chicken – *and* hawk.'

Mrs Susan Cartwright, the KGB Resident, drove her Austin Somerset at a careful forty miles an hour along the Oxford Road. She wore a tweed costume and a felt hat with a feather in it, and looked like a suburban housewife.

No-one seeing her would imagine that the car had armour plating under the floor and inside the doors. Beneath a flap in the right-hand door pocket lay a Mauser .38, and under the front passenger seat was a recording machine adjusted to pick up with the utmost clarity any conversation whispered inside the vehicle.

That morning, Mrs Cartwright had received a postcard, apparently from her sister in the Lake District, showing a coloured view of Coniston Water.

'Weather wonderful,' the typed message read. 'Must leave tomorrow. Hope you both can lunch with us at Compleat Angler, Marlow, Tuesday, one o'clock. Love, Priscilla.'

Mrs Cartwright immediately took the card up to her bedroom and examined it through an exceptionally powerful magnifying glass. She then removed one of the commas with a special pair of tweezers and enlarged the message beneath it. 'Layby, A40. 4 miles west Thame turnoff. Noon.'

The layby was in a brief section of dual carriageway, and a tanker lorry and two other cars were already parked in it. The driver of the second car had his bonnet raised and was checking the level of the engine oil. She pulled in twenty yards behind him, switched off her own engine and waited.

She had no idea who would meet her, perhaps one of these three drivers, or someone else altogether. Three minutes later, a Riley Pathfinder stopped behind her. She watched it in her rearview mirror, right hand poised over the door pocket in case of trouble. A man climbed out from behind the wheel, and flexed his arms as though he had driven a long way. Then he locked the front door, and casually walked towards her car. He passed the window, paused, and turned.

'Isn't it Mrs Cartwright?'

'Why, Cousin George! What a coincidence!'

'Your sister Priscilla told me where you would be lunching. How lucky to see you here.'

This was the first part of the dual recognition drill.

As the man walked round her car to the passenger door, she bent down and switched on the hidden recorder. He climbed inside, offered her a cigarette. Ten filter tips lay in the gold case. The second and third had their cork filters pointing towards her. This was the second recognition signal.

'You are leaving?' he began.

'Yes. I will be glad to get out of England. It's so small, so confined.'

'I know. A toy country. There is one last job before you go. A defector.'

'Permanently?'

'Yes. In London. A block of flats. The caller will go upstairs and knock on the door. Subject will be alone, but probably cautious. He will ask who's there. The visitor will say, "Special Delivery". Subject will be expecting this. Caller will deal with him as he opens the door.'

'Will no-one else be about?'

'Nobody. It's that kind of apartment building. Caller will walk down the stairs – in case the lift jammed or is stopped – and out through the front door. This can be opened from the inside. I will give you the exact time and date and address and apartment number later this week.'

They sat, looking at each other, wondering at their real and innermost thoughts, their true motivation. She saw a middle-aged man in a brown tweed suit, perhaps a doctor with a country practice, a solicitor from a market town, maybe a former army officer who had retired early.

'Any questions?' he asked.

'None.'

'Pity we can't meet at a more social level.'

'Perhaps we will, one day.'

He smiled, climbed out, walked back to his car. She thought of noting the registration number, but then decided against it. The plates would obviously be as false as the driver.

As Mrs Cartwright drove away, she switched off the recorder and turned on the radio. A news bulletin described how a Russian ballet dancer, number three in a touring Moscow company, had sought political asylum and had been taken to a secret address. She wondered whether he was the man she had to kill, whether in fact he was a KGB colonel, as the Americans claimed, or just a stooge to attract the attention of Press and governments while some real agent went undetected.

She would never know – any more than she would probably ever discover the real identity of Cousin George or the truth about the man she had orders to kill.

Nina jumped out of her bath when Max telephoned.

Wrapped in an initialled towelling robe she had bought that morning in Harrods, she stood admiring herself in a wall mirror as she took the call. She had immediately opened accounts at Harrods and Fortnums, and an interior decorator had already submitted plans for totally redoing her new flat in Cadogan Square.

'I had a job finding you,' said Max accusingly.

'I tried to ring you, too,' retorted Nina. 'But there was no reply.'

'I've moved to Grosvenor Square now,' he explained. 'I had an offer I couldn't refuse for Eaton Place.'

'And I wanted to tell you I'd also moved up in the world. I made a little money out of your TV shares.'

'So would you agree you owe me a favour – as an ex-wife to an ex-husband?'

'Within limits,' she agreed cautiously.

'Very modest limits,' he answered her. 'You know that fellow Carton, the Labour man who made such a passionate speech about the reasons behind the riots in Notting Hill? Well, I want you to persuade him to raise a question in the House about a building society. Two, in fact. The Union Flag and the Golden Star. Both have a lot to do with the trouble there. They're misusing funds, taking money from coloured investors under false pretences.'

'I'd love to help you, but you obviously haven't heard about Dougie. He's had a stroke, poor lamb. They think he'll live, but he's lost the power of speech.'

'Dear, dear. The very worst thing that could happen to a politician like him.'

'You sound very cynical.'

'No. Just realistic.'

Conversation drifted into generalities. Max replaced the receiver, thought for a moment, and then dialled *The Daily Sketch* and asked for the reporter whose wine he had once deliberately spilled in El Vino's.

'Yes?' said the reporter suspiciously. People who telephoned newspaper offices early in the morning were often time-wasters. Max could hear a mild clatter of typewriters in the background.

'We met some time ago,' he began. 'You helped me check out an American, a Mr Mulheim. We had dinner together in Soho.'

'Oh, yes. Of course. Mr Cornell.'

'I've a story for you, a thank-you for helping me then. You can't quote me on this, but one of your readers, a Mr Diaz, from Jamaica, now of Notting Hill, has been trying to withdraw his life savings of two thousand pounds from a building society. They won't pay. The man behind the society is the financier Sam Harris. And I believe that he has been misappropriating the funds.'

'How do you know this?'

'Mr Diaz is a friend of mine. I am sure that Harris is the man Mr Carton had in mind when he spoke in the House about the riots the other day. As a quid pro quo for your very valuable assistance to me, I can pass on the background to you, for what it is worth. Now, if you have your notebook, here are a few facts, figures, names and addresses . . .'

Max poured another champagne for Betty. They clinked glasses, and she crossed to the wide window that overlooked Grosvenor Square.

'I've never seen the Square from the inside,' she said.

'I'm just getting used to it myself,' Max admitted. 'I only moved in here last week. Bad news from Notting Hill these days, I see. Perhaps we are pulling out at the right time?'

'The trouble's mostly whipped up,' she said. 'Iron Bar and a few like him are behind a lot of it. White boys who've been living off girls are jealous now that the blacks have moved in.'

'They'll be more trouble,' Max said seriously. 'That's why you must start pushing more of our properties there up-market. Don't get rid of the blacks, but do get rid of the whores.'

'They will appeal to the Rent Tribunal.'

'Serve eviction notices on them first, then they can't. I know the law, too. When the houses are empty, strip them completely, then put in new plumbing and divide them into separate flats. Where you can, sell. A buyer is always better than a tenant. It'll keep a lot of the muck that's flying around Rachman's name off us.'

'What if they do have their rents fixed at a low rate by the Tribunal before we can get them out?'

'Agree with whatever rent is set. But those are furnished rooms. Make them hire the furniture. There can be no appeal against that. So we make the same amount either way.'

'You've most things worked out, haven't you, Max?'

'Some,' he agreed. 'But not the important things in life.'

'Isn't money important, then?'

'Only when you haven't got it.'

'Well, you have made me what I call a rich woman. And why? You never want any favours. You've never even made a pass at me.'

'Perhaps that's good – or bad?'

Max smiled.

'Sex has never bothered me much,' he said. 'I get my satisfaction from money, or rather the deal that makes the money.'

'And love? You've no place for that?'

'No time, possibly, is a better answer. How's your little girl these days?'

'Fine. You must see her some time. Let her meet the man she's beholden to.'

'I'd like to. Give her the best education you can, so that she'll have a better chance than we ever had. We're the last of the line to make money like this, you know.

'I made my first money under a Socialist government, remember. They were so busy nationalising railways and coal mines and gas works, they forgot the really important issues – and the rest of the world had a six-year start on us. But they will get in again at the next election, and then they'll change the rules for ever.'

'They'll never change you,' said Betty confidently, and smiled.

Max poured out more champagne.

A knock on the door; the manservant he had taken over with the flat entered and bowed.

'A number of gentlemen in the front hall to see you, sir,' he announced gravely. 'Gentlemen of the Press.'

'What about?'

'A matter concerning Pennine Television shares, sir, so they inform me.'

'I'll come down and see them. But don't let anyone into the flat.'

He turned to Betty.

'You won't want to get your name in the papers?'

She shook her head.

'There's a back entrance into Carlos Place,' he told her. They shook hands, and he walked down the marble stairs to the front hall. A babble of questions greeted him against the blaze of flashlights.

'Is it true you have already sold your holding in Pennine Television for five million pounds?'

'Are you keeping any shares at all?'

'What will you reinvest it in now?'

'Who were the buyers?'

'Why sell now when they are bound to go up?'

Max stood on the third step from the bottom and held up both hands above his head.

'Questions, gentlemen, but no answers. I don't ask you how you spend your salaries. Those financial matters only concern you and your families. Mine concern me. And no-one else. Good night.'

He turned and walked up the stairs, leaving them to shout their questions after him.

In Berkeley Square, other reporters were besieging Sam Harris's flat. They had brushed past the porter, and now gathered in the corridor, outside his door, taking it in turns to ring the bell.

Harris had locked and bolted the door, and stood by his study window looking nervously out over the square. The evening was touched with the melancholy of autumn. A mood of despair gripped him. Only weeks ago he had sat here at his desk and read and re-read Diaz's letters about withdrawing his wretched two thousand pounds from the Union

Flag Building Society. So much had happened since then that might have been in another life, another world.

Many Lesney Park tenants who had promised to buy their flats had taken fright at the Press disclosures about both building societies, and now refused to proceed with the sales.

Investors had besieged Mr Goudousky's office, demanding that he return their money. Appeals to reason – for if every depositor demanded back their money at the same time from any bank in the world, that bank must go down – produced only more frantic requests and threats. Letters and writs piled up like the autumn leaves in the square outside his window.

The newspapers had also given great prominence to Cornell's sale of Pennine Television. He had been the unknown man to whom Harris had lent so much money. Cornell could save him now if he repaid the loan, but Cornell was not accepting telephone calls.

Harris poured a whisky with trembling hands and drank it neat. The scheme he had devised in the taxi to buy off Iron Bar was still-born; events overtook him before he could even begin to put it into operation. Time had finally run out; the game was over – or up. The final whistle was blowing to mark the end of play.

His Spanish maid came into the room.

'A gentleman about the telephone, sir,' she said. 'He's in the kitchen. Came in through the staff entrance.'

'The telephone? I didn't know there was anything the matter with it.'

But perhaps there was? Perhaps that was why he could not reach Cornell?

'Show him in.'

Cornell came into the room.

'*You*!' said Harris. 'I have been trying to reach you all day.'

'I thought you might not let me in the front door, with all the reporters,' Max explained.

'Thank God you came. Whisky?'

Max shook his head.

Harris looked at him sharply.

'You have come to help me, haven't you? You are going to bail me out?'

'No.'

'What do you mean, no? You borrowed money from us . It's ours by right.'

'Of course. And I will pay that back – in time. But I am not paying out all those other investors whose money you used. This matter of Lesney Park, for instance.'

'What about it? That's a perfectly good investment. These are only transactions on paper, figures moved from one page to another. I control two damned good building societies.'

'Not any more. They are bust, and you with them. But I will bid for them when they go down – because I pushed them down.'

'You bastard. I gave you your first chance to make a deal. Remember those bets on the dogs?'

'I can never forget it. Or how you sent your creatures to do me up afterwards. I remember a number of other things, too. You killed my father. You and Paul between you. Maybe others helped, but you are the one I'm dealing with now. I thought of going to law about you, but the law takes too long. So I thought I'd deal with you in my own way. I set out to ruin you, and I have.'

'Wait a minute,' implored Harris. 'You've got it all wrong. We must work something out. I'll give you a major shareholding. Anything – anything you like. You wouldn't see an old friend go down.'

'I wouldn't,' agreed Max, and walked out of the front door, through the jam of jostling reporters, down the stairs and into the fresh, cool, evening air.

Blaikie sat behind his desk, facing Max.

'This will be the last thing we ever ask you to do,' he said.

'Isn't there anyone else?' Max asked.

'Vasarov trusts no-one as he trusts you. No good offering you money, of course.'

'Not any longer,' Max agreed. 'When you had the chance, you didn't take it. Now it's too late.'

'I thought so,' said Blaikie, revolving his pen slowly between the fingers of his only hand.

'Of course, we could help keep your name out of the papers

over these houses you own through various companies at Notting Hill. The cause of the riots, I understand?'

'Nothing wrong in owning a few houses, surely?'

'Nothing at all,' agreed Blaikie. 'But your partner, Mrs Betty Mortimer, is well known to the police as a prostitute. She's been on the game for years. Street-walkers use rooms in most of your houses – or they have done up till now. You know what the good book says? "A good name is to be desired above riches."'

'Not for me, it isn't,' said Max. 'They say, what say they, let them say. That's my motto. And I say a rich man's jokes are always funny. You can't frighten me, Blaikie. I don't give a damn about publicity – or anything else.'

'My dear Cornell,' said Blaikie quickly, at his most sincerely insincere. 'I wouldn't dream of trying to pressure you. I am simply trying to find a way of persuading you to undertake this last assignment which is desperately important to us. Of course, when you have so much money, there's really only one thing left that most people desire. A title.'

'You mean, a knighthood?'

'I mean, a knighthood.'

'You'll give me a knighthood if I get Vasarov out?'

'The gift of honours is not in my command,' said Blaikie sternly. 'But I would recommend you most strongly to the head of security. He would pass on the recommendation, with his own, to the Prime Minister, and so to the Queen. I think I can safely say that I see no great difficulty about it.'

'And this will be positively the last thing you ask me to do? For ever?'

'You have my word.'

'All right,' said Max slowly, making up his mind. 'I have always believed it was foolish to trust anyone. But in this case I will trust you – for the first and last time. Now, what exactly have I got to do?'

Mrs Cartwright dialled the number carefully and let it ring exactly seven times before she replaced the receiver. Then she dialled it for a second time and let it ring five times. At the third attempt, the number rang twice, and a voice said, 'Delicatessen stores.'

'Some instructions,' she said. 'Special delivery to Grosvenor Square.'

She gave him a number.

'The flat is on the fourth floor. No porter is on duty after dusk. You will have to deliver the goods to the front door. Press the bell marked No. 12. You will see there a speaker and a microphone. The tenant will then open the door for you by remote control. He is expecting a special delivery, so you will have no difficulty.'

'Shall I mention the delicatessen?' asked the man.

'Mention nothing,' she told him. 'Afterwards, you will leave by the stairs, in case there is any trouble with the lift. You can open the front door of the building from the inside.'

She replaced the receiver quickly before the man could ask any more questions. He also put down the telephone, but more thoughtfully.

He was sallow-skinned, and middle-aged, and lived in a two-roomed furnished flat in Kilburn, overlooking a main road. The room was in darkness, and through its thin curtains neon signs on a hoarding across the street coloured the ceiling red, then green, and blue, and red again.

He went into the inner room, unlocked a trunk beneath his bed and removed a pile of old shirts and socks. Underneath, wrapped in an oil rag, lay an automatic pistol, with a long silencer. He picked up this weapon, felt its weight, rubbed his thumb over the serrations on the handle. Then he began to dismantle it.

He cleaned his pistol every day, although he had never used it in London. Tonight, he had more reason. Tonight, he would be using it.

Mrs Cartwright dialled another number, counted the times it rang, dialled it a second time, and then a third.

Blaikie answered.

Vasarov walked down the Champs Elysees, past the open-air cafés with their bright awnings, on towards the Arc de Triomphe, where the giant tricolor fluttered lazily in the morning wind. He walked slowly, like a tourist glancing from side to side through his dark glasses.

When he had arrived in Paris with a trade delegation earlier in the week, he had complained to the embassy doctor that his eyes were inflamed. This was not unexpected, of course, since he had carefully rubbed pepper into them in the aircraft lavatory. The doctor had given him a phial of eye-drops and suggested that he wore tinted glasses.

He had no doubt that members of his own ministry were following him. He did not know them, for they would almost certainly have been brought in from another area, and they, in turn, would not know his real identity. He hoped that he had not given them the slip. It was essential for the success of the escape that they should keep him well in sight. That was why he walked so slowly.

He paused outside one café, reading the menu that French law insists every café must display, then walked on to the next, and finally sat down under the scalloped green awning of a third. He ordered a Pernod and sat sipping the milky yellow drink for eight minutes exactly by his watch; the time agreed, the time allowed.

Then he beckoned to the waiter, and asked him in poor French whether the café possessed a lavatory. The waiter nodded and pointed inside. Vasarov thanked him, put some money on the table to pay for his drink, hoping that the watchers had understood the dumb show.

Beyond the aluminium covered bar, where coffee machines bubbled and hissed, he saw a swing door marked "Hommes", and pushed his way through. As he had been told, there were two cubicles inside, both apparently occupied. He tapped on the left one.

'Butcher?' Max asked from inside.

'White.'

A click as the right-hand bolt slipped open. Vasarov went into the cubicle. A string led from the bolt over the top of the partition wall. Vasarov removed his hat, glasses, overcoat and suit, and handed them over the wall to Max. In return came a pair of flannel trousers, brown suede shoes, a corduroy jacket, a beret and spectacles with thick tortoiseshell frames.

Max came out of his cubicle wearing Vasarov's clothes, the brim of his hat pulled down over his black glasses. The swing door banged. Vasarov was alone.

Max walked through the café, bought a packet of Gitanes at the counter and sauntered along the pavement, glancing in shop windows. A taxi crawled by. As though on impulse, he hailed it, but to make it easier for the watchers, he discussed with the driver possible restaurants and decided at last on one in the Bois de Boulogne.

Halfway there, he changed his mind and took his time paying off the cabbie, long enough for another taxi to stop a hundred yards behind him. Then Max walked slowly along the road, pausing at a magazine and newspaper kiosk. He took off his hat, wiped his forehead, then removed his glasses, as though he could not read even headlines through such dark lenses. A man in blue jeans and a sweater bought a motor magazine. Another, wearing a neat blue suit and carrying a raincoat, read headlines over Max's shoulder. Max noted the surprise and dismay on both their faces. He walked down the stairs into an underground station, and took his time buying his ticket. They did not follow him. He guessed they would both be hunting for the nearest telephone booth to inform Control that Vasarov had somehow given them the slip.

Vasarov waited for the time previously agreed, then he came out of the cubicle, and glanced at himself in the mirror above the washbasin. From a pocket of his jacket, he took a gun-metal cigarette case. He dusted some grey powder on his hair, where it showed beneath the beret, and on his chin and his cheeks, to match his false moustache. Then he opened the door and walked slowly through the café, being careful not to look at anyone directly.

No-one appeared to notice him. More confidently, he walked out into the street. The air felt unexpectedly cold and he realised he was sweating.

Vasarov felt himself brace the muscles in his back as though this could protect him from a bullet or a knife. But there was neither. He relaxed, turning into a side street. This was jammed with cars. Apparently, a truck had broken down at the far end, and nothing could pass. Drivers were shouting, waving their fists, blowing horns. He had not expected this. How often in the past had he seen a totally unexpected incident or accident ruin the most carefully planned operation? As he paused, irresolute and fearful, a middle-aged woman carrying a shopping bag approached him.

'Excuse me, m'sieur,' she said in English. 'Do you speak English?'

'A little.'

'I am looking for the English butcher. Can you help me?'

He glanced at her and spoke the second part of the primary recognition signal.

'There was one in the Seventh Arondissement.'

'That is the fellow. A long time since I tasted Lancashire hotpot.'

For a moment, Vasarov could not remember the next response and stood looking at her stupidly. For some reason, he had not expected a woman like this to be involved. Then, like an actor recalling his lines, he said: 'I will walk with you. I am going in that direction.'

'Thank you, m'sieur. But I have a taxi.'

The driver of the cab caught in the jam was already opening the door. The woman gave him an address. At that moment, the truck at the end of the street began to move. Had the blockage been staged to help him, or was it an accident? Was the taxi genuine or also part of the plan? It was pointless now to wonder or worry; he was committed. The woman said nothing, but sat staring straight ahead of her.

They reached the southern suburbs of the city. The driver turned into an underground car park, tyres squealing on the steep ramp. Fluorescent white lights throbbed on grimy concrete ceilings. They drove down for three levels and stopped. The woman motioned Vasarov out. They walked between the lines of parked cars to a blue Citroën. She climbed in behind the wheel. He got in by her side. She looked at him critically, and then nodded.

'You'll do,' she said. 'As though you were appearing in amateur theatricals as a Frenchman.'

At the entrance, she showed a season ticket. The automatic barrier went up. Half an hour later, they were at the airport. She took him directly to the Spanish Airlines booking office.

'Say nothing,' she said, 'no matter what anyone else says to you.'

She produced a ticket.

'Can you please get this passenger on a different flight?' she asked in French.

The ticket clerk shook his head sadly.

'I regret it is too late, madam. That flight is closed.'

'We were delayed by traffic. It is imperative my friend is on that flight. He has an important appointment in Madrid.'

The clerk glanced up at Vasarov. He could see make-up dust on his face, his absurd beret and glasses, his obvious nervousness. He looked at the ticket: M. Louis Laburdière, single to Madrid.

'I am sorry, but there is another flight in two hours.'

'Can you not possibly help my friend? This is a matter of life and death, I assure you.'

The woman had a peculiarly penetrating voice. Several other clerks along the ticket counter were now looking at her. Vasarov said nothing, but he could feel sweat running down between his shoulder blades. He hoped she knew what she was doing.

'I regret, madam . . .'

'Then please book him on the next flight. But I will complain to your head office about your attitude. I am sure if you *really* wanted to help, you could delay the flight.'

The clerk stamped Vasarov's ticket, handed it back to the woman.

'No baggage, monsieur?' he asked, deliberately ignoring her.

'No,' she replied, picking up the ticket. She gripped Vasarov's arm and propelled him across the booking hall.

'Play-acting,' she explained softly. 'They will remember you – when it's announced that a diplomat has disappeared.'

She handed him a plastic carrier bag, stamped 'Prisunic', and a handful of small change.

'Go to the lavatory,' she ordered. 'Wash that make-up out of your hair. There's a red wig in here, and a different hat and jacket. I'll see you in the bar. Over there.'

Five minutes later, he joined her, outwardly a different man. She handed him a boarding card, and a British European Airways ticket in the name of Macnamara. Two luggage tags were clipped to it.

'Your two cases have already gone through. They are dark blue. Both are unlocked. Dutiable items are a hundred French cigarettes and a bottle of brandy.'

'I will be on my own?'

'Yes. But we have two people on the plane with you.'

'Where do I fly? London?'

'No. Manchester. You will be taken care of there.'

'What about White? When do I see him?'

'Later,' she said, and smiled for the first time. 'Good luck.'

She pressed a hundred-franc note into his hand, turned and was gone.

Vasarov had another drink, and sat watching the screen of flight departures above the bar until his number came up and the departure gongs sounded.

# Seventeen

After the rain, the sun had generously paved Sloane Street with slabs of gold.

Max walked to the bank, enjoying the warmth on his face. He carried a small brown-paper parcel the size of a book. All around him, men with briefcases were hurrying back to offices after prolonged lunches. He hated briefcases. How many of those who carried them only used them to transport that morning's newspaper or an orange or banana for a snack?

Max was late. He had been delayed by a telephone call from Manuela.

'Have you heard the news?' she asked him.

'About what?'

He answered one question with another, thinking she must refer to the announcement of Vasarov's death and his state funeral.

'About Dick. He died early this morning in the clinic. In his sleep. They operated, but found there was nothing they could do, so they simply sewed him up again.'

'I'm terribly sorry,' said Max. 'Is there anything I can do to help?'

'Well, there is one thing. Before he died, Dick told me you would help me. All our money is tied up in Spain, and the costs keep rising all the time. I don't want to be forced to sell out, and see someone else reap the profit. Would you be interested in coming in with me, say fifty-fifty?'

'How much is required?'

'To do it well, say two million pounds. I've got all the papers over here with me, if you want to see them.'

'Never mind the papers. I'll take your word, 'said Max. 'You've a new partner.'

'I thought you'd say that.' said Manuela gratefully. 'So did Dick.'

Max replaced the receiver, and stood for a moment looking out of the window across the square.

What a strange life he had led from the day he had first met Carpenter in Austria! One deal had merged with another, then into a second, a third. They were all separate and yet all linked together, like beads in a necklace. And in all these years he had made no friends, and, more strangely, had felt no need for them.

Max had married but never consummated the marriage. There were no women in his life, and he had not missed them. Was the brutality of the camp at Katyn the real and only reason, or was there something deeper? Had he deliberately or unconsciously sublimated all desire, even the normal human need for friendship, love and affection, into the pursuit of wealth?

And now that he had amassed all the money he could ever conceivably require, his mind was already fuming with possibilities for developments in Spain, about which he knew nothing at all except that the prospect excited him. He knew it would work, as he had known instinctively that the car auctions would succeed; the houses in Notting Hill, the offices he had built. Even the old cars would increase dramatically in value; he had the Midas touch. But then this gift had threatened to kill the old king; man could not live only on gold or by it.

Max did not need any more money, but so far as money was concerned, you either had none or not enough. The badger might not care to keep on digging, but if he stopped, his nails would dig into his own flesh. Now, at least, he was divesting himself of all his British shares. The future must be his to enjoy. But was he capable of real enjoyment? In the prison camps he had been alone among many; a crowd had never been company. Had he changed? And did he even want to now, if he could?

His manservant had knocked on the door.

'A gentleman to see you sir.'

The despatch rider, still wearing his crash helmet and black leathers, had handed him the parcel that he was now carrying down Sloane Street.

It had come from a safe house in the Midlands where Vasarov was being debriefed. It contained Vasarov's key to freedom; a list of all known KGB agents and sympathisers in the United Kingdom, including the name and address of the Resident. Some, as expected, were Members of Parliament, and trade union officials, but the more interesting traitors were the most unexpected: an earl; the managing director of an international banking consortium; the leader of a right-wing political group. Max had only time to skim through the first two or three pages, for the safest place for this catalogue of treachery must be in the bank, and he would have to hurry to reach that before it closed for the day.

David Graham, unusually for him, was standing on the steps, also enjoying the sunshine.

'You're late,' he said, glancing at his pocket watch. 'We shut in five minutes.'

'Just in time, then. I was waiting for this.'

Max held up the parcel.

'I want you to put this packet in a special deposit. No-one is to be allowed access to it except me on any pretext whatever. Even if they produce a letter from me, this must be not sufficient to allow them access.'

'What if anything happens to you?' asked Graham jocularly, only half believing him. 'You want it buried with you?'

'Some might be happier if it were. If anything happens, this must be delivered at once by personal messenger to the Home Secretary, and signed for.'

'Are you serious?'

'Deadly,' said Max.

They shook hands. As he left the building, the bank messenger locked the door behind him.

The rain was starting again; he hailed a taxi. The porter of his block of flats saluted as he opened the taxi door for him.

'Thought it couldn't last, sir,' he said.

'What?'

'The good weather. Nothing lasts for ever, so they say, sir.'

'You're right,' Max agreed.

It was true, of course, and Max had lasted longer than

most. The unexpected sunshine had again reminded him of The Hill of Goats; the promise of spring, the nearness of eternity. Somehow, he had escaped the fate of those buried in the long graves under the snow. They had died, while he had prospered. He thought of Iron Bar, poised now like a diver on the edge of a vast ocean of publicity. Soon, he would be embraced by the liberal-minded and the gullible. No doubt he would one day be Lord Diaz of Notting Hill. Well, if what Blaikie promised counted for anything, he would be Sir Max before the summer ended.

He thought of Nina and Rachel and the fatherless Robert; of Carton painfully relearning to talk; of his mother and the father he had never met, would never meet; and of Vasarov, whom he would meet within the hour. What a distance he had also travelled – from Katyn to the Connaught!

His manservant came into the room and coughed apologetically.

'I did not hear you return, sir. There is one telephone message. Mr Blaikie rang, sir. He will call you again. I have set out drinks in the study, sir. Will you be requiring anything else?'

'No. Nothing,' said Max. 'You go off early today.'

The man's wife was in hospital in north London.

'How is she?'

'Very much stronger, thank you sir. She should be coming home tomorrow.'

As Max poured himself a brandy after he heard the man leave, he felt curiously restless; probably reaction after the excitement of springing Vasarov. Yet that had been surprisingly easy. Perhaps too easy? He sipped his drink reflectively. The telephone rang.

'Blaikie here. Tried to get you a bit earlier on. There's something on its way to you about the honour I mentioned. Bit of bumf for you to fill in. Lots of checks to do. Being delivered in person, instead of using the post. The messenger will announce himself as "Special Delivery".'

'Thank you. You know I've already had something from Butcher? A parcel came in half an hour ago.'

'A parcel?'

Blaikie's surprise sharpened his voice.

'Yes. Personally delivered by despatch rider. You always said I was the only person Vasarov would trust.'

There was that word again; the forbidden word. Trust.

'What's in it? Bottle of vodka?'

'Something more valuable. A list of all the other side's friends and sympathisers here. Even the Resident – and all the contacts they use.'

'Have you read it?'

Blaikie's voice was unexpectedly tense.

'Not had the time. Some surprising names, though, in what little I did read.'

'You've got it with you in the flat?'

'Heavens, no. Too risky. I put it in the bank until I can hand it over to your people. Just got back, as a matter of fact.'

'I would very much like to look at it.'

'So you will. But my instructions to the bank are that I am the only person who can see it for the time being. It's pretty red-hot stuff, you know.'

'I can imagine. But what happens if you get knocked down by a car or something?'

'Then it goes straight to the Home Secretary. Personally.'

Blaikie replaced the receiver with a trembling hand. He leaned back in his chair, closed his eyes. He felt physically sick. He had been so clever, so certain he would win.

Ever since the war and the loss of his arm, which had changed his whole personality and diminished all his prospects, he had lived a double life of infinite danger and complexity.

Like Burgess, like Maclean, like Philby, he had fed to the KGB every item of secret intelligence that he felt could interest them. He did not do this out of any idealistic belief, but for the crudest reason of all – money. All around him, his contemporaries had steadily overtaken him. Financially, they now lived well, and in his view, he still lived wretchedly. They had no money worries, and often it seemed to Blaikie that he had little else.

Over the years, the Russians had proved ungenerous paymasters. The initial sums they had offered seemed large in relation to his regular salary, but as his own standards of living increased, they deliberately whittled down their bribes. After all, why should they run after a bus they had already caught?

Blaikie had to work twice as hard in their service to receive perhaps only half as much in real terms, and there was no hope of release. He had warned them about Tobler, about Crabb, about Vasarov's defection; about so much else, for he desperately needed their money. He had grown to rely on it.

Now Blaikie's usefulness to the KGB was almost at an end. What he considered to be a catalogue of coincidences pointed to two sources of their information: himself and Max Cornell. He had sown seeds of doubt about Cornell's reliability and loyalty in Reid's mind. He had planned to follow this through to its logical conclusion: he would have Cornell killed.

He could then produce a confession, in which Max would admit his guilt. In this lay Blaikie's dilemma. The unknown assassin was already on his way. He could not now be reached or stopped. The bullet that would kill Cornell would also finish Blaikie.

By tomorrow morning Vasarov's list would be before the Home Secretary. By tomorrow afternoon, he – and who knew how many others? – would be arrested. The irony was overwhelming. In destroying Cornell he would destroy himself.

He had chosen Cornell originally because he had no country, no roots and could not refuse the offer of British citizenship. He had regarded him simply as bait for bigger game; a chicken-hawk. Now the chicken had killed the hawk. Of course, it would die as well, but that was no comfort. One death could never neutralise another.

Blaikie could see no way out now, no escape. Slowly, but it seemed not altogether reluctantly, he opened the one drawer of his desk which he always kept locked. At last he had it in his power to act on his own initiative, not on orders from strangers, from people he would never know.

Under three empty files, lay his wartime Smith and Wesson ·38. He should have handed it in, of course, but he had kept it in the belief that one day it might be useful. Curiously, he had never fired it in anger during the war. Now the only man it would kill would be himself. He took it out slowly, loaded it.

Had he the courage to press the trigger? What if he did not die at once, but lingered on in unspeakable agony until the cleaning woman came into the office next morning and found him, still alive?

He wondered about his wife. If the Ministry paid her his pension or gratuity, she could at last afford to have the flat redecorated, and maybe some new chair covers and curtains made for the sitting room. She would probably move to somewhere smaller; it was really too large for one person on their own.

Blaikie opened a cupboard, took out a half bottle of whisky – how typical of his life that he could never afford a bottle! – unscrewed the top. Spirit ran like fire within his veins. Then he reached his decision.

As Max lit a cigar, a muted buzzer sounded on his desk. Someone had arrived at the front door. He flicked a switch.

'Yes?'

'Special delivery, sir.'

This must be the messenger with the papers about his knighthood. Better let him in.

Max pressed the button that released the electric front door lock. The porter had gone off duty an hour previously, otherwise he would have shown the man up. On his Harrow record-player a new record dropped and turned. The Vienna Philharmonic Orchestra began to play 'Voices of Spring'.

The music momentarily transported him back to the over-furnished flat in Prague. His father's former patient was at the front door to warn the doctor that if he did not leave at once, he and his family would be taken in for questioning.

That was the moment when Max had really started on his career. He had not followed it deliberately. Events had driven him along the road to riches. He had no remorse no regrets over what he had done or had not done. And yet . . . and yet . . .

Looking back, his life had been totally selfish, totally lonely. If history had been different, he would doubtless have been a doctor, and like his father, hard up financially. Instead, he had made millions. But which life would have been the more fulfilled, the more worthwhile, could never be in any doubt.

Well, now he had the money, he might do some good with it. He could afford to endow a university chair or a scholarship. He might not be a doctor himself, but at least he could help others – hundreds, maybe thousands – to qualify. He could even found a medical school, and live through these other young people by proxy, as a father sometimes lives through his sons.

A second buzzer sounded. The messenger had arrived on the landing outside his flat. Max carefully placed his cigar in a cut glass ashtray. With a brandy in his left hand, the strains of Strauss behind him, and his mind content for the first time since he had left Prague, Max crossed the hall to open the door.